A HUNDRED BREATHS

JEAN M. GRANT

To Lorraine, for reading everything!
Cheerleader, optimist, dreamer, journeyer.
Thank you for not sugar-coating.

SCOTLAND

The Western Isles, 1240

The people of the Western Isles go by many names: the Silver Folk, the Ancients, witches. King Haakon the Old of the Nord Land has heard rumors of whispering wind, life-giving water, and the intuitive strength of fire harnessed by this society. His predecessors had conquered and misused the western realm for nearly five hundred years. However, their hold on the Scottish isles has loosened as clans rise and retaliate. So King Haakon sends his unsurpassed warriors and mighty fleet to exploit these impressive Ancient powers and push back the Scots. One last foray. Little does he know, no amount of manmade force can breach the mystical Silver Veil.

CHAPTER ONE

Northern Uist, Scotland, Autumn 1263

Death came by sea.

Torchlight danced on the black calm of a predawn sea as the mainlanders' wooden rowboats drew closer to the shore on the fringe of the port town, Loch nam Madadh. The oars sliced soundlessly through the water. Each ripple hit Gwyn with waves of premonition as she watched from the shoreline with her sister. Though not a Seer like Venora, she knew the visions well. Venora always told her about them.

"Sit, Gwyn! Unless you want them to see us," Venora said.

Gwyn knelt lower behind the dune.

The hum of the water seduced her. She itched to let it flow through her fingers. She found herself rising again. Water was the channel to her ability. It cured. It didn't kill. She shuddered as the sea's waters lapped restlessly upon the shore. Death rowed through life.

"Gwyn…"

"Aye!" she snapped.

This was not a planned visit by the mainlanders, at least to her knowledge.

She squinted as the rowboats drew away from the cargo ship and closer to shore. "Six—no, wait, seven men?" she whispered. "Their ship doesn't belong to one of the merchants in town. Why are they here? Did Father arrange another exchange? Isn't he going to the market next week?"

"Sit, Gwyn," Venora snapped. Her cold fingers were talons on Gwyn's wrist.

She never dared doubt her sister's Sight. A reluctant sigh brought her squatting beside Venora in the long grass, and she drew her cloak tighter. Fear welled within her. Venora's fingers had done more than leave a pink mark. She rubbed her wrist.

Blood would be spilled today unless they acted.

Scottish blood.

As much as her father preached his hatred for the Highlanders from across the sea, she didn't hate them. She couldn't. Healing was her gift. She saved—despite the toll healing took on her own body. Instead of exploiting the gifts of her people, she harnessed them.

"Are you certain about the outcome?" she asked for the fifth time today, grasping at any possible alternative. "Perhaps they come to visit the MacRuaidhri clan? Trade with them, too? Yes, I see. Look." She recognized the dark shapes of barrels and crates in the rowboats. "They come only for trade."

Venora's silence was deafening. Finally she said, "It doesn't matter what brings them." She puffed a breath.

"It will end with blood. Yer mercy and hope has no place among their people," she chided. "It will—"

"Don't!" Gwyn said with a shudder. She didn't want to know her truth to come, and Venora was well aware of it.

A wind whistled across the grasses of the machair shoreline of Cuan Canach, the little sea. It was hardly little. But it *was*, compared to the large Nord Sea her father's men had navigated across nearly twenty-five years ago under the orders of King Haakon, bringing a throng of hungry warriors from the Nord Land.

"Perhaps...," Gwyn began again.

Venora held up her hand. "Stop. The Nordman's time has ended. Scotland will reign." She added, "But they have a bigger beast to contend with, south, for many years to come."

Gwyn shivered. "What about us? We're not Scots."

Venora shrugged. "The Ancients will always have a home in the isles, even if we must live in secret."

She prayed to the god Forseti that her father's bloodthirst would end. Regardless, her betrothed came from a strong and rich Norse bloodline, and he was coming soon to claim her. There was no escaping the Nordmen.

"Settle yer mind, Gwyn," Venora rasped. "By the gods, ye rattle me. Ye're all het up!"

Gwyn sighed and clenched a hand. Mother had taught her about the gift of the land. She'd taught her to connect to the power of the Silver Veil between their world and the other. She'd taught her to heal and not by herbals alone. She focused on mercy. If anything, it would calm the foreboding rising within her.

Venora inhaled sharply as a second strong wind blew past. She grabbed Gwyn's arm, her grip tight enough to cause Gwyn to gasp in response. "Ye wreak havoc upon me. Please," Venora begged.

Gwyn shifted to sanguine thoughts. Her gaze drifted across the coastline. Her hopes to gather meadowsweet this late in the growing season for her brother's headaches had been thwarted. She would ask Gunnar to purchase it along with burdock on the mainland when he went to the harvest market with their father this week. If only Father would let her go for once. Kendrick's condition grew worse each day, and she wished she could do more to help her brother before her father learned the truth. Her powers were limited on Kendrick, and it frustrated her ceaselessly. Healing him could take a thousand breaths from her. It could kill her. Her gift was both life and curse. One life for another was not the way, and healing Kendrick's blindness was not as simple as mending a bone or relieving winter's cough.

She cursed under her breath. How could this gift be so selective in its power?

"Gwyn...," Venora pleaded again.

She blew a breath. "I'm sorry if my thoughts unnerve you. Block them. You know how!"

Venora laughed wryly. "It's becoming difficult."

The Scotsmen drew closer, nearly to shore.

As the day announced its arrival by the ocher hue rising over the horizon, Gwyn peered into her sister's glassy eyes again. She couldn't discern if Venora was having another vision. An eerie cold radiated through her. It could have been the harvest's chill, but she was no fool. A low guttural moan escaped Venora's lips as her sister swayed slightly.

"Tell me," Gwyn murmured, wiggling a step away to avoid touching her sister during a vision.

Venora spoke, her voice brittle. Her statement was the same bone-chilling truth as earlier. "Death." She drew a breath in between gritted teeth and then exhaled. "We must warn Mother."

"You already told me all this. Is there more to the vision?" She gave a subtle head flick toward the men as they made landfall. Deep, grating masculine voices drifted over the dunes on the wind.

Why did she continue to doubt her sister's clairvoyance?

Venora chortled. "Sister, ye dare ask me again, and I respond the same. One of those Scotsmen will fall today. Crimson lifeblood will spill upon the doorstep of our home. And two of our own."

"What? Who?" This was new. Venora hadn't mentioned *their own* before. Gwyn swallowed, a stone forming in her stomach. "Us? An Ancient?"

Venora didn't answer. Perhaps her vision was murky? Or was she glad about their own falling? Would it be two of Father's Norse warriors? Or Father himself? Admittedly, neither of those was as unsettling as it should be.

She rubbed the Healer's stone in her deep pocket. Heat seared her palm. She briefly closed her eyes, allowing the warmth to surmount the ice emitting from Venora. She would need more than the stone, more than her mother's herbals and books, to help them. She was tied to them by blood. She *had* to help.

"Ye'll need to choose," Venora whispered.

The hairs on her neck prickled. "Choose?"

"Ye canna save them all."

She'd never needed to choose to save a life. It was not a negotiation. She just did it. The only choice she'd made was about her own life. Most of her healing had been minor. Twisted muscles or broken bones, a bairn's fever, or coughing fits. Saving a life in battle would take much from her. More than her strength. Palpitations quickened her heartbeat. How much breath would she lose for this healing?

Focus, focus. Her breath formed before her in a wet cloud. She shoved the thought aside. She could not think about *that. Slow, slow, slow,* she ordered her pulse. Saving was worth the escaped breaths with each healing, she reminded herself.

"Come. We must be ready for it," Venora said.

We? Venora had never lifted a finger in her life to save another. She refused to disclose Kendrick's path. Gwyn was sure her sister had seen it.

They rose from their vantage point and hurried across the dunes. Her glance fell again on the two boats docked by the bobbing mooring. The larger cog ship lay anchored in the harbor, idling side to side, waiting for the men's return. Intense conversations between the men were lost on the wind. One of them would not return unless she did something about it. *Two of their own.*

How could she possibly choose? How could she *not*?

She pulled the cloak hood over her head and followed her sister to their village. Venora was never wrong.

Simon MacCoinneach dragged the first boat to the sandy shore and clunked his oar into its bow.

Desmond grunted beside him and then retched in the grass.

Once he finished, Simon approached and clapped his brother on the back. "It's not that bad, is it?"

Desmond waved a hand in annoyance, wiped his mouth with his shirt sleeve, and drew upright. "Och, not at all." He grunted. "I'll be pleased to return home to Meredith and a hearthside instead of being tossed about on a leaky ship so we can attempt again to barter trade with these Lochlanach. Mark my words, this is my last visit here." He heaved a sigh. "Father is right though. We need to try." He drew a long gulp of whisky and returned the flask to Simon. "If anything...we do this for our clan...and for Mother," he added quietly with a nod toward their father.

"Pull them up farther, men. Secure them, over there," their father barked from behind.

"Aye, Master MacCoinneach," the soldiers said, moving in response.

Covering his nose from his brother's rank breath, Simon shoved his small flask of whisky back into Desmond's hands. Simon waited, then took it and, between guzzles, whispered hotly, "Perhaps Father is *not* right, Des. He thinks the Mad Jarl will continue to trade with us. What does he hope to achieve from an unannounced visit? War is inevitable." He rubbed his chin, surveying the cargo. "I'd prefer we brought more men."

Desmond scoffed. "Och, the blade is not the way. Not yet. Our king's attempt on Skye didn't end well when he tried to root out the Nordmen. You know that."

"Many Lochlanach met the tip of my sword with that cause. It's a win to me."

Desmond massaged his temple. "The devil's ships still roam our isles, Simon. Laird Donald brought news of some Nordmen reaching Loch Lomond this summer. We must make peace."

Simon corked his flask. He forced a steady breath. "I don't care."

Desmond sighed. "I'd bet all my cows King Haakon is sure to send more ships to the isles in retaliation soon. More than a rainstorm is brewin' on the outer isles, Simon. We must sway Laird MacRuaidhri and this Blasius the Mad—now."

"*All* your cows?" Simon said.

Desmond cuffed his ear. "Aye, all of them."

Simon snorted. Desmond liked his cows. "Meredith may behead you."

Desmond shared a laugh. "Our best hope is to press Laird MacRuaidhri to keep the isle clans strong and maintain a peace with the delusional Blasius and his Norse warriors." He shrugged. "Hope for the best. Futile as it is."

"Nothing is ever futile until the last man falls." Simon tapped the sword in his sheath.

"Always with the sword, you." Desmond gave a too quick smile. He brushed back his thick, dark brown hair as a sudden wind whipped past them.

"Our home is on the cusp, Des. If we don't use force, they'll encroach farther inland. The sword is the only way. Not grains and honey."

Desmond grunted. "I'm confident Father will prove his worth and we'll establish a stronger alliance here with the MacRuaidhris. Then King Alexander will see our strength and competence and reward us with the whole of Glen Shiel."

Simon fought the bile rising up his throat. "Stewards are not lairds." *Mercy gets people killed*, he wanted to add. They of all people should know.

"We'll reconcile that, won't we? Have faith, Simon," Desmond said. He rubbed his stomach, moaned, and straightened his back. "Trade until it comes to the sword."

Simon nodded in resignation, done with this conversation. "Indeed."

"One day my hope will rub off on you."

"Never," Simon said. He settled his own unruly coarse hair as it blew in the wind. Again, the thong had come loose. He cracked his jaw and yawned, passing a glance at their father, Alroy MacCoinneach the Red, the current steward to Eilean Donan. *Stewards.*

Simon leaned into the rowboat and withdrew sacks of oats and barley.

Desmond shuffled around the boat. "Here, these," he said with a gesture to Farlene, one of the younger men, as he pulled a barrel of whisky. Farlene doddered with the weight, almost losing his footing. "Careful. That's our best! Och, Henry, help him, will you?"

Simon bent and lifted two crates of apples followed by a clay pot filled with honey, distributing them to the men.

Desmond brushed past him to reach the other boat. "No, no! Not that. Here, let me do it. Half of these go to MacRuaidhri's keep and those there—yes, those—go to Blasius."

Their father paced the shore ahead, surveying the dunes and long grasses. "Desmond!" he bellowed. Even with age, he'd not lost his crow.

Simon took over unloading as Desmond hurried to their father's side. He continued with instructions to the men about sorting. They'd stop first in the port town, Loch nam Madadh, to obtain horses and a wagon, while also checking in with their local scout. Their father was acquainted with one of the merchants who resided in town, and he preferred to keep close eyes on the clans he did business with. Then they'd deliver the goods to Clan MacRuaidhri and trade for fish and salt, and lastly they'd visit Blasius of Varteig to barter.

"Futile," he mumbled under his breath.

Blasius the Mad had nothing they needed. His wife, Caoimhe, was known for her healing charms and herbs, according to his father. She was called "The Graceful One." He'd have to judge that for himself, for it had al-ways been just Des and his father on previous visits. This was Simon's first time here. He had usually been left to guard the castle, oversee the soldiers. His father brought unique isle herbs home from each visit as well, not that they did much for Mother's condition. Her illness was beyond medicinal power, or at least the kind of medicine they could afford. However, lairdship would bring not only prestige but accessibility. If only...

Simon shoved his mounting ire aside and instinctively rubbed his achy knee. A storm was indeed coming. They'd have a rainy return to Skye.

The wind rolled over the dunes, and a shiver ran down his spine as if he were being watched. His fingers flicked on the sword's sheath as he distanced himself from the boats to get a better look. Shadows danced in the predawn dimness, shrubs moved in the distance, and a breeze hissed ghostly stories to him.

His mind spun. Strange Norse words played on his ears.

Dauði. Blóð. Death. Blood.

He shook his head. Was he going daft now?

A'bheil thu a'tuigsinn? Do you understand me? she asked in Gaelic.

"Yes," he croaked, spellbound, and strangely, believing. Her voice was hardened, threatening, filled with foulness.

He drew angry fingers around the sword. *Try. Give me any excuse to slaughter you.* He whispered in response, "I'll bring death. I'll bring blood. Is that what you seek?"

The words disappeared in the wind. He stared into the distance, waiting for any movement. Any cause to pull his sword.

What the bloody hell was that?

The Nordmen were merciless and skilled. Did they also communicate upon the wind via their pagan gods? They had the ability to take their perfectly jointed longships out of the water and carry them across the land. The Nordmen who ruled the Western Isles were notorious in their obstinacy and ruthlessness, propagating fear. Blasius the Mad was no exception. Trade with him was *not* the answer. He and his kind deserved to meet their end.

Simon's family would lose their standing as capable leaders of Glen Shiel if they didn't act. This was their final chance. The Nordmen of the isles needed to die.

A fierce pain radiated from his swollen knee, and he buckled over like an old man and not the tall, young—and fully able—sort he was. It was like broken glass in his kneecap, never able to be healed, the injury moving around as icebergs in a cold sea.

Curse it. He withdrew his sword, slammed it into a sandy knoll, and used it to right himself. He chewed on the inside of his cheek to distract the pain.

They'd made it to the Isle of Uist without any attack from the sea wolves who patrolled the inner and outer seas. The Nordmen's ships were everywhere and had steadily grown in number. Luck had shone upon them with this sail. Perhaps fate would be on their side with the negotiation. Oh, how he prayed. He'd leave the prayers to the monks and abbots though. Where was God before?

"Simon!" His father's voice percolated the moist air. "Are you ready? Quit your foolin'!"

He blinked, warmth coming to his cheeks. All the men were already up the shore and staring at his lameness. His father gave him a dour look from beneath bushy auburn eyebrows and behind his graying red beard.

He squared his shoulders and trudged up the mound toward the waiting men.

Words were the weapons of the weak. Desmond didn't know how true his earlier spoken words were. This *would* be their last visit to the isles. Their chance for mercy was over.

Aye, he was ready.

The day drew on slowly, uneventful. Doubt carved a corner in Gwyn's mind. Perhaps the mainlanders were not coming to see them, and instead, had ridden north to the MacRuaidhri keep?

Venora was never wrong. Vague and unspecific sometimes, but wrong, no.

"Caoimhe!" their father bellowed, barging into the cottage.

Gwyn's hand skittered off the page, and she bumped the oak-gall-ink decanter.

"Graces, Gwyn!" her mother breathed, catching the bottle before it fell and spilled on the beaver pelt on the floor.

"Yes?" Her mother rose to meet their father at the door.

He drew her close with a firm grip on her arm, whispering heated, indecipherable words in her ear. She nodded, face blanched. "Yes, my jarl," she said, lowering her eyes as he was quick to depart the cottage again.

Her mother nodded and returned to her place by the hearth. "Where is your mind today, Gwyn? Certainly not on your work," she said sternly while pointing to the goatskin-covered herbal book.

"Sorry, Mother." Gwyn sought Venora's always telling eyes, but her sister readied a kettle by the hearth, her back to them.

"Thirsty?" Venora asked, but she made no move to get the wooden bowls or box of assorted dried herbs.

"Mother?" Gwyn asked.

Her mother waved a resigned hand. "Back to your work. The men will handle it."

"I'll get the lavender and dandelion." Fear lodged in Gwyn's throat, and she coughed as she made her way to her meager corner of their cottage for her herbals box. It was time.

She'd need more than herbs, ointments, and bandages. She traced a finger over the three concentric carved waves on the wooden lid.

Bylgia, goddess of water, and Eir, masterful Healer, bring me healing today, she prayed.

Hoping her mother would not question her, she lifted the lid. A whiff of bog myrtle and heather wafted to her from the box's contents. She withdrew a second Healer's stone, smaller than the one she always carried in her skirt pocket. It was black, striated with white, and flecked with silver shards. Gwyn was certain the stones had found their genesis at the Stones of Fhinn and the others in her box perhaps from the sea. A few, her mother had said, originated near the mystical Cuillin mountains. Whenever they rode across Skye through the Dubh Cuillin, the forbidding eeriness of the fang-like mountains filled her with a strange sensation. Not fear, but rather intrigue. It was like they called to her.

The dogs near the stable barked. She tucked a small vial of tormentil-infused water into her pocket.

Her mother didn't break her focus from her transcribing. "Mind yourself, Gwyn. Your father will meet with them."

"We told you what would happen," she protested. She approached her mother, her box's weight irrationally soothing as she pressed it to herself with a protective hug. "We may have an understanding with the MacRuaidhris, but we *do not* with the mainlanders," she added. "Harm shall befall them...and us."

Her mother moved with intentional poise. She turned a sheepskin parchment page, dipped her goose feather into the decanter of oak-gall ink, and continued. Gwyn eyed her mother with anything but fondness. She fumed. Once again her mother would sit idle, beaten to submission by her father's threats and manipulation.

"You mean to do nothing?" Gwyn pressed.

"What would you have me do?" She steadied her hand and wrote smoothly as if the gods held her quill. She lowered the feather, drew her hands through the lengths of her long, black hair, and threaded it into a braid. "This is your father's duty."

Her words said one thing while her mannerisms said another. Gwyn's mother, Caoimhe the Graceful One, would be ready to heal, too, or cast a charm if needed. She always plaited her hair when it was time.

Gwyn looked over her mother's shoulder at the drawing of a maiden and her thralls. *Eir* was written at the top of the page. Her mother had spent many hours transcribing her charms from their Ancient tongue to the Futhark alphabet of the Nordmen. Her father had brought Norse stone and tablet runes with him when he settled on Uist. He'd taught their mother the language of the Norse people. As a result, they were well versed in Latin, the Futhark of the Nordmen, and Gaelic from their encounters with Clan MacRuaidhri. Her father might be a manipulating fiend, but he took pleasure in keeping his people educated and prepared. Gwyn had yet to learn many words in Ancient tongue, though, beyond those needed for her healing charms.

She dropped the herbals box beside her mother with a thud and made for the door. Neither Venora nor her mother stopped her.

She strode through the cottage doorway with a determined step. Men, all of them walking, with a cart brimming with goods, entered their small village. The scent of evening meals permeated the air. How could there be blood today when they had clearly come to trade? She didn't know how Venora dealt with the knowing.

Despite the coolness of approaching dusk, sweat moistened her brow. Knowing would drive her to lunacy; it would send her leaping off the nearest cliff. It was pain enough Venora usually confided in her, perhaps as a way to cleanse her soul. Sometimes she didn't want to know the visions, the truths. At least Venora never shared Gwyn's intimate future with her. If her sister knew, she didn't say. They had drawn a line there with sharing. Gwyn couldn't know her own fate.

She shoved shaking hands into the pockets of her homespun skirt. One found her dagger. She slept and worked with it. Certainly she used its sharp blade for splaying roots and its hilt for grinding leaves, but it could and would draw blood when necessary. Not here. Not today. Not them. The Scots had never hurt her people. She drew one hand around it regardless. The other hand remained fast on the Healer's stone in the opposite pocket.

Kendrick was nowhere to be found among the gathering men. She hoped he was in the stable caring for the horses. He couldn't be around this. Let her father and Gunnar do it. It would not be Kendrick who would fall today if she had her way of it.

As expected, her father, her older brother Gunnar, and three of their warriors—Trygg, Rothwell, and Sigurd—flanked the mainlanders as they arrived. The Scots were the same group she'd seen on the shore: their older leader with graying red hair, who had come before, Alroy MacCoinneach, and two men beside him—his sons likely, she presumed by their similar builds, one with red and the other with brown hair—and four other soldiers. Seven men for trade? Her stomach twisted.

Gunnar passed her an icy-blue glare over his shoulder. This was not her place. She lifted her chin and hurried to the stable.

Therein was Kendrick, brushing one of the horses. Relief nearly collapsed her knees.

"The mainlanders are here," he said without a turn to her. He stroked his hand along the horse's back, drawing his fingers soothingly and with intention, a graceful habit he'd inherited from their mother.

"Can you sense their lifebloods? Does good lie within them?" She released her death grip on the dagger and tightened her hold on the Healer's stone.

"Aye. There is good, but there is also pain. One, och, his soul hurts so."

Well, she couldn't heal souls, only wounds.

She approached him and patted the horse, trying to distract herself from the men outside. "Mora's your favorite."

"She is." Kendrick turned to her, his youthful face always filled with kindness. The purple bruising around his eye startled her. He'd been hidden in the stable the past few days. When had their father done it this time? Her stomach knotted.

"Kendrick," she murmured, reaching to touch it. He stepped back and turned away with a shrug. "I can help," she added.

"It will heal on its own. You should go. There will be blood spilled today," he said, echoing Venora's words.

"That's exactly why I must stay. You should go, Kendrick. Please."

Even as she said it, she secretly wished for today to draw to a close, sparing everyone, and for Venora to be wrong. "Father won't know if you're gone. Please,

Kendrick. Go to the woods. Return tonight after it's over." She spoke to him like he was a lad, not the braw man of fifteen.

Milky blue eyes stared at her blankly. A sad smile formed on his hairless face. "I can't hide it much longer, Gwyn. He'll know soon."

She didn't know to what he referred: his worsening blindness or his Feeler ability. One trait her father would see as weak, and the other as strength he could exploit. Her mother had yet to write the Feeler's book into the Futhark for their father. Her father only knew about the Healing and Seeing abilities. He was unaware that Feelers existed. Yet.

"He won't need to know. I'll ask to go to the market next week and search for a new remedy," she said.

He shook his head, messy brown hair waving with it. He kept it shorter, refusing to grow it long or wear it in a braid or thong like Father or Gunnar. "Gwyn, we know it's inevitable."

She placed a hand on his arm. He winced.

Her pulse grew fitful. Later she could prepare an herbal tincture.

Kendrick was lean, not yet a man like Gunnar, but no longer a young lad. He stood on the precipice of manhood. He was as tall as her. He could fight like the best of her father's men. With his lessening vision, his gift to feel the life essence of those around him—their natural heat and their internal emotion—compensated for his blindness. He was no match for his father's drunken wrath though. Both he and Mother gave their bodies to Blasius the Mad, just in different ways.

He needed his ability more than ever. He had become adept at feeling his way around and fooled the likes of them. Only Gwyn, Mother, and Venora knew the truth. If their father unraveled their secret, he could do more horrible things. Yet if Kendrick didn't tell him, their father was bound to take his rage one step too far. There was no winning. She hugged him. "I wish I could—"

"Gwyn, you must cease these musings."

She shuddered as he read her feelings. Venora and her mind-reading and Kendrick with his feeling. Sometimes she felt raw and exposed, and she wished to be free from the mystical obligations of the Silver Veil. Eir and Jörd could find other tenants for their gifts.

He continued, "You can't. It would take everything from you. No. I won't allow it."

"Give me time, Kendrick. I'll find something if I can't do it myself. Please."

He shrugged from her embrace. "They need you."

No sooner had he spoken the words then the first raised voice drifted into the stable. "So much for negotiations," she said.

She emerged to the sharp clang of metal meeting metal. Who had drawn the first sword?

Men. Were they all heartless? Must it always end in blood?

Her breath hitched. Kendrick stood beside her. "Kendrick, please, go. Go!"

She didn't know if he listened for her legs took her directly to the fray's edge. She hurried past the two gardens and goat pen, and straight for their cottage.

"Get in here, lest it be *you* who falls!" Venora snapped. She yanked her through the doorway.

Horror rooted Gwyn's feet to the wooden beam across the threshold. "I must be ready."

She could do nothing until a man fell. Her prayers lifted to deaf gods. They would not intervene in battle.

She had taken up the sword with Gunnar in training. Norse women were known to be warriors. At least that's what the runes said. Certainly she was half-Ancient, but nevertheless, her father's blood flowed in her veins, too. She could embrace that part when necessary. She withdrew her dagger from her heavier pockets, weighed with two Healer's stones and her tormentil-infused water vial. She lacked a sword. Not that her father would allow her one. Her healing ability was too precious.

She winced as men crashed into each other.

"Why aren't they bartering? Look!" She pointed to the cart burdened with sacks of what had to be grain and crates of something else heavy. "They've come to trade again. Like I said."

"With seven men? Alroy MacCoinneach usually brings two," Venora countered crisply.

"He's been here before. Why would he change his stance?" Her mind raced. The MacRuaidhris ruled northern Uist in a delicate agreement with her family. King Haakon had paid both the clan and her family handsomely to maintain the northern part of the isle for the Norse crown. Her father provided men to Dubhgall and Alan MacRuaidhri whenever commanded, and the MacRuaidhri brothers in turn gave land, food, and work to those in need. It was a mutual truce, even if the MacRuaidhris had the advantage. Her father cared about one thing, his new, purer race—the mingled bloodlines of Ancient and Nordman.

She dreaded the day her mad father ordered their own warriors to kill the entire Clan MacRuaidhri. Venora hadn't seen it—yet. It was coming. Now, these men. The MacCoinneachs from the mainland. They'd never raised a sword before in their trading with her father and the MacRuaidhri clan.

A man cried. It was Sigurd. She stepped forward to help him, but Venora stopped her. "Not him. He will live...for now."

"Who then?"

Venora said nothing, but her gaze was rapt on their brother.

"No, not Gunnar," Gwyn cried. "No!" She tightened her grip on the Healer's stone. Gunnar was a tower of muscle and force.

Truth hit, a sickening blow to her stomach. Venora had *known* who of their kin would fall. She *knew*. She'd said nothing about who!

Gunnar fought against Alroy MacCoinneach and an-other, younger man. He had brown hair and similar gait, a less fiery expression than Alroy. He had to be one of his sons. He looked familiar; he'd likely come here before, but she couldn't remember. Her heartbeat skipped. Gunnar's red-blond hair was gathered in a warrior's coif, tied tightly and plaited. Blood splattered his high brows and sharp cheekbones. He was strong and able, fighting like a true Nordman. Would the brown-haired Scot fall with Gunnar?

Wide shoulders and breadth made Gunnar larger than those around him. He might not have inherited an Ancient's ability, but he was a warrior to the bone.

An auburn-haired beast of a man fought against her father and Rothwell. She wasn't sure, but his resemblance led her to believe he was Alroy's other son. Except for the gray in Alroy's hair, they were very similar in complexion and coloring. Bloodlust filled this younger man's expression. Equally robust, they dodged, deflected, and parried with their steel. The intensity compelled her to watch. Each face, each swift attack or counter. She stepped closer. Venora's grip tightened, burning into her flesh through the long sleeve.

There was no peace in bloody wars. She knew the history. The Scots hated the Nordmen. Her father's people would not stop with their conquests. The Ancients were caught in the middle of the fray, exploited by some, feared by others, and lumped in with the Nordmen, both groups referred to with that malicious word, Lochlanach.

She drew her hands out of her pockets, armed with stone and dagger. Life and death. She shifted, wanting so much to intervene.

Suddenly, several men fell.

The lean, brown-haired MacCoinneach son fell beside Gunnar, their blades and bodies locked. Gunnar recovered, righted himself, and stumbled backward.

Rothwell groaned from the ground. He held a hand high in retreat. "No!" he pleaded.

The other MacCoinneach son, thickset and muscular, with a wild mane of red-brown hair, stood above the fallen Rothwell. He didn't hesitate before running him through. She screamed, her voice unable to compete with their fighting.

"Control yerself, Gwyn!" Venora said.

Who? Who would she choose?

Rothwell gurgled, then was silent. She couldn't heal a dead man.

She broke from Venora's grasp and ran to the nearest injured man, the brown-haired MacCoinneach who had been fighting against Gunnar. Her brother hobbled away, sheathing his sword. She blew a breath. Gunnar would be well. She laid her stone-filled hand on the man. He was covered in blood. She couldn't even assess his injury. This would take many breaths from her and was beyond any herbal infusion. She'd be bedridden for days if she healed him. She centered herself anyway.

"Get off him!" a man said from beside her, raising his sword. She turned. He was the other MacCoinneach son. The red-haired beast. The one who had killed Rothwell.

She still held her dagger in one hand. "No!" she said, shielding herself from the incoming blow. Gunnar swooped in and shoved the man aside.

"Heathen! You go after a woman?" Gunnar hollered, holding his side and tottering. Gunnar. He didn't look well. But he still stood, she assured herself. He was well.

Metal sliced through the air as they fought.

She turned to the man on the ground and sheathed her dagger in her pocket. She ignored the hollers and curses. She could only help one at a time. Rothwell was lost. Killed mercilessly by that beast. How many would fall? She held the man's gaze. "I'm Gwyn. I'll help you. Lie still."

A painful moan escaped his lips. Then he said, "M-My Meredith. I must get to her."

"You will." She began, concentrating on Eir to prepare for a healing but was interrupted by a blur of motion and thunderous hooves.

Several men rode into the clearing. "Cease!" a voice bellowed from horseback. It was the MacRuaidhri brothers.

She pursed her lips, one hand frozen on her herb water in her pocket. This man needed more than her small infusion. She needed a greater source of water...a river, loch...

The MacRuaidhris had come too late. Unless they had come to issue harm as well, despite their deal with her father?

Silence fell upon the men as they halted.

Rancorous hate fueled her father's stance. "Dubhgall, you can't possibly think to negotiate further with these heathens. Their king attacked our men on Skye last year.

Now they come here with many men! There is no truce. Return to your home. This is our matter."

"Blasius, these men came to trade. They came to my keep this morn. We both have traded with them aplenty in the past. What the devil is going on here?" Dubhgall responded, dark-haired and threatening, not dismounting his horse. He gestured to the scattered, injured men.

Gunnar lay on the ground, the red-haired MacCoinneach above him, ready to strike him through.

She froze. Gunnar had fallen? Had it been the doing of the red-haired man or the senior MacCoinneach, Alroy? It had been moments—seconds—since Gunnar shoved the man away and taken a sword against him. He had been stumbling, gripping his side. Was that it? Had he already been mortally injured? Had she sentenced her brother to death by helping the mainlander instead? She chided her hasty choice.

The man before her whimpered, gurgled. She turned to him, beginning her healing chant although it was too late. The calm, the focus...was gone. She whispered, "I'm so sorry, so sorry..." She tried anyway.

He held her hand, the one resting on his chest, his eyes understanding. It wounded her more to see his own awareness of his impending death.

Her father spit, rage alight in his piercing blue eyes. "You can't be daft enough to believe they continue to come here for trade." He grimaced as Sigurd picked up Gunnar. Her mother emerged from the cottage and ran past Gwyn to Gunnar's side. She assisted Sigurd with bringing Gunnar into their cottage. Her father seethed, his sword shaking. He directed his venom onto Alroy MacCoinneach. "Never return here. Your goods are no longer welcome. If you should set foot on our soil again, I'll run you through."

The older man of virile health and steadfast demeanor stepped closer, his sword raised. "Let's end this now."

"Father, no," the man beside Gwyn said from the ground. His voice was weak. The other uncouth Mac-Coinneach son dropped to his knees beside her. He assisted his brother to their cart.

He stumbled and winced with a deep gasp as he lifted his brother. This man was also injured. Would he fall, too?

Was there *not one* unscathed man?

Hrmphm, well, her father and Alroy and the other Mac-Coinneach soldiers seemed to be in fair shape. The rest of her father's men rose, nursing wounded limbs and breathing hard.

Rothwell was dead, killed by the red-haired Scot.

Kendrick emerged from the stable but didn't approach. She doubted anyone saw him standing there, deadly calm, ever observant with his keen ability. Blind he might be, but his gaze was transfixed on her. He mouthed something she couldn't decipher. He then pointed to their own cottage. Venora spoke for him, "Gwyn. Come in. Now! Gunnar needs you."

Two of their own. Rothwell...and Gunnar? Her heart broke.

She paused briefly, sharing a look of confusion with the red-haired MacCoinneach son. He climbed into the bed of the cart with his brother, but not before he flashed her another look, one of the devil in his flushed face and copper eyes. The gravely injured brother lay deathly still.

She hurried inside. She had chosen.

CHAPTER TWO

"Stop! He can't take it," Simon said as the cart bumped along the road to Loch nam Madadh. "We need to care for his wounds."

"Simon, we can't. There may be help at the port." His father cast another look over his shoulder to the empty road behind them. The rest of the men were coming afoot and would meet them in town.

He caught his father's gaze. "Blazes, they're not following us. The MacRuaidhris have final authority here. We established our alliance with them today."

His father grumbled under his breath.

"Father, he won't make it to the port. I have to stop the bleeding. Here. Now." He turned to his brother beside him. "Des."

Desmond lifted a hand from his pressed abdomen. Crimson covered his palm and fingers as if he had dunked his hand in a bucket of blood. He winced when Simon lifted the shirt to inspect the slice.

Blood seeped too quickly with no pressure. Or with pressure.

Where was God? Curse that Lochlanach. May he die from his wound as well.

He took his brother's hands and placed them against the wound. They pressed firmly together. He had to stop the bleeding, and then determine how to suture it.

Blood leaked between both sets of hands. The shadows of dusk gave it a black appearance. The gratifying rush of killing that one Lochlanach was fresh in his mind: the heavy blade sliding through the man's gut, the metal tearing flesh, the fear and blood on the man's bearded face as death took his soul. He would have killed all of them if they hadn't been interrupted by the MacRuaidhri brothers.

Simon removed one hand, wiped it on his hose, and traced it across his brother's forehead, now smudged with grime and blood. Desmond's skin was clammy and wet. He didn't have long. Even if he *could* suture, his brother had lost much blood.

His vision blurred, and he clenched his teeth, sending an ache through his skull. "Which one of them did this to you? Was it that woman?" She had knelt over Desmond with her dagger.

Desmond gasped. "No, no. She said she'd heal me."

"She did a fine job."

Desmond winced again.

"Their men kill with sword, and their women with poison. I doubt she was going to help you."

"Simon, not everyone is evil."

They would never get to Loch nam Madadh in time, even if there were healers or herbalists available. He jostled and nearly fell backward when they rolled over a divot. "Father," Simon growled.

More curses from his father.

This was the end for Desmond MacCoinneach.

"I regret my words," Desmond mumbled.

Simon reached into the small crate and grabbed a clay jug of their best whisky, aged ten years. Their father had intended to give it to Blasius. "Bloody hell." He withdrew it, pulled out the cork with his teeth, and lifted it to his brother's lips. "Drink, Des."

His father halted the cart. The lateness of day shrouded them in black despair as the last glimpse of the sun slid behind the horizon. This was it. His brother was going to die in the darkness on this godforsaken rock.

"Don't stop!"

Grief had aged his father two decades in the past few years...in the past few minutes. He gave his son the look of a man who'd lost much already. First their mother and now Desmond. "Say your goodbyes, lads."

Simon turned to his brother. "Don't ever regret your words, Des. You've been a man of peace. I wish I could be as honorable a man as you." Shivers erupted within him. His knee throbbed and the wound in his arm stung, painful reminders of his truth.

Desmond swallowed. "Aye, not those words."

He must have looked confused.

"I said this would be my last visit here."

He tried to smile at Desmond's portentous words but found himself unable as his heart shattered into a thousand pieces.

In the face of his injuries, Gunnar didn't whimper or moan.

Gwyn hurried to her mother's side.

Gunnar was covered in blood. She wished Kendrick were here to read his lifeblood. Had it dimmed to a ginger glow? Kendrick had always said Gunnar radiated a red-hot center. Was his vibrancy gone? Did it fade as his body's life poured from him upon their beaver pelt?

"Here, Gwyn." Mother grabbed her shaking hand and guided it to Gunnar's side wound. She then drew her own hands over Gunnar's stomach. "Take your stone. The larger one. Yes. Close your eyes. Center and repeat after me."

She did as told. She'd done this many times, even if those healings were for minor cuts or complaints and once a broken bone. She'd never healed someone this badly injured. Never like this for her brother. Would she be bedridden for days after? She didn't care; it was worth it.

She closed her eyes and focused on his core lifeblood and the fluidity of water, for water was her conduit. The lifeblood was a person's essence, as her mother had taught her. She focused on the way Kendrick had described it to her. Red, flowing like a waterfall. Strong, cascading, ever-fed by the river. She breathed in and out, allowing herself to feel Gunnar's pulse beneath her fingertips. She gripped the Healer's stone as her mother poured a flask of herbal water on Gunnar's side wound. Her stone warmed.

Her mother uttered the words, "Breathe life into him. Water into breath. Earth into being."

The words she never said aloud, but she had memorized, Gwyn repeated in her mind. Her mother whispered them aloud in her own native Ancient tongue. Gwyn's knowledge of the Ancient language was limited to the handful of words required for healing, and she translated in her mind:

Pull breath from my body.

Heal this man with my own breath.

May it flow through his veins from my heart to his heart.

The sacrifice of a Healer.

May his days be evermore.

She didn't feel the breath escape her lungs like usual even though her heart rate quickened with the exertion. Nothing happened.

She repeated the Healer's chant aloud this time in Ancient tongue with her mother.

Again.

Nothing.

Gwyn opened her eyes.

Gunnar shuddered violently. He locked eyes with their mother, who had also ceased her chanting. She lifted her hand to her son's cheek. "May you feast in Asgard."

"Try harder! What good are you?" roared her father, an overbearing pacing presence behind them. Gwyn had forgotten he was there.

Calmly, her mother said, "He is too far, husband."

He stormed out of the cottage with a curse.

Venora rose and disappeared into the shadows behind their father. Outside to who knows where. Gwyn's bitterness rose. Venora had known. She had *known* and said nothing.

A small tear dribbled down her mother's smooth cheek. "Take the mercy of Eir, the peace of Jörd, and the glory of the Ancients as you pass through the Silver Veil. We will see you again," she said in a painful whisper.

Her mother had only mentioned Asgard for the sake of appeasing Father, for he scoffed at the idea of the Silver Veil. Caoimhe the Graceful One was an Ancient to her bones though.

Gunnar lifted a hand, squeezed Gwyn's tightly, then closed his eyes, and his grip slackened.

Silence engulfed them. Her mother rose with a gulping sob.

Gwyn couldn't pull herself from her older brother. She wiped the tears that had fallen down his cheeks, brushed aside his red-blond hair, and caressed his cheek. Bloodlust had killed him. Their father had slithered his way into Gunnar's soul, making him a cold-hearted beast thirsting for murder, like the rest of the Nordmen. He had yet to take a wife. He had no bairns. He died a warrior who had refused to learn the merciful ways of the Ancients. May the gods punish her father. He had poisoned her brother's mind with the glories of the afterlife, and there he was.

Gwyn didn't realize she was crying until her mother spoke again as she returned from the corner of the cottage with a woven wool blanket. She laid it over her son, covering his face. Fiery blue eyes forever closed.

"Gwyn, we cannot mourn for long." She sniffled.

"What?"

Her mother stared at her, green eyes aglow with introspection. "There is time to heal the other."

"I don't understand. Did Venora not say one of theirs would fall?" she reminded. "Damn them all." She hugged herself.

Her mother embraced her. "You don't mean that."

She was right. She couldn't let a man die when she had the power to save him.

Numbed from what had happened, but determined, she lifted her herbals box. "If Venora has seen it, then how—"

"Gunnar was not the one to be saved tonight."

"Did our powers not work on him? Like with Kendrick? Was he too far gone?"

Dark locks fell loose from her mother's plait as she nodded. "I don't have all the answers. Gunnar was not meant to be saved, and he *was* too close to the Veil. As for Kendrick," she began, lowering her voice to a quieter whisper, even though Gwyn's father was long gone, "his blindness is beyond our powers. It would take every last breath."

It would kill them. She didn't need to voice that horrible truth.

Gwyn pulled on her cloak, fastened the clasp, and made for the door.

"Take Kendrick with you, away from this," her mother said. "Be swift and discreet. I'll do my best to distract your father."

As Gwyn trudged to the stable, her herbal box nestled under one arm, panic gripped her. What if their father had stomped away to take his rage out on Kendrick? Her younger brother had not played a hand in the altercation. He hadn't cowered, but he hadn't taken a sword to fight by their side as any Nordman would do.

The stable appeared empty in the low light of dusk. She regretted not bringing a candle or lantern. She searched. Her father was nowhere to be found at least. "Kendrick?" she called into the stable, squinting past the first stall. Her muscles tensed, and she tripped on the hay-covered dirt floor as she pushed open each stall door. "Kendrick?" she called, louder.

"Here." He crept out of the corner.

She jumped and covered her racing heart with a hand. Dread was a heavy rock in her stomach. "Gunnar's dead." Her lip trembled on the words. "He—do you feel him?"

Kendrick jerked his head. "He's gone," he said with no remorse.

She held back the tears at his confirmation. "I-I need to find the other man who was injured. Kendrick, I must."

"They took the road to Loch nam Madadh. We can take Mora. She's fastest."

He didn't ask why. She didn't need to say more so they rode in silence. As night beckoned, doubt returned to her mind. What if he was already dead? "Can you feel him? The injured one?"

"Many were injured," he replied from behind her on the horse. "I'm far away. I can't sense any of their lifebloods yet."

What if they were already gone?

A short while later, they approached the port town, slowing the horse to a walk.

"You've never been like Gunnar and Da," she said.

She slid off first and allowed Kendrick to remain on Mora as she guided the mare along the path. Moving kept her legs busy and quieted her mind.

"I may be going blind, but I'm well enough to see right from wrong. Not every man thinks the same as our father. There are honorable men."

"You've always been the precocious one. Not necessarily with skill, but in wisdom." She wanted to add, 'Tis a shame Father doesn't see it that way. The red-haired MacCoinneach's eyes, hell-bent on death, taunted her memory. "You're a rare one, Kendrick. Few men think like you. It need not matter if it be Scot or Nordman." She quickened her step. "There!"

The Scots' cart, still filled with goods waiting to be traded rested outside one of the merchants' taverns. She handed Kendrick the reins. The mare ducked her head and nibbled the long grass. "I think you should wait here."

"Why?"

She shrugged in the evening shadows, knowing full well he couldn't see her. His vision was so impaired he hardly saw movement, let alone any sort of detail. "What if they think we sought retribution when they see both of us, and you on horseback and a man? You're not exactly a wee lad anymore. They could see us as a threat."

He nodded. "Aye."

"Do you sense any darkness?"

He pressed his lips together. "No. I'll wait here, but if I do sense something, I won't be far behind you." His eyes glazed over, and he gripped his head. "Och."

"What is it?" she whispered. She steadied him on the horse before he could slip.

He muffled a moan. "'Tis too late. He is dead, Gwyn."

A stab of defeat held her immobile for a moment. "There were others injured?"

"I'll be well," he answered her unspoken question. "Go, check. Do what you must."

She straightened her shoulders and rounded the cottage. *Grant me mercy and strength.*

One last look at Kendrick, who nodded his approval, and she entered the tavern.

"We need to sail tonight," barked Alroy MacCoinneach to a weather-battered man at the table. She didn't recognize the man from the original crew who had landed on the machair shore. She had a skill for remembering faces, and she knew many in this port town. Was he their captain?

"Aye, I ken well enough, sir, but there's a storm stirrin' and it may sink the ship. Besides, a fleet o' the wolves patrol these waters. We do not sail at night. We leave in the morn, sir." The captain took another drag from his cup.

"I paid you handsomely. We need to leave tonight. Those Lochlanach are of no concern. We sailed last night and fared well."

The place reeked of sweaty men, boiling fish, and strong mead. Haggard, grimy men sat around tables, drinking. The scents were overwhelming, and Gwyn sneezed. Surprised scowls of townsfolk, and some Scots, glared at her. So much for discretion.

She gave her best apologetic smile as they returned to their drinks and conversations. All seemed well. She was a local and had healed many of them. The glower from Alroy was a look that could kill. His was the only gaze that had *not* left hers after a moment. Where were the injured ones? The brothers? She opened her mouth to ask but instead slipped through the doorway to look elsewhere.

One was dead, Kendrick had said.

Just as she stepped outside, she bumped into the gruff, red-haired MacCoinneach. "Umph!" she said, taken aback by his size and startled at his sudden appearance.

His halting voice was venomous. "What the devil are you doing here?"

"I-I've come to help," she muttered. She had secretly hoped to help the other MacCoinneach brother, the one with a heart. Her cheeks heated with that shameful thought. He was the dead one. She blinked, sending a prayer for his soul.

"Haven't you done enough?"

His words stung more than his grip on her arm as he led her away from the cottage and Kendrick. Her brother was dismounting as she waved a hand at him. "I'm well," she said in the choppy Old Norse tongue to Kendrick.

"Are you?" the man countered.

Her breath halted. "You know the Nordman's language?"

"Enough to know when they're lying to me," he said through a scowl. "Where's Blasius? Did he send you to finish us with your poison?"

"I've come to help," she repeated. "I have no poisons."

"Your people have done enough. Go home." He loosened his hold on her arm with a wince and sigh.

She released her secret grip on the dagger in her pocket. Her knuckles hurt. She shifted on her feet but didn't retreat. "You're hurt, too. Please, let me help you. I can heal." She touched his forearm, heavy with matching auburn hair. No gooseflesh rippled his skin despite the chill in the air.

"Is that what you were doing with my brother?"

Her resolve fractured within, but she firmed her voice, wavering as it was. "I tried. He was too far gone," she lied. She didn't have the *chance* to heal him. Alan and Dubhgall MacRuaidhri's sudden arrival had interrupted her. She still clung to the hope that he had been savable. That she *had* tried. However, trying wasn't enough. Then Gunnar. Anger burned within her. "My *bróðir* is dead, too. Was it your hand that struck him down?" She shuddered, reminded of poor Rothwell, who had held up his hands in helpless defeat while this red-haired devil sent him to the afterlife. There had been no mercy in that kill.

The man's eyes blazed with a flicker of satisfaction. He gave no answer.

Perhaps she should let him die from the arm wound. Let it fester and take him.

"Go!" he said again, limping toward the doorway.

She muffled a curse under her breath. Was he hurt in his leg, too? He seemed right in body, except for the blood painting his tunic sleeve and his staggered gait. There was a chance he'd die from infection on the voyage to the mainland though. There were no Healers like her in the port town, and the wound needed suturing, dressing, or more. Her dislike of him put aside, it was her responsi-bility—her burden—to heal.

"Let me help you," she tried again.

He turned on her, bringing his face a breath's distance from hers. He smelled of mead and glared with threat. "Help me? What of my brother's soul?"

She whispered, "I can't help with that. But I can help with this." She swallowed and laid her hand on his arm. She met his dark brown eyes, then closed hers, not releasing her grip on his arm. She breathed two deep life-giving breaths.

Pull breath from my body.

Heal this man with my own breath.

A thermal life filled her fingertips as she clasped the Healer's stone in her pocket. For something small, water was not necessary. However, if the injury were left unat-tended, it could and *would* kill.

The man faltered but didn't move from her light grasp. Wind rustled her hair as Eir surrounded her. Unlike her mother, she never plaited it for healing. She liked to feel Eir's fingers upon her and the fiery rush of healing as it flowed through her arms to the injured person, as the wind lifted her hair, announcing its presence.

"What the—?" He drew in a sharp breath.

She mouthed the rest of the chant, invoking the goddess's power. She moved closer to him, their bodies an intimate—and stirring—distance apart. His nearness captured her breath, and not just from the healing.

"What are you doing?" His words said one thing while his body said another. He didn't step away. His breathing hitched and then steadied.

"It's not the devil's works," she clipped.

"Then what in the devil are you saying? That's not Norse."

She ignored him. He placed a gentle, nearly sedated hand on her free arm in protest, but he did nothing. Her healing had a way of stunning and spellbinding her charges. It was working.

A long moment passed. She opened her eyes and stepped back, releasing her hold. He let go of her other arm and immediately reached to touch the wound. Her stomach twisted as she broke from the enchantment. This was her father's enemy, a murderer. Finished with her prayer, she stepped away, hit with coldness.

"No need to touch it. It'll be sore, and you'll need to have it stitched properly when you return home or on the ship if possible. I have needle and fibers in my box. If you wait, I can do it. Where else do you hurt? Your leg?" She reached for his thigh, but he shifted out of reach.

"Leave it."

She retracted her hand. "I can—"

"Simon!" Alroy called from within.

He regarded her with indecision. His thick brown eyebrows curled; he stroked his throat and grimaced. He then went inside.

She turned toward a silent, observant Kendrick, but she stumbled. She wheezed and allowed placating thoughts to ease her discomfort as she leaned against the outside of the tavern. Two quenching breaths and she hurried to meet her brother.

Kendrick offered a hand to her as she lifted herself in front of him on the saddle. Fatigue railed within her lungs.

"You should have let him suffer," he said bitterly. "I don't like to see your breaths taken, Gwyn."

His remark surprised her. Kendrick was not one to wish ill or hold grudges. Then again, these men had murdered Gunnar. She said, "Is he well?"

"Aye, he is. Glowing like amber, steadfast and true. Gwyn, he is the one I mentioned. He is the one with the hurting soul that no amount of healing can mend."

She resisted the urge to look back. "Perhaps, but no soul is unredeemable. You've even said it. Now haste us home before Father learns of this."

Gwyn and Kendrick returned to a darkened village. A quiet mourning had fallen upon their small community composed mostly of the families of the Nordmen who had come to Uist nearly twenty-five years ago with their father. Their village on the outskirts of Port nan Long was not far, less than an hour by horse, from the eastern ports.

Each step lightened as Gwyn recovered her stamina after the healing.

Near Sigurd's cottage, the chisel of hammer against stone beat in rhythm with her heart. Her father had been quick to order their smith to prepare Gunnar's rune stone. What else was a father to do once his eldest son died?

Speaking of the mad devil...

Their father paced in front of the stable. Dread surmounted any hope she had acquired after healing Simon MacCoinneach.

Her father grabbed Kendrick by the leg and pulled him from the horse. Kendrick grunted as his body hit the ground. He righted himself and stiffened, readying for the next punch, his face drawn to the ground.

"Where were you?" their father hissed, balling fists at his side.

Gwyn made to step between them, but her brother shoved her aside as he took the first punch to the gut. Then another to the face. He remained standing but dared not fight. It was not his place. Nor hers.

Belatedly she said, "We were gathering herbs to prepare Gunnar's body."

Another wallop to his side. With each one, the breath was sucked from her as Kendrick swallowed his moans and squinted with pain.

"Stop, Father!" she cried.

Her brother fell again. Their father kicked him in the side with a sickening thud and then spat. His slender face crinkled with distaste. "Only the strongest hail from the Nord Land! Ha! You're not a Nordman...you're not even a man! Where were you when your brother fought and died for his people? You carry on with these *women*...women who have abilities you could only wish for! You're a disgrace. You can't fight, and you've yet to show any Ancient power. What good are you?"

Kendrick didn't whimper or cry. He absorbed each blow of body and word.

"You've not learned the sword like your brother. What use are you? I'd be better training Gwyn and Venora than you. You tend *horses*. You're no better than a *thrall*." He slicked his long hair back from his face. The fumes of drink saturated his breath as he paced like a mad dog.

Kendrick remained quiet.

Like all frenzied dogs looking for a fight, their father eventually simmered when his opponent didn't take the bait. He gave a quick disgusted snort and stalked away in a huff toward Sigurd's cottage.

Gwyn reached for Kendrick, and he shrugged her away. "Leave me. These wounds will heal on their own," he whispered, slinking inside the stable.

She slowly made her way to their cottage. Inside, her mother and Venora prepared Gunnar's body for burial.

"Gwyn, you must be more careful." Her mother strode over to Gunnar's body with a wet cloth.

She heaved a sigh and approached the hearth. "You told me to go." She didn't ask if her mother had heard or seen the attack at the stable. They all knew.

Her mother dabbed at Gunnar's bare chest. "That is not of which I speak."

Venora shrugged, tight-lipped and resolute, her focus elsewhere.

Gwyn rummaged through her box for the herbals needed, her spirit crestfallen for her brothers: one dead, one forever tormented by their father.

Gunnar would have a Norse ritual, and not being a jarl, he would be buried with a rune stone in the small cemetery instead of being commemorated with a ship fire. Her mother would want him bestowed with Ancient rites, too. They moved methodically, cleaning, rubbing ointments, and dressing him down to the last buckle and pin. She drew an antler comb through Gunnar's thick locks, inherited from their father, richly golden with shimmers of red. He had been a handsome man, with high cheekbones and commanding presence. A wife would have done him well. Perhaps it would have changed his tainted mindset.

She placed a silver arm ring with a dragon at its terminus, on his right forearm. Her mother positioned his sword, bejeweled with amber and jet on the hilt, upon his chest. "Why is it broken?" Gwyn asked, running a finger along the sword where it had been cleanly divided with a chisel. This was her first family burial aside from the young infant her mother had given birth to last year, its breaths never taken. She was not unfamiliar with bestowing the dead with accouterments as they made their way into the afterlife but a *broken* sword?

In a resigned voice, her mother said, "A Norse warrior must visit Asgard with his weapon killed as payment for entry into the afterlife."

Gwyn sighed. The Norse ways were founded in foolish myths and superstitions, and she suspected her mother agreed. Mother always did as told though. She had learned quickly how to survive and acquiesce after Blasius of Varteig brought his warriors to her homeland and forced himself into her bed. Gwyn wondered if her mother ever truly loved him or if he loved her mother in return, beyond her gift and body. There was nothing to adore of the man who waved a madman's fist over the entire village. Had her father once possessed a loving soul?

"Mother, why couldn't we save him?"

Her fingers paused in preparation. "Gwyn, you have questions for which I don't know the answer. He was too far gone for even our combined powers."

Gloomy and quiet, Venora prepared a kettle of water to boil.

Gwyn caught her mother's look upon Venora. "You knew," she accused her sister. "You knew and did nothing. You let us try. Now Gunnar is dead," she gulped, grief overcoming her. "That other man, the red-haired man's brother, is also dead. You knew *who* and said nothing!"

Venora turned with a huff. Gwyn caught her shoulder.

"We cannot alter fate." Venora regarded her with unwelcome frankness, her mouth downturned. "It is my burden alone."

"We could've saved the other man!"

"Ye chose."

Her sister's words were ice down her spine. She wanted to smack her. "You're a simple-minded, self-righteous—"

"Gwyn!" her mother interrupted. "Enough. This was not our place. Gunnar wasn't ours to save. Do not question your sister's visions or her loyalty."

She shared a look of contest with her sister. Sharp blue eyes, lost against a sea of pale complexion, stared at her.

Venora raised her voice. "Ye want to ken only when it's convenient. Ye're an idealist, ye with yer *mercy*." She pinched her lips together for a moment, a hundred tight lines. "Impetuous to act, never seeing the full picture. Ye don't want to ken." She frowned. "A Seer's burden is not the same! I see death every day. It torments my sleep. So much blood and lust and when they die, I feel it, sister. Gunnar's soul tore through me. Kendrick feels it, too! You...*you* are spared! Ye moan about not being able to pour breath into another body. Try having the wind whirl through ye like a maelstrom, helpless to stop it!" Venora tossed her hands in the air, her voice rising and shaking.

Muscles throbbed in Gwyn's arms and legs. A striking humiliation stole her words. Shuddering, she hugged her arms to her body. Belatedly she countered, "You don't lose your life bit by bit with each vision, as I do with each healing. One day it may just kill me."

Venora plunged on, her stare fixed on Gwyn. "Something bigger is coming. A vast fleet of the dragon's teeth will sail across the Nord Sea." Pink filled Venora's cheeks.

"What?"

"They come to die. The Norse reign will meet its end."

Gwyn blinked, stunned into silence. Her mother's resigned look confirmed Venora's prediction.

"King Haakon's realm will be defeated on a shore near the Isle of Cumbrae on the second day of the tenth new moon, the morning after a great gale."

Gwyn quickly calculated. That was a month away. "How is that possible? His fleet is infinite. His men fierce. They control many of the isles. And..." She paused, reconciling the information. "My betrothed is coming for me. Is he not?"

Always gracefully submissive, her mother shrugged. "I do not know."

"A Seer cannot lie, sister. It is my *gift*," Venora said, nearly spitting the word. She added, bitterly, "It is my curse."

Gwyn was surprised at the mixture of fear and relief within her. An end for her father's people was near? What about their family? Would they be safe on Uist? Or would the Scots use the opportunity to exploit the Ancients, too? Her betrothed...perhaps he'd also perish in the fight. The thought was not entirely displeasing. She'd never met Leidolf of Reindalr, but her father had boasted of Leidolf's prominent family. Her stomach turned. He was just another Nordman.

Simon MacCoinneach's fuming face entered her mind. Brown eyes filled with hurt and indignation. Hair like a wild beast.

"One more thing, sister," Venora said, rocking side to side, her voice brittle.

Gwyn twisted her fingers together and then drew a hand into her pocket, her palm seeking the comfort of the river stone to balm the unease.

"That red-haired one, the son of MacCoinneach, he shall perish in this great battle. Ye can do naught about it, for saving him will take a hundred breaths."

The following morning during the burial, Gwyn's father was fully drunk on mead and slurred his way through the ritual prayers. Her mother, always steadfast in her role as dutiful wife and parent, stood by his side at the open grave, the tangible distance between them able to be cut through by a blade. She did not cry, for her puffy eyes held no more tears for her eldest son.

They lived in a cramped cottage of two rooms, and Gwyn heard and saw it all, even on the nights when her father, inebriated with drink, sought comfort beneath the animal furs with her mother. An uncomfortable quake rumbled through her. Soon enough her betrothed would arrive from the Nord Land, and she'd create her own family. Would Leidolf of Reindalr, a man she'd never met, also be a drunk? Would he slide between her legs without a care of her own needs? Would he be a savage beast? Or would he love her the way a man should, the way men did in the stories her mother shared?

Or was love something that only existed in the Ancient stories or beyond the Silver Veil?

Sigurd and Trygg lowered Gunnar's wrapped body into the freshly dug hole beside the grave of his infant brother. Rothwell's wrapped body was lowered next.

Gwyn blinked through fuzzy eyes. She had not slept much, and when she had finally succumbed to sleep, nightmares of Gunnar and the red-haired man beset her.

She didn't know what incensed her more. Her father's lunacy and provocation of the mainlanders? Certainly they *had* come in peace. Her mother's pretense of unruffled obedience? Or Venora's chilly words of premonition? By the gods, all of it.

What about her own behavior? Had she done enough? Had she chosen wrong?

Kendrick stood close. Akin to his feeling ability, he also radiated heat. He squeezed her hand and then let go. He hunched over to hide the black and blue bruises. That MacCoinneach son entered her frayed thinking. Simon. Her blood boiled with his part in this, too.

They all had a hand in these deaths, their consciences soiled.

Quiet tears found their way down her cheeks, but they weren't just for Gunnar. What about Kendrick? She had spent her life protecting him. What would their father do now? She swiped the tears and summoned strength.

She hadn't been able to save Gunnar, but she could save Kendrick. She had to.

Their small community lacked a temple or priest so her father stumbled through the prayers. He spoke in his native tongue, rambling about the greatest warriors in Norse history, of prosperity and honor. Rain pattered upon the brown grasses and her battered soul. What now?

As he continued, the rain grew heavier. She let it soak her skin. It wet her hair and dribbled down her neck. The coldness of it, usually a comfort, was anything but. She let the rain be her tears. She sobbed for their unknown path.

Nordmen didn't cry. There were no words of grief to be shared, only boasting and glory. Sigurd and Trygg and the rest of the Nordmen, about ten of them, stood with their families. They were dressed in their finest warrior's clothes, decked with weapons, carefully groomed beards, and silver and bronze bracelets. As were their sons. No pure Ancient men remained in her village anymore, long since slaughtered. The lucky few had fled.

Who needs weapons at a funeral?

Later tonight, the men would raise drinks to Gunnar's new glory: afterlife in Asgard. Norse women were not to shed a tear either. She was no Norse woman. Curse those beasts. Curse them. She hugged her arms against her stomach. Tonight she would find comfort in the sacrament of the Ancients. The women would gather at the stone circle, embrace Jörd's inner peace, and celebrate Gunnar's life.

Moreen approached Gwyn from behind her parents, Eskil and Lavena. Despite the rain, her friend placed an arm around her, her usual pluck replaced with solemnness. She said nothing. Her comfort was enough to awaken a glimmer of hope within Gwyn.

A few minutes later, after the last rites were completed, her father drew near. She straightened her shoulders and dabbed her face with a wet hand. Kendrick kept his posture straight and rigid, hyper-focused upon the burial mound before them as Trygg and Sigurd shoveled.

"Gwyn, you will go with Venora to Àrasaig in Gunnar's stead, on the morrow to gather the winter provisions."

She blinked and nodded. "Yes, Father."

"Trygg and Sigurd will escort you."

She nibbled on her lip. "Yes, Father."

Her father clapped a hand on Kendrick's back. Kendrick pressed his lips together, his posture stalwart. "We've much work to do here."

Inside, Gwyn wept.

"Come, Gwyn! Gather yer wits. Ye lie like a sack o' oats. We ken how they fester when left to be a wet muddle." Moreen poked Gwyn.

"Soggy oats?"

Moreen gifted her with a wide, large-toothed smile. "Aye."

Gwyn couldn't help but laugh. "You and food. You'll make a delightful wife one day. All your ingenious concoctions. Just don't serve him soggy oats." She then moaned and curled farther beneath the comfort of her fur. She was still in her damp funeral clothes.

"Aye, my husband shall be as fat as a pig!"

Gwyn resisted smiling. "Bannocks, mutton, and the best bread in the village," she said dully, but factually.

"Come. Ye're to be off t'morrow. We must go to the stones tonight to remember yer brother, Gwynnie. First," she said with a wrinkle of her nose, "ye need dry clothes."

Gwyn nudged her face from the fur. "You've not called me that in years."

"Well, ye're actin' like a wee thing, Gwynnie, not the woman of twenty-two and soon-to-be wife that ye are."

She tossed the fur aside. "Aye. You're right." She rose, stretched, and located her dry gown. She then hung her damp gown beside the hearth and changed, her fingers still ice-cold despite the warmth beneath her animal furs.

"I ken ye miss yer brother. Now we do our part for his spirit."

She sniffled. Heartache encircled her more than the cold. If it was a chill, a dram with garlic would work to nip it quickly. She hurried through kirtle and gown and a brush of her hair. "Let us go." She left her herbal box behind, pulled on her cloak, and followed Moreen from the room. She *was* acting childishly. Certainly they were all mourning. Hers held guilt, too. She sucked in a breath of smoky peat-filled air. She clutched the stone in her pocket. No herbals were needed for this part of the Ancient ritual. They relied solely upon the gods and goddesses.

She had to forgive herself. There was healing to be done. She had been bestowed a remarkable gift. She could do good. Barbarian though he might be, she had saved the red-haired MacCoinneach. If that meant anything in the grand scheme of things. Broken bone or broken spirit, all healings held significance to her.

Her mother, Venora, and Moreen's mother, Lavena, already awaited them outside by a cart. Her father hadn't allowed them to bring Gunnar's body to the stones last night, but they could still perform their own last rites today for the warrior lost too soon.

Gwyn hopped in the cart, and they rode as the afternoon sun peeked through the gray clouds. It would be a sunset ritual. They bumped along, none speaking, but all aware of each other's presence. She wished Kendrick could've come along, for his own abilities were enhanced at the stones. Once when they'd gone alone, the two of them, he fell to the ground overwhelmed with the penetrating colors of life. The stones were powerful. Their father had already left with Kendrick to ride to Port nan Long to meet with the MacRuaidhri clan this morning. She hated to contemplate what plans were being formulated. Would her father retaliate against the MacCoinneachs? What about Kendrick? How much longer could he hide his impairment?

A short while later, they reached the stone circle. This place of worship had been built long before her mother's birth. Her mother had taught her to harness the earth's energy here. Mother Earth, Jörd, provided gifts to those who sought her. Each gift utilized an element. Kendrick's gift was nurtured by fire, and Venora heard the whispers of the wind. Water was Gwyn's element.

Always a bubbling spirit, Lavena chatted with Gwyn's mother as they ambled up the small ridge to the circle of stones on a wide, flat, raised mound. Her mother even laughed as the longtime friends leaned against each other, their arms linked.

"Your ma has such a spirit, Moreen."

Moreen nodded, her wiry brown hair bobbing with it. "Aye, 'is a shame Jörd never bestowed her with a gift."

"Laughter is her gift," Gwyn said.

"Aye."

"As is your pluck."

Moreen jabbed her. "Pluck is not exactly a gift."

"It is to me."

Her friend smiled widely. Although younger than Gwyn by a few years, she was a genial soul. Kendrick said her lifeblood was a tawny, earthy ale. Like her mother Lavena, Moreen possessed no gift, but she had a strong connection with Jörd. She homed in on the truths life played, reading people and seeing things, similar to a heightened form of intuition.

They held hands and found their way to the first stone, the massive blue-streaked one.

Gwyn laid a hand upon it. A humming filled her soul, and she breathed in the life around her. This stone exhibited the strongest healing sensation.

Venora and her mother assembled the fire in the middle of the large slabs of stone, building it of rowan and oak branches. Lavena sprinkled a mixture of dried roses, thistle, heather, mugwort, and hazelnuts in a circle around the wood. Once the fire was lit, they held hands and stood around the small blaze. Her mother prayed in the Ancient tongue, most of the words unfamiliar to Gwyn. Some words were Norse from the Futhark alphabet, and she had to wonder how much of the ritual was Ancient Silver Folk and how much was Norse-influenced. Although Nordmen held their beliefs in the gods and goddesses, the Ancients did as well. The Ancients' deities bore no actual name until the Nordmen had come, so they had adopted those names. To the Ancients, there were the elements of being: wind, fire, water, and Mother Earth.

Her mother translated for them.

"Mother Jörd, of our uncultivated earth. Daughter of Night and Water. We bestow upon you the soul of Gunnar of Varteig, your son and our brother. Draw him into your embrace as he crosses through the Silver Veil. May his flesh bring fertility to our land, fruit to our trees, and new life to our people."

Lavena then spoke. "Our sisters of Fire, Wind, and Water are with us. Rise, fire goddess," she said, as they lifted linked hands, palms up. Their fire goddess lacked a name. Kendrick was the only one in their village with fire's gift. The flames flickered, a welcome warmth on Gwyn's chilled skin. "Njord, our wind goddess, our winds are your winds. Blow around us, fill us with your Sight of introspection and premonition. May we use it for good. Steer our paths on The Way."

The wind quickened and whirled around them.

Venora's eyes were closed, and she swayed.

Lavena continued. "Bylgia, let your water billow in waves on our sea, rain upon our land, and stream through our villages. Assist Eir, our goddess of mercy, with your healing. Together, bring mercy to one and all."

Gwyn ignored the rest of the prayers and chants as she moved in remembered ritual from their seasonal prayers.

Mercy for one and all? She squeezed her eyes shut and did her best to feel the earth's hum, allowing compassion to settle into her essence.

She shivered with the thought of mercy and healing, a sobering reminder of how limited her gift truly was.

Leidolf of Reindalr left his spot at the steerboard to pace the deck as the longship sliced through the turbulent Nord Sea. Sea spray dampened the planks, and the stones filling the keel rumbled with jolts. A few carelessly anchored crates slid across the deck.

"Tie those down, lest we lose them!" he hollered to two crewmen. The men rose from their rowing bench and hurried to the wayward crates.

They had made it through the night's squall. Morning's first sign, a sliver of gray, rose over the seemingly endless horizon.

The ship cut through the waves with each stroke, his forty men tirelessly rowing at their benches. Leidolf quelled the frustration rising within his chest. If his father had provided him with the full capacity of eighty men, they would have already reached Uist. Instead, he had overworked, disgruntled men.

He pressed his lips together and stifled a snort. Why would his father send his youngest son with ample warriors and supplies when they'd do better in service to his more honorable sons, Magnor and Hallbjorn, who were finishing this year's raids on the south land?

Leidolf ran a finger along the deck rail, the smoothed oak consoling his anxious mind. A third of the way to the stern, his finger found the first runic symbol. He paused, traced the familiar lines of a cross and diamond, and then he moved on to the next one at the halfway point. He paused, traced, and moved on to the third. Aware of the eyes upon him, his pulse flickered, but he continued his routine until he reached the bow. Only once he touched the dragon's head and ran his calloused hand along the six raised circles down the beast's neck, could he release his breath. Relief poured through him, not unlike when he was with his whores. Less pleasurable, perhaps, but it steadied his mind, brought him to a sharpened focus.

The wide rectangular sail flapped in the wind, ballooning to full breadth from the massive mast of unseasoned oak wood. Aegir had not gifted him with decent wind through the night, and his men grumbled with discontent. Perhaps the ocean goddess had also thought as little of him as his own father.

As the sail finally caught, he barked orders for half the men to rest. They rose without moaning, locked their oars, and made for the center of the ship where they'd rest for a few hours. Their warship lacked the freeboard of his father's cargo ships, so the men were forced to rest where they found space on the deck. Leidolf bent over the deck rail and breathed in the familiar, briny air. Streaks of pink scattered the gray clouds as dawn made room for day. No birds joined them as the bow carved through choppy whitecaps. Wind drafted through his hair and chilled him, but he welcomed the cold. It kept him alert, kept him awake. He needed to focus on his task.

For, these weren't *his* men. These were his father's warriors, men bribed by greed and the promise of glory. Men who paid homage to Magnus of Reindalr, not to his third-born son with naught to his name *except* for his name. He had to declare his worth to his father. In a few days, Leidolf would retrieve his promised bride, the enthralling beauty Gwyn, daughter of Blasius the Mad. Then he'd kill the Mad Jarl and his sons, maintain proper rule over their village, and prepare for the rest of King Haakon's fleet. Much of the king's fleet was dispersed throughout the isles and had begun congregating south, near Cumbrae. After the Scottish king's attempt to root them out on Skye, King Haakon had taken no more chances. Many ships, thousands of Nordmen, were gathering. Their opportunity was coming.

He inspected the sail as the lines grew taut. He drew the sunstone from his pocket, awaiting the sun to rise higher from the fog so he could determine their direction.

The red wolf's head, a symbol of their bloodline, snarled at him from the sail. Soon, he would carve out his own den, eradicate contenders, and rise as a leader, showing his father a lone wolf could be as ruthless as the rest of the pack.

CHAPTER THREE

After his brother's funeral, Simon lumbered out of the newly built small chapel and directly to the village healer. He'd heard enough about God's blessings and the fruition of a holy life for one day. He stretched his arm and shoulder. They no longer ached, and the wound looked clear. The captain's wife had used a suitable bronze needle and thread to stitch it before he departed on the weeklong journey home to Dornie. It would surely leave a scar, but he was not unfamiliar with those. He moved his shoulder in a circular motion, testing it. Och, it was as if he'd never been cut.

He reached Mervyn's cottage and hesitated. The place always smelled rancid with jars of herbs, vials of strange concoctions, and burnt plants in aromatic discord. What could Mervyn do anyway? He'd visited the healer many times since the incident nine years ago, and Mervyn always told him the same thing, handing him the same weak tincture. He turned to leave, but the door opened. Damn, had he sensed him?

"Ah, Simon, how fare ye?" a disembodied, nasal voice came.

He grimaced and turned. "Good morn, Mervyn. Was walking past."

"Yer father mentioned ye might need attention. Come in, come in. Let me see. Do ye need more musk mallow?" He waved a knobby hand, swollen with age and work.

Simon relented with a nod. "Aye." He slouched onto a stool near the low-burning hearth.

Mervyn tottered around, led by his walking stick. "Could I offer you some spiced honey water?"

"Nay, I must be on my way. I was"—he grasped at any excuse—"going on a hunt. The red stags have been prime this month."

Mervyn nodded as he prepared a kettle. "Anything new that ails ye? This foul weather is surely flaring yer knee, sir?"

"Aye." He gritted his teeth but decided not to correct him. They were humble stewards to a castle and land with no clear laird. He was no "sir." The former steward, God rest his soul, had ordained his father the steward nearly ten years before. Certainly the MacCoinneachs performed the tasks of a ruling clan: run the castle, maintain the village and fields, collect taxes for the crown, and uphold traditions. All without a title. He wasn't sure if his father was truly a patient man or a fool, hanging on King Alexander's empty promises. Their glen was one of the few remaining without a lairdship.

"Just this," Simon said, rolling up his sleeve.

Mervyn inspected the injury.

One last effort, his father had assured him before they went to Uist. He balled his hand into a fist. Now his brother was dead and they were no closer to kinship with the MacRuaidhris, and they had dug a deeper chasm of discontent between them and the Nordmen of the isles. *May the devil take the lot of them.*

Mervyn prodded with a calloused fingertip around the sutured area. "Does this hurt here?"

He shook his head.

"Here?"

"No."

He continued to poke.

"Any fever? Warmth on the arm? Irritated bowels?" Mervyn rattled on, his attention engrossed by the healed cut.

"No. I feel well, considering."

Mervyn rubbed his chin. "Interesting."

Simon rose to leave.

"Wait." Mervyn held a hand up. "You need a tincture to stave a fever in case."

"I have no fever. I've traveled a week. I'm well."

"Who tended yer wound?" Mervyn eyed him with hooded suspicion beneath furry white eyebrows.

He swallowed and pulled away from Mervyn's scrutiny. "The captain's wife stitched the injury before we boarded the ship."

Mervyn pressed his lips together, wrinkles drawing together on his upper lip. His face blanched to nearly match his white hair. "This was a deep wound, Simon. Stitching alone was not enough for it. Ye lost a lot of blood?"

"Not as much as my brother," Simon retorted.

Mervyn didn't retreat. His voice penetrating, he said, "I daresay ye met with a Healer?"

He controlled his frustration with a grimace.

"Not one like me." Mervyn waved a hand to his vials. "My knowledge ceases at herbals and infusions. This here was the work of an *isles Healer*," he said with clear emphasis. "I've heard about the life breathers of the isles. They're said to rely on the water and earth goddess for their powers. Ancients. Ye're familiar with them?"

"You speak blasphemy, Mervyn."

Mervyn snorted, shuffling around. "I speak truths."

He stood. "I won't repeat this to my father or our priest."

The old man eyed him with fascination as Simon tried, and failed, to instill a threatening countenance. He mumbled under his breath and left the cottage. "Good day, Mervyn."

A few days later after another unsuccessful hunt for stag, Simon made his way to the keep, two mountain hares in his hand. Small catches would have to do until he could kill another Nordman.

He found his father, thick in his cups, in the kitchen. He plopped the hares along with his short bow on the table board.

He then made to return to the gardens, anything to avoid the inside of the castle. A castle they resided in but would never rule.

"Simon."

He lowered his head, paused, then lifted it and straightened his shoulders. "Aye, Father?"

"You can't avoid it forever."

"Avoid what? I'm hunting for our people, while you sit here in your cups again."

Commanding eyes glowered sharply as his father grabbed the whisky bottle and refilled his goblet. "I'm well of my wits, son. I've news."

Neither spoke of the heavy sorrow residing between them since Desmond's death. It was he and his father now. His mother, Margaret, rested in Dryburgh Abbey, south of Edinburgh and far away from the madness...fighting her own evil spirits. Since the worsening of her condition, he could no longer bring himself to visit her. Guilt stabbed him. Had his father sent a message to his mother that her eldest son was dead? Would she blame Simon? He shook his head to dislodge the painful thoughts creeping in.

Reluctantly, he asked, "What news?"

"I received a message from Farlene this morning."

Interest piqued, he said, "And?" Farlene had stayed in the port town on Uist as a listening ear.

"The Mad Jarl has sent his two daughters and two of his men to Àrasaig for the harvest market this week."

Simon shifted on his feet and cracked his knuckles.

He wanted nothing else to do with the Lochlanach, especially the Mad Jarl. Hadn't they already done enough? Mother. Desmond. His knee throbbed again, and he stifled the sensation by grabbing the whisky bottle from his father and sipping a hefty gulp without a goblet. He should have taken a swallow of Mervyn's musk mallow tincture instead. "What would you have me do? Blasius will no longer trade with us. The MacRuaidhri clan is a lost effort. We need to focus on the clans here if we are to win King Alexander's favor."

"No, there is much we can still do. You are to go to the market."

Simon perked up. His fingers itched, vibrated. He steadied them. "Want me to kill those two men? Send a message to the Mad Jarl?"

"No! There's a better way."

Another sip. It never dulled the pain. The whisky burned. A sweet burn.

His father tightened his voice. "You're to go to the market, steal one of his daughters, and bring her home to Dornie. Wed her, and Blasius will be obligated into an alliance with us."

Simon coughed on the whisky. "What has the kitchen wench been putting in your brew? That's sheer folly. You're as mad as he. We don't steal women. I will not force a woman against her will."

"Blasius is a cunning devil. He plays games. We'll reach a consensus with the MacRuaidhris, give that time, but with the Mad Jarl, we must play like him. Besides..." He lowered his eyes, lost in memory. "We know what these jarls and Lochlanach can do. Your mother, Simon. We must do this for her."

Simon fumed and opened his mouth to speak but was rebutted by his father.

"Blasius is a heartless beast. I saw you with his daughter, the one who came to the tavern in Loch nam Madadh."

Simon swallowed, remembering her fiery touch. "You saw us?"

"She seems bonnie enough. She captivated you, did she not?"

Aye, you could say that. There was no way he was going to tell him about her healing his arm. Instead he said, "Grandda is in agreement?"

His grandfather, Lonn MacCoinneach, had not left his bedchamber since Desmond's funeral. Old Mac-Coinneach the Fierce refused to let his body catch up with his deteriorating mind. Desmond had been his favorite, the chosen one to succeed after their father and grandfather.

"Grandda is in agreement."

Simon muffled a grunt.

"The witch sister, the other one, can take care of herself. Gwyn, his other daughter...we can protect her from Blasius's fist. I've seen what he can do."

"I've seen my share of the Nordmen's cruelty. You know that."

"Aye, I do."

"I know as well as you how pressing this is, but I can't steal her, so don't try using that ploy on me. To save her?"

he scoffed. "She seemed competent to me." He turned to leave.

"Simon, you will not walk away from me!" He slammed a hand on the table. The bottle fell to the floor with a loud crack.

"This is futile, Father. You're as foolish as Desmond to think we can negotiate our way to lairdship! I doubt stealing her would induce him to strike a deal."

His father rose and approached. He drew shaking hands through his graying red hair. He held his son's gaze. He echoed Desmond's words. "The sword is not the only way, Simon."

Simon sighed.

"We must try. We can offer her safety and anything else she wishes. You know well what they will do to her eventually."

Simon relented. There was no arguing with his father. "I'll only marry her if she consents." Had he really just said that? He wrapped his hand around his dagger hilt for comfort. He would never strike his father nor would his father raise a fist or sword to him. The blood pounded in his temple. He tried again. "His son is dead, and you suggest we take his daughter?" The image of her determined face, dark lashes falling over enchanting eyes as she closed them and healed him with her touch, entranced his memory.

Damn him to hell for thinking she could do more with her gift. She was a healer, after all.

Damn him to hell for not ever wanting to touch a woman after what happened to his mother.

Damn him to hell for wanting to slit every Nordman's throat.

In a fragile whisper, his father said, "It was not your fault, Simon."

He snarled and heaved a loud breath as his tenacity crumbled. Bile rose up his throat, and his knee crippled him. He grabbed the edge of the table. "Yes, it was. She's sick because of me. Desmond is dead, too. Mercy gets people killed. Mercy betrays."

His father's unfaltering, astute gaze bore into him.

Simon gulped for air. "They're the enemy. All of them. How could you betray Mother and Desmond by suggesting we ally with them? After all they've done?" His stomach hardened with his father's proposition.

His father turned from him and brushed past the entering kitchen servant. He paused in the doorway. "They can and will do much more." He cleared his throat and added, "We can make it right, Simon. Go to the market. Get the lass. There's a chance to win them over and claim our right."

Gwyn weaved along crowded dirt roads, the people moving in a fluid dance of peddler and customer as she took it all in with awe. Cobblers, smiths, fishermen, and merchants alike conducted their business from stalls, wagons, and building fronts. The rocky coastline, dark sea, and rugged mountains lured her.

She shuffled around the fishmonger's barrels brimming with mackerel, herring, and eels. The salty sea air blew past, ruffling her gown's skirt. She lifted the hem and stepped over a muddy puddle.

"Down this way, right?"

"Aye, that way toward the potters and weavers," Venora said.

Gwyn was eager to remove herself from Trygg and Sigurd's overbearing presence in search of new herbals, even if for a short while. They hadn't stopped overindulging in the strong bog myrtle ale for the entire length of the sail! At least they kept their hands to themselves.

"Slow yer step!" Venora hollered from behind.

Trygg and Sigurd had already stopped in a tavern for drinking and information gathering. The men hadn't come along as protection alone, or if at all. Norse women were fully capable of protecting themselves. Gwyn had heard about many Norse women warriors. Of course Father's men were as narrow-minded as the rest of them and would not admit the *fairer* sex could hold their own or even captain a ship. Mother had shared stories she'd passed on from other Norse women who'd visited the isles with their warrior husbands. She'd shown Gwyn and Venora old runes with women warriors, dressed in full glory, axe and shield in hands and blood at their boots. Some boasted of seeing women among King Haakon's famous *berserkir* and *úlfheðnar*, his coveted warriors cloaked in bear and wolf furs.

Àrasaig was a small seaside town, a safe blend of Nord-men and Scots working in solidarity for profit. Suppos-edly, the markets in Edinburgh and Glasgow were more bountiful and the gossip and political discourse thicker. She and Venora were safe here, though. Deeper inland if they were identified as Norse, less scrupulous people would not be kind to them. However, here they were just two women eager to make a deal and stock their pantries.

A woman's voice came from the stall beside them. "Dame! Hold this fine silk! Only two shillings for the length o' it."

Gwyn shook her head and continued on her way. After locating her herbs, she'd tend to her mother's wish list: wool and linen, threads, bronze needles, candlesticks, cloves, ginger, and other goods harder to come by on Uist. After gathering their information, Trygg and Sigurd would scout the best deal for iron, pigs, sheep, and can-vas.

A packhorse and cart loaded with chickens rolled past as the driver barked for people to get out of the way. Venora pulled her to the side before a loose, snorting pig nearly clobbered her.

She exhaled. The busyness was invigorating. She'd nev-er seen so many people in one place.

"Ye'll lose yer head if you dinna watch yerself. Dinna act like a wee lass and not the woman ye are. Trickery thrives here. Best ye remember. Come, Gwyn. This way."

She followed Venora past the potters and sacks of grains. Finally, they reached a quieter area of the market, almost on the edge. She blew a wisp of moistened hair from her brow. An attractive woman nearby haggled with the herbalist.

"Dame, I already give ye a bargain! If I go any lower, I make nil. How 'bout I include cinnamon? The finest in Scotland."

The woman, dressed in a thickly woven and decorated blue silk gown and beaver fur-trimmed cloak, waved a hand. "Just the musk mallow. Ten pence." She moved with elegance, reminiscent of Gwyn's mother. Her long, dark hair rippled down her back and was not gathered up in the way traditional ladies wore it. She was stunning and regal, and Gwyn struggled to pull her gaze away.

"Och, Milady Montgomerie, ye do press me, but aye, aye." The vendor shook her head.

Satisfied, the lady handed over the coins and tucked the pouch of herbs into her pocket.

Venora pinched her sister's elbow. Gwyn drew her look to the herbs in front of her. She searched her mind. Musk mallow was used for swollen joints.

The lady offered a courteous smile, and Gwyn returned it. The woman scanned the crowd, puzzlement furrowing her refined face. "Ali? Alasdair, my love?" she called, searching. A lad, maybe two years old, with floppy, dark hair emerged within the bustling crowd, carrying a squawking duck. Another younger woman, simply dressed, stood beside him, frustration turning her brow down.

"Milady," she said with an exasperated breath to the woman beside Gwyn.

The lad waddled, weighed down by a duck half his size. "Aye, Mama!" He presented the bird. It struggled in the boy's grasp and broke free. It gained flight.

"Och!" he said, frowning.

"Ali, you worried Mama! Come, love. We need to go," the woman said. He shoved his small, chubby hand into hers. Pausing, she whispered to Gwyn, "Don't let old Effie here swindle you. Her goods are the best, indeed, and worth the coin. She is always willing to negotiate. A shilling per bag for the best herbs." The boy wiggled on his feet, impatient.

Gwyn smiled, wrapped in a strange sense of euphoria as the boy departed with his mother, hand in hand. The other woman, clearly a maid, for Scots didn't possess thralls, followed.

Venora inhaled sharply beside her as she scrutinized mother and child as they quickly disappeared among the crowd.

"What is it?" Gwyn asked quietly, pulling Venora aside. Her sister had an eerily familiar look in her eyes. "Is it the boy?" Unease rattled her stomach as she dropped her hands from Venora. Touching her sister while she had a vision was unwise. "Don't say he—"

Venora snapped out of her Sight. "No, no. *He'll* be well." She blinked and turned to the herbs. "What are we looking for?"

She sighed. Venora would eventually tell her what she had seen. Or not. It was Venora's way. Always censoring her visions. Gwyn surveyed the open bags of fragrant herbs. "Feverfew, hemlock, and betony." They were balms for the headaches Kendrick got frequently. There was no cure or treatment for blindness. Her mother's herbal books had mentioned bilberry, not native to Scotland. Bilberry grew in the Nord Land.

They negotiated an acceptable price for the herbs. "Bilberry?" she asked.

The old crone curled her lip and shook her head. "Ye'll na find any Lochlanach poisons here."

"*Hrmphm*," Venora said. "Come." She drew Gwyn away.

Her enthusiasm withered. She had hoped to find something new here for Kendrick. Instead, it was more of the same. He'd been alone with their father for over a week. She hoped Trygg and Sigurd would find all they needed today without hassle. She had an ominous feeling being away from Kendrick for so long especially since Gunnar's death.

A man approached as they left the herbalist. "Ye seek the whortleberry?"

"Excuse me?" she asked.

"Whortleberry? Bilberry, ye call it, aye?" Handsome eyes on a cleanly shaven face regarded her.

"Come, Gwyn," Venora chided, eyeing the well-dressed merchant with sharp scrutiny. A sword was strapped to his side, not an uncommon sight. All men here were well armed, and some even better dressed than this man. His face reflected friendly confidence.

"Yes," Gwyn said without hesitation.

"Aye! I ken where ye can find it." He flicked his chin in the direction down the cobbled way. "There," he said, pointing through the crowd to an indistinguishable location. "Get my own herbals there. She drives a hard bargain, but 'tis worth the haggle."

"Venora, come. We're here. We might as well try," she said as she followed him through the crowd. He turned left, then right, and kept waving them on. She almost lost him at one point, and her heartbeat fluttered.

"Gwyn," Venora said, her step hurried behind Gwyn. "Stop! This is—"

She ignored her sister. Animals grunted, merchants negotiated, and smiths hammered in their stalls. The busy market hummed around her. She needed bilberry. This might be her only and last chance to acquire it.

He turned down an alleyway between buildings, and her curiosity morphed into heightened wariness. Where was the herbalist? Belatedly, she searched for possible exits from the shadowy alley. He quickly spun on them, drawing his sword. She gasped.

Venora cursed, clutched Gwyn's arm, and tripped backward. "It doesn't take the Sight to ken ye've been tricked. Och, Gwyn, yer desperation has fooled ye," Venora murmured. She thinned her lips and glared at the man. "What do ye want? Our men will be here shortly, and yer blood will fall on these stones."

The tan-faced man smiled. "Nay, I dare think not. They're too full in their cups."

Gwyn stifled a yelp. "What are you talking about?" How did he know which men were with them? They had parted ways with Sigurd and Trygg long before they'd reached the herbalist's booth...

Her stomach was suddenly heavy. "You were following us?"

A familiar voice came from behind them. "Thank you, Hugh. I've got it."

The red-haired MacCoinneach, Simon, came around on Gwyn's side. The heaviness in her stomach deepened.

He laid a strong hand on her arm. He didn't unsheathe his sword, but he didn't need to. His grip was a claw on her arm, and he stood taller than her. He nearly blocked the light spilling into the alley with his size.

"You! After I healed you!" she said, spitting the words.

The handsome trickster disappeared into the crowd.

"You may go. I only need her," he ordered Venora.

Gwyn's pulse quickened. "What? Unhand me!" She struggled in his hold. He tightened his hand on her arm, so much so it pinched. She kicked. Her aim landed on his knee instead of his shin.

He muffled a groan and a foul curse. "Blazes, lass. I shan't hurt you. But you're coming with me." He directed his frank, focused look at Venora. "Are you the witch, *ehm*, the Seer?"

A thundercloud passed over Venora's expression. Her scowl deepened.

He nodded, formulating his own answer. "Tell your father." He handed her a parchment scroll. "Here are our offers of truce."

Venora took the scroll and stepped back. She chuckled with derision. "Ye ken by now that our father doesn't negotiate. But I'll share yer offers."

"No, Venora. Don't go!" Gwyn cried, fighting to no avail against Simon MacCoinneach. They could handle him. Two of them against him...if she could just reach her dagger...

Venora blinked, spellbound. *Oh, not now. Not now!* A cloudy hue passed over her seaweed eyes. She froze. A blink. Then it was gone. She nodded. "It'll be all right, Gwyn. Ye'll be safe with him. I'll see ye again soon."

Then she slipped away.

"What? Venora! No!" she shrieked. The red-headed beast dragged her through the crowd of people, her kicks and screams ignored by all.

Simon tugged the lass along, her stubborn heels continually finding the ground and halting them. "You'd do well to come willingly." He lowered his voice to avoid attention, but he kept a firm hold on the squirming woman.

"Why would I do that?"

He grunted and zigzagged through the crowd. She screeched and clawed at him. "Help! Help!"

One man stopped and sized up Simon with a frown.

Simon said, "Never mind my wife. She didn't get the pig she wanted, and she's succumbed to fits."

The passerby smirked, nodded in understanding, and turned to his own cart.

"I am not your wife! You're the pig," she said through gritted teeth.

"Pig or not, the first will be remedied when you return with me."

"What? *What?*" she said shrilly.

They emerged alongside the Scots-run tavern only a foolish Lochlanach would enter. He was well in the clear from her protectors. He approached his tethered horse out front. He dropped a coin into the hand of the young lad he'd ordered to watch over the horse. "Be off," he said. The lad scurried away.

The lass fought him again, stamping her heel on his toes. He ground through clamped teeth, "I don't hit women, but if you do that again, I may take you over my knee."

"Och, your good one or bad one?" she snapped.

He grunted. Tart lass.

She backed into the horse's belly, refusing to climb into the saddle. "No."

He withdrew his dagger and raised it but not drawing it close to actually harm her.

"You wouldn't," she said, her mouth tightened in defiance.

"I wouldn't? You murdered my brother."

Fear welled in her eyes, and her face turned ashen. "That wasn't me. I tried to help him. I heal."

"We'll see about that." He shoved her on the horse, his hand pushing on her bottom through layers of ruffled skirts.

"*Hrmphm!*" she said in surprise but positioned herself in the saddle. "Where are we going?"

He mounted behind her, took the reins, and clicked for his horse to walk. "To your new home, Eilean Donan."

CHAPTER FOUR

After hours of the red-haired beast answering Gwyn's questions with grunts or snarky retorts, they stopped for the night. "There are mountains in both directions. The Camerons patrol the south and MacDougalls the east and north. Both would be delighted to bring a bonnie healer like you to their lairds," Simon condescended. "I suggest you dare not try to run off on me tonight. You're safer with me than you are with them."

"I don't believe that."

He sniggered. "Try and see."

"You wouldn't want your prize harmed, aye?" she countered as she dismounted. A dull ache rode up her backside. Long distance rides were worse than bobbing on the open sea. Her knees creaked, and she massaged her wrists from holding onto the saddle.

Silence.

"Am I to be your prisoner?"

He glared at her.

She pressed. "My father doesn't negotiate."

"I'm well aware."

She heaved a sigh. "Then let me return to my home! I can make the ship before my father hears of this."

His jaw clenched, eyes narrowing. "It's too late for that, lass."

"Our men will come for me."

"No, they won't."

She threw her hands in the air. She marched back and forth across the small clearing while he prepared a fire and meal of salted venison, apples, hard cheese, and a loaf of bread he'd pulled from his satchel.

"Sit," he said finally.

She did so and huffed. "Please, I *must* return home."

He handed her the meal upon a clean cloth napery. "I've ale, here, too." He plopped the flask beside her.

Her stomach churned, famished from the day's ride. She bit into the salty meat and tried not to eat too quickly. Deer was hard to come by on the isles. She grew tired of oatcakes, porridge, and fish. Protest like a bairn as he did, her father relied heavily upon trade with the mainlanders and seasonal trips to the markets. The apple was an explosion of sweetness she'd not enjoyed in a long time.

After a quiet meal spent sulking, she tried again. "I must go home. You've taken me against my will, and if you think this will lead to my father being your ally, you're gravely mistaken. You've just started a war."

"We're already in the middle of a war."

She stuck her chin out. "Did you kill my brother?"

He returned her boldness with a hateful glare. "Did you kill mine?"

"No! I was—" The last bit of apple lodged in her throat, and she coughed.

He waved a mocking hand. "Trying to save him. Aye, you've told me." He pushed the ale flask closer to her with the tip of his boot. "Drink."

He hadn't answered her question. She said, "My brother did not deserve to die."

"Nor did mine."

"Nor did Rothwell."

"Who?"

"The man you killed."

He scoffed. "He was another Nordman. They all deserve to die."

"So now you've resorted to stealing their women as well? And they call us brutes."

He snarled as he bit into a piece of dried meat. "My father believes we can form an alliance with your father through our marriage. I don't question him."

"You always follow his orders?"

Simon released a sigh. "Don't you follow your father's?"

She shivered and pulled her cloak tighter. She had nothing with her but the clothes on her back and the small parcel of herbs from the market. Even her beloved herbals box remained on the ship.

Dusk's arrival cast smudges of night upon their campsite. She discreetly eyed her munching companion. Did the MacCoinneachs know King Haakon's fleet would be upon their shores in a few weeks? That, in fact, a large fleet already roamed the Western Isles and more were coming? Certainly the Scots were no fools. They knew something was amiss.

A full bushy head of wavy, auburn hair fell around Simon's face, loose. Crimson stubble upon his chin twinkled in the firelight. His piercing, brown hawk eyes caught her looking at him.

She diverted her gaze. "How's your arm?"

He chewed slowly, giving her a calculating stare. "It is well."

"Did it get sewn?"

"Aye, lass."

More chewing. They called her people uncivilized!

"My *name* is Gwyn."

"I know."

She blew an exaggerated breath.

He sighed. "I'm Simon."

She pursed her lips. "I know."

"Well, now we're acquainted."

That was that.

She refused to be his bartering piece. If she escaped tonight, she could still catch the ship home.

All men needed sleep at some point, and even the stonyhearted man guarding her had to succumb to night's lure. So Gwyn waited. She rolled to her side on the bedroll he'd provided her. Chilly from the lack of fire, she drew her cloak to her chin. Her captor had kicked dirt on the fire after their supper and now sat silently against a tree. No blanket. No offer of anything.

Brute.

He watched. Unwavering.

She curled herself into a ball, trying to summon heat from within, her back to him. A nearly full moon lit the clearing. Early harvest's wind encircled her, howling like a hungry wolf. She shivered. At least the cold would keep her awake. Perhaps if she closed her eyes for but a moment? She blinked. No, she had to stay awake.

Hours passed and although he was quiet, he wasn't asleep. The occasional shift of weight, the flick of finger on blade, the clearing of his throat, and the sip of ale.

Did the man not sleep?

Was he still watching her? She dared not turn around. She yawned.

Perhaps a moment of rest...

She startled awake. Curses, she had fallen asleep!

Heaving a sigh, she rolled over.

He was gone. She sat up and listened in the darkness. The pitch black of night had passed, and gray light hinted dawn's pending arrival through the trees. The sun would rise soon.

She stood, stretched, and peered around. Not a rustle. Even the wind had died.

The horse nickered as she approached. He wasn't gone then. No man would leave his horse behind. Nor his captive.

Well, curse him for going to relieve himself from drinking too much ale! His mistake. She oriented herself as she gathered the horse's reins. It nickered again, and she hushed it. She'd have to guide it through the thick brush first to get to the road. It was bold, but she needed to be faster than him.

The sun had been to their left when they arrived near sunset, so that was where she needed to go. They had ridden along a rudimentary road for most of the day, and she'd made mental notes of landmarks. She would follow the road south, then west. She wasn't sure but presumed they were in the Lochaber region and she'd locate the harbor town where they'd made port. It was a risk, but she had no other choice. She couldn't return to Simon's home with him. Kendrick could only hide in the stable from their father for so long. There was nowhere for him to go on Uist.

She guided the horse over errant roots and branches. No sooner was she in the thick woods of tangy hemlock and dominating oak, did she hear voices. She stopped and bent an ear to listen, heartbeat quickening.

Male Gaelic voices argued with each other from the main road. She could barely see the men. She lifted a foot to step forward, then stopped. This was not Uist. This was the mainland, and these were foreign men. Even if they had been Nordmen, it didn't guarantee her safety. Too many devils roamed the earth in the form of landfarer or *wicing*, as some would call the sea Nordmen.

Alone was the safest way. The horse blew a snort.

She patted its nose, shushing it again.

The men argued with each other. Her pulse raced, and she swore it could be heard outside of her body. *Make haste, you dolts!* Surely, by now Simon would've noticed her missing. She slid her hand into the pocket with her dagger. She might have to make a run for it without the horse.

Finally, the men veered toward the road. She breathed a sigh, released the dagger, and clucked softly for the horse to continue. She was almost upon the simple cobble and dirt road when a hand grabbed her by the waist and pulled her.

She fell in a thicket of prickly bushes and landed upon a large body with a thud. Recovering her wits, she scrambled out of his grip. He turned, rolled over on top of her, and clamped his hand over her mouth just as she released a scream.

Simon pinned her to the ground with his full weight. His breathing was heavy upon her. "Hush!" He murmured pacifying Gaelic words to the horse. The horse danced slightly on its hooves but didn't leave.

She wiggled beneath him and fished inside her pocket for her dagger again.

His eyes were black pebbles in the shadows, his hair mad about his face. It brushed against her cheeks, smelling of fire smoke and salt. He pressed the full length of his body against her but didn't make a move to rise. She gasped for breath.

"Quit your fussing," he ordered.

Her fingers searched. She tightened them around the dagger's hilt. She withdrew the dagger and swiped with no directed aim. With his other hand, he grabbed her wrist and smacked the hand against the ground. The dagger tumbled loose.

She coughed, his weight pressing the air from her lungs. "I—can't—breathe."

He shifted to give her room, but kept his hands upon her, one on her mouth, one on her wrist. Her gown's hem was caught on his boot buckle and was halfway up her leg. She blinked, and then closed her eyes. His heart raced against her own, his breath hot and ragged.

Her tousled hair fell into her face. To her surprise, he removed his hand from her mouth and brushed her hair aside, the touch of his fingers on her forehead and cheek gentle and rousing. It was the same sensation she'd felt when she healed his arm. It stirred her insides with an unfamiliar something. A man had never touched her in such a way. Even if he did have her pinned to the ground.

A moment later, he released her and she pulled her knees up, fixed her disheveled skirts, and swiped leaves from her sleeves. She vibrated as the encounter rushed through her veins.

"Bloody hell," they said in unison.

She belatedly felt around for her dagger. He scrambled, snatched it, and thrust it into his belt. "No. It's mine now."

She was surprised he'd not searched her earlier for it. Perhaps he was new at stealing women.

He rose and offered her a hand, but she stood on her own.

"You were going to take your chances with them after I warned you?" he said.

The commotion had drawn the other men's attention. They conversed loudly.

"Ye hear that?" one said, closer now.

"Aye. Who's there?" the other asked.

"Come out! Show yerself!" the first said, even closer.

She froze. Simon froze. She prayed to the gods the horse wouldn't give them away.

Simon slowly unsheathed his sword. He raised it, stance ready.

"No, please," she whispered. She laid a hand on his forearm and squeezed. "They've done nothing. Please. Not everyone needs to be killed, S-Simon," she stammered on his name, the sound of it too personal, too much for her to give her captor, but she said it regardless.

He ignored her but didn't move a step closer.

His arm muscle tensed.

"Please, Simon, please. I won't run off again if you do this for me."

Finally, after a long moment, the men turned and continued on their way.

He replaced his sword in his sheath. Her heartbeat pounding in her head, she pressed a hand to her stomach, turned, and trudged to their camp.

Once daylight broke, Simon guided their horse to the main road north. They would reach Dornie by evening supper if all went well. Gwyn rode in front of him in the saddle. Every bump of the dirt road rubbed her backside against him, and it rained havoc upon his weary mind. Last night, he had waited for the stubborn woman to finally fall asleep before taking a moment to relieve himself behind a bush. Christ, and he must have fallen asleep for a few moments against the tree. Then he'd heard the men on the road and found the empty clearing. She was a daring lass to steal his horse.

"Why do you wish to return home so eagerly? You can't possibly like living under a madman's rule," he said, shifting himself in the saddle again.

"That madman is my father."

"So? He's still a madman. We can offer you safety. My father's told me the stories of your mother and her people. Your father came and killed the men of her family, forced her to his bed."

"Aren't you doing the same?" she countered.

"I'm nothing like your father. I'll never force you to my bed. As I said, my father wishes a truce. I've yet to kill all the men of your family."

"No truce can come from this," she said.

Silence skulked into their ride, and when he thought she'd fallen asleep in his arms, she spoke again. "I need to go home."

"So you say."

"It's barbaric to steal women."

He guided the horse around a large sinkhole, clicked under his tongue, and then said, "I don't want this either, but my—"

"So let me go," she interrupted.

He lowered his voice. "I can't." Och, he was exhausted. "Mind you hand me that flask, there?" He leaned forward, pressing his chest against her back.

She reached and unbuckled the flask from the horse's satchel.

His fingers brushed hers when she passed it to him. Her fingers were cold. Instead of taking a drag himself, he handed it to her. "You might need it more than me."

"I'm well, thanks."

"Drink. It'll warm you."

She heaved a sigh and took it. After sipping, she handed it back. He drew a long gulp, wondering what her lips would taste like.

Devil, he *was* tired. Never before had he been this near to a woman. He left the whoring to the others.

"So I am to return home with you?"

"Aye."

"Then what?"

"If all goes as the elder MacCoinneach proposes, we marry in a few days."

She shifted in his arms. "We will not!" Dark hair caught in his mouth as she squirmed. He tightened his hold on the thinnest part of her, consciously aware of the curves jostling against him.

"Gwyn, quit your fussing. You'll bring us both down!"

She elbowed him.

"Ooof!" He tightened his hold on her. "Give it a chance, lass. Let's see what our fathers agree upon."

"I am no pawn."

"I'm afraid we both are. You know this as well as me."

At least her fussing had helped knock the drowsy from him. They had hours to go. He needed to stay alert. He swallowed. "So, you heal?" he said, lacking disdain.

"Yes, as I've told you."

"Are you a witch like your sister?"

She stiffened. "Is that what you mainlanders always assume? That a person with a special ability is an evil-caster?"

"Your people believe in many gods," he countered.

"My mother is one of the isle-folk, an Ancient, and we have only a few deities."

"So you *are* a witch."

She released a gurgled moan. He lessened his hold on her. "No."

He was unapologetic. He mulled over the plausible versus illogical.

She exhaled loudly. "There is a delicate balance between order and disorder. My mother is descended from a people who've been able to breach the Silver Veil, harness the powers of the mystery for good, mind you—and bring energy to man."

He was quiet. Had she cast a charm on his arm? Even with the haphazard stitching by the captain's wife, it should have taken longer to heal. Her brother had cut him deeply. This healer had been correct in her assumption he should have caught fever with it, if left untended. It healed in days. Practically nonexistent now. Just a minor scratch and irritation remained. Had it been more than God's healing?

"What is the Silver Veil?"

She took a moment before saying, "It's hard to explain. It's the fragile line, the margin of being between our world and the next."

"The line between earth and heaven?"

She shrugged. "I suppose."

"That's blasphemy."

Her shoulders slumped. "You men and your one God. Can't the Norse gods, the Silver Veil of the Ancients, and your God not be one and the same? We only see it differently."

"If that were true, then why don't my people have these abilities?"

She didn't answer. Perhaps she had none.

They rode for hours, each lost in their own thoughts.

He tried again, the absurdity of it all nagging him. "So your *power* is to heal?"

"Yes," she whispered.

"What about herbalists and our healers? Do they weave lies?"

"No. There are proven herbs and remedies man has accessed to care for the ill. They can only do so much, though. What I do is much more."

"What about—"

She held up a hand. "No. I refuse to answer another question. Not until you agree to let me return home."

Admittedly, he'd considered letting her return and forgetting his father's fanciful plan. However. Not only would she safeguard their destiny, but he was also bringing home a healer. Burn him in hell for believing her, but if it meant healing his mother, then may he dwell in flames eternal.

They came upon Simon's village as the last shards of daylight left the sky. The people moved about, finishing their daily labors in the fields and preparing suppers near their cottages. Smoke saturated the air, damp and dank from the afternoon rain. Clouds obscured the lustrous mountains protecting the dale. Gwyn had only learned about this place from others who had ventured here, mostly from the sea captains or merchants in Loch nam Madadh. The air around them reminded her of the smooth energy in the village near the MacRuaidhri stronghold, but it was a vastly different place.

Crags rose to surround the town, instead of endless machair and flat moors. In place of the open ocean battering the cliffs below the MacRuaidhri keep on Uist, a loch lapped gently alongside the isle where the mighty keep stood. Oh, and what a keep, Eilean Donan! A magnificent stone tower house rose on the lush green isle.

They stopped in an outer stable to dismount. Two lads approached to take the horse. A younger man exited the stable. "Ah, Simon, you're back," he said. "Shoo, lads. I've got it." He took the reins.

"Aye, how fare ye, Finn?" Simon slid off the horse first and then offered a hand to Gwyn. She took it only because she wasn't sure her legs would handle the jolt as she dropped to the ground after the long ride. Simon had stopped them only twice during the day.

"Good day, my lady," the man said with a freckled smile and head bob.

"Good day," she said in return, her attention too rapt on the isle across the small bridge. The MacRuaidhri keep was modest and homely, nothing like this castle. Simon looped his arm through hers to guide her across the bridge, and she was momentarily stunned with the breathtaking beauty to protest. After hours in the saddle, she'd become accustomed to his nearness, too.

Her amazement with the splendor around them didn't last long, as Simon said, "My father is waiting to see you."

She tugged at her tight high-necked dress, shakes rippling through her. She moved to pull from Simon's grasp, but his arm didn't budge from hers. In a quaking voice, she said, "That he is. What now, S-Simon?" She wanted to call him a red-headed brute but suppressed the urge.

"That's up to you."

"I wasn't aware you intended to give me a choice."

"I won't force you to wed me nor into my bed, as I said."

"*Hrmphm*. Oh, but you took me without asking permission. I had no choice. Now you give me a choice?"

More silence.

Her lungs tightened. "What if I wish to be returned home? Can that be an option?"

He said nothing, and she turned to face him.

She blew a breath, exasperated. "Simon, please. I must return home. There has to be another way."

"I'm afraid not."

Truth filled her as she recalled her mother's Gaelic teachings. "Your priest would not marry us without my full covenant."

"I suggest you consent then, Gwyn."

Her mouth dropped open, and she clamped it shut.

Contemplation played across his face. "It is done. You might as well comply."

She tried again. "I need to go home, Simon. Please."

"Tell me why."

"My brother needs me," she blurted, on the verge of tears. They stopped midway across the bridge, neither making an attempt to move onward again. She placed her other hand on their linked arms.

His muscles stiffened beneath her touch. "Your brother is dead," he said.

She swallowed. Pleading was beneath her. Telling him about her needs was not what she wanted. She wanted to be home to care for Kendrick.

As the forbidding fortress loomed before her, both lovely and life-sentencing, she had no other card to play. Simon seemed to have cared about his brother. Perhaps he'd find compassion for her own sibling obligation.

With an acute sense of purpose, she said, "My other brother. He is younger. Not yet a man. He is but fifteen."

Simon eyed her, dubiousness furrowing his brow.

"He is ill."

He stared at her for a long moment, chestnut brown eyes unrevealing.

They began walking again.

Nothing. Not a compassionate bone in his body? A lost soul, like the rest of them. Kendrick was right. This man was beyond redemption.

She could not believe what she said next. "Simon, promise him protection. Bring him here. There is room in the keep for another able man. He is a braw fighter, even with his ailment." *Mother and Venora, forgive me,* she prayed. Her mother and sister were capable of escaping her father's hooks. They played well under his rule. Kendrick was too fragile. She could save him before it was too late. One day their father could strike the mortal blow. "I will comply if you bring him here."

He guided her through the inner bailey, silent in the evening's shadows, not a servant to be seen. He licked his lips. "He ails, and you cannot treat him?"

She pressed her lips. "No, not his specific disease."

Simon muffled a grumble. "I need you to heal someone for me."

She halted and faced him again. "Who?"

He cleared his throat but didn't reply.

She spun it differently. "I don't barter my healing."

"I don't help the Lochlanach, but look at what I am doing."

"You call this helping me?"

Face determined, gaze directed into her eyes, he said, "Aye, I do."

"I give of my own accord," she said.

"You healed me."

"That I did." Her own words continued to stun her, for she would never withhold her healing from an ailing person. "Then we are at an impasse."

"I dare say."

The silence was painful as they maneuvered through the bailey to the main house.

"Simon."

He responded in a gentler tone. "Yes?"

"Did you kill my brother Gunnar?"

He ushered her through the main entranceway. "Come, my father is eager to make your acquaintance."

A lump of despair rose in her throat.

Just as they entered, he said quietly, "It wasn't I who sent your brother to his grave."

"Who then?" she dared to ask, tingles erupting along her arms. Was he presenting her to her brother's mur-derer? Alroy MacCoinneach?

He said, flatly, "My brother Desmond."

She inhaled and said no more.

He led her into the hall of the castle.

Simon took Gwyn directly to the hall, where Alroy MacCoinneach sat at a large wooden table, alone, and reading over a stack of parchments.

She briefly closed her eyes and took a calming breath. She could do this.

She searched her memory. The MacRuaidhris on Uist were a clan with a laird. Was Alroy also a laird? Living in such a grand castle, he had to be. "Laird MacCoinneach," she said with a gamble and a curtsy. That's what Scottish women did, aye? Curse her thoughts for having wandered during her mother's teachings. At least her Latin and history were sharp. Customs and manners though...

Alroy rose from the table and approached her. "No need for formalities. Just Alroy, Gwyn." He took her hand, despite its grime from travel, and kissed the knuckles. He snapped his fingers and a servant appeared from the shadowy corners of the large hall with a cloth and a basin of water.

The servant nodded at Gwyn, basin out in offering.

Gwyn wasn't sure what to do. Was this water for cooking? Was she expected to prepare their meal, too?

Simon stepped forward, brushing close against her shoulder. He washed his hands in the basin, dried with the cloth, and then lifted his eyebrows at Gwyn.

She washed, feeling like a fool, smiled, and said, "Thank you."

Alroy waved a hand to the table. Only three place settings. "You must be famished. Come and eat."

Instantly, Gwyn's wariness peaked. Where was the lady of the keep? This was an impressive hall in an equally stunning castle. Didn't others attend the meals?

"How was the market?" Alroy asked Simon.

"Fair."

Quite thirsty, Gwyn willingly took the goblet of wine Alroy poured for her. She wished for a rose and lavender herbal drink or perhaps sage wine but dared not ask. The heavy drinks of ale, mead, and wine made her head spin. She sipped slowly.

Several servants appeared and brought a scent-heavy meal on platters: garlic and rosemary on fowl, a yeasty bread, and a bowl of boiled onions and a mushy root vegetable. The herbs stirred her stomach with hunger and reminded her of her own home. She swallowed the strength from the wine as they set the meal down. Waiting for the servants to leave, she gathered her gumption and said, "Alroy, I've been taken against my will. This is a misunderstanding."

She didn't share a look with Simon, who sat beside her. He was as quiet as a moor in winter. He'd be no help in her cause.

Across from her, Alroy scooped food into his trencher. "There is no misunderstanding."

She suppressed a cry. The goblet, suddenly heavy, slipped from her hand. Simon caught it before it spilled.

"I don't understand. Your grievance is with my father."

Alroy's cold blue gaze fell upon Simon. His son nodded. Alroy then said coolly, "We've provided your father with our requests."

She raised an eyebrow. "Requests? You mean that parchment Simon gave my sister? Does he have a choice? Do I have a choice?"

"You'll be protected here."

"I don't need protection. I was well in my home," she countered, losing steam. She sipped again and again. The wine lost its bite. Her head grew heavier.

"Were you?" Alroy asked.

He was right, though she refused to admit it. Kendrick was repeatedly beaten by their father through the years...and her mother was forced to give her body to a man who treated her no better than a dog and exploited her powers knowing with each healing it brought her closer to death. No, she was not safe. She and Venora had been mostly spared from her father's wrath. For now. What about when Gwyn was offered to her betrothed, Leidolf?

The lack of food and increasing fatigue was a rock in her chest. Dizziness spun her head. She pushed the goblet away. Weakly, she said, "I don't need to be saved."

Simon scooped meat into her trencher and ripped a heel from the bread. He passed her the bread. She forced food into her mouth, unsure it if might come back up. She tried once more. "I must return home. I thank you for your hospitality, but I must—"

"You will stay, as I said. For your own safety. Eilean Donan and her kin welcome you. Simon will take care of you," Alroy said, his voice unbreakable.

There was no choice. She was stuck here. She wept inside.

Simon led Gwyn to a bedchamber, his mind a muddled mess. The remainder of their meal's conversation had been lighter talk about the market, the affairs in Glasgow and Edinburgh, and the fall harvest.

No more discussion about the truth. He had taken her against her will.

What kind of a coward stole his bride? He was as despicable as *them*.

He was a liar, furnishing her a meal in a hall belonging to nobody, escorting her to a bedchamber not theirs to provide, hosting his captive in a castle named, but not claimed. Och, they had been stewards for so long the people respected them, revered them, and paid homage to them. All they needed was King Alexander's final blessing. All he needed was the lass to agree to marry him so an alliance could be forged with her devil father. Would it be enough for their king? Would it be enough for his father?

He rubbed his temple and yawned.

"Does your head ache?"

He cracked his jaw. "I'm well."

The hearth had already been lit in the bedchamber. He darted to the dressing cabinet and opened it to display numerous of his mother's gowns. He eyed Gwyn, still bonnie enough after a day and night of riding. Her own gown hugged curves. Mud lined the hem, and dirt smudged her skirt though. Her cheeks were rosy, hair loose about her shoulders but flowing like a river down her back in richly brown, nearly black, waves.

Where was his head?

He finally turned back to the dressing cabinet. "There are gowns and—" What did women wear beneath skirts?

He'd never seen a woman's layers below their gown and apron. He didn't allow himself to think about the finer half and physical pleasures. Not even when Des had encouraged him to seek the hand of Meredith's younger sister, Mildred. Heat filled his cheeks, and he'd soon have a predicament if he didn't swing his mind to the mundane. "*Ehm...*" He rubbed the stubble growing on his chin. Shifts? What were all the layers called, dammit? "The rest of your attire," he said. He glanced at her, certain his face matched the color of his hair. "You seem a similar fit."

"To your mistresses?" she asked.

"Heavens, no," he said, sputtering over the words. "This room is—was—my mother's."

Her lips curved into an O, but she said nothing. She approached the cabinet. "I can't stay here then. Surely, there's another more humble chamber or a cottage in the village?"

"No, she's, *ehm*, no longer with us. Take what you please. She wouldn't mind. Do you need a servant to help you?"

"No. We Lochlanach know how to dress ourselves."

Och, there she was again. The tartness had left during the meal. It'd been painful to watch her plead with his father. He'd sat there like an arse, not speaking up for himself or for her. Daft as it seemed, he enjoyed the return of her sharp tongue.

"Simon," she said, turning to him. The light caught flecks of green in her deep blue irises.

He fought the urge to touch her. He already missed her being in the saddle with him. Holy God, he was tired.

"Aye?" He shoved away the impurities leaching into his mind like they were poison.

"I have no things, naught but the herbs I acquired at the market. My own personal belongings. An herbal box, my own clothes."

"I can provide all you need."

Frustration wrinkled her brow.

"Do you wish to send a letter home to your sister or mother? They can send your things." He pointed to the desk with parchment, ink, and feather. He quickly added, "I can call for a scribe."

"I can write."

"Ah."

He expected protest, for they had yet to forge any covenant.

She blinked, eyes wet. "Will I be here long?"

He chewed his lip. "I don't know. My father is adamant with this cause. There will be no persuading him otherwise."

"What about you? Do you agree with his plans?"

He paused and lied, "Yes."

She heaved a sigh, and he couldn't help but notice how it lifted her breasts up, then down. *For all that is holy.* "Good night." He closed the door behind him as Errol, one of his father's soldiers, came to take the first guard shift. Heavy steps and an even heavier spirit brought him to his own room. This plan grew more wearisome by the minute. How could his father possibly think Blasius would make a deal with them after they stole his daughter? He repressed his angst with a tight fist.

He would not wed her. He couldn't do it. After he took her to Dryburgh Abbey to heal his mother, he'd bring her home to Uist. Then the madness would end by sword as it should. His father might eventually see the other side.

He slammed the door behind him and approached his bed. The chamber was aglow from the lit hearth. He unbuckled his belt and removed his sword and sheath. He rested it on the side table with a clunk. The iron gleamed in the firelight. It called to him. He had killed many men in the name of Scotland and in the hopes the crown would deem the MacCoinneachs worthy. Last year on Skye, he had slaughtered many Nordmen. That other man, Rothwell, killing him had been vindicating. So many Nordmen and Scots had gone astray.

He'd not forgotten. Mercy injured the ones you loved. The blade would always be the way. It had to be.

Leidolf drummed his fingers on the deck rail as the ship approached Uist. Aegir had brought him safely across the Nord Sea, thanks to his uplifted prayers. The heavens shone on him in favor. This would be a fruitful visit, he was sure of it. He ran a finger along the half circles on the dragon's neck as the sail flapped in the wind on their approach. He twisted his lye-bleached beard, fiddled with the silver rings on his two fingers, tightened the leather strap across his vest, and adjusted the sword at his side.

He resisted the urge to dip his finger into the wolf's blood vial in the pouch at his side. Not yet. When the timing was right, he would unleash the inner wolf and do what was necessary. He needed to be ready to kill when the time came.

He shouted orders as men rowed, controlled the tack and sail, and steadied the ship for landfall. "Aft to port, Steinthor!" he said, making his way to the steerboard. "Steady! Steady! Bring her up."

Landing the large warship upon Uist's flat shores was easy. He was a master seaman, and when needed, his crew would take the smaller coastal river ships upstream upon their backs. This isle was different, flat and dismal. His homeland was rich in bog, forest, farmlands, mountains, and lakes. However, that was not truly his home anymore. Let Magnor and Hallbjorn fight over their father's land. Uist was his new home. For a land of his own, he would get used to flat and dismal.

He squinted ahead at the shoreline. Did they even have animals in their forests? Did they *have* forests? Foxes, reindeer, elk, wolves...how could beasts of such grandeur call this barren isle home? Or did they only roam on the Scottish mainland? He couldn't live where he couldn't hunt. He exhaled, and then inhaled the scent of salt and upcoming glory. All wealth must be seized. He'd share a horn of ale with Blasius, feast in celebration of their union, and perhaps best some of his men in contests of wit and bow, for he was the best bowman in Reindalr. Then he would take the land and move to the south with King Haakon's fleets to conquer the rugged mainland.

First, he needed to greet his bride and bring warmth to his bed.

CHAPTER FIVE

When the sun rose, Gwyn opened her eyes to her new truth. She moaned. It wasn't a horrible dream. She sat in the feather-filled bed and stretched, willing herself to emerge from the coziness of it. It was plusher than the flattened cot and furs she was accustomed to. Heavenly, almost, though she hated to admit it, given the circumstances.

She wrapped bedclothes about her and shuffled to the writing desk. She tapped a finger on the parchments. There was a pile of them, crisp and awaiting ink. Parchment was hard to come by on the isles. She nibbled a lip and yawned. Somebody had been in the chamber recently while she slept. A hot kettle and cup for a spiced drink, she presumed by the earthy aroma, sat beside the parchments. She whiffed barley and sage with a touch of sweetness.

What could she say to Venora that only her sister would understand? Her father was well educated on Futhark runes, Gaelic, and Latin. As children, she and Venora had created their own unique code with numbers and symbols. She rested the feather quill. There was nothing she could say he couldn't decipher. He was too cunning.

If she was going to stay here for however long, as the men fought their skirmishes of words and bickered over negotiation, then aye, she'd need clothes and her herbal box. What she wanted to do was ask about Kendrick. Was he safe? If she couldn't return home, then Simon could bring her brother here. If they could just agree.

Words unwritten, she laid the feather down. It was futile. She would help Simon with whatever healing needed to be done, and then he'd send for Kendrick. Or better, she could return to her brother. If healing was what Simon truly wanted from her, once she obliged, he would gather his wits and let her be gone. A marriage accord need not be struck over such a thing.

Need it?

Och, well, it did according to Alroy MacCoinneach the Red. *The Red*, well he earned that name, even if he was graying. His overbearing son was just as mighty and red, albeit also a grumpy arse.

Curse her upbringing. Her mother had done nothing to help her with these types of situations. Give her herbs or people to heal or words to transcribe. Aye. Give her questionable warrior Nordmen to contend with. Aye, she would have done her duty. Give her a fight of the hands, and she had her dagger...

A knock on the thick oak door scattered her thoughts. A young woman entered, carrying a pewter pitcher.

"Mistress, I am Gildy. I'm here to help ye dress."

She rubbed her eyes. "I don't need help."

Gildy pointed to the soiled gown, a crumpled heap upon the rushes. "I will wash it, mistress, and ready ye in another gown."

Gwyn shivered in her thin shift, even with the bedclothes around her. She sipped the spiced water and contemplated.

Gildy set the pitcher beside a basin and turned to the hearth. She placed logs into a neat stack and prepared a new fire.

Gwyn poured the water, still tepid, into the basin and splashed it against her face. She wiped it dry with a cloth. A bath would be lovely, but she ran fingers through her long locks instead.

"Master Simon said ye may wear any dress from the cabinet. The lady shall not mind," Gildy said, gliding over to the simple dressing cabinet. She passed a look at Gwyn and then to the clothes within. "With yer eyes and fair complexion, the blue silk would match lovely." She chose the gown and laid it on the bed.

She'd not mind? So she was alive. Where was Lady MacCoinneach, though?

"I can't possibly," Gwyn said with a sigh. She picked up her soiled gown and her homespun kirtle. "This is suitable."

Gildy was persistent. She took the gown from her. "He insists."

Instead of leaving, the young woman stood by as Gwyn pulled on her own kirtle, tied the bodice, and then stepped into the lace-embellished gown. She frowned when she realized the lacings went up the back.

Gildy cleared her throat.

Gwyn resigned herself to the servant's help and allowed her to lace her in and fluff the skirts. She was about to pull on her boots when Gildy stepped forward with a pair of fine slipper shoes. "You can't possibly expect me to wear those? They'd get muddy the moment I step outside."

Gildy knotted her hands together and drew her look away. "There is no need for ye to go outside, mistress." Without looking upon Gwyn, Gildy opened the shutters on the window. A draft of cool morning air blew in.

Hands on her hips, Gwyn said, "Whyever not?"

Gildy said no more. She picked up Gwyn's cloak and hung it beside the gowns and kirtles in the cabinet. She then curtsied and departed with the basin of water and soiled gown.

Irritated, Gwyn marched out of the room only to be stopped by a guard. "Unhand me, please!"

"Milady—"

"I'm no lady, sir, or whoever you are. I am captive here. Did you know that?" She pulled roughly from his light grip. His fingers stirred over the hilt of his sword, still sheathed. "Och! Of course you did. Why else would you be guarding me? Do you think I'm going to hurt you?" She glanced at his dancing fingers and then to his confused face. He was but a lad, no older than Kendrick.

"Ye're not a Norse warrior?"

"Do I look like one?" She blew an exasperated breath and tucked errant strands of hair behind her ear. She should have plaited it.

"Weel, I dinna ken. Aren't all Lochlanach warriors, even the women? I heard tales of seamen's vessels overtaken by the dragon women..." He stumbled over his words while trying to keep pace with her as she hurried down the corridor.

"Then where are my sword and shield?"

He grimaced, his face, ears, and throat flushing pink. "Och, aye."

"I suppose we breathe fire out of our arses, too."

She halted, unsure which way to turn. There were two sets of stairs. She steadied her valor and offered him a smile. Sweetly, she said, "Is there a meal in the hall?"

Understanding lit his eyes. "Aye, mistress. I shall take ye there."

"So you shall."

Nobody greeted her in the empty hall.

"Where is Laird—um, your master?"

He bore confused doe eyes once again. "Mistress?"

She strode to the heavy oak table and ran a finger along it. "Och, no laird resides here. I mean your, hmm..." What was the word her sister had mentioned? Caretaker? A keeper? "Warden?" she tried.

"Master Alroy MacCoinneach is steward to the castle and village these past ten years, mistress. Do ye seek him?"

She nodded and thinned her lips. "Ah, yes, the steward."

"I'm afraid he's not here."

"Then his son, Master Simon?"

Sweat beaded on the guard's brow. She reached into her pocket. She could manage one man, easily. She'd never killed a man, but maybe a slice to give her the moment she needed to run.

Her hand found an empty pocket.

She reached into the other one. No healing stone.

She muffled a curse. The stone and empty sheath were in her gown Gildy had taken to clean. Simon had her dagger.

Her gaze flitted quickly around. Candlesticks, thick decorative banners on the walls, a jug on the table. Nothing. Hmm, it was a heavy-looking clay jug. She could...

The guard licked his lips, sensing her unease as her hand hesitated near the jug. His fingers found the hilt of his sword again. "Mistress, might ye take a seat?"

Simon entered the hall, his deep voice echoing off the high rafters and ceiling. "Errol, return to your post. Thank you."

Hope dashed, she settled into a seat at the long table. Though if she kicked Simon again in his bad knee...

Simon came beside her, then sidled around to the opposite side, sat, and shared a long look with her.

"Do captives get a meal?"

"Only if they don't try to run away."

She chewed the inside of her cheek and felt the burn of her galls. The silken gown weighed her down nearly as much as her spirit, and she tugged at the lace on the end of the sleeve near her wrist, anything to avoid Simon's stare.

He tipped forward, poured two goblets, and handed her one. Cloves and apples wafted to her.

"It's cider ale. Try it."

She was thirsty so she drank. It wasn't unpleasant even if its flavor accompanied her soured stomach. "I much prefer herbal drinks or oat milk."

"Did Gildy not bring you any in your chamber?"

She pressed her lips together.

Simon wasn't much for conversation as he sat and stared at her. Would it be a clash of looks, then? She crossed her arms and held his gaze as well.

She heaved a sigh. "Now what?"

He rubbed his cleanly shaven chin, all signs of the red stubble gone. His hair was wet, too, half brushed back over his ears, thick and wavy. His high forehead, darker eyebrows, deep-set brown eyes, and grumpy demeanor might rattle his guards or keep people in line, but they failed to intimidate her. Well, they *did* affect her, but not in that way. She chose to ignore the arousing sensations his nearness gave her. "Well?" she said.

A smile broke through, surprising her. "We have our own chapel here."

Her breath was squeezed from her lungs, stolen by the implication of his words. "You said you'd not force me."

"That I did."

"I don't have much of a choice."

He said, "Choose as you wish."

"I want to go home."

He sipped from his goblet before saying, "That is not an option."

His attentive eyes never left hers, and she grew uneasy with his blatant attention. She broke from his stare and followed the lines of the room with her gaze. The hearth, banners, and tapestries...the lofty windows...the door leading to the bailey.

This game tired her. She held out her fingers and counted on them in exaggerated irritation, her tone high-pitched. "My choices are to marry you and heal someone. Or to not marry you and heal them anyway. If I choose not, you won't let me leave. There is *no* choice. My *only* option is to heal some stranger *and* marry you. If I don't agree, then what? Shall I live locked up and join you for a meal each morn until my father comes to free me?"

He swallowed, rubbed his chin again. "Your father won't come for you."

Exasperated, she said, "Will you bring my brother here if I marry you and heal this person?" She could not believe she was negotiating. What of her betrothed, Leidolf? Surely, he wouldn't like to share his wife. It wasn't uncommon for a Nordman to have multiple wives, but none shared their wives with another man. She didn't think Scotsmen had more than one wife.

A servant entered the hall with a platter of food. Gwyn's palms grew slick with sweat, as the woman laid bowls for each of them. The servant looked to Simon for permission to serve them. He waved a hand, and she curtsied, nodded, and left.

Despite her hunger, Gwyn didn't reach for any of the food. She stared at her hands in her lap. She was getting nowhere.

"Lass, it's easy. Marry me, heal this person, and I shall send for your brother."

His coolness irked her. "Who am I to heal?" she asked again.

He frowned. "It doesn't matter."

Truth dawned. "The scroll you sent with my sister Venora. Your 'offer of truce.' There was no offer, was there? You had sent along your demands, your plan of action? You expect my father to acquiesce."

He held her gaze.

His lack of words said enough.

"Simon," she began, drawing his name out deliberately slow and mild. "I am promised to another."

"No longer."

"Then more hell than you could ever imagine will rain upon you. Your brazen idea will yield only death. He is a Norse warrior! From a distinguished bloodline!"

He slathered a bannock with butter and took a bite. "Sometimes death is the way."

She slammed her hands on the table, regretting it as pain rode up her arms and her goblet tumbled. Her pulse soared. The cider pooled next to her empty bowl. She squeezed her aching hands into knotted balls until they throbbed with her pulse. She shot upright, the seat falling behind her. She clamped her hands onto the edge of the table to control herself from scratching him and from succumbing to her shaking knees. She said, "Then I am your prisoner because I will *not* be your wife."

They shared a long look.

She stormed from the room to the hallway leading to her bedchamber. Simon didn't stop her. She heard the scrape of utensil against bowl as he served himself.

Gwyn's fit had accomplished nothing except to leave her hungry. She was in a foreign land with a stubborn arse of a man who thirsted for blood along with his unrelenting father. Kendrick was without her protection. Her father was still a madman. How had things come to this? Only a week ago, she had been home, Gunnar was alive, and, with her help, Kendrick was relatively safe from their father.

The day passed slowly, and she thought she might go daft with boredom and mounting ire over her situation. No books, no herbs to grind, no clothes to sew. No place to go. A knock on her door jarred her to the present. She threw it open, not knowing or caring who might be standing there. Perhaps Gildy the handmaiden or Errol, the freckled guard who blushed easily.

Dizzy with fatigue and hunger, she faltered when Simon appeared in her doorway, carrying a tray of food. She caught herself against the door jamb. She swallowed, her throat dry despite Gildy having brought her some honey-sweetened oat milk.

She eyed the covered food.

Simon hesitated. "May I come in?"

She took the tray from him. "I think not."

She uncovered the food and sat at the dressing table. A decadent meal of pheasant, apples, hard cheese, bread, and stew filled the tray alongside a goblet of dark wine. The food smelled divine, and her stomach growled.

Simon entered, ushering the guard in the hallway downstairs. "But—" the guard began. He was cut off by the thud of the door closing.

Reflex brought Gwyn's hand to her pocket. Still not there.

"Here's your stone," Simon said, handing it to her. "Heavy thing to be carrying around with you. What's it for?"

"My dagger?"

He smirked. "Not yet."

She suppressed a moan and instead of arguing she ripped a piece of the bread and dipped it into the stew. "The stone is for healing."

"Stones can't heal."

She turned away from him while eating. "Some can. With the right person. I'm a conduit of healing."

"A what?"

She waved her hand. "Never mind."

"Nobody is keeping you in your room," he said, approaching.

His nearness sent her mind spinning.

"Oh? Then why do I have men posted at my door?" She chewed, refraining from licking the grease from her fingers indelicately as she took a large, unladylike bite of pheasant. To Simon, she was a heathen or the word they used, Lochlanach, and she didn't care what was ladylike or not. She was *not* a Scottish lady.

"For your safety."

"You do like to remind me how safe I am here. Ever consider perhaps I was perfectly safe in my home?"

He hovered. No response.

She glanced behind her at the other stool. "Is your plan to stand there and watch me eat? There is a seat, you know. Might tire standing after a while."

"I best not stay."

"You best not then."

He shifted on his feet, the rushes crinkling with his movement. She didn't turn around and felt him move no closer. "We can walk the grounds after your meal, if you'd like. I can show you the beauty that Eilean Donan has to offer. Can't be pleasurable alone in here all day."

"What do you know of pleasure?"

Silence. Had his parents not taught him proper conversation or manners?

She turned to him again. Was that hurt in his deep brown eyes? Something about them drew her in, and she was surprised at her feeling. Well, she wasn't being the most obliging either.

The food caught in her throat, and she sipped the wine. She straightened her shoulders and held his gaze in return. "Yes, I'd like to go for a walk."

Simon began with a walk of the castle.

He felt like a fool. How could he convince her she was no prisoner, that she was safer here?

How could he convince *himself* of it?

What did women like to do?

He entered the buzzing kitchen. "Here's our kitchen."

"So I see."

"And the pantry here."

His mother had hardly spent time in their kitchens or pantry. She was likely to oversee gardens, visit people in the village, or attend the markets.

The cook and servants appeared surprised at his presence. "Och, Master Simon, is there something ye wish?" one asked.

He scratched his chin. "Nay, sorry to be a bother."

She curtsied. "Never a bother, sir."

He guided Gwyn by the arm to the inner bailey without much idle talk. He led her past the seawall under construction. "Do you like gardens?"

Brilliant blue eyes glimmered with interest. "Aye. Most Healers do."

They stepped onto the dirt path through the nearer gardens. "It's been a wet year. Our crops have not fared well, but we do what we can and trade special herbs at market along with our harvests. Our true asset is the grain from our fields." *And our fortified keep to block the Nordmen from pressing further inland*, he wanted to add.

"Do you have a village healer?"

"Mervyn is well learned. He's an able surgeon and prepares formulations for the ailing, but..." He floundered over his words. The urge to touch the wound she had healed by hand alone gnawed at him. "Would you like to meet him?"

"Perhaps not. His ways are different from mine."

He nodded. "Aye. He is open to the, *ehm*, unique."

She pressed her lips together but said nothing.

They walked for a long while, his thoughts a storm of questions and growing frustrations. After reaching the edge of the village beyond the miller's cottage and near the rye fields, he turned so they could continue their way back to the isle.

Her mood softened. She seemed less ready to bolt. Perhaps fresh air did help clear the mind, though his was a jumble.

"What is a steward?" she asked.

He cringed at the word. "An undervalued caretaker, I suppose."

"Your father is not a laird? Does he not rule?"

A heaviness filled his body and tethered his breathing as he explained. "The earl rules the region, and clans have taken hold of parcels of lands throughout the country. Clans are ruled by lairds. The former king never declared an official lairdship for this region. A few score years ago, the area lay empty and was guarded by a handful of men, and a steward rose up to take that leadership role. But he is dead now, and we're back to where we were before. The king thought it best to fortify the isle Donan against intruders." He stopped, chewing over his words.

"Like the Nordmen," she finished, hate noticeably absent from her tone.

He led her down one path between cabbage and onion beds. "Aye, yes. It's the gateway to the mainland from Skye and the isles. The men—some call themselves kings or lords or jarls—of the isles have ruled for many years but continue to press inland. The Scots were here long before your father's kind came. It is our land." He quickly added, "Just like your mother's folk were there long before the Nordmen came."

"I agree, Simon. It seems like man is never content. Always conquering," she said, disdain coloring her words.

He waved a hand. "Not all of us. My father and grandfather have been honorable stewards to the castle for many years. We do as a laird does. We provide for our people and ensure their safety. We do not encroach on another's lands."

"You fight with sword though. You seek the Nordmen."

"Only because they have overstepped their own territory," he defended, self-reproach rising up his throat.

"So you fight *only* for the protection of your people?"

He'd killed men for less. The devils had robbed him of a healthy mother. He'd been complacent for far too long. Let peace be for foolish dreamers. "Aye," he lied. He hastened his stride, leading her to the keep.

"She is *where*?" Leidolf asked.

Blasius repeated, "Alroy MacCoinneach and his son have taken her. She's at Eilean Donan Castle, at the mouth of Loch Duich, on the mainland. My man, Sigurd, has returned from the harvest market and reported the Scots stole her away. They presented us with their demands. Trygg stayed behind to follow them."

"*Taken*? They stole her? Why in Odin's name would they have stolen *my bride*? What right do they have to make demands?" Leidolf wanted to hit something. Or someone. Even if Blasius was twice his age. First, he'd arrived to find his bride not in waiting. Now...Sigurd returned to tell them she'd been stolen?

A thin smile slithered across Blasius's face as he held out the scrolled parchment. "Read for yourself."

Leidolf wanted to snatch it from him but stroked his beard instead.

Blasius sighed with feigned exasperation. "We had a disagreement when they came here to trade last week. They bested one of my strongest men and hastened my son's journey to Asgard."

Leidolf grunted. Fortune shone upon him today. Two fewer men to slaughter. Gunnar was supposed to be quite the warrior. He'd picked up on the man's absence upon his arrival but assumed he was elsewhere. Praise the gods. "You trade with the mainlanders?"

A bleak frankness filled Blasius's face. "No longer."

Leidolf's fingers found his sword's hilt. His axe was aboard the ship. He wanted to hack something. He traced a thumb over the engraved wolf's head hilt, followed by the amber jewels. Touched them each twice, and then resumed his grip on the hilt until his knuckles hurt. "How far away is this place? Don't our Norse brothers have a holding on Skye?"

"Aye, they do, despite the Scottish king's failed attempt last year."

"So then passage should not be a concern."

Blasius shifted from his spot near the hearth. His wife Caoimhe and daughter Venora had already left them alone in the cottage. "It may be too late."

"It's never too late," Leidolf assured.

"What if MacCoinneach has already bedded her? Would you still want her, Leidolf? Is she worth that?"

A raging fury tingled his fingers and pulsed in his veins. "Would your daughter do such a thing, Blasius? Is she not devoted to her Norse kin? My family is descended from the wolf god Fenrir himself. Lest I need to remind you?"

"Of course she's devoted, and she is well informed about the superior bloodline she will marry into." A snide smile spread Blasius's unkempt face as he drew a long gulp from his goblet. "Please, sit, Leidolf, descendant of Fenrir and son of Loki, and tormentor of the nine worlds, if you are to be my son." He poured a goblet for Leidolf.

Leidolf resisted the urge to punch Blasius and took the offered goblet instead. This Blasius was a brash bastard. Leidolf twirled the dark red wine in the goblet, wishing it was his wolf's blood.

"How do Magnor and Hallbjorn fare this season?"

There it was. "They fare well," he said, keeping his cringe internal.

His skin crawled with the mention of his older brothers. Blasius was no fool. Mad, yes. Foolish, no. Third-born sons were never favored; they were a drain upon their disappointed fathers. First- and second-borns were enough to rule and plunder: one to carry on the name, and a second should the first happen to fall. In place of a third son, Magnus of Reindalr would have much preferred a daughter to marry off and join forces with another Norse family. His father made that notion clear with every breath he took. Leidolf's mother had died shortly after his birth, and he'd been suffering for that wrong every day of his life.

"Good, good," Blasius said smoothly, rubbing his chin. His blue eyes blazed with intoxication and delight.

Unlike the other Nordmen, Blasius wore no plaited beard or even bracelets. His reddish hair was naturally blond, not in need of lye, and he wore but simpleton's clothes. Clearly, he'd spent far too many years on this desolate isle, allowing himself to be corrupted by their Ancient ways. During the past few days, as Leidolf await-ed his bride's return from the market, he'd learned much about Blasius the Mad. All the whispers were true. When in his cups, which occurred daily, Blasius rattled on about the purer Ancient race, the superiority of this Silver Veil, and his plan.

Leidolf had always been a keen listener, so he took it in. It was about timing. The wolf waited for the right moment. Even if he lacked a pack, he was the best hunter in all of Reindalr.

Killing the Mad Jarl would not be too hard. The Scot brothers north would prove challenging, but he had able warriors with him to handle that siege. His father had not sent him with many men, but the ones who'd come across the sea were chosen for their strength and killing skills.

They held no remorse. Leidolf had promised them much in gold and silver. It would all fall into place...soon.

He drew a long breath, coercing the unease that boiled within him to settle. He brushed another hand along the leather strap across his chest, then downed the drink. He wrinkled his nose. It tasted like rye water instead of a good wine. "How can you be assured in your daughter's faithfulness?"

A snicker escaped Blasius's lips. He staggered to the door. "Kendrick, come," he barked through the doorway.

The younger son, who had been outside tending to the horses, hovered at the entrance.

"Inside, son," Blasius said.

Kendrick stepped tentatively inside, hands balled in front of him, face downturned.

Leidolf gave him hardly a glance. He was a young lad, not properly groomed in the Norse way. Nordmen never cowered. However, he was skilled with horses. Leidolf considered sparing him when he felled the village. He would need a stable master.

Blasius put an arm around him, and the boy immediately stiffened. The madman's grin widened, his eyes alight with malice. "It appears I have exactly what I need to ensure my daughter's return. All families have their weak foals," he said.

Leidolf scoffed, feeling the cut with Blasius's undertone. "He's a lad. What of him?"

"Gwyn would not want to see him harmed."

Leidolf crossed his arms as he sat, ready for another one of Blasius's drunken ramblings or backhanded punches. He listened anyway. Soon Blasius would be dead. Leidolf wouldn't be able to rouse and lead his men until morning. They were in the village somewhere, seeking women or wrestling with Blasius's warriors. They needed the respite. He flicked his fingers for Blasius to continue. "And?"

"My wife cannot heal the boy."

Kendrick quaked beneath his father's presence. The boy's gaze fell upon the hearth and then Leidolf, but there was a distance in his eyes. Bluish bruises circled one eye, and reddened fingerprints marked his neck.

Leidolf's frustration mounted. Blasius enjoyed beating his son? The pleasure he'd get from running Blasius through rose within his chest. If he didn't need him, he'd do it now.

"Is he a Seer, too?" If it wasn't for Gwyn's supposed beauty, he would have been content taking the Seer, Venora, to his bed. She was equally striking, but he imagined he'd find a dagger in his back come morning if he did so. She needed taming, a lot of it. Perhaps he'd have both daughters. Arousal awakened within him. Did Blasius not own a single thrall? He hoped his men left a few of the women for him. He shifted in his seat.

"No, he's not a Seer."

Leidolf tired of this roundabout talk. Blasius's wife Caoimhe the Graceful...she was a remarkable creature. She was a Healer, like Gwyn, or at least that was the promise Blasius made about his betrothed. He contemplated who would make the better second wife: Venora or Caoimhe.

His father would be pleased to know he would conquer such a people with their exquisite beauty, good breeding, and mystical gifts. Exhaling, he said, "What ails him so much so the sacred Caoimhe cannot heal it?"

"Sit," Blasius ordered Kendrick. He shoved him toward the hearth. The stool was on the other side of Leidolf, in the opposite direction. The boy stumbled on the beaver pelt, arms out before him, feeling for something, anything. He found the wall, drew himself upright, and whirled to face his father. He blinked and gripped his head as if it pained him.

"My son is blind."

Leidolf was unimpressed. So much for his stable master idea. "So?"

"Healing him would take a thousand breaths."

He crossed his arms. "And?"

"She would die, and I cannot have that. Caoimhe has more work to do for me."

He gnawed over the information while Blasius continued, "My daughter has kept this secret from me. I just discovered the truth of it. She will return home, or I will kill him."

Leidolf searched Blasius's eyes, clouded with drink. Gwyn would be a fine asset. She hid this secret from her father for years? Aye, she was a striking woman. Cunning woman. His arousal grew. "You're confident she would return for him? What if MacCoinneach has swayed her to stay?" Not that Leidolf could possibly imagine what a Norse woman would want with one of the lowbred Gaels. They hid from the English in stone castles and rode across their drab moors to bicker amongst each other. Nordmen would just take what was rightfully theirs. He rubbed his plaited beard.

"Their blood bond is fierce. Aye, she'll return home for him. She'd do anything for him. She's like her mother," Blasius said.

"Sibling blood goes deep, but I daresay she'd not die for this louse," Leidolf said, thinking of his own brothers who used to burn his hair as a lad, send the dogs chasing after him, or lock him away for days while their father was away.

"I am certain. Venora has seen it."

Leidolf couldn't help but smile. If the witch had seen it, then so be it.

"And Trygg? He stayed behind?"

"Yes. He will seize the moment to retrieve her, but he is one man."

"A Nordman with a family of *úlfheðnar* in the homeland, you know. He has virtuous blood," Leidolf assured. He heaved a sigh. Retrieving Gwyn was his responsibility. As was slicing to bits the Scot who had taken her. "Let's review these demands and ready a ship to retrieve my wayward bride and kill a few Scots, shall we?" This put a wrinkle in his plans, for the rest of King Haakon's fleet would be there soon.

The days passed slowly and routinely while Simon waited.

He waited for the Nordmen to make the next move, so he could kill again.

He waited while his father had gone south to visit with Mother.

He waited for Gwyn to warm to him.

Life was too much waiting.

Her companionship, ruffled as she was, made his step lighter, and she was a bonnie distraction. Each day he greeted her for a meal and then took her around the grounds. Each afternoon, he'd hunt, but he still had yet to kill a stag this season. Then they'd have their supper together, alone, and she'd retreat to her chamber for the night. His father would return from Dryburgh Abbey soon.

Then they would marry in the chapel if he could get her to consent.

Until then, he waited, for their priest had gone to the abbey with his father to deliver the news of Desmond's passing and to visit with Abbot Oliver and his monks. He was grateful his father left, giving Simon time to try his best to coerce Gwyn into saying yes. If his father had his way, the two would have already been married.

The imagined look of his mother's reaction when she would hear the news of Desmond's death haunted Simon's dreams, waking him in fits and sweaty bedclothes. The illusory image of his mother in the damn dreams, for she was fair and young and untransformed, drove the pain deeper. She was the mother he knew of his childhood before the incident. Before an incurable disease percolated through her body. Before mercy and innocence had served him a fist of truth.

He stumbled in his steps in the garden's overgrowth.

Gwyn prevented his fall through their linked arms. "Something ails you, Simon?"

How he loved it when she said his name. Over a few days, her words had changed from accusations and acrimonious retorts to sincere friendliness. With Desmond dead and his mother lost to the illness that ravaged her body, loneliness dominated everything else...well, except for his desire to kill. Des had wanted peace, some wee bairns. Now he was in the ground. If Simon had been faster on his feet, killed more Nordmen, would his brother still be alive?

Simon cringed and rubbed his knee again in reflex. Even the stags and roes hid from him these days. "I'm well," he said, snappier than expected.

Inquisition lay in Gwyn's eyes as her eyebrows shot up. "Does that always bother you?" She reached for his knee and then retracted her hand.

He flinched from her near touch. "Not always. Usually in foul weather." *Except for when I am reminded of why it hurts,* he wanted to say.

She blew a wisp of hair from her face, tucked it behind her ear, and said into the misty air, "Well, that's always. The sun doth hardly shine."

"When it does, we are certain to make use of it."

She laughed lightly and kept her arm linked in his as he guided her past the garden. Had he made her laugh?

He'd initially asked her to keep to his side, arm in arm, for her security and for his own reassurance. When she was in his presence he'd not have her run off on him. If he hadn't entered the hall at the precise moment on that first morning, when Errol was guarding her, he wondered if she would have taken the cider jug to Errol's head and been gone without haste. Ironically, a grin curled his lips with that image.

He'd already made a deal with the devil when he agreed to take her by force. There was no turning back. God forgive his soul. His smile disappeared.

Therefore, he made sure to keep her in sight, and when he hunted or slept, he left his men guarding her. She hadn't tried to bolt again. Was she taking a liking to him as well?

Their conversation reached a lull. He didn't say much anyway. She was hard to ignore. He stifled a moan and cracked his neck.

They walked through the village. It wasn't a market day, so it was quiet. He passed the miller's cottage. Meredith approached, carrying a heavy sack of grain. She tripped, floundered, and he came to her assistance. "Here, let me help."

She blew a breath, her cheeks rosy. Although she was a bonnie woman, her wrinkles now made a permanent home at the sides of reserved brown eyes since Desmond's death. Her hair was disheveled and loose beneath her cap. She forced a courteous smile. Her face was pale, her shoulders hunched. "Aye, thank ye kindly,

Simon. My cart is there," she said with a point. She huffed and splayed hands on her hips.

After loading the sack, he said, "Meredith, I'm—" He rubbed the growing stubble on his chin, dryness stealing his voice. "I can send Errol or Henry to come help you."

"It's not needed, but thank ye kindly, again." She accepted his offered hand and climbed into the cart. She snapped the reins and was off toward her small cottage. She and Desmond had never lived in the castle. Des had preferred the crofter's life, even with Father's grooming for lairdship. Physical confrontation was never his way. Des would have been a righteous chief.

That responsibility now fell upon Simon.

As they returned to the hall for the evening's meal, Gwyn spoke again. "Who was that, Simon?"

"Desmond's widow."

"Oh."

Her arm slackened. He looped it tighter into his, not for fear of her fleeing—she had long since proven to be less resistant—but he liked her touch. She soothed his soul, which was worrisome in and of itself. "Was your brother Gunnar married, too?" he asked.

"Nay. He had a warrior's heart."

Simon knew too well how much a warrior sometimes yearned to be turned from such a path. Could Gunnar have also felt that way?

Not since long ago had he felt remorse for killing.

Now...now, it besieged his heart.

CHAPTER SIX

Simon awoke, slick with sweat, his pulse galloping within his chest like horses' hooves.

There it was again. The slice of steel, her piercing scream.

He jumped from the bed, leapt over to his scabbard, and withdrew the sword in lightning reflex.

He clutched the hilt until the pain in his palms awoke his senses. He wasn't in the forest. Nay, he was naked, soaked with sweat, and crouching beside the near-dead hearth. The last log he'd put on was charred to crunchy pieces. One final hiss, then it was gone, and the room went dark.

As he rose and slid the sword into its home, he approached his bedside table. He lit a candle, poured a goblet of ale, and downed two hefty sips, hoping to stay his dream and steady his mind.

He'd done a fine job repressing the memory over the past few years. Limiting his visits to his mother helped. Hunting anything he could kill in the woods helped. Killing intruders on the Dornie limits helped. Running that Nordman, Rothwell, through had felt good. He hungered for more.

Why had he agreed to one simple voyage with his father and brother to that godforsaken isle? Look where it landed them! Hell had been unleashed in a matter of moments with the Nordmen—again. Now the memories infiltrated his mind like the disease that stole his mother's life away from them each day.

He slapped his knee, which burned fiercely as a rainstorm pattered the side of the keep. He wished for musk mallow. If what Mervyn said was true about it being a spirit wound—and spirit memories—both would fade if he left them alone—then why did they haunt him? There was nothing wrong with his knee, for it had healed nicely from the wound. He grimaced, rubbing it again. His head grew dizzy.

He dropped the goblet on the table and burrowed beneath the bedclothes, ignoring the heat they manifested. He curled himself tighter, muffling the ache within. The memory flashed again behind his eyes, suppress it though he tried. Was God reminding him of his wrongs? Did his Holy Father damn him to hell for the men and animals he'd killed in the past nine years? Or for not being able to protect his mother?

Or was it the work of the devil, luring him in?

He'd been younger when it happened. Not young like the wee stable lads, but not a man either. A young daft fool of fifteen. Old enough to fight well with the sword but not experienced and keen enough to realize mercy was for the weak-hearted and some men were pure evil.

The Nordmen had not come in their impressive warships. No, they sailed in a smaller coastal river ship, one decorated with the hideous dragon-head, shields mounted broadside, and a white sail emblazoned with the snarling red wolf's head. They were nameless. They were traveling along the southern coast near Loch Shubhairne. One man was injured and alone beside the ship put ashore on a sandy embankment.

Simon and his mother came upon the injured man while riding home from the market.

His mother pleaded for Simon to continue on—for they hadn't been seen—to not trust this man. She said he was Lochlanach, a people who lived on the Western Isles and Skye, a people not to be reckoned with. Simon was naïve, filled with too much compassion, and not educated upon the cruelties of the world. At that time, he wasn't aware there were two types of isles people: Nordmen, demonic and ruthless, and the Ancients, like Gwyn, rational and merciful. All isles people were Lochlanach, were they not?

What harm was there in one man, alone, and injured? His mother was adept with the needle, and she stitched the man's wounds upon Simon's insistence. As they turned to leave, the rest of his group returned.

They were not just any Nordman. Not soil tillers or jarls. No, they were warriors. The *úlfheðnar*. He'd heard of both the bear-pelt wearers, the *berserkir*, and the wolf-hide wearing *úlfheðnar*, sickening select groups who were unleashed for the most important battles. The ones who invaded nightmares with their bloodthirst, the ones his father had warned him about. The ones who drank animal blood and killed with an appalling lust.

He remembered too vividly their purple faces twisted with a maddening rage, skin streaked with blood, embellished beards, and wolfskin clothes.

They were surrounded, and he was helpless to do anything.

Simon fought the memory. He cursed under his breath.

He punched the pillow and hollered as the pain rose from his knee to his chest, taking his breath from him.

He'd fought as any young man would. They left him there, bleeding, his own dagger stuck into his knee. Why they hadn't killed him, he would never know.

He could hear his mother's screams as they pulled her away into the trees, as she clawed at their throats and arms, but there was no stopping men drunk with frenzy. The leader had dark black hair and sharp blue eyes. He would never forget the man.

Opening his eyes, he tossed the bedclothes to the floor, and rose. He wanted to punch something—anything. There was naught but the stone walls.

Never again.

There was but one way to deal with them.

Gwyn yawned as Simon ventured farther from the keep on their daily walk. He led her beyond Dornie today, to the foothills of the mountains, and despite her fatigue, she took pleasure in their time outside. She breathed in the fresh, wet air.

"What are these mountains called?" She stared in awe at the craggy points beyond the glen. No such massive mountain existed near her home on the isle. Moors, bogs, meadows, and water in all directions made up her home, save for a few mountains far away she'd never been allowed to visit. Once she and Kendrick had attempted to reach them, only to have Sigurd and Trygg drag them home.

Simon scratched his head. "It's a pagan story," he said, cheeks flushing.

Gwyn laughed lightly. "Stories are stories. I'd love to hear it. Besides, don't your people have pagan roots?"

He released a long sigh and said, "The story states that five maidens awaited their princes to return from the land across the sea. Two of a powerful chief's daughters were already wed, and their husbands sailed across the sea to bring back their five brothers for the five remaining daughters. But the princes were lost to the sea."

"How sad," she said.

He nodded and continued, "The maidens waited to no avail. Thus, they asked the Gray Charmer, a magical man, to turn their vigil into forever, to preserve their exquisite beauty. So he created them into these stone memorials—mighty and striking mountains—to make the maidens immortal. Now they wait for eternity for their princes."

"Love," she said with a sigh in the moist air before them.

He wet his lips and pinched his nose before saying with resignation, "Legend says each of the five sisters of Kintail has a special power: protection, fruitfulness, divination, memory holder, and healing." He shrugged. "The crofters heed a host of superstitions for fertile harvests and believe these powers to be why our glen is fruitful. Like I said, a foolish story."

"Belief in something beyond one central god does not need to be pagan or foolish."

"Well, och, the church would not agree with you."

"The church seems to determine your mind a lot. Who is to say a man speaking the words of a god is correct? I would love to read your teachings," she said.

"Perhaps the monks and priors at the abbey can enlighten you?"

"Abbey?"

"You don't have those?"

She shook her head.

"They're religious sanctuaries where our priests and monks reside, pray, and transcribe and study the holy texts. Holy places. Do you not have those in your religion?"

She waved a hand. "Aye, the people of the Nord Land have holy places, temples. The Ancients rely on the earth to be our spiritual haven. The earliest people created shrines with stones, into grand circles. I don't know what they mean, but when I visit the stones near our home, the earth hums, the wind whispers, and the world tells me its..." She drifted. He stared at her, his forehead thickly furrowed. Perhaps she *was* the pagan one.

She stepped over a wet puddle as they made their way on the outskirts of the village. "You have your written stories, like us. The Norse people have the skalds and runes. You have your *monks* transcribe words of your god, aye? My people, the Ancients, we share our stories and write our own books. Are we not the same?"

Simon's brows turned down as he rubbed his forehead. "Perhaps. It is not my place to interpret things holier than I."

She relented, "Mayhap. Where is the abbey? In Dornie?"

"No. We'll ride south."

Her pulse fluttered. "We must journey there?"

"Yes. A few days."

"Why?"

He cleared his throat. "The healing, remember?"

Her pulse grew fitful. She hadn't considered that the person to be healed was located elsewhere. "Who is the person I must heal, Simon?" she asked again. Was it a friend hurt in battle? Family? She swallowed a thickness in her throat. Or perhaps a lover of his?

"Somebody dear to me. She is ill."

She pressed her lips together, frustrated. *She.*

Sister? Lover? Mother? Daughter?

Simon's silence crept under her skin. A bird cawed above them, and a drizzle pattered the ground. She turned her face heavenward for a moment, letting the droplets hit her skin. She licked her lips before returning her gaze toward Simon, opening her eyes. This water had a different taste to it, like smoky peat. Water gave man life. Water was the thread to Eir's merciful healing.

She lifted her chin and held Simon's look. Yearning curiosity burned in his eyes. He closed the space between them, his hand sliding from her arm to elbow. He brushed a wet lock of hair from her forehead with his other hand, his fingers pausing a moment on her face. He leaned even closer. She stepped in, smiling up at him with his touch on her skin. Oddly, she enjoyed his nearness. His touch sent shivers through her.

She blinked, his look fast and hard on hers. Then he broke away and walked on, letting go of her arm.

She drew her cape over her head and hurried to catch up.

"Is something wrong?" she asked. She almost wanted his touch on her again. In fact, after the last few days of walks, she found herself looking forward to their time together each day.

"Nay. Is your healing conditional?"

She held her tongue. Why would he ask such a thing? "Healing is my gift bestowed to me upon my birth. Be it from your god, the Norse deities, or from the Earth herself, it's true to my blood. It runs through me like life-giving water. No, I will heal any who seek it. I will heal this woman."

He nodded. "Then I will bring your brother to my home if you wish."

Cooperation was all she had. She might never see her home again, and so she said, "I do."

"After my father's return, we'll journey south to the abbey."

There was no talk of marriage today. Simon looped his arm through hers and guided her along the path. She wondered about the rest of his family.

Just as she settled her mind so she could enjoy the remainder of their walk, Simon unsheathed his sword and spun around to face someone or something behind them.

Winded and shocked, she turned after him.

"Step back!" Simon ordered Trygg, who had materialized from the woods flanking them.

Gwyn gasped. "Trygg!"

His face flared with threat. He was filthy, his dark hair oiled, his beard long and plaited. Had he been in hiding all this time? She'd been here, imprisoned at the castle for days. A week? He chose now to show himself?

"She returns with me to our home, and there will be no harm against your clan, MacCoinneach," Trygg said, gray eyes narrowing. Fatigue and anger filled them. Trygg was older than them, nearly her father's age, but still possessed the Norse stamina. His sword was raised and ready.

"We sent our requests and offer of truce. This is not your matter. Speak with your Mad Jarl," Simon countered, stepping closer to Trygg.

"Oh, we sent your offer of truce to our jarl. He shall not negotiate. I don't leave without her," Trygg said with a chin flick toward her. A muscle twitched in his jaw.

She stepped nearer to Simon, reached out, but retracted her hand. "Please, Simon. Let me return home. I can help you later with—"

"No."

In a flash, he lunged toward Trygg. Negotiations were over. Now she knew why Simon always wore his sword.

They traded blows mixed with curses in Gaelic and the Norse tongue. Simon was half Trygg's age but fought with equal vigor and deathly accuracy.

Trygg tripped and caught the blade on his upper arm. He retaliated and barely missed Simon's ear. Simon dodged, grunted.

"Please! Please! Let me go with him, Simon! I can return to help her!" she pleaded.

"No!" Simon growled. The same man she had witnessed murder Rothwell with not a shred of mercy danced and countered before her. His shoulders were set back, his legs moving with each parry. He was maddened by the confrontation. He and Trygg locked together, swords ringing, sharp poison on her ears. It was painful to watch, but like other battles, she was unable to pull her gaze from it.

One would fall. Who?

Her answer came soon enough.

Trygg yelped. Simon didn't even hesitate as he released their locked embrace and plunged the sword in deeper.

Trygg's cry went silent. He gurgled. He wheezed.

He was dead.

Heedless, she ran to his side, thrust her hand into her pocket, wrapped it around her stone, and chanted her healing words. She placed a quivering hand on Trygg's gaping chest wound.

Simon hovered behind her, the stench of male glory falling off him. "Do you bring men back from the dead, too?"

She cried through her prayers.

Simon sheathed his sword.

She rose, her hand bloody. "You. You!"

His voice eased. "He wouldn't have left without you. My father doesn't take Nordmen as prisoners."

"I could have gone! I promised to return!" she countered. He handed her a kerchief from his pocket. She wiped the blood off her palm.

"That was not an option."

"How could you?" she said through a whimper, shuddering.

He made to walk back.

"We can't leave him here!"

He heaved a sigh, taking her arm. "I'll send a man to fetch his body. Give him a burial, is that what you want?"

She nodded. "I need to say the Ancient prayers over him."

She expected an argument. Instead, he said, "Whatever you wish. All men deserve final rites, even Nordmen, I suppose."

As they walked, his limp grew noticeable.

For the first time, she wished Simon pain.

"As I said, Gwyn. I can't bring you home. I need you."

A heavy cloud of dreariness fell upon Gwyn as she replayed the moment over in her mind for faults, what she could have done better. There was naught.

Upon their approach to the castle, there was commotion at the stable as horses and riders were being settled. Simon's arm stiffened in hers, and his feet slowed.

He didn't look at her when he said, "My father has returned."

"Sir, sir!" Errol ran into the hall, waving scrolled parchments.

Simon turned from his conversation with his father. Errol bowed with a rolled parchment outstretched. "A message, Master MacCoinneach."

Simon's father excused Errol, opened the scroll, and read it. His face changed from concerned to interested to…delighted? He smiled as he handed Simon the message. "Well, my plan has fared well." He lumbered to the doorway nearest the stairs to his chamber, noticeably tired from his long journey. He paused. "I'll have the priest ready the chapel, Simon. Go find your bride." With that, he was gone.

With shaking hands, Simon unrolled the parchment and read. It was in Latin and he skimmed to the bottom where it was signed V.

He read it from the beginning. His father had wanted Blasius to come in full glory, ready for a fight or negotiation. He wasn't sure if Venora having sent a letter to Gwyn was a secret warning or their madman father's ploy. Either way, they'd be ready. Given the time it took for emissaries to sail from Uist and ride across Skye, Blasius and Leidolf of Reindalr, Gwyn's betrothed as stated in Venora's message, would arrive upon the morrow or the day after. If it was a fight he wanted, then his father would get it. Perhaps that's what his father hoped for all along...that the idea of a marriage alliance had been a farce. He wanted to lure the Norse fiends, bring them here to their own territory.

He hadn't told his father about killing the other Nordman. There was no undoing it. The madman and his new son were already on their way. Simon turned down the hallway to locate Henry, one of their best soldiers. He'd help him bury the poor bastard before the wedding.

"I will not!" Gwyn said, again.

She stared at the parchment in her hand and read it again and again.

Simon glared at her. "You can read Latin?"

She stuck her chin out. "My father saw me learned. And my sister addressed this to *me*."

He exhaled and paced over to her window with crossed arms, keeping his back turned to her. "Gwyn, there is no other way. We must marry tonight. The priest is ready in the chapel. My father will not allow you to return home."

"What about you?" she asked, her hands shaking as she dropped the letter from Venora to the floor.

"It doesn't matter what I want."

She approached him and laid a hand on his arm. "Yes, it does. Talk to your father. Let me go home."

Home.

Her heart went out to Trygg. The burial for him had been swift, silent. Two of Simon's men had brought the body, dug the hole outside of their town's cemetery, and interred him. A light rain had fallen to match the tears she'd shed. She never liked Trygg, but all men deserved a full life. After, there were no more words between Simon and her about what had happened.

"I need you to come with me to the abbey."

"Then I can return home after?"

His look remained directed outside. "What about your brother?"

She pinched the bridge of her nose and huffed. "I don't know. He's not safe with my father. Simon, please reconsider! There has to be another way other than an unwanted marriage and needless deaths! I already promised to help the woman you wish me to heal. Isn't that enough?"

He finally faced her, taking her elbows in his hands. "I said I would not force you to wed me, but my father will not relent, Gwyn."

"Neither will my father. Or Leidolf!"

"Tell me about your betrothed," Simon said, releasing her elbows.

He drove her daft. "I don't know much about him. Why do you ask?"

"You've not met?"

She lowered her gaze and paced before the hearth. She stopped and stared into the low flames. "We were promised to each other at our births."

"Hasn't your father spoken about him to you?"

"Yes, plenty about his glories. My father has only sailed to the Nord Land twice since my birth. He holds no love for that country."

Simon waited, silent and as unwavering as an ox.

"Leidolf comes from the house of Reindalr. His father is Magnus, and he has two older brothers, Magnor and Hallbjorn, both of whom are already wed and readily pillage distant countries." She eyed him briefly. "I believe he is about your age. How old are you, Simon?"

"Four and twenty," came his terse response. He didn't ask her age.

She held in her frustration. Well, at least she wasn't to be married off to a man many years older, like some of the women in her village. "They are a powerful family and rule with blood. I know nothing else."

It wasn't the complete truth. The Reindalr family was known for their atrocities. Seafaring to distant lands, raping, burning. She shivered. Had Leidolf's family been to Scotland before? Did they, too, paint their skin with ink, wield chiseled axes with deathly accuracy, and conquer any land they came upon? The ancient runes told of Norse warriors and of a lofty kingdom, but years of greed and lust for glory, in addition to retaliation from superior English and French armed forces, had diminished their hold on distant shores. The sea kingdom had seen its finest days already. What was embellishment by her father versus truth? Perhaps, as Venora had foreseen, the Scots would rise and the Norse culture would assimilate. Or be decimated in the process.

"Why does your father not care for his country anymore?"

She shrugged. "I know not. He's a distant cousin of King Haakon. He was appointed many years ago to journey to Uist and oversee part of the isle dominion." *And exploit the powers of the Silver Folk. Brutalize our people. Until Haakon's return,* she wanted to add but did not.

Venora's premonition echoed in her mind: *Haakon's realm will be defeated on a shore near the Isle of Cumbrae on the second day of the tenth new moon, the morning after a great gale.* She counted the days in her mind. A fortnight. Where was Cumbrae? Her father had taught her Latin texts and rudimentary Scottish history, but no charts or maps of the mainland country.

Simon turned on his heel, ready to go. "Gwyn, the priest is ready. I *will not* force you, but I can't say the same about my father. I promised you I'd bring your brother here. I stay true to my word. We shall marry, and I'll send word to your brother. You can write the letter now if you wish. Then we leave for Dryburgh Abbey."

The door closed with a grating thud behind him.

She stewed for a while. Pacing accomplished nothing, so she sat. She stared at Venora's letter again, the words blurring together like wet clouds. Simon seemed an honorable man, even if pigheaded.

He was a murderer. Rothwell and Trygg were almost as evil as her father, but they hadn't deserved to die, even if it was *justified*.

She weighed her choices, and each time she ran through them, her hope dwindled.

She could leave and marry Leidolf, if he prevailed against the MacCoinneachs. That wasn't even a real choice. Simon and Alroy would never let her leave.

What of Kendrick? What if her father discovered his blindness, or worse, his ability as a Feeler? She had to go home. She rubbed her empty pocket, itching for her dagger. The Healer's stone sat in the other pocket.

She could stay here and marry Simon, and he would bring Kendrick to her. Marriages were often made with far fewer accommodations. What if they were too late? Confrontation would surely ensue between her father's men, Leidolf's men, and the MacCoinneachs. Who would win? Venora hadn't warned her.

King Haakon was already on his way. To be conquered by the Scots as Venora had foreseen. Their end was coming. Was Leidolf one of them? Would her betrothed also meet a warrior's end?

Could she keep Kendrick safe until then? What if she married Simon and he died in battle? Then, she could return home after the battle. Her father need not know what she had done if it meant safeguarding her brother. Would Simon's kin care for Kendrick? Or could she find a home for him elsewhere on the mainland?

She hung her head in her hands as tears found their way down her cheeks. Although she didn't care much for the man, she didn't wish for Simon's death, nor anyone else's.

Simon waited in the chapel.

And waited.

Evening had fallen, and the priest circled around the sanctuary lighting candles. His father rose from a wooden bench.

"Enough! She's not coming. Simon, can you not do this one thing? I've left you alone for the week while I visited your mother, and you have yet to convince her?" his father said, voice thick and gruff. "Let's go." He made for the door.

Simon followed, relieved she had not shown herself. Strangely, also disappointed. Despite their blooming friendship, she hadn't wanted to put her trust and faith in him. He didn't blame her.

"Father, you, too," his father said to the priest.

The priest glanced around the empty chapel as if for answers. He blinked, opened his mouth to speak, and then clamped it with a squish of his gray eyebrows. "Yes, sir."

"Father...," Simon fumbled in protest.

His father snipped, "If she doesn't come to us, then we go to her. Come."

Gwyn paced her chamber. Hours had passed. She couldn't bring herself to go to the chapel.

"Curses!" she said, tossing her hands in the air. Decision-making had never been a strength. Give her a person to heal, aye. Give her this choice—which was in truth, not a choice at all—and the wheels spun in her head violently. Queasiness rolled in her stomach.

Her skin prickled with an odd sensation. She heard their boots in the hallway before they entered. Hugging her middle, she readied herself.

Alroy opened the door, barging into the room with nothing short of controlled fury. "My lady," he snapped. Simon followed him, haggard in visage despite being dressed for a fine occasion in a clean linen shirt with ruffled sleeves, deep green tunic highlighting his broad chest, dark brown hose, clean boots, and dagger in his belt. His ruddy hair was swept back from his shaven face. He beheld her with fearful clarity—or was he just as nervous? It was hard to read his hawk-eyed expression.

She released her grip from her angry stomach and balled her hands. The priest entered behind father and son.

This is not happening.

Simon opened his mouth but nothing came out.

Alroy's tone lost some, but not all, of its hard edge. "Lass, we have offered you safe refuge from your mad father. As my son has informed me, you also request sanctuary for your brother. If you do honor our request of marriage, your safety and your brother's well-being will be granted. We request this *now*."

"I was taken by force," she said, clamping her jaw.

"It was for your own security. Do you want our protection or not?"

"We know it wasn't for my safety alone," she said through gritted teeth. She thought of asking about Simon's healing request but hesitated. Simon's deeply dipped frown said it. His father didn't know. *So it is a secret lover.* Had she been sent away to the abbey to raise a bastard bairn and had grown ill with complications? Maybe Alroy didn't know.

She raised her gaze to meet Alroy's, and said instead, "War is coming, Sir MacCoinneach."

"I am well aware."

"There are many forces you may not be aware of," she countered, focusing on controlling her breath. Her heartbeat flitted madly in her chest.

Alroy's gray-streaked eyebrows curled, his face twitched. "Do you know more?"

She swallowed, unfaltering. "No," she lied, not knowing exactly why she didn't tell them about Venora's premonition of King Haakon's gathering fleet. Did she secretly wish to see the Nordmen fail? Or did she wish for them to succeed, so she and Kendrick could lose themselves among the disorder? Perhaps they'd find refuge with another isle's people or in the south? She tightened her balled hands. No, she wouldn't tell them about Haakon. Not until Kendrick was safe.

Alroy's look was palpable. After a brief moment, he waved the priest over. The thin, graying man approached with a slow gait and placed a parchment on the table. "My dear, if you could please sign the marriage contract? It must be your decision. You shall not be forced." He didn't look at Alroy when he said these words, spoken crisply, but kindly. He handed her the quill.

Her vision blurred the words before her as she read.

"Och, put your mark to it."

She turned her head to Alroy and snapped, "I am reading it!"

He scoffed. "You can't possibly know Latin."

She fell onto the stool and drew the parchment closer to her face, forcing her hands not to shake. "I daresay I do. Do you think all of us heathens? Why else would my sister have sent me a message in Latin?" She read through the rest of the agreement. Submission. Duties. Faithfulness. Heirs. All men were the same. The mainlanders were no different from her father's people. Perhaps foolish men would eventually realize the futility of their barbaric ways and embrace the beauty of what nature had provided them. Perhaps then they might listen for a moment to ask what a woman wanted.

Simon finally spoke, his voice an isle in a storm. "Please, Gwyn."

She rubbed her nose with a hand, steadied her posture, and dipped the quill in ink.

"My brother?" she asked, face turned to Alroy.

"Yes. Our word. We shall provide him protection."

"Bring him here?"

"Yes."

She then marked her name in the Latin way.

She turned to Simon with her glare as she rose. "You better be prepared, because my father's men—and my intended—are coming, and they won't relent."

The priest swept the parchment off the desk and reviewed her signature. "Aye, sir. I approve. Now, Master Simon?" He handed the parchment and quill to him.

Simon hesitated, but then took the quill, bent over the desk, and signed.

Alroy smiled. "You will not regret it."

"Aye, but you may," she said.

Alroy cleared his throat. "Good, then. Father?"

She stumbled. "What? Now?"

"Now," Alroy said.

The priest objected, "Sir, this holy sacrament must be performed in a house of our Lord."

Alroy pressed his lips together. "This chamber is Lord's house enough. Do it now."

Simon stepped forward and stood beside her. He looped his arm into hers, the nearness of his body infusing her with mild comfort like it had all week. The hearth crackled and candles flickered as a breeze blew through a slat in the shuttered window.

The priest began in Latin, and she did her best to follow along. Although her reading skills were adequate, she hardly ever heard the words said aloud.

Her stomach twisted, her mouth dry.

The priest said their names and began the prayers. "...give thanks to the Lord, who is good, whose love endures forever. Let the house of Israel say: God's love endures forever..."

Her heartbeat drummed in her chest, her cheeks burned, and a claw scratched at her skull, sending the hairs on her neck to rise. She blinked and straightened her posture, ignoring the hot heaviness in her head.

"...and the two will become one flesh..." The priest continued, his articulate and steady voice echoing in the small chamber. He read through a psalm from a book in his hands, although she paid no heed. She wasn't sure what a psalm was. The words whirred in her ears, and she rooted her slippered feet to the floor to remain upright. She stole a glance at Simon, breathless. He stood respectfully, his look distant even if his eyes were squarely aligned with the priest's.

They exchanged no rings or offerings. The priest seemed unaffected and continued with his recitations.

Simon added his own words at the end of the vows. He turned to her, taking both her hands in his own. Uncertain dark brown eyes bore into hers. "Place me like a seal over your heart, like a seal on your arm; for love is as strong as death, its jealousy unyielding as the grave. It burns like blazing fire, like a mighty flame. *Thugaim mo chridhe dhuit.* I give my heart to you."

Her knees wobbled with his words. The priest's eyes gleamed with approval. Were these more of the words of his god, his priests? Simon hardly seemed a man of such eloquent phrases.

The priest cleared his throat and continued: "Simon Kenneth MacCoinneach, son of Alroy Kenneth MacCoinneach and Margaret Mary MacCoinneach, grandson of Kenneth Lonn MacCoinneach, wilt thou have this woman to be thy wedded wife, to live together after God's ordinance in the holy estate of matrimony? Wilt thou love her, comfort her, honor, and keep her, so long as you both shall live?"

"I will." Simon's voice was deep, firm. His hands, though equally firm, were sweaty in hers.

The priest repeated the question to her. "Gwyn of house Varteig, daughter of Blasius of Varteig—" The priest looked to her. "Your mother's name, mistress?"

Alroy interrupted. "It doesn't matter. Continue."

"It does matter," she said, her pulse quickening. Her mother lacked a surname. "My mother is Caoimhe of Uist."

The priest awaited Alroy's decision. Alroy nodded.

Hesitating, the priest slowly continued, "Daughter of Caoimhe of Uist, wilt thou have this man to be thy wedded husband, to live together after God's holy estate of matrimony? Wilt thou love him, submit to him, honor and keep him, so long as you both shall live?

Gwyn paused. Simon's vows lacked *submit*. Alroy coughed. "Speak up, lass."

Simon's eyes never left hers. They were as vast as the sea. Perhaps she was his isle in the storm, not the other way around.

Her whispered words caught in her throat. "I will." It was done.

"Our help is in the Lord, who made heaven and earth," the nasal priest said, taking both of their hands into his cold ones. "Blessed be this union."

Simon didn't release their clasped hands. He stood unnaturally still, his face expressionless. Her own hands trembled.

"Kiss your bride, Master Simon," the priest encouraged.

Simon bent his head and turned it to the side, closing the space between them. She tipped her chin up and allowed his lips to meet hers. She had never tasted a man's lips before, and it was the briefest of moments. She'd expected ale or perhaps pungent cider, but as she pulled back and he released her hands, all the taste that remained with her was of fear.

And not just her own.

Their interlocked hands broke, and he stepped back, his breath slightly heavy.

He nodded to her, blinked, and then turned on his heel and left without another word. His father followed, brimming with satisfaction, and lastly, the priest.

Once again, she was alone in her room. Alone on her wedding night, a Norse-Ancient woman the new lady of Eilean Donan.

Simon found his father alone in the hall the following morning. He slid onto a bench and poured himself a drink. His father didn't look up at his entrance.

"How is Grandfather?" he asked, staring at the spread laid before him. Their cooks were the best in the glen, but he held no appetite. Gwyn hadn't emerged from her bedchamber, and he hesitated to disturb her.

"He's as can be expected."

A thickness rose in Simon's throat. He'd tried to visit his grandfather every day this week, but the bedchamber's door had been bolted shut. When he knocked, Old Lonn MacCoinneach berated him, mumbled, and cursed. He refused most visitors except for the chambermaid and his father.

He doubted Grandda was well. Desmond's death had pushed him over the edge. His wits were gone. Simon couldn't help but blame himself for that, too. First his mother Margaret, whom Old Lonn had adored as his own daughter, and now Desmond. The fate of Eilean Donan and the MacCoinneach clan lay on his shoulders alone, and if history was any judge, he'd likely spoil this, too.

Simon swallowed. "The men are ready?"

"Aye. On every post. Laird Donald's men arrived last night."

"They did?" He rubbed his jaw, his teeth aching. How had he not heard them? Och, well, nightmares had plagued him while entrenched in a catacomb of sleep, laced with strong ale. Memories scratched at his soul whenever he slept now.

The Donalds were Meredith's clan. Well, certainly they'd be eager to avenge her husband's death at the hands of the isle Nordmen. "How many?"

"Forty. With our soldiers, too, if Blasius brought all his men, we'll outnumber him."

"What about the MacRuaidhris?"

His cleared his throat. "They don't want to be troubled with this. I doubt they would come against us."

"What if this Leidolf of Reindalr has a great number with him? Their longships can hold a hundred men."

His father scoffed. "Then we're ready, and we'll do it your way. I doubt it will come to that. If so, we have the fortress on our side. We have the advantage."

His blood boiled. How he'd love to kill them all with one fell swoop and be done with the back and forth nonsense.

Just be done with it.

Bloody hell, he had a wife.

"What do we intend to do when they arrive, Father? She's no longer a prisoner. She's my wife, and her intended won't be pleased."

His father scooped an egg onto a crusty end of the bread and took a bite. He chewed, gulped cider, and then said, "We do nothing."

"Nothing? I thought we were to negotiate a new trade with Blasius."

"It appears there is more going on as the lass implied."

"What do you mean?" Simon twirled the goblet in his hands, watching the ribbons of liquid spin. He itched to be on his way to Dryburgh Abbey with Gwyn, for her to uphold her end of their agreement. He needed to determine when to take his leave. Every day was another day his mother was closer to death.

"While I was south visiting your mother, I passed through Edinburgh. Rumors flourish among the court that King Haakon may make another pass at the mainland sometime soon."

Simon rubbed his temple. "His forces are limited in Scotland."

"I've heard that he's rallying his fleet. Our king's futile attempt to root out these Lochlanach incensed the Norse king."

His pulse spiked in memory. Last year on Skye, even though he killed a handful of men, they'd fought with aptitude. They were able and ruthless fighters. There would be much blood spilled if they returned to Scotland with a greater force. "Aye, but there are always whispers in court and in the Highlands, Father. The sea wolves roam the isles already. They're *always* coming, and they never succeed, even with their pressing inland near Loch Lomond. When they do try, we crush them. Why should this be any different?"

His father narrowed his eyes. "Our fate hinges on this if a battle should arise on our shores. King Haakon will bring more ships, more men."

Simon pinched his lips together to prevent from saying something else he might regret. "Aye."

"After Blasius and Leidolf arrive and we negotiate, I must go to Edinburgh again. We need to be prepared if strong forces come. I need to confirm these rumors. King Haakon might not arrive until spring given the rougher autumn and winter seas, but we need to be ready. You'll see things here are cared for?"

"You're confident their arrival won't be met with blood? That Leidolf and Blasius will indeed negotiate and let us keep Gwyn, this Nordman's betrothed?" Simon scoffed, the jadedness rising in his voice.

His father smiled cynically. "Nay, but we are ready if it should come to battle."

"Aye." He rubbed his knuckles on his thigh. He was fully convinced this had been his father's plan all along, for Alroy MacCoinneach held his own grudge about what had happened to his wife. Negotiation was likely never in his plans. He had poked the snake. Now he was waiting for the snake to unleash its venom.

"Simon?"

He turned from the cold, soggy food.

"She is not your wife until you take her to your bed. The marriage must be consummated for it to be true."

Simon nearly choked on the sip of ale bubbling in his throat. He patted his chest and set the goblet down. "I know."

His father tempered his tone. "Women like to be courted. Your mother, och, did she enjoy our time together before we wed. Listen to the lass. Be kind. You may have a warrior's mind, Simon, but your mother is right. You've got a good heart, son. Go share it with the lass."

Simon stared at his father, spellbound.

His father added, "Also, see if you can get information from her. She knows more than she lets on."

Ah, that was the man he knew. "Yes, Father."

His father finished his meal, nodded, and left the hall.

Simon's grip tightened on the goblet. He sank his head onto his resting forearms, beleaguered with what he had done and what he had yet to do.

Labored steps brought Simon to her room after his morning meal. She'd not come down to eat. He carried another tray of food for her.

Henry stood at his post in front of her door. He nodded and straightened at Simon's approach.

His father's orders resonated inside his skull like one of the minstrel's off-tune songs.

"G'morn, Henry. You may take your leave. Send Errol in an hour, aye?"

"Aye." The strapping man nodded and departed. Henry was one of the best. Quick with the sword, but even quicker with the mind.

He waited for Henry to descend the stairs before opening the door to her chamber. He steadied his gait and breathing, forcing valor to replace unease. He expected a tossed chamber pot or cider jug. Instead, she was sitting at the window on a stool, her gaze lost on the distance across the loch.

Not turning, she said, "I'm your wife, and still I am guarded?"

Simon shrugged though she couldn't see. He'd given up on excuses.

"What must I do to prove I won't flee? I signed your marriage contract. I said my vows." Her voice broke on those words.

Was she crying?

He laid the tray of food on her table and approached. He didn't touch her, as much as he wanted to link his arm within hers as they'd done during their walks. He reached inside his ganache and withdrew her small, simple dagger. Unadorned with jewels or carvings, it possessed a bone hilt and a blade worn from use. Likely from tree limbs, flowers, and household use. His smith had sharpened it and cleaned the hilt. "Here," he said, placing it in her lap. Gildy had retrieved the sheath from Gwyn's laundered gown.

Gwyn stared at it, her fingertips dancing butterfly wings hovering over the hilt. After a moment, she drew her hand around it and pulled it from its leather sheath. She rose and whirled on him, the dagger pointed out before her, barely pressing into his chest.

He didn't retreat as he met her fiery, misty gaze.

She made no move to remove the dagger's tip.

"A smidge to the center, Gwyn, and you'll be square over my blackened heart." He held her glower. Heat blazed in her entrancing blue eyes like the devil. He fought a smile.

The door opened, and Gildy popped in with a basin of water. "Mistress, I've got yer—" She froze, nearly spilling the basin. "Och! Master Simon, I—"

"'Tis fine, Gildy. Please leave the basin and go."

"Och, but sir—" her tremulous voice wavered.

"We're well, Gildy," he said again, not moving. A small step closer and the pointy tip would puncture through his overlayer and into skin.

The door thudded shut.

"Do you wish to be a widow so soon?" he asked Gwyn.

She pressed harder, but hesitation flickered over her face. "I wish to no longer be a prisoner."

"You've always been free. I've not shackled you to your bed."

Her. In his bed.

She gritted her teeth. "I'm always to be chaperoned and watched?"

He lifted his shoulders, drawing his chest out. The dagger pricked, its new sharp tip penetrating the thick overlayer but not breaking skin.

He placed his hand over hers on the hilt, tightly wrapping his fingers around hers. "Do it."

She shifted on her feet. "You wish for death?"

He didn't respond.

She heaved a sigh, and her hand loosened beneath his. He released it and both of their hands fell to their sides. She slid the dagger into its leather sheath and dropped it into her pocket.

"Something pains you more than your knee."

He grunted and sat upon the bed, allowing his heart rate to slow. *In. Out. In. Out.*

She sat beside him, the mattress creaking slightly beneath their combined weight. "What now, Simon?"

Heaven, she said his name again in that way...no challenge, no hate. Sweet and silvery.

He wiped a damp palm on his thigh and faced her. Her lips were rosy and alluring, shaped like a heart, and even if it'd been a stiff, required matrimonial kiss last night, he'd felt her lips melt when he'd pressed his against them. He wanted more of them despite everything he told himself.

He locked eyes with her.

"Oh," she said, her cheeks blossoming with pink.

He couldn't—he wouldn't—force her. He'd never lain with a woman before. He'd seen no need to.

"The law requires it," he said, meekly. God, he was a coward.

Her eyebrows lifted, but she didn't retreat. "The law is not in our bedchamber," he added.

She laid a hand upon his and squeezed. Neither made a move.

He wanted to taste her again.

She blinked dark eyelashes over bejeweled eyes.

Well, he'd never consummate the marriage if he didn't act. He placed a hand behind her slender neck and drew her closer. Her body stiffened against him, and he stopped, his lips a breath from hers. He lowered his eyes and pulled away. "Not like this. No. I'm sorry." He rose.

He swallowed and couldn't look at her. "I brought you a meal. I-I'll be downstairs."

Shouts echoed through the window from the inner bailey. He regained his wits and rushed to the window. Ten men on horseback rode through the village and toward the bridge. The Donalds and MacCoinneachs stirred within the bailey. Men emerged from the hall and made their way to their waiting spots along the battlement and at archer's holes. He squinted to see men materialize from within the lists in the village, where the majority of the Donalds were sleeping. They assumed their posts, swarming around the enemy's small group in a matter of seconds.

This was all the men Blasius would send?

Gwyn was quick to his side. "What is it?" she asked, pressing near him so she could look outside.

"They're here for you."

He spun to face her and wrapped an arm around her waist. He drew her close. She inhaled sharply, nearly squeaking. The thought of losing her to these Lochlanach spurred a new purpose within him, taking him to uncharted places. "Hold fast to that dagger. I'll send for Henry to guard you. He's one of our best men."

"Shouldn't I go, too?" She searched over her shoulder into the gray morning's mist. "What if my brother isn't with them? Oh, heavens, what if he *is*? We've not sent my letter!"

He drew his hand halfway up her back, fingers running along her spine. "Gwyn, this is my doing. You've done your part. Now let me do mine. I promise. I need you to stay here no matter what happens. Can you do that for me?"

Her breathing was erratic and riled, but she nodded. "Aye. Simon..."

"Yes?"

"Don't kill him."

Christ, woman. I'll try.

Instead of responding, he threaded his hand through the length of her unkempt hair and found her neck again. Agilely, passionately, he drew her to him and kissed her, for it might be his last. He made it count. A muffled gasp escaped her lips, but she indeed kissed him, too. She was the sun to his moon, the light to his darkness.

After a moment, his eyes still closed, he held her close. He rested his forehead upon hers. Her ragged breathing matched his own. Then, reluctantly, he let her go and tramped to the door. "I *will* return."

If things went awry, Henry knew exactly what to do to protect her.

He licked his lips, wanting to remember the kiss.

CHAPTER SEVEN

Gwyn dashed to the window as soon as Simon left the room. Through the smoky haze, thick from yesterday's rain and the smoldering morning hearths, the Nordmen approached. They snaked around cottages and buildings and found their way to the main road and bridge leading to the keep. Like ants to a morsel of bread, the Scots surrounded her father's riding party.

She blinked as Scotsmen appeared in every corner.

Men approached the Nordmen from the soldier barracks in the village. More of them moved about in the bailey and made their way to posts on the small battlement. Who were these men? Certainly the MacCoinneachs didn't have such a force. She'd not seen half these men during her walks and explorations. Not once since arriving had there been an elaborate evening hall meal.

Had another clan arrived? Did clansmen do such a thing for each other? She remembered Simon's warning about the other clans on their journey through the glen.

Suddenly dry mouthed, she licked her lips as a strange sensation—relief?—overtook her.

The Nordmen rode without banner or flag. Yet, she knew her betrothed's banner. Correspondence to her father had shown the Reindalr emblem on the parchment: a growling red wolf's head. It was on the marriage contract between Varteig and Reindalr she had yet to sign.

Her stomach twisted with the reminder.

Only ten men. She squinted and didn't see Sigurd, her father's last strong man. Simon had killed both Rothwell and Trygg already. Her father never traveled without one of his best men.

In fact, the men who arrived were strangers. They were all Nordmen, but not men from her village. Her father wasn't below.

Neither was Kendrick, Venora, nor her mother.

She quivered and ripples of gooseflesh erupted upon her arms.

Unless they had a hidden force somewhere in the depths of the forests beyond, or a longship coming down the loch's channel, she doubted they'd breach the keep. Men awaited them at every turn, outfitted with spears, axes, and swords. In a matter of moments, men dotted the entire length of the wall with bows ready.

Battle. They were ready for battle. All she could do was watch and pray.

The Nordmen drew closer, but they stopped at the bridge. Which was Leidolf? From the tower of the keep she had a bird's view, but she couldn't discern faces or hear anything. The man in the center of the group was moderately built, blond-haired, and bearded like the rest of them. Her father never wore a beard or embellished himself.

Why were her father and his men *not* there?

Cowards.

Her father knew. Yet...he hadn't come. Had he laid his confidence in Trygg alone or were more waiting in the thistles? Was this display below only a ruse?

Sickness turned her stomach. He didn't come. He didn't care.

Her gaze was transfixed on the exchange below. Alroy and Simon exited the portcullis. Simon wore his sword sheathed at his side and an axe strapped to his back. Unexpected concern filled her as the man who was now her husband—dear Mother Earth, her *husband*—strolled with robust confidence. He was attractive, she'd admit, even for a Scotsman. Broad and muscular, rough-edged, and wild with his coarse auburn hair and gold-flecked brown eyes. That kiss. She touched her lips.

A few of the soldiers, other clansmen, closed in behind Alroy and Simon, all of them with their swords drawn. Leidolf's men were outnumbered. They'd be slaughtered if they fought. This was not a negotiation. This was a confrontation. She didn't need her sister's Sight to know this would end poorly if someone swung the first blade.

She hurried to her door. Surprised to discover it unlocked, she flung it open and found Henry standing guard near his window viewpoint at the end of the hallway. He was upon her in a swift moment.

"Milady! You must stay."

Henry was nearly a foot taller than she and far stronger. She shoved him anyway, meeting a wall of muscle.

"Milady! This is not your place. Our men are able. All should fare well, mistress."

"I must go! Can't you see? They—Simon's men—they're going to kill them! The Norse are outnumbered." She kicked his shin. He didn't budge. He held her back, large hands pinching her arms.

"No need to worry about your husband. Now quit your fussin'!"

She groaned and huffed. She withdrew her dagger. "It's not him I'm worried about!"

He quickly disarmed her. "I can't hurt you, mistress. You must stay. I *will* lock you in your room if I must."

He restrained her, and she bit his hand. He carefully dragged her into the room without a sound. He plopped her on the bed, tossed her dagger beside her, turned, and was out the door. She bolted upright and chased him, but he was faster, locking the door from the hall.

Once again, she was alone in her chamber, unable to do a thing.

Two red-haired brutes approached Leidolf from across the bridge.

The steward and his son? A graying, glowering elder and a younger fox with sharp eyes. Aye, father and son, indeed. *This will be entertaining.*

Leidolf scanned the isle. Hunter's eyes gave him a rough count of men: all afoot, no horses, but at least fifty or sixty. Movement behind archer's slits, across the battlements that encircled the inner courtyard and tower house...and more motion afar, hidden in the village, but oh, he was well aware of them all. He'd brought a fraction of his men, not expecting a man of such a meager castle and village to have many warriors. How could they have gathered so many if they hadn't known they were coming? Well, he wouldn't make that mistake again. Even if his warriors could kill four or five each.

Oh, but somebody had told them. Alroy MacCoinneach, he was a cunning *bacraut.*

The gods had gifted Leidolf with ample time to ponder the Scotsman's motives. For what other purpose would he steal his bride than to stir a war? He couldn't possibly think it would trigger a peaceful negotiation with Blasius the Mad. Was it blood he sought? He almost snorted. Perhaps this fool had not known Gwyn was betrothed. He hid a smile as the connections burst in his mind. Hmm, perhaps he did?

"Are you Alroy MacCoinneach, the *steward* to the castle?" He directed his question to the elder. He held in his grin. Steward. Not even a jarl or laird.

"Aye." The man puffed his chest.

Good, ruffle away, red rooster.

"Where is Gwyn of Varteig, my promised wife?" he asked, stepping no closer. He counted the slits again, fingered along his leather belt. One, two, three holes. The rough edges of the amber eyes in his sword hilt comforted his fingertips. He traced them three times. It eased his mind. Focused him.

No change in Alroy's stance. He had known she was betrothed. Daring bastard.

"She is not here."

So it would be that way. He pressed his lips together. "I denounce this monstrosity. She was taken by force. This matter will go to your king, Alroy. Last I heard, it's not an honorable Scots trait to steal what belongs to others."

The man beside the elder was silent, seething. Was he the man who had stolen *his* property? Alroy was too round, too old to have done it himself.

"Who are you, sir?" Alroy asked him.

"I am Leidolf of Reindalr, and son of Magnus of Reindalr, Jarl of Øystridalir."

A shared dissonance flickered in Alroy's eyes as well as in the man's eyes beside him. His son, most definitely. The younger man put on a front beside his father, but their faces and even the way they stood was disparate. The younger was hard to read, his face rigid and controlled. Try though he might, Alroy didn't mask his feelings well, which was excellent for Leidolf. "You've heard of me?" Leidolf cracked his jaw and fingered through his beard.

"Should I have?"

Leidolf chuckled within. Oh, yes, play the ignorant fool, Alroy. He wondered where Alroy might have heard of him before. Or perhaps it had been his father Magnus? His father had since forgone his pillages abroad, but he had been quite the Norse warrior in his prime, sacking and plundering along the western and northern coasts of Scotland. It was where his father had acquired the best thralls to bring home.

Alroy drawled composed words. "The lass came of her own accord."

"I doubt a Norse woman would willingly leave her countrymen to reside with Scotsmen. Where is my bride, MacCoinneach? She returns home. Now. You can resolve the other matter with Blasius. She is no concern of yours. Release her, and we'll be lenient with the repercussions."

The man beside Alroy sneered, his eyebrows twisting and hand dancing on his sword's hilt. *Do it*, Leidolf willed with his glare.

"She is not yours to take," the younger man said, stepping forward as he resumed his stiff posture.

Oh, Leidolf enjoyed him immensely. The red fox's façade was not working. "Who can say that? She was promised to me."

"A promise that will no longer be kept," the man said.

Alroy stepped in front of his son, hand outstretched. "You're outnumbered, Leidolf. Return home. Tell Blasius we wish a truce, a union between the isles and our homeland. His daughter came willingly in order to forge our alliance."

Although he knew it to be a lie, doubt slithered into Leidolf's mind. Would the woman be so daft? To come willingly? To these *Scotsmen*? His gaze drifted around and settled on the keep. Was she ensconced in the tower? "She'd dare not do that against her father's wishes. She is to be *my* wife."

The young bold one spoke again. "Well, she already *is* my wife. Our union is legal."

How he wanted to cut the man's throat, to see the blood on his hands. Instead he rubbed his beard, neatly plaited. The man would die for saying such things, for doing such things! He calmed the inner wolf. He *was* outmatched. He refused to die for a dimwitted woman. There were ways to honor his birthright, to clear Blasius and his men from their land. There was another way to reclaim his promised bride with her special abilities.

He appraised his opponents. Yes, the rooster's throat could be easily slit or neck broken, and that fox though, ah, he would be some work. A good hunt indeed.

"That can be remedied," he responded, trying—and failing—to cool the riotous boil within him. He slid his hand into his pouch, the wolf's blood enticing him. Just one taste...but no. It wasn't time. He had to wait.

The man snorted. "It won't be."

His heartbeat raced. He quieted it with every shred of control. "Oh, it will."

The man drew his sword. "Enough. Be gone! We will speak with Blasius. Not you."

"Simon," Alroy chided his son.

Leidolf stepped even closer to the burly red-haired fox. "Oh, to be brash, *Simon*. You think Blasius is going to join you now? You stole his daughter." He shook his head. "Oh, no, no, no. Hell comes for you."

He was close enough to Simon to smell the temper within. Ah, but better, he also sensed fear. Like any hunt. His family wasn't "of the wolf" for no reason. He enjoyed a hunt with bold, wild prey. There was no animal he couldn't kill. Man was just another beast.

Simon growled, "Be gone."

"Oh, such a simple request." He took a moment to smile at them, making a point to show his teeth, as wolves often did, though his weren't chiseled to points like some of his warriors. "You will return my bride."

Simon stepped forward menacingly. "Never."

Games of the mind were nearly as much fun as physical ones. Time for the kill. "Oh, you will. It appears Gwyn holds a tenderness for her younger brother Kendrick. I hear Kendrick is not a healthy lad. Oh yes, we know about his *ailment*," he continued, "that Gwyn has hidden from her father."

Simon's scowl deepened, eliciting a sweet satisfaction in Leidolf's gut.

Leidolf drew in a deep breath and said, firmly, "If my bride is not returned to me, *virtue intact*, then I'll enjoy slitting Kendrick's throat myself. Then *your* blood will meet my sword, Simon MacCoinneach."

He turned on his heel and nodded to the closest men. He mounted his horse and looked over a shoulder. "You have a fortnight, MacCoinneach. Return her to Uist in two weeks...untouched. Or else the lad is dead."

Leidolf was pleased with himself as they rode from the keep. Perhaps Blasius was correct about Gwyn's love for her brother. He'd make sure Kendrick was on display for his sister to see. Then he'd slit the boy's throat in front of them. Let his disloyal bride learn her place quickly.

The red-haired fox couldn't know the entire force of the Nord Land would be there to greet him. Soon the Scots would be a nuisance no longer.

"I wanted blood, MacCoinneach!" Laird Donald said after Leidolf's departure.

Simon's father strode to the portcullis with a confident gait. "That will come, Hamish."

"They killed my daughter's husband. *Your son.* What is she to do?"

"She's a bonnie woman, Hamish. I'm sure another arrangement will be made."

Hamish narrowed his eyes. "We don't want an arrangement. My daughter loved yer foolish son. Now she is a widow, and with no bairns!"

His father stiffened but carried on through the bailey. "He was not a fool, Hamish, and I'd remind you to never speak ill of him again. He desired peace."

"Peace go' him killed."

"No, the devil got him killed. It wasn't Leidolf's men who killed him. It was Blasius's son who sent him to his grave."

"I want blood," Hamish said, curling a fist at his side.

"You will get it. There will be plenty of Nordmen to kill. Be patient. Soon."

Hamish paused, his boots kicking loose stones in the dirt. "What do you mean?"

Simon's father placed an arm around the laird's upper back and guided him through the main hall doors. "Come, there is much afoot. First, a meal? Some drink."

Simon caught up to them. "Father, what about the lad? Gwyn's brother?"

"There will be no return or exchange. She is already your wife. There will be no bartering for her brother."

"You'll let an innocent lad die?"

His father's shoulders slumped, his voice mellowing. "'Tis out of our hands. The Lochlanach won't hold true to his word. Send the letter for her brother if you feel it can help him. We will do what we can, but I can't make promises."

Simon sheathed his sword belatedly, the weight of its iron heavy, shaking in his hand. He wasn't sure why his father was pleased and, frankly, acting like an arse. This was not like him. He'd never leave a man behind. Then again, Kendrick was not theirs. He was a Nordman.

Not only had there been no negotiation, there had been no blood. They could have easily killed those Nordmen and been done.

In the hall, his father continued with grand ideas as Donald and MacCoinneach together dined around the long oak tables. Servants brought heaping platters of food for the midday meal. Simon raged with the rush of a near-fight...that hadn't happened.

"I believe the Norse king will make landfall soon," his father said in between gulps of mutton stew and mead.

"Some Lochlanach have already been sighted near Loch Lomond. Their ships patrol many of our Western Isles. Their numbers are increasing. The war is coming," Hamish concurred.

"Indeed it is readily upon us," his father agreed.

Gray eyes sharp, and voice sharper, Hamish replied, "We must relay word to King Alexander then, if this is true. Rally all the clans. Be ready and stay one step ahead."

"Aye, aye!" others cheered, raising goblets and bowls and scarfing food.

Hamish released a garbled groan. His weary gaze slid over to Simon's father. "Alroy, are you certain of this? It's not uncommon to see them along our coasts."

After a long drag from his goblet, his father said, "I'm not, but I rode south of Edinburgh not long ago and stopped in court. My sources wouldn't lie."

"So the rumors *are* true?"

"I daresay they are. Why else would so many ships be sighted on the seas and now, before winter?"

Nobody asked the reason why his father had been riding south of Edinburgh. All knew. Like many around the table, vengeance had burrowed itself deep within his father's heart as well.

"Not Drummond MacRae again? Ye know ye canna trust a word he says! In his mind, the Lochlanach are *always* coming. They never do. The western and isle lairds and jarls have remained peaceful," Hamish said.

"Until our trip two weeks ago. My son is dead."

Hamish scoffed, "At the hands of a madman long since dissociated from his people. You can't think the brash

Leidolf, too, poses any risk to our holdings? He comes just for his bride. Blasius is the one who deserves death."

His father smirked and raked a hand through his hair. "He's a foolish jarl and will fall with the rest of them."

Hamish said quietly, raising his goblet, "May you finally have peace, Alroy. Time to cull them all. We will be ready when they come."

His father nodded and raised his goblet. He swallowed, silent.

Simon cracked his knuckles and sipped mead. These conversations were nothing new. He didn't bother to argue with the already drunken, raucous men. Let them cheer and jeer and curse. He'd have none of it, though his sword was forever ready for if and when.

He searched his mind for an excuse to leave and speak with Gwyn. He rose. "Father, I—"

His father waved a hand. "Aye, go check on your wife. Be sure to do as I ordered," he added.

Simon found himself taking the steps slower and with another full tray. He'd snatched one of the cook's best apple tarts. He didn't know what to say to Gwyn. The encounter with the bleach-haired barbarian had left him with a sour taste. There had been no deal. No fight. Even Blasius the Mad had not come.

Simon would go daft trying to decode his father's intentions. Before Desmond's death, his father yearned for continued, peaceful trade with the isle rulers. He'd never once called for blood for the wrong done to his wife. After Desmond's murder, and after drowning sorrows in drink, a beast arose in Father's glower. Alroy MacCoinneach had changed. He'd always been the voice of peace. Or perhaps he'd wanted blood all along and he'd been biding time with the trading front. There was no doubt his father cared about the security of his people, but Simon worried his father was driven by revenge now more than safety and kinship.

For once, it wasn't only Simon who thirsted for it. Oddly, it unsettled him.

What had just happened? No fight. No negotiation. He swallowed the bitterness.

What was his father up to?

They had promised Gwyn's brother sanctuary. Now he denied it? Gwyn was but a pawn in his plans.

It appeared, so was he.

Dejection filled Gwyn, but she didn't cast her negative energy upon Simon when he returned. Instead, she steadied herself and her mind, sat on the bed, and said, "What now?"

She'd seen it all. None of her family had come. Only Leidolf of Reindalr and a handful of his men. She secretly thanked Eir for no bloodshed. She wouldn't have been able to heal any of them from her prison. No fighting, no injuries, no barging into the keep to rescue her. Did her father care so little of her?

The breath was crushed in her lungs.

"We leave on the morrow for the abbey," Simon said, not sitting. He diverted his eyes, purposefully focused on the low-glowing hearth.

Her hope couldn't have dropped further. "Can I then go home, Simon, after this journey?" She added in a desperate plea, "I *need* to go home."

"Returning you home was never part of our bargain. Besides, we're now wed."

She swallowed. "Aye, but what about my brother? Did they say anything?"

He turned away from her and rubbed his knuckles. "No."

She exhaled loudly. "Then he's probably still safe."

"Aye."

"Good. Then you will send for him as promised?"

He nodded. "Of course. Write a letter to Venora, and I shall send it with my messenger right away."

"Leidolf? Did you tell him about us?"

He brushed a finger along his nose. "Aye, he knows."

Her pulse spiked. She rose and approached him, her shoulder near his. "And? He can't be pleased with the arrangement."

"He raised no sword."

She crossed her arms, shivers rippling within. Her words caught. "Are you telling me the full truth, Simon?"

He turned to face her, tucking his upper lip in. He held her look. She returned it with her own, her tenacity fading, seeking truth in the brown enormity of his eyes. She was too exhausted to press him further.

"Yes, 'tis all. He was outmanned and outwitted. Your Leidolf left like the coward he is." He then strode past her and departed the room.

"Leidolf, shouldn't we do something?" Steinthor asked as he shuffled his feet and hugged himself to get warm in the crisp, early dawn. "King Haakon arrives soon. We should return to Uist to your father's men as well and wait."

Leidolf wanted to smack the insolent man. Instead, he counted to ten forward and backward, then responded. "We wait. The elder MacCoinneach is readying to depart. See," he said, pointing through their covering in the forest on the edge of Dornie. Men prepared horses at the outer stable. Sunlight broke over the horizon. Leidolf suspected Alroy MacCoinneach would be riding south to their court in Edinburgh to relay news of their arrival to his lairds and king. *Good, let him.* They had no idea of the force coming across the Nord Sea. "You and Donner will follow him. Do not kill him. Gather information and meet me near Edinburgh, at the Norse-run tavern along the mouth of the river near the city. An old warrior, Halvor, owns it. He has one eye and a crooked gait," he said, relaying information his father had given him. "Seek him."

They both nodded.

"If something happens or if there's a change, I'll leave you a message with Halvor. You'll need to cut your beards, cover your markings, blend in. Our Norse brothers are settled mostly on the western shores, and if my prediction is correct, the elder is heading to their court in Edinburgh. If you do see our countrymen, thank the gods for their greatness at providing you refuge."

"Yes, Leidolf," both said with a nod. Each took their short daggers and sliced away at their plaited beards.

He suppressed his urge with a groan. Neither referred to him as the jarl he should and soon *would* be once he took over Blasius's holding. Years of observing his father and brothers taught him in spite of the commanding presence and sheer violence many Nordmen exhibited, the best way to keep your allies *and* adversaries close was with controlled benevolence, even if it was a front. Brutality only got you so far. Then, when they drew close and dropped their guard or trusted you, then the wolf can make the kill. So no, he would not throttle the men as much as it burned him. Years of being beaten, ignored, and disregarded helped in his ability to blend in, observe, and remember.

"I will wait for the younger Scotsman to make his move," he added.

Simon, oh simple-minded Simon. Leidolf had enjoyed their encounter on the bridge. He would surely enjoy this hunt.

Honor and obligation told him to return to Uist and wait for the fleet to arrive. He needed to secure Blasius's land. His men were ready to follow his orders at the flick of a finger. Wolves might be pack animals, but he was a wolf of the gods and men would do his bidding even though they acted for his father Magnus, not him.

Something else, something primal, told him to wait and see what progressed at Eilean Donan. He had a bride to locate and bring home. If he returned to Uist empty-handed, it would be his end. He had but one mission: to wed Gwyn the Healer and murder all the men and children in Blasius's village, sparing the women alone. Certainly most of his warriors already had Norse wives, but let the women maintain their homes in the Nord Land while their husbands claimed second wives on Uist.

So, no, he couldn't return to Uist without her. This was the last chance for him to prove his worth. There would be time to recover her and kill the red-haired fox who laid claim to her.

Therefore, decision made, he'd already sent the remaining men back to Uist yesterday to relay the message to Blasius. Mad as the man was, he was easy to understand and even easier to manipulate. Blasius would meet him south on the coast of Cumbrae in two weeks, as they had arranged, where Blasius, his men, and that blind son of his would be culled after their glory against the Scots.

All men were predictable, the MacCoinneachs not excluded. Simon would never return Leidolf's bride to him. Why should he? He already had his prize.

Leidolf considered himself a master at quick assessments. Simon was no coward. So Leidolf watched and waited to see when the fox would make his escape.

Gwyn had nothing to pack, so she layered herself in her cleaned green gown with shift, kirtle, boots, cloak, and dagger the following morning. There hadn't been an evening meal the night before. For a husband, Simon hadn't exactly been the most hospitable. Was this how Scottish men treated their wives? Certainly she'd seen her father's lack of care for her mother, except for when it suited him, of course.

Her mother found solace in friends, other women, most notably Lavena. Oh, how Gwyn missed Moreen's humor. Melancholy struck her as she prepared to leave.

Her mind catapulted her down a path she tried hard to avoid.

She fell onto the bed and opened the small pouch of herbs she'd acquired at the market. She lifted them to her nose and inhaled the woodiness of the betony, allowing its fragrance to calm her.

Alone. She was alone.

Yet, she had been alone in her village, too. Surrounded by her mother, sister, brothers, a handful of friends, and Eir's healing with Jörd's constant guidance...the loneliness still pervaded her spirit. A part of her—a naïve, daft part certainly—had believed she'd feel complete when her betrothed eventually came for her.

She snorted, and the betony tickled her nostrils. "Foolish," she murmured to herself. She would be a fool no longer.

She *had* accepted her role as soon-to-be wife and mother. She'd even accepted the inevitable duty that came with being a Nordman's wife. He might have taken more than one wife, though her father never had. He might have not treated her with the kindness she'd hoped for. She would have been a worthy crofter, a loving mother to her bairns, and would have sought a somewhat pleasant life.

Leidolf had come to retrieve her from the Scots. Even from afar, she had seen his imposing demeanor, his sheer determination. She possessed no Feeler abilities like Kendrick, but she swore she could feel the ugliness within Leidolf's soul. She shivered. He was like the other Nordmen. It was then, belatedly, she'd realized perhaps she hadn't been ready to marry him and to submit to him as was expected. Marrying Simon *had* saved her from a potentially painful situation. Perhaps he and his father were correct. She had needed to be saved.

Yet, she was still a prisoner, was she not?

Were they all beasts, Nordmen and Scots alike? So few of the men in the Ancient bloodline remained. Although most of the abilities were bestowed upon women, Kendrick had also been born with a gift. She wondered if other men, too, had been gifted. She had no answer, for her father slaughtered them when he'd come to Uist. Those who had escaped retreated to the southern isles. Her mother's father and brothers were dead. Gone.

She was determined to build that family again. No matter whom she married, she'd raise bairns and teach them the gifts of the Ancients, for even if she mingled her blood with Norse or Scottish, the traits would carry on. Her mother had birthed three children with such blessings. She would do the same.

Och, the thoughts wouldn't cease. Her mind wreaked havoc upon her.

Now she was a Scotsman's wife. Now she must ready to ride south to an unknown abbey in the lowlands of Scotland to heal a woman. She'd nearly convinced herself the woman in need was his sister. Or maybe his mother. Anything, anyone, other than a lover. No women roamed Eilean Donan's halls, except for servants. Who could be her confidant and friend here as she assumed her new role as his wife? Even the soldiers cast their eyes away from her. She was no witch.

She was more alone here than she'd ever been.

Maybe one day Venora or Moreen would come here. Also, well, Kendrick. She'd have him.

Wrapping her fingers around the healing stone in her pocket, she prayed silently to Eir. With it, her fingers tingled. She itched to heal again, despite the detriment it played upon her body. Even if a few breaths of her own life were cut short with each healing—forever taken away—she still healed. Larger healings took more, smaller healings less. She'd never allowed herself to heal somebody who was so close to death that it would steal years from her. Desmond and Gunnar had both been too far gone. Rothwell and Trygg had already crossed over the Silver Veil. She was no match for men intent on killing each other.

So much death. And more to come.

Her lungs rattled, a potent reminder of the power of the breath within. Erratic pulses replaced her usual rhythmic heartbeat.

She whispered, "Bring me the mercy of Eir, the peace of Jörd, and the glory of all the Ancients, as I do thy Earth's bidding. May my breaths bring me to the Silver Veil when my earthly journey ends."

Gildy knocked. Perhaps she had learned from her last visit.

"Come in."

Hastily, Gwyn tucked the betony away and grabbed another gown from the dressing cabinet, though she hated the idea of wearing Simon's mother's clothes.

Gildy entered and nodded. "Your husband awaits, mistress."

Aye, that he did.

In his usual manner, Simon was quiet. Gwyn rode alongside him, her mare clopping in a hypnotic rhythm. They traveled farther south than she'd ever been. "How long will it take us to get there, Simon?" she finally asked, unable to take the silence any longer.

"Two or three days." He leaned back in the saddle as the downward grade increased. They rode on a path through the mountains, thick with brush and forest and craggy peaks. It was a slow, tedious ascent and descent on pebbly paths.

She repressed her frustration at his constant vagueness. She followed suit on her horse as she maneuvered through the narrow part of the trail. Stones skittered down a steep slope on her left, and she tightened her hold on the reins. The horse tossed its head at being reined in. "How long will we stay there?"

"Must you ask the same questions?"

"Yes."

"I've sent an emissary, an able man, Niall, with your message for Venora. She will relay word to your brother."

"And?"

He grimaced. "It will fall into place."

"How is your man going to get the message to my sister without my father knowing? Kendrick has nobody there who can help him except for my sister or mother. He can't journey far by himself. I should get him myself. I've told you, Simon."

"Why can't he journey?"

"What?"

"You've said he needs you, he's ill. You said he'd be a braw fighter? Is this untrue?" he pressed. "What ails him, Gwyn?"

"Does it matter?"

The bleakness of the conversation depressed her spirit. They rounded a bend and reached the bottom of a gully where the path widened.

"Can you not heal him?"

"No, I cannot, as I said."

He scoffed. "Well, wife, I certainly hope you can remember how to heal when we reach the abbey."

"You don't need to be an arse about it, Simon." Her knuckles ached. She hurried her horse to bring it abreast, and she nearly spat her next words. "Not everyone can be healed, Simon, as I'd warned you."

He drew in a breath and then released it, abating his tone. "You said he would be an asset to my home, yet he is ill and beyond your healing scope? What ails the lad?"

She took a hard, obvious swallow and then said, "He is blind."

"You can't heal that?"

It was hardly the full truth when she said, "No, and it is why I must go home to him. He is not safe."

"Why?"

Now he was interested in the answers to these questions? Now, after he had coerced her into marriage, sneered at her betrothed, and decided to drag her on this long journey south to the lowlands? She fumed. "It doesn't matter, does it? You won't take me there."

He huffed but prodded no further as the day drew on.

Their horses trotted along. The five sisters of Kintail faded behind them as they rode through the heart of the Highlands, surrounded by jagged gray-brown mountains. Misty fog curled along the trail, and at moments she feared they were lost, as the trail meandered or disappeared.

"'Tis the hardest part here," Simon said to her "*hrm-phm*" of discomfort. "Not rugged on Uist, aye?"

"No."

She found herself dizzy from effort, wet with sweat, and achy from the stop and go and imbalance. "I daresay you're leading me in circles."

He didn't respond.

After hours of riding, one quick rest, and a stop to water the horses alongside a loch, they reached a green vale between mountains. Her body thanked her. The wind whirled around them, fluttering her cloak. She shivered regardless of the sunlight. The wind had done a fine job of whipping against her skin in the mountain pass and had etched its marks on her cheeks.

Here in the vale, puffy clouds danced across the sky, casting deep shadows upon the slopes of the mountains flanking them. They rode on a beaten dirt path, edged by longer grasses. Boulders dotted the countryside. She couldn't suppress her appreciation for the pleasurable beauty of Scotland. First, it was the sheer grandness of the mountains. Now, it was the sweeping splendor of the moor and lochs. Machair and moor carpeted Uist, with few mountains. Here, they rode between deep, ridged mountains. Despite the majesty around her, her truth was eerily suffocating...she journeyed across the Highlands with her Scottish husband.

For so long she had been confined to Uist. She had been surrounded by the sea, with the ever-present threat of the wolves of the Nord Land coming to claim what they desired and obliterate any who rose against them. Now, she breathed a small sigh of relief for her assured safety here. Leidolf would never venture far inland, certainly not for her.

By Jörd, it was a selfish thought. The wind howled, but a shameful flush rose to her cheeks. Had she felt a moment of contentment? Sure, Simon was an evasive, crabby ox, but he also kissed with fire, held a deeper pain beyond his aching knee, and was loyal to his family and people. He'd also shown no ill-intent toward her well-being.

That kiss. She had the gall to enjoy it. And want more.

He'd yet to demand her to come to his bed. Unease rippled through her. These next few days could prove otherwise.

Her eyes gritty, her soul weary, she tried again as they stopped for the night in a small, wooded alcove sheltered from wind and rain. "Simon?"

"Aye?"

"Who am I to heal at the abbey?"

He took her hand as she dismounted her horse. Her boot tip snagged in the stirrup. "Oh!" she said as he caught her. His hands remained on her shoulders as he steadied her on the ground.

He didn't release her. Instead, he held her gaze and his hands moved down her arms to her elbows. Red flecks of beard growth speckled his wide, round chin.

She didn't move away.

A long moment passed, and she hoped he would kiss her again. He broke their shared look, took her horse's reins, and guided the animals to a grassy area. Finally, he said, solemnly, "We go to see my mother."

CHAPTER EIGHT

S imon was broadsided. Gwyn's brother was blind.

By going along with his father's plans, poking that beast Leidolf, and not sending his soldiers along to retrieve the lad...he'd just sentenced the young man to death. Then he lied about it to Gwyn to make matters worse. Leidolf's threat was a coiled snake around his thoughts. Simon squeezed a fist so hard it hurt. The pain distracted him from his own moral wrong.

No, his conscience reminded him. He had allowed Gwyn to send a letter to her sister through one of his best emissaries, Niall. Kendrick would be warned. He could try to escape and make his way to Eilean Donan for refuge. Simon regretted not sending his own men to extract her brother, but there were none he trusted for this type of mission, except Henry, and Henry was halfway across the mountain pass with his father to Edinburgh. It left few men to guard the keep. The people of Dornie were his priority, not one Nordman.

Errol was a strong fighter and skilled at rousing men on the quick, even if he *was* a daft tongue-tied fool around women. It was a risk even riding to Dryburgh when his father needed him home, but Errol could hold his own and summon the rest of the able-bodied men who resided in the village. The Donalds were a quick ride away if need be.

He assured himself he had done all he could. He had given Niall instructions about getting the message into the hands of Gwyn's mother or sister, and they would relay the message to the lad. It would be fine. The lad would be well. It was all he could do!

Christ, if he had known the lad was *blind*, he would have sent another man and ordered an escape, not just a letter.

He tossed two logs into the pile in the middle of their camp. Errol had Eilean Donan covered, Niall was en route to Uist, and his father was a half day ahead of them to rally the king's men.

All would be well.

Would it?

He dragged a hand across his forehead and rubbed his eyes. Would he hand Gwyn over to her family if this went sour? Could he? Did he want to? An annulment was not impossible.

She approached with leaves and bark for kindling. She was quiet as she worked to form his angrily strewn logs into a triangular, tent-like gathering for a fire. She seemed capable, so he refrained from assisting.

Och, he was a stubborn fool. His mother's care could have waited a few weeks. He should have gone to help the lad and stuck a sword through Leidolf and Blasius. By God's bones, what if he'd lost Gwyn somehow? What if she had escaped or Leidolf had succeeded in taking her? Mervyn had tried every ointment and concoction known to man on his mother. The priests at the abbey had also done their best. Her disease was incurable by man's power alone. It required more. Curse him for believing Gwyn might use her enchantment on his mother. He had to try. He needed her. His mother had been too close to death's clutches on his last visit.

His muddled mind refused to admit perhaps he needed Gwyn beyond her healing powers alone, too. That kiss...

He dug into his satchel and removed cured, salted venison. He withdrew two apples, hard cheese, and a loaf of bread.

Gwyn sat across from him with an exaggerated breath as the fire lit.

"Tomorrow's ride will be less taxing," he said. "The steepest mountain pass is behind us."

She nodded and pulled her cloak tighter around her shoulders after a stretch. She bit into an apple and released a silky moan.

"Good, aye?"

"Aye. We don't get much fruit on Uist."

"Our cook chops 'em, mixes with oats, cinnamon, figs, and lard, and bakes it. Ah, like that apple tart I brought you."

"That was delicious. Moreen would love to concoct something as pleasing on the tongue."

"Who's Moreen?"

Gwyn smiled, but it was shaded with sadness. "She's my oldest friend. And quite skilled in the kitchen. If she saw the grand kitchen at your keep, she'd lose her wits."

He licked his lips, enjoying the salted meat. "Is that so? Our cook also makes meat tartlets. Hearty and delicious." He found himself blushing. "Och, well, I like food."

"Our food choices on the isles are limited by what we can trade for at the markets or make ourselves. My mother has a garden of vegetables and herbs, and we have trees, but we usually use them for herbals, not food."

"You'll not want for anything at Eilean Donan." He'd meant the food, but his mind jumped to family. She had nobody here. He wanted to say he'd be her family, but he didn't.

He shifted in his spot, relaxing as the fire soothed achy muscles and the food filled his belly. "So you use both herbs and this, *ehm*, ability? In your healing, I mean?"

"Yes. Not everything requires a healing from across the Veil, as I told you. I make curatives and tonics when that's all is needed."

"How can you tell? How do you know the difference?"

"I don't always know. I've pored over my mother's healing books, and I know what aches to look for in easier conditions. I can sense it, I suppose."

He rubbed his upper arm subconsciously. "This was more than tonic or curative, was it not?"

She held his look, the firelight dancing in her mossy eyes as she bit into the chewy venison. "Yes. A fever would have snared you on the ship home, and with no Healers nearby, you would have succumbed to it."

"You didn't know."

She paused and waved a hand. "No, not for certain. I can't see what lies ahead."

"Then why ride to the port to save me after your brother fell?"

She swallowed, drank a long sip of the cider he handed her, and said, "I'd gone to the port to save your brother Desmond."

His throat thickened. "Could you have saved him? If we had stayed in your village?"

She nibbled on her lip, affliction crossing her face. "I don't know. I hoped I could, if he wasn't already too far gone. It is my responsibility to save any and all I can. I do not barter. I do not choose."

"Who says? Your gods?"

Her brows knit together.

He raised a hand, relaxing his tone. "I mean no disrespect. Your beliefs are yours to have."

She shrugged. "It's both a gift and a curse. A calling. I must do what I can when I can, for not everyone is given such an ability."

"How do you see it as a curse? Healing is a great power. You hold a man's life in your hands."

"Many have exploited such powers."

He let that assertion find a resting spot in his mind. He grasped at anything to say to ease the sadness growing on her face. What could he say? *I'm sorry I stole you from your home. I'm sorry I've put your brother in a worse predicament. I'm sorry war is upon us. I'm sorry you're married to a foolish, cowardly murderer. I'm sorry I don't have the confidence to make you my wife in body.* He wanted her more than anything. "Do others have the ability? You mentioned your mother."

He crossed his legs and groaned as the kinks loosened in his muscles. A part of him missed the ride with her in his saddle from the market. Less space in the saddle perhaps, but also a lovely bottom against his body and her fragrance in his nose. *Think of other things, Simon.* Horse manure. Cold winter nights. A warm bed. With Gwyn in it. He rubbed his face again. Redirection never worked with his mind.

She was quiet for a long moment. He resigned himself to the fact she wasn't going to answer, when she finally said, "Yes."

"Are you all Healers?"

She shifted and put down her napery of half-eaten food. She met his eyes straight on and responded with her own question. "Tell me about your mother, Simon. What ails her?"

Well, that released the desire growing in his groin. Tension seized his stomach and his dinner didn't sit well. "There's no name for it," he lied. *The Frenchman's disease.*

She tapped a finger to her chin. "Was she born with her condition?"

"Nay," he said, his breath catching.

"What about your own healers or these priests? It is beyond their scope?"

"Aye."

Her look was pensive but compassionate. She then smiled. "I will do my best to heal her, Simon. It doesn't need a name to be healed."

"How does your healing work?"

"It's a spiritual connection between the Silver Veil and myself by way of the mercy goddess, Eir. She is the one who allows me to heal. I pray to her, and her powers flow from me to the one being healed. I heal through water; it is my way to access her healing. Water in its purest form works best...rain, river, or herbal infusions."

He bit his tongue. If that wasn't witchery, he didn't know what was. God pardon his soul. Better, God *take* his soul. It made no difference. He'd already lost it years ago.

He nodded without words, running a hand through his hair. A sharp pain swelled from within his knee, and he winced. He made to rub a hand over it but was keenly aware of Gwyn's watching eyes. She slid over beside him. He tensed at her nearness but then relaxed as her shoulder brushed his arm. He had to kiss her again. He wanted to touch her skin. He had always wondered what it would be like to take a woman to his bed, and now more than anything, he yearned for it. He yearned for Gwyn alone.

"Simon, may I touch your knee?" she whispered, though there was no need for the decreased tone. They were not near a settlement.

He closed his eyes, the ache in his soul too much. "Yes."

She laid a hand on his knee.

The gentleness of her touch was enough to penetrate his throbbing heart. He flinched.

"It will be fine." Sweet apple fell off her breath.

She murmured words he couldn't decipher, her touch soothing and heady. *God save my soul if she's the devil's work.* Men made deals with the devil all the time, he reasoned.

She shifted closer, her nearness pushing his thoughts elsewhere again. He sliced them from his mind as much as he wanted to take her on the ground then and there.

A wind rippled his shirt, and prickles rose on his thigh and leg.

She drew in two deep inhalations and then let them out. Then again.

She removed her hand from his knee.

Darkened despair lifted from his chest. He cracked one eye, then the other to find her wheezing but beholding him with a glassy gaze.

"You are healed," she said.

Firelight drew shadows of brown and yellow upon her round cheeks. He wanted to run his hands through her hair. It cascaded down her shoulders, dark and mysterious. "You didn't need water?"

"Not for this one."

"Thank you," he exhaled. He rose and readied a bedroll for her, the eternal ache within his knee gone.

An unpleasant familiarity awoke Gwyn at dawn. She was on the ground. On her way to an abbey to heal a woman she didn't know. Simon's mother. She didn't rouse herself to flee again. As much as she wished to take herself home to care for Kendrick, she had to see this through.

Daunting though it be, it was not the reason she had awoken affright.

Simon lay beside her, a homespun plaid tossed over both of them. His arm rested upon her hip. She had gone to sleep in her full attire, too afraid and too cold to strip to shift or kirtle. She sat up, now sweating from his shared body heat, despite the autumn nip in the air.

Aye, as unnerving as it was...his nearness, the knowledge of whom she was to heal...neither of those things evoked her attention.

The crunch of steps in the forest had drawn her from her slumber.

She drew a hand around her dagger with instinct. She listened. Simon's stern warning from last time froze her to her spot.

Shards of white sunlight penetrated the morning's shadows, enough that she could see well around their site.

There it was again. Steps. Stumbles. Mumbled curses. Was it just one man? Alone? On this path through the Highlands? She didn't know where they were. They had traveled inland, away from the coastal towns like Àrasaig, and away from the Nordman-controlled coastline. She was thick in clan territory. Were these the clans Simon had warned her about? Her gaze darted around the clearing. They had camped a short distance from the main path.

She nudged him in the side. "Simon! Simon!" she said in a raised whisper.

He murmured, groaned, but then his eyes shot open. "What is it?" Before she could respond, he leapt to his feet, sword drawn from the sheath at his side.

"I—"

"Shh!" he cut her off with a warning hand.

He stepped to the edge of their camp.

The stumbling stranger cursed, his voice echoing off the oaks and beeches. A twig snapped.

"I think it's just one man," she said.

"Stay here," he ordered, heading toward the direction of the sounds.

Ignoring him, she followed.

"Dammit, Gwyn. I said stay," he chided under his breath.

"You might need me."

"Are you willing to take a life?"

Well, at least he hadn't said she'd get in the way. Or worse, she was just a woman. She exhaled. "Yes."

"It's not safe."

She groaned. There it was. For a short while, she had held hope for Simon to be different. "I'm quite able."

He heaved a sigh and brushed aside low branches. "Step where I step."

She did so as they weaved through the wood and closer to the road. The man was tangled in a thick gorse bush, cursing and fussing, a hand to his thigh.

Simon approached the solitary man and said, "What business do you have here?"

Shock lit the man's dirty face. His brown hair was disheveled, his tunic and hose torn, and he was alone.

"What business of that is yers? Leave me be, ye dun-derhead!" He gave a hard squint and then winced as he applied pressure to his leg.

Gwyn approached him, and Simon grabbed her arm so hard she gasped. "He's injured," she said.

"Leave him be. He doesn't want help."

She pressed her lips together and gathered her fin-gers around the Healer's stone in her pocket. Balmy and smooth, it ceased the rattling within her soul. She wished she had a vial of rose and saffron-infused water. "Unhand me, Simon."

He began to drag her away from the clearly hurt man.

"He's alone!" she snapped.

Simon's usually ruddy face had gone pallid. Baring his teeth, he said, "Let's go." His grip tightened on her arm, and he jerked her farther away.

She fought against him. "This man is not your enemy. He's but a fallen man, and he's alone." She turned to the man. "Please, sir, what happened?"

The man's voice lost its edge, and he said in a whimper, "My horse threw me. Smashed my leg."

Uncertainty crept across Simon's face. He dropped his grip on her arm and drew his sword upon the stranger. "Where is your horse then?" he snarled.

"Simon, no!"

His blade's edge hovered dangerously close to the man's throat. His muscles stiffened in his back, and his hand clasped the hilt in readiness. Was he truly prepared to run the man through? Yes, yes, he was. Rothwell. Trygg. Even those other clansmen on the journey back from the market; he'd been ready to kill them, too. Was Simon always ready to kill?

Gwyn knelt beside the man. "He's alone and hurt, Simon."

"How do we know he's alone?"

The man flinched as she touched his hand covering the wound. "Let me see. I'm a Healer," she said with earnest.

"Och." He didn't loosen his hold on his thigh.

Through tight teeth she said, "He's no Nordman, Simon." She pressed the flat undersides of her fingers against Simon's sword. "Please."

He finally stepped back but did not sheathe his sword. "Are...you...alone?" he asked the man in a raging, ragged breath.

What in the heavens was wrong with Simon?

The man pressed his lips together. "Aye, I was returning home from Àrasaig. My horse spooked and tossed me. Now that *bowfing* beast is gone and my goods wi' it. Oof!" He inhaled sharply as Gwyn removed his hands.

"Where is home?"

"Loch Moy."

Simon tensed again. She held a hand up. "Enough. I care not who he is."

Simon said, "He's a Cameron."

The man's face drained of color. "Aye, I'm John Lonbie of Clan Cameron. What of it?"

Gwyn's stomach churned. Simon had warned her of the Camerons. She tried again. "Simon, he is *alone*," she said, drawing it out. She directed her words to the man.

"John, I can heal you. Please, close your eyes, and focus on breathing. Imagine you're breathing in life."

He closed his eyes in a painful squint, his hands upon his wound. "Och, all I smell is blood. I think I may retch."

She tightened her grip on the stone, allowing its energy to heat to a near scalding temperature in her hand. She turned to Simon. "Have you any water?"

He paced, his gaze darting around the trees. "Nay. Cider and ale?"

"No, those won't do." She needed water in its most natural form. They had not stopped near a loch or stream. Beside her was a patch of thick, broad leaves. The night's dew had collected in their palmate surfaces. She folded and cupped a few of the leaves, and poured the droplets into her palm.

She knelt beside John again. "Eyes closed, John. Breathe. Think of sweet water being poured down your parched throat. Yes, yes. Remove your hand, John." He did slowly, his hand slicked with blood. She took her own dew-moistened palm and laid it upon his wound, firmly and without hesitation.

This level of injury was deep. She need not look at it or probe it. Instead, she pressed her hand resolutely to his wound. He winced. She concentrated on the body beneath her hand. It was either a deep gash or a broken bone. He'd bleed to death or need it set. She couldn't fix a bone or gash with what she had in her satchel. She prayed in her mind. A delicate wind rippled her arms and the warmth of the rising sun touched the back of her neck.

Pull breath from my body.

Heal this man with my own breath.
May it flow through his veins from my heart to his heart.
The sacrifice of a Healer.
May his days be evermore.

Heat flooded her hands, but it was not the gush of blood. Spirit, breath, life. Down through her arm, beneath her palm, and into his wound. She repeated the prayer. More lifeblood and breath escaped her. Wheezes rattled her chest. Her lungs quivered, releasing their energy to the man.

She paused, head dizzy, her lungs burning as though she were on the winter moors of Uist. She shivered, released her hand, and rocked backward.

Simon's sword thudded to the ground, as he caught her before she tumbled. "Gwyn, what's wrong?"

She held up her hand, shaking. The other was deeply lodged in her pocket, adhered to the Healer's stone. *Release!* She ordered it, and it fell free. She withdrew the hand from her pocket, and Simon took it in his.

"Blazes! Your hand is like fire!"

She blinked. The other hand was covered in blood. Simon removed his tunic and cleaned her hand.

"It's fine, 'tis just blood," she said with a gasp.

John coughed and gulped in deep breaths. "The bleedin's stopped." He drew his hands to his wound again.

Gwyn didn't need to look at it to know the tear was closed and the bone repaired. She rested against Simon's thin linen shirt, her heart hammering, her chest fighting for breath it would never have. *Let it go, let it go,* she told it. She steadied her mind and breathing. Simon's own pounding heart beat into her back. Together, their rhythms synced. He held her tightly, wide strong arms around her in a protective embrace.

"W-We...he needs to be carried. He mustn't walk too far. It needs time," she said finally after a long moment. "The wound is sealed but needs time to fully mend. It needs sewn, too."

"No," Simon said.

John said clearly now, "I-I thank you. What did you do?" Amazement shone in his eyes.

"She healed you, you dolt! Now be gone," Simon said.

She raised a hand, but it held no strength and it flopped back into her lap. "Simon, he mustn't—" she protested.

John slowly got to his feet like a newborn foal. He rested against a tree. "No. He's right. I'm well. Thank ye verra much. My home is far, but I hiv family past the wood. That's where I was headin'. A shorter way, beyond the dale. I ken they'd tend to me. They're not far. My mother's kin."

"Your horse, your things...," she said, swallowing, panting. "Please have somebody sew the wound."

"Come." Simon urged her to stand.

She handed his soiled tunic back to him, and he shrugged into it.

They rose, and John clasped her hand. "Mistress, bless ye."

Simon kept a wary eye on him as John made his way to the road.

Gwyn stepped to walk to their camp but stumbled into Simon's arms.

"Christ's bones, lass! What happened to you?"

She shook her head, mute. He wouldn't understand. Every healing took her breath. John's injury was worse than she had imagined. Even now, she was not certain it had been just a cut and small fracture; deep breaks had been hidden beneath that mess. Regardless, he could now walk, and the wound was closed. All her healings took hours to days to fully set, but he would make it to his people where he could rest and recover.

"Come. You look a muddle. You need a drink."

Simon didn't ask any questions but kept a firm embrace around her as they made their way to the camp. The scent of his sweat and heightened energy emitted from him. He would have killed the man if she hadn't intervened. Did Simon hate all strangers so much? Did he thirst for the kill? She stole a glance at him as he set her on her bedroll and reached into his satchel for his flask. What had a stranger done to warrant such intense hatred?

As the sun rose, Simon moved through their preparations with haste. There was no telling if the injured man had told the full truth or if he'd return to their camp with his brethren. Clan Cameron was a vicious lot, almost as notorious as the Nordmen. His pulse drove into his mind like a hammer and nail. What if something had happened to Gwyn?

Just like before.

"Must we rush?" she asked.

"Yes."

She didn't question him further as she knelt and rolled her bedroll haphazardly. She huffed a "*Hrmphm.*"

He strode over to her. "Here, you're winded. I'll help you."

She placed a hand on her chest and sat back. "Aye."

"Does that happen every time?"

He didn't need to specify, for the question hung in the air, thick as mud. She gulped another drag of the cider, scrunched her nose, and said, "To an extent."

"But you recover?"

She nodded.

Her eyes said otherwise. He didn't press the matter.

The sweat at his brow chilled him as his body reset from the upsurge. The injured man, John, had not been *that* man. The dark-haired scowling beast with icy eyes.

It hadn't been the same situation.

By God's bones, it was. Or it could have been. He tied her bedroll, then shook out his own, rolled it, and cinched both to his horse's saddle. His gaze kept darting around the clearing, falling on trees, bushes, and shadows deep within the thick wood, waiting for the man and others to reappear.

They didn't.

"That wasn't wise, Gwyn," he finally said.

"He was alone and hurt."

He bit his tongue. She didn't know. "It's not the same here as it is in your home. Men here kill each other over simple squabbles."

"Do you not show mercy to your neighbor?"

He swallowed the bile-laced taste creeping up his throat. "Mercy gets you killed."

"Mercy saves." She crossed her arms, shivering.

He grabbed her cloak beside their dead fire. He drew it around her shoulders and clasped it. His hand found her face, and he cupped her chin. Her skin was smooth beneath his fingertips and cool to touch. Damn him, for he was about to do it again. Her lips tasted like the heavens when he bent his head and claimed them. She muffled a surprised moan but returned the kiss. Oh, how he'd love to do more than kiss.

He pulled his face from hers, their mouths close, his hand upon her chin. "Mercy *will* get you killed," he repeated. "Remember that when you are with me. I can only protect you so much, Gwyn."

They were off.

What he didn't tell her was *why* he drove them harder, faster this morning. Aye, part of it was the other clansman and the uncertainty of whether he would return with more Camerons.

However, while Gwyn had refreshed herself beyond the bushes, he had done a cursory check of their perimeter to be safe.

What he found were the cooling remains of a fire not too far from their own camp. It had clearly not been the injured John's fire.

No, they were being followed.

The day passed quickly as they rode through the foothills of the Highlands and pressed inland. This part of the route was worn from hooves and carts, but Simon drove them hard. Gwyn did her best to keep pace.

Gooseflesh rippled upon her arms with each squawk or rustle in the woods. Simon's words had burrowed into her confidence. Perhaps she was naïve, having lived a sheltered life with men who would defend her at the first bolt launched or fist thrown. She always had an unfair advantage—a sister with the Sight. Although Venora couldn't predict every misfortune, she was irreplaceable. Here, Gwyn rode, blindly reliant upon her new husband's instinct and experience.

"Let's rest the horses." Simon's words intruded on her musings.

She gladly dismounted but had to first dislodge her gown, it having been tucked around her legs to fit in a man's saddle. Pain slithered up her backside, in her legs, and radiated down her arms. This journey pushed her limits in a saddle.

They guided the horses along a vast loch. Brown windswept grasses danced against her gown's hem. It was as rugged and as stunning as the Glen Shiel region, with meadowland, dark, jagged mountains, and a cerulean sky filled with sunshine that shimmered on the loch.

Not a cloud was in sight, yet droplets of rain dotted her dress. She eyed Simon with hesitation, wondering if his knee bothered him again. He had said foul weather, or the approach of such weather, triggered his aches.

He neither winced nor cringed.

She masked her smile for she hadn't healed him as she had said. Not that she didn't want to. This wound hadn't required healing. When she had rested her hand upon his gnarled knee, the ripples of scarified skin released a burst of negative energy associated with the wound. She often wondered if a smidgen of Kendrick's gift also ran through her blood. Her mother had told her part of each of the gods' powers was in all of them. They were gifted with higher access to some powers over others. Not even a pinch of the Sight ran through her. If anything, she was adept at never seeing far enough ahead. It was forever her downfall.

She'd known before even uttering her prayer breaths that it was a phantom wound, which wasn't to say he'd not been hurt, but the remaining pain was in his mind. So she had lied because something awful tormented his soul. As a Healer, she wished nothing more than to free her charges from their binding shackles, whether they be physical or of the spirit. She wished Simon would confide in her.

"How does your knee fare?" she nudged.

He rubbed it instinctively and cast a smile in her direction. "It fares well. Thank you."

She locked eyes with him. "You're welcome." She licked her lips, remembering his upon hers. The idea of consummating their marriage grew less intimidating the more time she spent with him, which confused her. There was no denying part of her yearned for his hands upon her skin again. His gaze, like a caress, lit tingles of desire in her stomach. Suddenly aware of his nearness and their aloneness, she drew her attention to the path before them. She tugged at the collar of her gown and coughed.

She was Simon's wife and soon would be his wife in more than name. It was inevitable. He would never return her to Leidolf. Oddly, the idea wasn't unpleasant. All she could do now was rely on Simon for protection and pray her letter reached Kendrick. Then, her mother or sister could plan his escape. She would suffer the consequences from her father and Leidolf. She wanted to ask Simon to bring her mother, sister, and friends to Eilean Donan, but it was too much to ask.

Hope was all she had these days. She shivered.

"Are you cold?" he asked, stepping closer as he dropped the reins; the horse sipped water on the loch's edge.

"Hmm, aye." She hugged her arms to her stomach.

He drew her in, slipping his hands between her cloak and gown.

She anticipated the kiss now. A craving lit his eyes. For a man of such a robust façade, it dissipated when he gathered her into his arms. She melted in the embrace surrounding her, tipping her head upward and seizing his lips first. His kiss emptied the twirling thoughts from her mind. She lost herself in it, and he parted her lips with his tongue.

He tasted of the apple they'd shared, tart and sweet. His light beard tickled her chin and cheeks. She drew a hand behind his neck, urging his tongue to explore. He moaned, embracing her tighter, chest against chest. One of his arms slid from her back to her hip, and then slowly trailed up her side to below a breast. She inhaled, but his hand moved no farther. Their hips were intimately close, his proximity potent.

He unhurriedly pulled his face back and lowered his hand to her hip, his chest still pressed against her breasts. His heart pounded against hers. Through deep breaths, he said, "Och, woman, you'll be the death of me."

She blinked, swallowed the last taste of him in her mouth, and looked, unsure if he'd given a compliment or curse. His eyes were a storm.

"Come, we can make it to Ceann Loch Raineach before nightfall. There are safe lodgings in the village."

He didn't whirl on his heel or turn away from her, stomping in his usual withdrawn evasion. Instead, he held her hand as they walked the horses for a while along the loch.

His words struck her, and she squeezed Simon's hand tighter while they walked.

Venora's clairvoyant message rang in her ears: *That red-haired one, the son of MacCoinneach, he shall perish there. And you can do naught about it.*

They reached the tavern after sunset, clear of the Cameron territory, safely to the small village of fishermen and crofters near the open moor and loch. Simon's unease had nearly pressed his resolve to its brink today. He would never allow another woman in his charge to be afflicted with the brutality his mother had endured. Especially Gwyn.

"Are you well, Simon?" Gwyn asked as he helped her dismount. She settled her disheveled skirt and released a moan as she pressed her balled fists into the base of her back.

"I'm sorry I rode us hard," he said.

A smile parted her lips. "It's no bother."

"Ample food awaits within. You'll soon forget your aches."

"You do like a good meal," she jested, brushing a hand on his shoulder.

He ran a hand through his hair, thick and in need of a wash. "Aye, I do." He secured the horses' reins to the outside post. "Come, they're hospitable here. I'll get us a room upstairs."

He motioned for her to enter first as he paused at the entryway. He cast a look over his shoulder to the surrounding trees. *One more look.* He'd seen no further sign of being followed, but it didn't mean anything. He'd keep the lass close to him tonight and the sword closer.

He stepped through the front door and into the main room. Two tables were pressed along one side, each with three stools, and a door led to Geordie's meager kitchen, where his wife Edina conjured her delicious meals. To his left, a staircase rose to a second floor consisting of three guest rooms and Geordie and Edina's room.

A lone man sat at the table closest to the hearth, most likely drinking Edina's cider. Simon nodded to him in courtesy. "Have a seat, Gwyn."

He walked to the kitchen door. He cast a look within. "Edina?"

Edina poked her head inside from the rear door. "Oh, Simon! So good to see ye. Ye'll be looking for Geordie, I suppose?"

"Well, aye. We also need a room for the night."

Edina stepped in, arms overflowing with a cluster of vegetables. Simon didn't offer to help. The old hen got all het up when he did. She shuffled to her cutting block and dropped the assortment upon it. An onion rolled onto the dirt floor. She swiped it, cleaned it on her apron, and then wiped her hands. She approached Simon and pulled him into a fierce hug, despite her leaner, bony figure. He was reminded no man should be fooled by her stature. She was nearly his grandfather's age and could put up a fight against the best of them.

She studied him with a grandmotherly eye. "Ye look leaner. Ye're in luck tonight. I made a mutton stew and my raisin-nut rye bread. Slaughtered our fattest sheep. Lots o' fat to put on yer bones."

"You're too kind, Edina." His stomach growled. A fragrant aroma bubbled from the pot on the kitchen hearth.

"We?"

He wrung his fingers. "Aye, there is one with me."

"Och! Is it Henry? Now, that lad needs meat on his bones!" she said merrily, life swaying in her eyes.

He rubbed his chin, the new beard growth prickly. "Nay." He paused and said in a fast breath, "I brought my wife. We're going to the abbey."

Well, that did it. Edina brushed past him and into the main room, where Gwyn stood beside a crackling hearth, rubbing her hands together. Surprise, followed by pleasure, filled Gwyn's face as Edina hurried over to her. Gwyn succumbed to Edina's poking, fussing, and questioning.

Geordie then appeared behind Simon and surprised him with a clap to his shoulder.

"Wheesht, Pinkie!" Simon said, pulse racing.

Geordie laughed. "How fare ye?"

Simon admired his bride. "Aye, I could be worse."

"Why do you call him Pinkie?" Gwyn asked as Simon led her into their shared room.

"Och, a funny story," Simon said. He closed the door and approached the bed, the only furniture in the room. It wasn't a large bed.

He didn't sit.

The idea of a mattress was appealing, so she did. She sighed and loosened her plaited hair. She ran her fingers through it, unknotting tangles, and brushing it the best she could. Gildy had insisted on packing combs and ribbons from Simon's mother's room, but for now, Gwyn used what she had on hand.

Simon paced across the room, something she observed was a habit regardless of what kind of mood he was in. The floorboards creaked beneath his steps.

"Aye, I've known Pinkie, *ehm*, Geordie, and Edina for a long time. Their family resides north, near the Donalds. They used to come through Dornie. They found love in the mid-Highland lands. Better weather here," he said, face animated. He waved a hand. "Anyway, they opened the alehouse to cater to people passing through to the south. They appreciated our hospitality in Dornie, so they chose to reciprocate the gesture to others going yonder to Edinburgh and such."

Simon was rambling. She'd never seen this side of him, and it was adorable. Pink tinged his cheeks and the tips of his ears.

"Anyway, one day, Geordie got too close to Edina and her kitchen knife, and you saw how she is about her food," he said with a tap on his stomach, "and his finger got in the way of her wrath—" He stopped to look at her.

Her bottom lip dropped. "She didn't?" Did Geordie have any fingers shorter than the rest? In her tired fog, she couldn't remember noticing. Edina's food had been tasty and her incessant talking a welcome but also draining. Gwyn had fought to keep her eyes open.

The bed lured her...

Simon released a belly laugh and sat beside her, held her gaze, and said, "Nay."

She swatted at his shoulder. "Simon MacCoinneach, have you a sense of humor?"

His brows lifted then fell, and there it was. His usual somber look had returned. "Sometimes. My mother could tell a good yarn." He cleared his throat. "Truthfully, you've seen how he squints when he gets full of drink and excited?"

She nodded.

"'Tis from that. There's a sickness that makes your eyes crusty and pink. You squint a lot until it resolves. Have you heard of it?"

"Oh, yes."

"Well, that's where we got the name Pinkie." He brushed a hand through his coarse, wavy hair. "Daft when you think of it. There you have it."

"Charming. I think," she said through a smile. "I do like your other story for it. Even if it's a ruse."

She caught him with a kiss. His lips were tangy from Edina's cider. She laid a hand on his thigh. She enjoyed the taste of him, his nearness, his male scent.

Sighing, she slowly retreated, as much as she wanted to not.

He released a quiet rumble from his throat and stared longingly.

She began to speak, but he took her lips again with a need more dire. Winded, she fell back upon the bed. He lay atop her, chest against chest. He lifted a hand to her breast, cupping with urgency, as he pressed against her, stirring her senses. His kiss grew harder.

She moaned and felt him stiffen against her...lower. Her pulse raced.

Abruptly, he pulled back, his hand falling off her breast, brushing her waist, then drifting away.

No, she wanted more…

Her breast tingled from his caress through the layers of fabric. She wondered what else he could do with his hands.

He sat up, leaving her lying upon the mattress. She blew a frustrated breath and sat upright beside him.

"Sorry," he said.

"Don't be."

The crackling sound of the hearth filled the room as they sat in silence.

"Simon?" she finally said when she couldn't stand it any longer.

"Aye?" His eyes were alight with life, something she'd not seen much from him in the past few morose weeks. She hated to put a damper on it, but something had been gnawing at her.

"Do you not want me?"

He rubbed his chin and turned. Intense eyes stared at her. "I want you more than anything. I don't want to hurt you."

She nodded, unsure what to say or do. The mood was broken. She ventured another question because she had a sneaky suspicion she knew the answer and had made the connection. "What happened?"

"When?

She swallowed. "With your mother?" She wanted to ask about his knee, too, but she'd bet the two were related.

Now she asked about his mother during an intimate moment. Surely, she was a novice at this.

He stiffened but didn't retreat for once.

"'Twas nine years ago, when I was your brother's age. An impetuous lad who thought he could take on the world." His voice faded to a hushed stillness.

She drew his thick hand into both of hers and laid them, clasped, on her lap. With a gentle finger, she traced over his knuckles, some scraped from manual labor. She remembered his caresses upon her. Simon could be gentle when he wanted.

Bitterness spilled from his voice. "We encountered trouble. A lone man, at first. My mother wanted to leave, but he was injured. I was young and foolish and insisted we help. Then the rest of them arrived, maddened as if possessed by spirits. Raging, ravenous, grunting madmen, wearing wolf skins and acting like dogs, covered in the blood of whomever they had just attacked. She," he said, pausing, chest rising, "...was gravely injured. My injury left me to walk another day."

She was stunned to silence. That explained his behavior with the injured man, John. Heaviness welled in her stomach at his description of the men. There was no doubt who they were.

Simon rubbed his chin. "Och, well, I'll let you sleep." He stood and made for the door again.

"You're leaving?"

"That's a wee bed. I may toss you from it when I roll over."

She saw through his humor. Their shared moment had been lost as soon as she'd asked him about his mother. Curse her curiosity.

"We are wed. Don't you want to—"

He coughed. "You need your sleep. Rest, Gwyn. We leave early in the morning. Edina's oatcakes and meat pies will not leave you hungry on the morrow."

She nodded. "After tonight's meal, I can't wait," she said, patting her stomach. "Where are you to sleep?"

"Don't worry about me. I'll find a place, but I will stay close."

He averted his gaze from hers and angled his body away to look out the small, square window.

"Simon?"

"Aye?" his voice cracked.

"Who were they?" Simon had said his mother was ill with an unnamed disease. He acknowledged strangers had caused her condition. What kind of illness was this? Had she been beaten, bones unrepaired? Skull fractured? Burned? All the possibilities raced through Gwyn's mind, increasing her pulse. Was his mother sick with another contagion she had acquired naturally? She was stupefied. She hated pressing him for details.

His breath hitched and shoulders slumped. He spun around. A frightening despair dwelt in his eyes. "It's my fault."

She protested, "You can't blame yourself. Many people get sick or injured. Men are barbarians."

Unable to hold her look, he stared through the doorway into the dark hallway. "She was violated. I couldn't protect her. Demons have taken her body and spirit. A horrible disease courses through her body, affecting her bones, skin, and mind."

Violated.

The blood drained from her fingertips. She rasped, "W–Who?"

"The Nordmen. The *úlfheðnar.*"

She said nothing. The *berserkir* and *úlfheðnar* were demon-enraged Norse warriors.

"I've never learned their names, but they traveled under a banner of a red wolf's head. One day, I shall kill them all."

He strode from the room, leaving her once again alone. She flopped onto the bed and clutched her aching chest, for she had no breath.

CHAPTER NINE

Leidolf hovered on the forest's edge, his stare fixed on the tavern before him. He'd lost their trail briefly in the mountains, but being an astute hunter, he found it again quickly. He remained vigilant, considering his next move, waiting for the right moment.

He tapped his fingers on the sword's sheath, moved to the hilt, and touched each amber jewel on the silver wolf twice, then adjusted the axe and waited. The plan was all-consuming, a frantic black vortex in his mind. Every detail had to be considered.

He stared at the wolf's head on the sword's hilt, which matched the carved wooden hilt of the dagger. He had studied the wolf in its natural environment in Reindalr. A wolf's body was made for the hunt. Pure muscle, lean, and created for powerful sprints. Usually the largest dominant male was the leader. Instinct, glory, and lust drove the wolves to their prey. The pack consisted of a blend of families—adults, juveniles, and pups. They were territorial, social, and highly defensive.

Always ready for a hunt and chase. Always ready to take what was rightfully his. Always. Ready. Lone wolves had to be or they would be killed over being adopted into a new group.

He straightened his shoulders and imposed a practiced control upon himself. He inhaled the scent around him. A hunter and his surroundings merged into one. He tasted smoky peat and cooked animals from the village's hearths.

Blinking, ever watchful against beckoning sleep, he reached in the pouch at his side and slid two fingers around the small vial of wolf's blood. Not yet. Not yet. He might need it later in battle. Just a few drops would bring him to the sublime state of being where he and the god Fenrir were one. Let his father have his coveted reserve of *úlfheðnar*. He had his own powers to unleash. Soon. Soon.

The Nord Land was rich in fjord and mountain, with wolves, foxes, elk, and reindeer aplenty for hunting. The Reindalr brood was never short on food when he was around. He was a hunter like Fenrir. He would be a provider for his Uist brides.

Gwyn would be quite the bride. Her healing abilities on that man in the woods were truly a gift from the gods. The control of her powers would bring him the glory he needed. With her ghostly allure, oh, she would also be divine in his bed. He hoped she'd yet to be soiled by that fox's seed. Based on their interactions at each of their camps, he suspected not. He needed her soon, or else he'd have to find one of the servants at an inn. They'd surely open their legs for a coin or two.

Something stirred outside the alehouse.

Ah, there was the red-haired fox. He paced out front. Why was the fool not in bed with his wife?

The fox's time would come soon. Very soon.

When he least expected it.

Simon had become predictable, always glaring into the woods, waiting for something or someone to jump him. Blasius had warned him of Simon's fighting ability. As much as Leidolf had wanted to sneak into their camp and slit the man's throat in the night, a wolf never behaved that way. The prey needed to know they were being chased.

So he stalked. He followed. He hunted.

He purposely left the remains from his salted fish dinner and then stepped into the forest cover.

After their conversation about his mother, Simon resumed his usual sullen mood, and Gwyn was relieved when they drew closer to the abbey. He purposely avoided Edinburgh via a roundabout route. She stopped asking him why. Slowly, the pieces to his story found their places.

They rode through the southern uplands, green and lush. Her aching body thanked her for the smoother ride. No rocky passes or deep thick woods where she constantly got tangled in the overgrowth when her horse seemed to forget its rider's added weight. A river murky with silt churned slowly beside them as if a guide to the abbey.

She squinted ahead. Spent, invigorated, and increasingly wary at once, her heart spun to Kendrick. Every day that passed was another she was not there to care for him.

She prayed she could heal Lady MacCoinneach and return home before the battle. It had already been far too long. Where would Kendrick go if he got Simon's warning? Would he arrive at Eilean Donan to find her absent? Would they see him as another invading Nordman and turn him away? No, *no*. They would welcome him. Simon had promised.

She tightened her hands on the reins, and the horse snorted. She muffled a curse.

"Dinna worry," Simon said. "I know how sorely you wish to return home."

She frowned and added reader of minds to Simon's growing list of traits. "How can you be certain I will return? Neither of us can foresee our paths."

He furrowed his brow. "I don't know. Do we ever know anything for certain? I've given specific orders to Errol about your brother. When Kendrick gets the message from Niall and finds the moment to get away, he will be cordially greeted by Errol and the rest of our men at Eilean Donan. I've told you every day since we left," he added, not hiding his exasperation. He drew his horse alongside hers as they slowed their gait. He took her hand in his. "I promised. We won't be here long, aye? A few days. The horses will need to rest before our return. If you wish me to send for your mother and sister, too, I shall."

She forced a smile. "Aye, but they won't leave." Then added, "What if the letter doesn't reach him?"

"What if the sky falls tomorrow?"

She heaved a sigh. "You belittle my feelings, Simon."

He shook his head. "Nay, I don't. I see how important his well-being is to you."

"You don't mind having the Norse people and my father's men as your enemy?"

He shrugged. "I'm not unfamiliar with enemies. Besides, they've always been our enemy."

"What if more come?"

"More to kill."

"Your arrogance will be the death of you, Simon Mac-Coinneach."

He glared at her with derision. "Your blind faith in humanity and mercy will be yours," he said in repeat of his earlier omen.

She huffed and tried to gain speed. He was quicker, riding abreast. "Gwyn, please. Trust me. You have faith in others but not in me?"

She met his glower with silence. In her mind, the retort remained: he'd taken her against her will and coerced her into a marriage she did not want. He showed no mercy for her people or plight. He was like the man she had never wanted to marry.

Yet.

Mercy had nearly gotten him and his mother killed. Mercy had ruined his family's life.

He eased his voice and softened his shoulders. "All will fare well."

Help the ones you can, her mother's words echoed. *Leave the rest to the fates. Show mercy. Be compassionate. We all have our stories but cannot change our destiny.*

What lay in the stars for her and Simon?

Their horses approached the lofty arches of Dryburgh Abbey's impressive cathedral, and Gwyn's breath stalled as she momentarily forgot all else. It was as if the house of worship reached to the heavens, declaring the abbey's allegiance to its celestial creators. The abbey was unlike the castle fortresses of Scotland, as Gwyn had seen a few great strongholds on their journey south. This was far grander.

Simon gave her an oral account of every part of the abbey. The largest section of the cathedral engulfed the surrounding buildings, finished to perfection, with high transepts, as he called them. The roof was a gray-pink stone, chiseled and new, a commanding presence over the meadows and trees.

The horses slowed to a walk on the slight hilly incline. "What is that?" she asked, pointing to intricately carved stonework far above their heads. It was a flower of sorts, with twelve petals, massive in size, and filled with gorgeous colored glass.

"A rose window. The radiating spokes represent the twelve apostles of Christ. The glass is new. Do they have glass on Uist?"

She tapped her chin. "Not much. The MacRuaidhri keep was recently furnished with glass last year. I don't journey to Port nan Long much." They dismounted and walked the horses to the small stable.

"Come," he said, guiding her by the hand through a grassy area within the outer walls of the abbey. Stone slabs were situated throughout the knoll, in table and chair style.

"A cloister," he said. "For studying, copying texts, and praying."

"Ah." She nodded. She couldn't resist running her hand along the stone. It was both smooth and rough and vibrated with the hum of Jörd.

Smaller buildings and rows of manicured gardens completed the abbey. The size of it overwhelmed her. Not a soul walked among the gardens or grounds. No guards. No defensive posts.

"They leave it unprotected?" she asked, turning over her shoulder to cast a wary look about. A nearby yew tree whispered in the gentle breeze and the echo of the river drifted across the grounds. The presence of water always brought a flooding relief to her spirit.

"This abbey is inland and close to Edinburgh. Nothing poses a threat here. The English may sack our castles along the border, but they leave God's people alone," Simon said.

His unspoken insinuation rang in her ears. The Norse conquerors never left religious sanctuaries intact in their plunders. They robbed and burned even these holiest of places. They killed all. She took a deep breath and steadied herself as they continued their walk through an archway. "Where are the holy priests?"

"It's midday. They, the canons, are likely in Mass."

"Canons?"

He waved a hand. "They're priests."

"Ah."

"Mass? Is that their ritual?"

"So to speak. The abbey is overseen by an abbot. These priests spend most of their day in prayer, tending fields, selling to local markets, healing those they can, copying religious texts, and reading."

"How do they heal?"

"Not like you. Traditional herbals coupled with prayer."

She nodded, unsure if that was an accolade to her ability or criticism. "Prayer can heal?"

He scoffed. "Not always." He continued, "Here are their residences. There's a special dormitory"—he pointed toward a moderate-sized cottage not far from the forest's edge, but isolated from the primary buildings—"for visitors. I reside there usually when I stay. There are extra rooms inside. You can stay there."

Her belly twisted. Simon, her *husband*, hadn't shared a bed with her, except for the litter-covered forest floor. A few passionate kisses, and then she'd ruined it with her talk about his mother. She fluffed her hair and swiped at invisible wrinkles in her skirt. Was she not appealing to him? Heat stung her cheeks. Although she had always hoped Simon might let her go with an annulment after this unrest subsided, a part of her secretly wanted him to take her to his bed and make her his true wife. Even he had admitted to his desire. Perhaps she was wrong about her idea of marriage.

Simon rattled on about the building. For a man of few words, he sure was talking a lot. Stories, food, and walks...that's when the happier Simon emerged. She liked it. She liked him.

As always, her thoughts strayed to the dark. How often had he come here to tend to his mother? Her mood shifted from a flowering interest in her husband's touches upon her to something far more dreary.

Violated.

Lady Margaret MacCoinneach had been violated. Gwyn was no fool. His mother had been raped. By Gwyn's own kind. The red wolf banner. Leidolf's crest. It had been nine years ago. She didn't even know her betrothed's age, but she assumed he was her age or a few years older, like Simon. Perhaps the attacker had been one of his brothers or his father even? Leidolf was the youngest of three sons. Besides, Simon would have recognized Leidolf on the bridge at Eilean Donan; surely Simon MacCoinneach didn't forget faces.

What had befallen Simon's mother after the violation for her to be housed here, away from her clan, kept under constant treatment and supervision by these priests? Her spirit ached for Lady MacCoinneach. Did she have the strength to heal her? She half listened as Simon spoke and pointed. The wind blew through a chime dangling from the nearby willow tree, its harmonious melody permeating the air. A few stray chickens scurried across their path. It was indeed a heavenly place. Finally, she said, "Simon, when can I meet your mother?"

"They'll be convening for the midday meal in the refectory shortly after Mass," Simon said, hopping over a muddy puddle. Gwyn walked around it. He looped his arm into hers and led her to the main building.

"Your mother?"

He didn't hide his unrest. "Soon."

Tucked in behind the cloister were the library, chapter house, and abbot's parlor, which were interconnected by stairs and breezy hallways. Finally, they reached the embodiment of the abbey. The nave, choir, and chapel created the cathedral. "It's in a shape of the cross if you looked from above like a bird," Simon said.

He hesitated at an entrance. Pleasant music resonated from within. "We can't go in now since they are mid-Mass. Let's wait in the cloister."

She uttered undemanding, hushed words, slowly. "Shouldn't we see your mother first, while we wait?"

He made a hard, obvious swallow. "She's probably resting. I'd like to speak with Abbot Oliver first."

"I see."

They sat and waited in the outdoor cloister. Then, the bell tolled and men, dressed in white tunics—*habits* Simon called them—and hoods or cloaks, exited the cathedral and strode through the cloister toward the refectory, which was like a hall. A few nodded to Simon, but most continued on their way, silent and solemn, disregarding Gwyn's presence.

Her ears burned. Was she invisible even to these holy men?

A slender aging man, adorned in a simple and crisp white habit, emerged from the chapel. He ambled as if in reflection. His fair eyebrows lifted as his soft look fell upon them. He approached with a nod and wave. "Simon, my son. I pray God's grace has shone upon your journey here. We didn't expect to see you."

Simon nodded. "Thank you kindly, Abbot Oliver."

The older man, skin aged with wrinkles and sunshine, drew his head slowly to the side and took in Gwyn. A smile and light blue eyes greeted her. "Milady."

Simon gestured with his hand toward her. "This is my wife, Gwyn."

She curtsied and returned the smile, aware Simon hadn't elaborated upon her full name, for it would allude to her heritage and kinship. She was a foreigner even here. Her chin trembled. Was she not worthy, even for Simon? Why did she even care? It's not like she loved her husband. "Good day, Abbot Oliver," she managed to say, calming her irritated heartbeat.

"Welcome, Gwyn. Our home is yours. Stay as long as you need. Always a pleasure to have a shining spirit in our presence." Abbot Oliver bubbled with a serene friendliness, his expression clear and genuine, not dubious. He reached forward and took her hands in his. They were cool and bony.

She squeezed back. "Thank you."

He turned to Simon. "The midday meal is served. Please join us."

Nobody mentioned Lady MacCoinneach as they followed him and the other priests to the large dining hall. Gwyn was nothing short of eager to have a meal by a fire followed by a plush bed. With or without her husband, the lure of a bed was rousing.

Abbot Oliver and Simon carried on a quiet conversation beside her as she enjoyed a meal of salmon, eggs, bread, cheese, and a burgundy wine. Most of the men ate in subdued conversation, unlike the boisterousness of the men from her village or the Scotsmen. The scrape of utensils and plates mingled with low voices. It was soothing and hypnotic. Regardless, her skin itched for conversation. She was the only woman, except for Simon's mother, wherever she might be.

"Milady?" A man beside her held a pitcher.

"Yes, please. Thank you."

He smiled, filled her goblet, and then turned to the companion beside him.

Simon spoke of amiable topics with Abbot Oliver, circumventing the questions of why he was visiting, how his mother was doing, or anything beyond weather and harvests. When the meal drew to an end, Gwyn said quietly to Simon, "Shan't we meet with your mother soon?"

He lay down his goblet after a hefty swing. "Aye. I wanted to let you eat and rest first."

"I'm well fed, and rest can come this evening."

Simon meditated upon calming thoughts as he led Gwyn toward his mother's chamber. Abbot Oliver had gladly relinquished his own dormitory for Lady MacCoinneach on the second floor. It was above the warming parlor and the rising heat from the double fireplace eased her aches. They climbed the spiral staircase, each of his steps heavier, yet somehow lighter with hope. His palm grew slick in Gwyn's hand, and he withdrew it, wiped it on his leg, and reached for the door latch. Would his mother be sleeping? Moaning? Or was she in the midst of the delirium caused by the medicines the priests provided her daily? What would Gwyn think? His pulse raced and hands tingled. Meditative thoughts, his arse. They never worked. Hate. Anger. Vengeance. Yes, those worked. The barbarian who had done this to her would die one day by his hand. Yes. Yes, that worked.

His pulse settled into its uneven cadence as his muscles shuddered. He pushed the door in halfway and stopped. "Gwyn, I..."

She laid a light hand upon his shoulder. "I've seen many people ill from disease or injury."

Her words and sweet voice were a mild comfort to his eternal ache. Regardless, he said, "She's disfigured from it. The disease has spread. Her skin...I should've told you more."

Gwyn pushed open the door for him. "Your mother and Eir will guide me in what needs to be healed. First, let's at least offer our greetings. Then you and I shall talk, aye? I will need to know more about it."

He nodded. "Aye."

He followed her into the dimly lit room. The scent of the sickly ointments the priests used upon his mother's skin wafted across the overbearingly hot air and stung his nostrils. He swallowed his gag and immediately marched to the closed window. He drew the drapes apart and pushed up the wooden shutter to allow in light and air.

Finally, he turned to meet his mother's welcome.

She was asleep.

Gwyn approached and sat beside her on the bed. "'Tis not pestilent?" Her hand hesitated midair for a long moment, before she finally placed it into her lap with her other one, knitting them tightly.

"No, you can't catch it by touch."

With a heavy, beleaguered gait, Simon approached and stood behind Gwyn to gaze upon his mother. Whenever he visited, she looked worse than the previous time. He almost couldn't bear to come anymore. She lay buried to her neck beneath bedclothes, but the pustules covered other parts of her body not readily seen.

Red-gray spreading bumps rounded over her nose, across her cheeks, on her lower lip, and to her hairline. Her usually elegant, smooth dark auburn hair lacked its luster, appearing like dried burnt wheat, tucked haphazardly beneath her cotton bonnet. Was she even eating these days? Gaunt bones protruded from a formerly vibrant, healthy face. She'd aged decades in a matter of years.

All because of him.

His wife—heavens, *his wife*—tilted forward and swiped a gentle hand across his mother's saggy skin on her cheek.

"Gwyn, perhaps you shouldn't."

Tears pooled on the emerald edges of her blue irises. "Simon, please don't worry. I must touch her. You said I couldn't catch it."

His shoulders slumped in wordless acquiescence.

Instinct told him to pull her hand back, for he truly did not know how contractible it was. Abbot Oliver had assured him there was only *one way* to contract the Frenchman's disease.

"She's a bonnie woman, Simon," Gwyn whispered.

"She was," he said in a ragged gulp.

"I may not be a Feeler, but I can almost sense the life that once shone from within her," she added. "She has a tough spirit."

He nodded, even if she couldn't see him. Her gaze was rapt upon his mother. He remembered his mother's tall tales, always bringing smiles to the men around the hall table. "What's a Feeler?"

She continued to stroke his mother's face, avoiding the hideous bumps and the ulcerated pustules or the spot in her cheek near her nose where the bone caved in. Gwyn tucked his mother's hair into the bonnet and adjusted the bedclothes. "It's another gift of my people. My mother and I are Healers. Venora is a Seer. She has visions. Kendrick is a Feeler. He can sense the essence in every person, their lifebloods. Every person emits an energy he can feel. He also can feel a person's inner being, good or bad, and their emotions."

Simon was awestruck. "That's an incredible ability."

She heaved a sigh and turned to him again. "A powerful one. One that can be exploited. My father doesn't know of Kendrick's gift nor of his blindness. He has hidden both well these past few years. My father already uses Venora's visions to his advantage." She added, quietly, "My father treats Kendrick like a dog." She hesitated before saying, "He beats him. Horribly. I fear for his life. Do you see why I must return?"

Simon's mind stirred. Strangely the first thought was whether their own children would have any of these abilities. *Our own children.* But what monster beat his son? Ire grew within him.

Now. Now, of all times she told him all of this? Well, he'd not been the most forthcoming either. He had muddled this entire situation. That lad needed his help badly, and he had been selfish, whisking Gwyn off for his own needs. He rounded the bed and sat on the other side of his mother. He took her cold hand in his. "I'm sorry I've been an arse, Gwyn. I should've asked about your family. I do want to help you." By the Lord, poor Kendrick.

"I wish for your help, Simon."

Her words nearly crushed his soul. They sat silently for a few minutes as Gwyn seemed to be considering his mother's ailments.

"This disease has no name?"

He had lied before; it was time for truth. "They call it the Frenchman's disease. Have you seen it before?"

She threaded her fingers together in contemplation. "No."

"I've also heard it referred to as the *Gor*. It's a pox from raiders, not native to England and Scotland. It runs rampant in France. There is but one way to contract it."

Truth hung in the air, thick and suffocating.

"What are her other symptoms?" she asked.

He rose. "Come, let's talk about it elsewhere. We can then return after she wakes."

She stood, tucked the bedclothes around his mother, and followed him downstairs to the parlor. Despite the chill in the day, he wiped sweat from his brow. The hearth blazed. He swallowed, his throat dry and his spirit sore. He paced as Gwyn sat beside the hearth, quiet and patient. A grave frown parted her lips, her skin paler than usual.

He exhaled and said, "She has aches and pains in joints, her fingers, knees, elbows. These pocks, wretched and foul smelling, bleeding, all over her body. She suffers from repeated fevers. She cries at night mostly, saying her bones hurt her. She used to have a plump, full face. It's withered away to naught but skin and bone."

She nodded, eyes distant.

"Can you heal her?"

"She's been afflicted for many years?"

"Yes. It began within a year after the attack. That was nine years ago."

She was silent.

His face heated, the hearth unbearable. "Can you heal her, Gwyn?"

"Water is my wellspring, my assistant, you can say. It complements my ability. I'm without my special infusions. I've naught but my healing stone. Perhaps we could bring her to the river and I can do it there? The fresh moving water of a river is especially potent. Is she able to walk or be moved?"

"Aye, I'll fetch Abbot Oliver to help. She usually has her wits about her in the afternoon after her morning dose of poppy has worn off."

He took her hand, his voice cracking. "Can you?"

She stared into his eyes. "Some are beyond my ability, Simon. It is not up to me, as I've told you. Jörd and Eir decide it. I am at their mercy. I will try my best, Simon. I will try my best."

Oh, how Gwyn longed for her herbals box.

Lady MacCoinneach moaned as they eased her to standing. Her shift hung loosely from her frail frame and didn't hide the sores, abscesses, and pustules rising from the neckline and under the cuffs of her sleeves. Her breasts sagged beneath the thin fabric. Nobody mentioned her near nakedness in front of the tending audience. The abbot brought her a simple gown. He skimmed it over her head. She wore no special plates or bones beneath like many ladies. Even Gwyn chose to wear a gown with minimal boning sewn in, for her selection of clothes were not as fine as a lady's. "I can help her," she said, stepping forward.

Margaret didn't seem bothered by her lack of modesty. The lady had remained mute.

Simon said at her side, "The priests and Abbot Oliver oversee the abbey's maintenance. I'm afraid there are no maids here for my mother. We had one, but she, *ehm*, she left when it became too difficult." Embarrassment colored his cheeks, but he swooped in beside Margaret. "Here, Mother. Let us help you. It's me, Simon. I'm here." He held her upright as Gwyn tied the lacings and fastened a belt.

"She has a mantle here," he said, shuffling toward the modest dressing cabinet. He withdrew the brown garment and shrugged his mother into it, leaving it loose and open in the front.

Margaret locked eyes with her, belatedly noticing her presence.

"Who are you?" she asked, her voice raspy.

"I'm Gwyn. I'm a Healer. I've come to help you, my lady, but we must get you to the river."

Glassy eyes regarded her. "I don't like to swim."

Gwyn suspected they had given her a heavy dose of a henbane and poppy tincture along with whisky to keep her numb, but she didn't ask.

Thankfully, the abbot and priests made no protest to her unique healing method. Had Simon taken them aside and warned them? Regardless, all were willing to see her work and provided no opposition. In fact, all eyes in the room were upon her.

Simon drew an arm around his mother's waist as Gwyn knelt and slid slippers upon Margaret's feet.

"Mother, Gwyn is more than a healer. She is my wife, like I told you already."

Gwyn rose, built-up emotion whirling within her. She curtsied and avoided Margaret's gaze.

His mother gasped and then released a breath, rank and sour. She clutched Gwyn's hand. "Wife?" she croaked.

Simon added, "Aye, Mother. I told you already."

She found herself eye to eye with her new mother. "Aye, my lady."

Tears brimmed in Margaret's brown eyes. She tightened her grip, bony yet firm, in Gwyn's hand. "Has my son been treating you well?"

"Aye, Lady MacCoinneach."

Margaret nodded. "He can be a bit of an arse."

"Mother...," Simon said, blushing.

Well, he had said she was a plucky woman. A chuckle rose in Gwyn's throat.

"Please call me Margaret," she said. Her face pinched from a spasm, but she straightened, shifting from helpless sufferer to authoritative lady of a manor. "Shall we?" She looped an arm within Gwyn's as they exited the room.

Jarred from her stupor, or perhaps the herbals had worn off, Margaret chatted the entire walk to the river, although it took much effort, evidenced by pants and gulps. "How did you meet my son?"

Gwyn coughed. "*Hmm*, that's a long story."

"I'm sorry to have missed your ceremony. My husband told me nothing about it. He visited me recently."

Simon followed in step behind them, speaking about the abbey's business with Abbot Oliver, yet Gwyn knew he was listening.

Their hasty wedding wasn't one she'd like to discuss with Lady MacCoinneach. In fact, probably nothing would be a comfortable topic. Their brothers' deaths, their forced marriage, a war with the Nord Land...

She grasped at anything with a shred of hope. "This abbey is relaxing and lovely to the eye."

Margaret nodded. "Aye, indeed. It was constructed nearly a hundred years ago. We always find generosity here. The former abbot was a friend of Alroy's father, and they did business together. So we naturally carried on the kinship. Scots are steadfast beings. You'll learn soon enough."

Gwyn flinched. Had Simon told his mother about her upbringing? He had disappeared for a short time, leaving Gwyn to peruse the library for an hour while she waited for Margaret to wake. She shoved a hand in her pocket and ran her thumb over the stone.

Margaret's small birdlike voice said, "You're not a native mainlander. You're from the isles, are you?"

"How could you tell?"

She rubbed two fingers on her temple. "I may be lost in oblivion from these tinctures the priests give me every day, but I've got my eyes and ears about me. You speak differently. You carry yourself differently. Plus, while you were in the library Simon told me. Och, I remember it. These curatives. I get holes in my memory." She sighed.

"Tell me about your family, dear. I would love to know more about you."

I'd rather not. Her father's lunacy. Seers. Feelers. Healers. Humming stones. Blood. Death. Red wolf's banner. Rape. Haakon's growing fleet. She wanted to fade into the surrounding trees, but there was no escape.

Margaret must have sensed her hesitation for she said, "Let's start with the easy things, sweet dear. Do you have a mother? Siblings? Your healing. Do you use herbs, too?"

Gwyn guided her around a mound on the grassy slope. "Hmm, well, I've a sister and brother, yes. Well, two brothers, but one has since passed."

"I'm sorry." A long pause. "Who taught you the healing?"

"My mother. She also has the gift."

A coughing fit seized Margaret, and they halted. She lifted a kerchief to her face. Gwyn now saw why Alroy MacCoinneach chose to entrust the priests with her care. Certainly he cared for his wife, from what she could deduce, but these men of religion were not disgusted by her deformed figure, and the air here *felt* clean. The scent of the river, fresh and pure, drifted to her on a breeze.

Bring me mercy, Eir. This healing would take many breaths from her.

Simon hurried to their side. "Here." He handed a flask of what smelled like a fragrant wine to his mother. She sipped, took a deep breath, and they continued.

"This healing is a gift? You are not learned like our healers and priests?"

Gwyn shrugged. "Well, aye, I'm learned. My mother taught me much about herbs and their healing properties." All ears were upon her. She consciously forced her limbs to relax.

Simon corked the flask and took his mother's other arm. "Gwyn utilizes the gifts of water and earth's elements. The Ancients have strong, unique abilities. Gwyn can heal. I told you she was special."

Her jaw dropped. He shared a look with her, eyes glinting, auburn-stubble chin spreading in a smile. Only a few weeks ago, he'd insisted her work to be heathen and blasphemy of his one god, and now he spoke the contrary. Did he finally believe her? Or had he believed all along, hiding it beneath an exterior of stubbornness?

His affirmation negated her theory he was ashamed of her origins. It warmed her spirit.

"She healed my arm from festering, and she healed my knee," he added.

Margaret's mouth formed an O, and she nodded. "Divine intervention. God works in miraculous ways. You're an inspiring woman, Gwyn. I'd love to learn more."

"I'm only a conduit for greater powers, my lady." Her chest tightened with palpitations. His knee had not been healed. It had been a ghost wound. His mind and heart needed to release the lie he told himself about the knee, and that was all she had done. Guilt plagued her nonetheless.

"So you use water for healing, Gwyn?" Margaret asked. "That's why we're going to the river?"

"Yes, my lady."

They drew upon the shore, and thankfully the questions ceased. How could she possibly explain the mystical power of water and her gods? That a few simple chants, water, and touch could make a lame man walk...and could heal the disease within. Margaret's condition was unlike anything she'd seen before. It also appeared to be in a later stage. Frenchman's disease. Gor. That's what Simon called it. Given Margaret's state, it looked like it had chewed away at her bones, and only the gods knew what else it had done internally. This would take many breaths. It would leave her bedridden for days. Graces, it *might* work.

"Simon, please sit with her here, on the shore. My lady, may we dip your feet in? I will then use water on your skin." Simon sat on the grass and his mother reclined against him.

Margaret nodded. Abbot Oliver removed her slippers. Gwyn thrust a nervous hand into her pocket, seeking the stone. As if it knew, it emanated a strong heat already.

Her pulse fitful, her breath catching in anticipation, she knelt beside Margaret. "There, there," she said, guiding Margaret's feet into the water. She withdrew the stone and rolled it around in her palm. She then dunked it into the water and used it to drip water on any exposed area of Margaret's body...her ankles and toes, lower calves, hands, neck, and finally her face. "Close your eyes and breathe. Focus on your breathing. Take deep inhalations and exhalations. Imagine you're breathing in new life. There, yes, like that."

Nobody spoke.

She channeled Jörd, Eir, and Bylgia...earth, healing, and water in one. It was a different trinity from the Scots', but a powerful one. She reached into the water count-less times with the stone and her other hand, cupping the fresh river water and trickling it over Margaret. She repeated her words in her mind until she spun with dizzi-ness.

Pull breath from my body.

Heal this woman with my own breath.

May it flow through her veins from my heart to her heart.

The sacrifice of a Healer.

May this woman's days be evermore.

The wind whipped around her, the earth hummed, and her breath escaped. Her chest quivered as the heat sliced through her core. Her heartbeat was a hundred hooves, her head a thumping drum. *One more time, one more time,* she told herself. She reached into the water with the stone again, her entire body shaking, fingers chilled despite the burning in her palm. Her soul drained from the effort.

Yet again, she said in her mind:

Pull breath from my body.

Heal this woman with my own breath.

May it flow through her veins from my heart to her heart.

The sacrifice of a Healer—

Then all she saw was darkness.

CHAPTER TEN

Still beleaguered by healing Lady Margaret, Gwyn was hardly aware of her chamber door opening in the dimness. Was it night? And what night? The hearth sizzled. She grew flushed from the choking heat in the room, and her mouth was parched. How many days had it been? A log popped, fell off the burning pile, and the light from it quickly reduced.

The opening, then closing of the chamber door provided a moment's rush of respite. She had slept, dreamless, in a nearly dormant state.

Perhaps one of the priests had come in to check on her? To tend the fire? She stirred.

Nay, the man, for there were no other women here at the abbey except for Lady Margaret, approached her bed evidenced only by his dark, wide outline. Simon? Palpitations erupted within her chest. How she secretly longed for him to come to her. Not now. She was so tired.

Oh, but that he did.

She brushed the bedclothes aside, too hot, too delirious to say anything. Nor did *he* speak as his hand fell upon her ankle. She wore only her shift, and his other hand found the hem of it and pushed it halfway up her thigh. His lips found her calf and kissed it. Confusion rippled through her. She swam in and out of murky haze.

Memories flooded back to her. First the healing at the river. She remembered Simon bringing her here to rest. It had taken many breaths from her.

This man climbed upon her bed and kissed her legs in anything but a gentlemanly way—

This was not like Simon. She was in no way recovered enough to do this. What he required as her husband, she had to remind herself. It was not her place to deny him. When her stamina returned, she would delight in being with him. She longed to be distracted from the eddy in her soul.

Not like this.

She swallowed as both his lips and his thick beard tickled the inside of her knee. Something wasn't right. Trembles stole the heat from her skin. Simon lacked a full beard. Had she imagined that sensation?

"Simon...I...oh...," she said through a choked groan as he shoved her shift up to reveal her nudity beneath. She laid her hands on his head, then his shoulders. "Perhaps when I feel better. Oh!" His mouth was on her inner thigh.

She pushed him away. He grabbed her hands in one of his, pinching, and pinning them to her chest. One hand came and squeezed her breast until it hurt.

His face was buried between her thighs, and she wiggled. He fought her movements and licked the inside of her thigh. He bit, and pain pierced her skin. His mouth then moved higher.

Her mind sharpened in a fraction of a moment, and she shoved him off her with all the strength she could summon before he could reach the part of her meant to be shared with only her husband.

This was not Simon.

Caught off guard by her quick move, he tumbled with a grunt on the bed.

She leapt to her side table to locate her dagger. Instinct told her it was there, always a breath's distance away, and always unsheathed. Yes. There. *Thank you, Simon.* She wielded it in front of her with shaking fingers. Through blinks, she saw the intruder clearly as her eyes adjusted to the dim room.

Leidolf rose from the bed and stood before her.

He chortled. He then licked his lips. "You give me but a taste and then deny me?" He stepped closer.

She swiped blindly.

He sidestepped but did not pull his own weapon.

He laughed again.

She swiped with intention.

The dagger caught his arm. He winced, and then laughed again.

What kind of sick beast was he?

"Get out of here!" she screamed. Who would hear her? Margaret was probably in herbal-induced oblivion and Simon was residing in the guest house outside, from what she could remember in her foggy memory. The priests and abbot roomed on the lower level. She had nobody. The priests had no weapons or guards. Why was Simon not in the main building, guarding her?

"Not until I get what is rightfully mine!" He lunged. His audacity startled her, and she tripped on the rushes and collided with the stone wall. He fell against her. He was a larger man up close and stronger than she anticipated. Bog myrtle ale filled his breath.

He grabbed her wrist and smacked it against the hard wall. The dagger tumbled to the floor in a thump and it was swallowed by the rushes. Pain shot down her arm. She squelched a scream, stamped her bare foot on his boot, and released another cry. His fingernails bore into her skin.

She prayed for the powers of the earth and fought him.

He pinned her to the wall. She grew dizzy with the effort. His bearded mouth claimed hers, and she thought she might retch. She altered her strategy and slowed her fighting. She tabulated the rest of the assets in the room: pitcher, water basin, candlesticks, and the fire poker beside the hearth.

She drew a hoarse breath as he pulled his mouth back. "All right. Yes," she said.

Dumbfounded, he stopped. His eyes were black and unfathomable. Resolve forced her to steady herself. She could do this. Truth hit her. Leidolf had tracked them. He followed them, found them here at the abbey. Had he been watching all along? Had he been *hunting* them?

She lowered her hands, palms up in offering. "It is me you want." She tried to smile coyly.

"You *are* mine."

"Then you may have me," she said, creeping around to sit on her bed. She sat near the head of her bed, beside the table, and nearer the thick clay water basin. She dropped a hand to her shift's loose V-shaped opening at her neck. Her hand shook as she distracted his gaze with her fingertip sliding down her neck.

He then loosened his hose, all the while their eyes locked on each other.

He knelt before her, placed both hands on her knees, shoved up her shift, and parted her quaking legs to continue what he had begun earlier.

It was the moment she needed.

She beckoned Jörd. She grabbed the basin with both hands, lifted it, and smashed it upon the crown of his head. Bits of clay flew everywhere.

He slumped to the floor, motionless.

Wind flew into the room as the door flung open, and all blurred before her as several people stormed in. She jumped to her feet and made for the hearth. She grabbed the poker and spun to face the doorway, ready for another attack.

Simon led the charge, and she dropped the poker, falling into his arms with utter relief and exhaustion. Her lungs rattled, her mind spun, and she passed out.

Simon tossed Leidolf down the steps into the dungeon. It was ironic the abbey had such a place. With the raids unleashed upon the mainland over hundreds of years by the Nordmen and other invaders, it was a necessity, sadly.

Now one of those same invaders rolled to a stop and hit the stone wall with a thud. Blood smeared a path down the roughly chiseled stone steps. He was still unconscious.

Why wouldn't the beast wake? Had Gwyn smashed his wits completely from him? Simon wanted to beat him to a mash and then run him through. The priests and Abbot Oliver would have no such sacrilege on their holy property. So the dungeon it was.

Oliver placed a hand on his shoulder. "Come, Simon. Let's get him on the cot."

"He deserves no such thing." Simon shrugged from the touch. He trudged down the stairs and stood over Leidolf. He knelt and removed Leidolf's sword and dagger, then patted his body for any other weapon. He fought the temptation to cut the bastard's nasty beard off while he slept.

"I'll take those."

Simon plopped the weapons into Oliver's small hands. Oliver laid them on a chair beside the cell's door. He paused, then squatted and drew his hands under Leidolf's armpits. He huffed and made little progress on his own, for Oliver's strength was his words, not his muscle. He was older than Simon's father, almost too slender from fasting, and wrinkled beyond his years. What he lacked in girth, he made up for in spirit though.

He heaved an irritated sigh and gently pushed Oliver aside. "I'll do it." He dragged Leidolf to the simple cot and dropped him upon it with one quick motion.

"I'll bring food."

"No." Simon gritted his teeth and paced, his heartbeat roaring in his skull. Visions of the incident in Gwyn's room flashed in his head like a nightmare.

Oliver pressed his lips together and glided to the sconces nearest to the cot. He drew a flint from his pocket, poured oil into each from an urn on the floor, and then lit them. "Every man merits compassion."

"Not him."

"Yes, even him."

Simon drummed a finger on the door while Oliver pulled the blanket over Leidolf's limp body. Finally, Oliver returned to the hallway and closed the door. He pulled a key ring from his pocket.

"I'll have Bernard stand guard and bring things to clean his wound—"

"No."

"Simon."

"Food and drink, through the lower slot, that's it. That bastard will wake and strangle you if you tend to him. Let his wounds hasten his journey to hell."

Oliver sighed. "This man was alone?" Oliver fiddled, trying to find the right iron key. The key ring clattered against the heavy oak door.

"Aye. From what I know." His fist ached from clenching. He'd seen both the doused fire in the Highland pass and the meal remnants outside Geordie's ale house. They had been followed. Both had been left there on purpose. Gwyn could have been hurt or far worse. God's teeth, this man was cunning. Simon had underestimated him.

He measured the room through the small circular peephole in the door. Barely three fingers could reach through. It, along with the slender food slot near the bottom, provided enough air for a prisoner. There was no escape. No windows. The cell was made of solid stone, deep in the belly of the abbey near the west door of the nave.

"I'll wait here for Bernard," Simon said.

Oliver nodded and ascended the stairs to the exterior door, his habit swishing with carefully placed steps.

The priests had nothing in the way of weapons. Simon rubbed his temple and paced in the narrow hallway as he discerned any possible way Leidolf could escape. He'd search the grounds for evidence of any others. Bernard would likely have a dagger, though he wouldn't employ it. The entranceway was hidden from outside at least. He could use Errol or Henry right now. Priests couldn't fight an intruder with prayers. He had only priests and an injured, spent wife. Though she *had* done a fine job smashing the clay basin on Leidolf's head.

The thought brought a small satisfied smirk to his face. It quickly disappeared. She'd been asleep for nearly two bloody days. When she'd explained before that healing taxed her, he didn't think she meant like *that*. He should have known after seeing her fatigue when helping the man in the woods. Yet, fool that he was, he'd kept insisting on her healing his mother. Christ, what if she hadn't awoken in time when Leidolf came in?

What the hell was he to *do* with Leidolf?

Keep him here? Send a messenger to Eilean Donan? Side trip north to Edinburgh and seek his father? Tie up the bearded fiend and drag him to Eilean Donan?

Or run the Lochlanach through?

His eyes swam with red. This entire thing could end now if he killed him. So what was stopping him?

Goddamn mercy.

It would be the death of humankind.

He squinted through the hole at Leidolf's unconscious form.

And seethed.

A hand on his shoulder jolted him to the present. He whirled to see Bernard standing behind him, pale-faced. "Och, sorry, Simon. Didn't mean to startle ye."

"You have a dagger and the keys?"

Bernard nodded. He drew his hood over his head and sat on a nearby chair. Tucked under his arm were a Bible, parchment, and quill. "God is with me."

Simon grunted. "Aye. Any disturbances from within, come get me."

"Of course."

Despite the uneasy dread in his chest, Simon climbed the steps, his mind churning. He settled on the most civil option. A messenger. His father was staying in Edinburgh for a few days. The message would find him. He'd know what to do. Then they could kill him together.

After checking on his dozing mother and searching the grounds, Simon made his way to Gwyn's room.

Buried within a thickly-woven wool blanket, she sat in a chair beside the crackling hearth. The priests had already cleaned the clay basin pieces on the floor. He rubbed a hand across his face. What the devil time was it anyway? He suspected the sun would rise soon. He entered, mindful of his steps. "Gwyn?"

She turned to face him, her hands cradled around a goblet. "Simon."

He closed the door. His jaw ached, and a pinching headache spread across his forehead. The only door with a lock was the dungeon. Oliver had quite a few keys on that key ring though. That issue would need to be remedied. These priests were naïve. An attack could come. He approached her. A steamy and aromatic brew with spiced apples emanated from the goblet, likely from one of the priests' ciders. He was glad they had brought something to calm her.

"I'll stay with you the rest of tonight, aye?" He hovered near.

She nodded and sipped. "What did you do with him?"

"He's in the dungeon."

"The abbey has a dungeon?" She rose and approached the bed. Forgetting modesty, she tossed the blanket on the foot of the bed and climbed beneath the bedclothes in only her shift. She moved fluidly, sedately. Simon tried to not notice the outline of her breasts, the curve of her hips, and the thinness of the material. The priests had likely given her a nip of whisky in her hot cider. Perhaps she was also still fatigued from the healing?

He cleared his throat...and his mind. "Aye, it does. For contingencies. Gwyn, are you well?"

She lay back on her pillow and curled to her side. Her hair fell about her face in torrents of black. Firelight reflected in her smooth skin. "Yes."

"Truly? You're not hurt?" He suppressed the temper rising within.

"No, I'm well, Simon," she murmured.

His heart rate didn't slow. "I'll find blankets and sleep beside the hearth."

She stared at him. "On the cold stone floor and rushes? No. This bed is awfully comfortable. Please, Simon." She lifted the bedclothes open.

He tilted his head to the side, weighing his choices. "I can—"

Her brow furrowed, and hurt welled in her eyes. "Just sleep, Simon. We both need it," she said, her voice small, breathless. "You won't toss me," she teased.

"Och, aye." He turned away and kicked off his boots and then unbelted his tunic. Untucking his long tunic shirt and allowing it to fall loosely to mid-thigh, he slid out of the hose and tossed them beside the boots.

He slipped beneath the opened bedclothes and faced her. Unease burned his ears, and he was grateful for the minimal light the fire provided so she couldn't see his awkwardness mingled with arousal. He made room between them.

"Gwyn."

"Yes?"

"You had me scared out of my wits. You were asleep for nearly two days," he said, fighting for composure. Christ, he thought he'd killed her. Well, not him. His request. For his mother. He breathed heavily.

She closed her eyes. "Och, well, yes. Healing does tire me. I should be better by morn."

Tire her? She'd nearly died. Two days asleep. Not asleep but in an exhausted state. He wanted to argue, instead he said, "Sweet dreams, Gwyn." He brushed a hand down her cheek.

"Good night, Simon," she said, her breath fragrant with apples and whisky.

He lay there for a long time, watching as she fell into a disturbed slumber, her breathing ragged at times. He pushed loose tendrils away from her forehead, his finger lingering on her cheek. The desire to kiss her pounded in his core, but that would have to wait.

On the morn, he'd send a messenger to his father. The Nordmen had destroyed many lives already. He couldn't bear it if Gwyn had also been hurt. Aye, this madness needed to cease. If war didn't come to them, he'd bring it to their shores.

Leidolf awoke to a splitting headache. He cracked his sore jaw and licked dry lips. Where the hell was he? He blinked several times, and each time, the amber-rust blobs in the darkness across from him flickered but resumed their obscurity.

He closed his eyes and listened, trying to drown the ache within his head.

Dripping water. A light breeze whistled in a narrow passageway. He rested his hands at his sides upon a scratchy wool blanket. A man coughed from nearby, keys jingling.

By the gods, he was in a cell.

Dark oblivion swept him away again.

He kept waking to horrible visions. Bloody battles. Wolves' teeth. His father beating him to a pulp using the wooden shaft of his spear in front of their entire village. Magnor and Hallbjorn locking him in a chest once for days, to be left in a putrid puddle of his own filth. Another time they barricaded him in one of the outbuildings.

Memories he had shoved away long ago came bubbling to the surface in infernal and constant nightmares.

His hand glided to his side. His dagger and sword were both missing. He had no axe. All he had was his belt and pouch. Instead of running his fingers over the gemstones to ease his muddled mind, he undid the belt.

That whore. She was no better than a common thrall. To think he was prepared to treat her as his queen while he ruled over Uist.

She would pay.

He slipped his hand down his hose and brought himself quickly to a stiff longing. He thought about how he'd slowly kill Simon in front of the witch. He'd let the blood spill over her naked skin, yes, then while the fox was still dying, ravage her in front of him.

Soon enough.

If Steinthor and Donner had reached the set meeting point at Halvor's tavern outside Edinburgh, they'd find the message he'd left for them. After discovering Simon and Gwyn at the abbey, leaving a message for his men had been a wise move. He thanked the gods for that insight. They would come here to break him out of this hell hole. Or so he hoped the two dolts would make sense of it.

Soon.

Morning came and went.

Finally, when the rays of afternoon brightened her room, Gwyn stirred from bed as the door creaked open—and with it, a rush of vivid, painful, disgusting memories.

She shot upright and lunged for the dagger that had found its place again on her side table.

She spun to face the door to see a startled Simon frozen in his spot, a tray of food in his hands. "'Tis me."

Her heartbeat frantic, she drew herself up and brought the bedclothes to her chest. She remembered Simon sharing the bed with her the night before. She placed the dagger upon the table with a shaking hand.

She swallowed, encouraging the soothing idea of him in her bed last night to suppress the memory of Leidolf's touch upon her skin.

Simon approached and laid the tray on the table. He remained standing. "You must be hungry and parched. You've slept all day again."

She nodded. "Aye." Trying for lightness, she said, "You're always bringing me food."

He rubbed his chin and shifted his feet. "Well, it's something I'm good at. Some other things...not so much."

"Sit, Simon."

He did but not close to her.

"What is it?" she asked, picking up a piece of toasted bread. She spread a berry jam, bit into it, and moaned, realizing her hunger. She'd not eaten in two days.

"Why didn't you tell me this happens? After a healing? And did he...did he..." His cheeks flushed and eyes sharpened like a bird wanting to kill something.

"No. He didn't do anything. Just grabbed at me." Well, that was a partial truth. Sickness joined hunger in her stomach. "Some healings take more from me. Your mother's illness was in its later stages. It took many breaths from me."

"What do you mean? Many breaths?"

She deliberated. "It's hard to explain."

"I've time."

She wet her lips. "Whenever I heal, it takes some of my breaths."

"You said. You always recover, aye? It just winds you like you've been punched?"

She sighed. "Not quite."

He furrowed his brows.

"I lose some of my breaths permanently," she said, sipping an herbal infusion. Spicy, it was a welcome on her palate. She tasted a nip of whisky in the drink.

"For all that is holy, what does that mean, Gwyn?"

"It's too hard to explain."

He crossed his arms. His brown eyebrows dipped deeper. "Try."

"It means I lose moments or years off my life. My heart grows weaker. Is that what you wanted to hear?" she said, raising her voice.

"Sweet Christ," he murmured. Then he was quiet, restive.

There it was—the look she didn't want to see in his face.

He took her hand in his. Slowly, he drawled, "How do you know?"

"There are benefits to the gifts of the Ancients. There are also sacrifices. My mother has told me, for she is descended from Healers, and she has seen with her own eyes the toll it takes on our kind. She personally has given many of her breaths. She cannot possibly give more or it will be her last," she said, a heaviness filling her chest. "That's why neither she nor I can heal Kendrick."

She took their linked hands and traced over his fingers, each stroke a slow caress with her other hand. Auburn hairs shimmered on his knuckles. "Kendrick, as a Feeler, his fate is uncertain as few Feelers have lived as long as he. I often wonder if his blindness is related to his ability or had arisen purely by chance. He gets awful headaches with his gift, and he can feel the pain of the dying. If he's around too many deaths at once, it can wreak havoc upon him. Seers, I've been told, could lose their power to foresee, or it could become hazy and ambiguous if used too often...and could tell lies. Venora's ability is strong. Healers like myself, well, our hearts grow weak as each breath of our energy is shared to heal others. The more demanding the healing, the more breaths. At some point we must stop, or it will kill us."

Simon's voice was slow and agitated. "I forced you to heal my mother. You've lost some of your life because of it. Because of me."

She squeezed his hand tighter. "I *chose* to heal her. Nobody can force me, Simon. Not even you," she said with a nervous laugh.

"I'm sorry, Gwyn."

She raised a hand to his cheek. She loved the heat of it beneath her palm. "I chose to do it. I do *not* regret it. I don't regret any of my healings. It's my fate."

"But you—"

She stopped his words with a kiss. His lips were tender and receptive in return. She drew a hand through his coarse hair, then to his cheek as she pulled back slowly. "No regrets."

He swallowed, deep eyes boring into her. He heaved a sigh. "How are you feeling?"

She licked her lips and inhaled. "Better."

"Would you like an afternoon walk before the sun sets?"

"I would. Simon?"

He rose and turned. "Aye?"

"How is she? How is your mother?"

He smiled. "Resting, but she's not asked for any poppy today or yesterday. She seems alert, more alive than I've seen in years. You did this."

Gwyn breathed a sigh of relief. Good. She couldn't tell Simon she had been deeply concerned Margaret's condition was too far gone for even the power of Eir.

After tucking Gwyn in for the evening and promising to return momentarily, Simon made his way to the dungeon. The memory of sharing the bed with her last night filled his body with a renewed energy. He wasn't sure how much longer he could wait before he made her his wife in body. What was stopping him?

He sighed. He was a fool. Any other man would've bedded her as soon as the vows had been spoken. Yet, she was a precious jewel that needed to be treated as such. If he waited much longer though, he'd likely find himself burst into pieces.

Good sense told him to wait to confront Leidolf until after his father arrived in a few days—it would take time for the messenger to get to Edinburgh, locate his father, and then return to the abbey. Yet here he was, descending the slick stone stairs, carrying a lantern. Distracted with his riled thoughts, he slipped on the wet bottom step, caught his hand on the corner, and righted himself.

Bernard looked up from his reading. "Och, Simon. What brings ye here? We've already served him his supper."

"I wish to speak with him. He's awake?"

Angst wrinkled Bernard's leathery brow. "Aye, he comes and goes. Mumbles and curses. Nothing the Lord won't forgive. He paces. He stopped banging on the door an hour ago." He rubbed the back of his head, where his brown hair thinned from the habit. "He certainly tests a man's vow of silent observation."

Simon grunted. "I want to go in."

Bernard tucked a hand in his pocket, where surely the keys resided. "Abbot Oliver said nobody goes in. We serve his meals through the slot as ye requested. He has a chamber pot and blanket for comfort. A flask of wine should last a day or so."

Simon gritted his teeth. He knocked on the heavy wood. "Wake, you dolt!"

Leidolf cackled. His laugh held an eerie familiarity, but Simon couldn't place it.

A sour taste slid down Simon's throat and settled in his gut, upsetting his evening meal. "Coward, come speak with me."

"What's there to speak about, my fox?"

Fox? What the devil? "We had a deal."

"A deal you'd never see through. You think me dimwitted? I knew you'd take her away from me and never return her. Isn't that why you came to the abbey? To hide your prized hare?"

Simon grunted.

"Does she know you've sealed her brother's fate with your own selfishness?"

Simon peeked through the small, round hole to find Leidolf reclined in his cot, hands behind his head and sneering at him. "You and I both know that agreement would have never seen fruition."

"Her father planned to kill the lad if I didn't return. I've sent my men in my stead to Blasius. Kendrick is as good as dead. In fact, my men are likely already there, and I gave them orders. Kendrick is dead because of you, Simon MacCoinneach."

Bloody hell, Leidolf needed to stop using his name. "Let's take up swords now, coward." Simon's fingers danced on his sword's hilt.

Bernard coughed nervously behind him.

Leidolf grinned, the low light from the sconces twisting his face, giving him the look of a demon.

"Do you not know how to kill a man, Leidolf?"

"You know nothing about me, red fox. I enjoy sinking my teeth into my prey."

Simon felt the vein pulsing at his temple. This man was madder than Blasius.

"So what say you? Swords, here?"

Leidolf closed his eyes. "Your day is coming. Sooner than you think, fox."

Simon slammed a fist into the door, not caring that it bloodied his knuckles. He stormed up the steps. This was falling apart, and he fully regretted asking for his father to come. A quick kill and it could be over. Until his father's arrival, he'd wait. If no further news, then Leidolf would die. To hell with mercy.

"Blessed morning," Simon said, entering the library.

Gwyn yawned when she looked up from the pile of books and parchments splayed before her. "Good morning, Simon."

He cast a look at the parchments, and then shared a grin with her. "I've something to show you. If you'd like to take a break? If you are well?"

Her spirit lifted. Simon had been quite dour, but now he seemed more cheerful and she gladly welcomed it. "Another treasure trove of books?" she asked. She'd grown mystified by the abbey's hidden riches. The priests kept immaculate records. Over the past day, she'd pored over the books while she recuperated. It had certainly tested her knowledge of Latin, but she was able to make sense of much of it through the drawings and notes. She wanted to learn all she could about Margaret's condition. When she'd breathed life into Margaret, her focus was on the core of the disease Simon had told her about: the skin lesions, her bones, aches, and fevers. She had prayed for peace to return to Margaret's mind. Despite the healing, she couldn't fight the suspicion there was more to it. What if there were additional unknown symptoms that her healing hadn't addressed?

"Even better, I hope," Simon said.

"Now I'm intrigued." She rose, and he slid his hand into hers and guided her through the door, down the hall, and past the parlor and chapter house. They strolled through the cloister, empty of men but filled with chants echoing from the nave in morning ritual.

"How is your mother today? I was waiting for her to wake before I checked on her again."

"She's well. Her skin is clearing. She's asked to see you."

Gwyn nodded. "Good. I will visit her soon." She was eager to see her charge again, now that she herself was recovered. A quick visit yesterday afternoon found the lady sleeping, but already vibrant, healthier. He led her past the dungeon, and she couldn't help but shiver. "Have you seen him today?"

"Not yet. One of the priests will bring him his meal after their prayers."

"He's said nothing else?"

"No."

He could stay in the dungeon forever. Or ship him home to the icy Nord Land. After his attack, she was ever more grateful she had not returned to Uist to marry him...and that she was Simon's wife. In fact, she'd spent much time pondering it. She had grown fond of her Scottish husband and anticipated all their moments together.

They walked in the dewy morning grass past the west door of the nave, along two thick hedges and came upon a circular landing with a stone bench. A deeply lobed green vine climbed the trellis behind the bench. Its blooms were long since spent, now brown and unidentifiable.

"Where are we?"

"It's another prayer spot."

"It's peaceful." Her gaze went beyond them to the round hills giving way to the forest. The babble of the river sang up to them. The fresh air outside tickled her nose, and she inhaled deeply, full recovery expanding her lungs.

"I love to come here."

Simon had smiled twice in one day. It was like a new part of him appeared since Lady Margaret's healing. His spirit had emerged from a shroud, even if a dark evil lurked below them in the dungeon.

"There's something else," he said, stepping behind the trellis. He felt along the stone wall for a handle, pulled it, and a small hidden door creaked open.

She inhaled. "What is this?"

"The first abbot built this room as a safe place over a hundred years ago."

"A safe place?" Even as the question left her lips, she knew why.

He took her hand and guided her down the steep, narrow staircase. He drew a flint from his pocket and lit the sconces on the wall as they descended. The light behind them crept into and illuminated a room outfitted with three cots, feather-filled mattresses, a table, wax candles, and numerous urns, jugs, and crates.

"In case of attack, the abbot and a handful of priests could hide here."

Her stomach twisted. The Nordmen had destroyed many Scottish monasteries. The runes her father had brought from their homeland boasted of such "glories." What glory was there in killing unarmed holy men?

Dungeon. Safe chamber.

"Oh, Simon, my people have done yours so wrong," she said in a sorrowful whisper.

"Not you. Not your mother's people. Don't apologize for them. You are nothing like them—" His words caught.

She squeezed his hand. "Kiss me, Simon."

He did. His lips helped her release her pain and feel only sweet joy.

He threaded his hands through her hair and pulled her face to his. Wanting, passionate lips took hers. Although he shaved frequently, small hairs had already grown in and they tickled her chin in a welcomed familiarity.

She drew her hand boldly lower down his back to his backside. She knew not what she was doing, but she quickly prayed to Jörd to guide her and for Eir to help her heal his heart. There was no more waiting. Somewhere in her sleepy recovery, she had come to the conclusion there'd be no annulment. She was Simon's wife and he her husband.

It was time.

He quivered in her embrace but didn't move his own hands beyond the nape of her neck.

"You've not done this before?" she asked.

Instead of drawing his look away from her, he pulled back ever so slightly. His heavy, wine-laced breath fell on her cheek. His gaze impaled her. "No."

"We can learn together."

His heart drummed against her breasts. "I'm sorry, Gwyn. I can't."

"What if I said I wanted to?"

"I'll hurt you."

She took his hand and placed it on her hip. "Killing men and animals require a man to be a warrior. You need not be a warrior with me. You will not hurt me." Now she understood. Now she saw why he shied from intimacy and armored himself with indifference. It was because of what happened to his mother. Contrary to the guise, he was a passionate man.

"He could have hurt you. What if I hadn't come in?"

She raised a hand to his cheek. "You did. We can't ordain our own fates, but we can guide them. I'm skilled with the dagger, you know. And apparently a clay basin."

He suppressed an awkward laugh. He remained engaged in their embrace, life vibrating from his body. He kissed her again, and then pulled away with a heavy sigh. "I'm lost. It's too late for me. But not for you," he said through gulps. "You can find someone better. I can return you home."

She lifted her chin and took his lips in hers again. Breathless, she whispered, "I want *you*, Simon."

Simon's poor heart needed forgiveness, release of blame. *Let me heal his soul with my own*, she prayed to Eir. "It wasn't your fault. You must release the pain, Simon."

His kiss grew urgent.

"I want you. Now. Simon." She turned around to face away from him and held one of his hands, guiding it to her lacings.

His trembles became driven touches as his hands fumbled down the back of her gown and he untied the lacings. She let him, delightful shivers of desire coursing through her at his gentle, careful work. Her pulse throbbed in her ears. A hot ache grew in her fingertips. He slid his hands inside the opening of her gown, ran them to her shoulders, and paused. She laid her hands over his and helped him push the length of the gown down and caught it before it hit the dirt floor. She then turned to face him and tossed the gown on a nearby cot.

As he unlaced the ties of her undergown, the kirtle, she reached forward and lifted his shirt over his head. Her hands fell on his heaving chest, sprinkled with bristly, auburn hair. He gasped with her touch as she outlined his chest muscles. Her touch fell to his stomach, tight and firm. He froze in his untying. She finished for him and stepped out of the kirtle. Her shift was loose, and the cold dampness of the private chamber rippled gooseflesh upon her skin. The firelight in the sconces danced in a breeze floating down the stairs. Water dripped into a nearby pot.

It was oddly arousing to be in the damp, dark, quiet place of refuge. It invigorated her senses: the nearness of water, the coolness upon her flesh, the scent of herbals in one of the nearby boxes. It helped to be away from the scene of the attack. She didn't know if she could feel the same way standing in the same room, lying in the same bed. This was a new, special place, and she gloried in it. It could be their place.

She was no longer a captive. She wanted to be Simon's wife.

With a bold, deep breath, she led him to the nearest cot and removed her shift. Fully naked, she lay back and pulled him atop her. He propped himself on his elbows so he didn't pin her. She studied his face. Every errant hair, smooth curve, and sharp edge.

"I-I don't know how to—"

She silenced him with a kiss. Her hands found the top of his hose. "I'm willing to learn."

"Together," he added, hoarsely.

She slid her hands down the back of the wool hose, admiring the feel of his chiseled, taut backside beneath her fingers. She was highly aware of where his hard flesh touched her body as well. A puddle of desire radiated from within her, and she wanted nothing more than to feel their bodies interwoven as one.

She couldn't believe her own audacity, and yet, she couldn't *not* give in. For she knew he wanted it, too.

He inhaled sharply and kissed her in return, his lips longing, yearning, and passionate. He cupped her breast, and her skin tingled with his caress. His kisses drifted down her neck. She wanted his hands everywhere. She wanted to consume him, to surrender to him. He not only touched but kissed her nipples, and her mind soared to new heights.

He drew his face to meet hers.

"Blazes, Gwyn," he moaned. His chest pressed upon her. Skin to skin, breath against breath.

His rawness compelled her to capture his eyes with her own. Shadows and sconce light danced across his face like ocean waves. She spread her legs around him, clutched his backside, and guided him toward her.

She bit her lip on the momentary pain, but soon it was replaced by pleasure.

As he made love to her, Jörd hummed within their joined bodies. The sweet morning air tickled her skin, the water pinged on the walls, and the song of the distant river encircled them. Vitality's breath returned to her, strong and vigorous. They moved in a cadence of harmony as Earth's glories blessed their unity. Never before had she felt such power from the Earth. Never before had she felt such love.

CHAPTER ELEVEN

After the midday meal, which they enjoyed in the privacy of their chamber under the comfort of bed-clothes, followed by more kisses and touches, Gwyn made her way to visit Margaret, who was a short distance down the hall, while Simon went to see Abbot Oliver.

A rush bloomed within her from the intimacy of Simon's touch upon her. She hadn't expected lying with a man to be so easy or pleasurable. She could almost feel him within her still. Her knees nearly gave way remembering it. They were now married in body. *You are now his.* Her insides vibrated as she bit on a smile.

She knocked on the door. She fluffed her full skirt, straightened her back, and blew a breath as she awaited Margaret's greeting.

"Come in," Margaret's cheerful voice said.

She entered and curtsied, with another swipe of loosely plaited hair. The lass in her wondered if Margaret would know. She stumbled upon her own words. "M-My lady."

Margaret waved a hand, slender fingers a bird's wings. "Please, Gwyn, come in."

Gwyn tucked her arms at her side and slid onto a nearby chair in a whoosh of both skirt and breath.

Margaret tapped the bed. "Come."

She drifted over and sat. She shifted her mind's focus, springing into her role as Healer. Her gaze caught Margaret's effervescent brown eyes. A smile twisted its way from beneath healing sores.

"How are you feeling?"

"Very well. The fevers haven't returned. My body is far less achy than it's been in years. How do I look? I'm afraid the priests took away my mirror years ago." She tsked. "A woman knows when she appears wretched, especially with these sores over me like the worst boils."

"You look beautiful." She did not lie.

Margaret laughed. "That is doubtful. I thank you for your compliment. You have an astounding ability, Gwyn."

A breath crushed her ribs, and she clutched her stomach. "It's nothing."

"You know it's not *nothing*."

Gwyn traced a hand along her gown's skirt, following the twirling design her mother had sewn in for her. Thread rippled down the length of the green linen to end in a pool of flowers and waves to match the whitecaps rolling within her. "It is something, indeed," she admitted. What was wrong with her? She had never let humility steal her confidence. She wanted to impress Lady Margaret. The lady of Eilean Donan was Simon's mother. He had been carved within her womb. He had fought to protect her in every way, both body and soul, and had suffered greatly for it.

Could she heal him? Was she enough to conquer his raging, battered soul with her healing touch? Kendrick had certainly been correct about Simon's hurt soul.

In words a Seer like Venora could have uttered, Margaret said, "My son adores you. How did you meet?"

"Aye, well, I'm fond of him, too." She decided to sweeten the story for Margaret's sake. "He came to our home with your husband for trade." She prayed Margaret would not inquire about the brevity of their courtship...

The light in Margaret's golden eyes dimmed, and their resemblance to Simon's struck Gwyn. "My Desmond was lost in that negotiation. Alroy told me. I'm afraid I wasn't well enough to attend his funeral."

"I'm sorry. My brother died, too."

Margaret sniffed, holding back tears. "A horrible misunderstanding. Des was a good man with a good heart. Look at the union that resulted from that meeting. You and Simon. We must only look ahead now."

Gwyn nodded. "Aye." Her own voice lost its vigor, and a flood of words fell forth. "I tried to help Desmond, but he was beyond my healing ability." Her gaze returned to the hands cupped in her lap, vision blurring with tiny tears.

"Simon didn't tell me that."

"I'm sorry," she said again.

Margaret reached forward and held her hand. "Don't be sorry. When our end comes, there is nothing we can do."

"Some like to think we convey miracles, but we do not. We use the gifts bestowed upon us and harness the energy of the earth, wind, fire, and water. The rest is up to a power greater than I. We can only do so much."

"I understand."

Her face didn't lie. She understood. Oh, if Simon could see the truth. If he could see how mercy was also a way to heal. He was dead set on revenge. What would he do when he discovered Leidolf's family had been responsible for Margaret's condition? He might breach the point of darkness where there was no redeeming. Pain gripped her, replacing the beating wings of fulfillment with something vile. She needed to tell him.

"Will you and Simon be returning to Dornie soon?" Margaret asked.

Gwyn shrugged. "I don't know." She doubted Margaret knew of their prisoner in the dungeon or why he was there.

"Well, I should like to spend time with you, but I doubt I am well enough to return home yet." Her face beamed with untethered honesty.

"But you will?"

Margaret nodded. "Aye, when I am ready. Tell me more about your family."

Gwyn shifted her weight and considered what to say. She poured two goblets of the cider on the table and handed one to Margaret. "What would you like to know?"

"Are you all able to heal? What is the significance of the water? I'm afraid I don't remember much of our conversation before the healing."

Gwyn drew in a breath. She'd already shared this truth with Simon, and Margaret didn't seem like one to persecute differences. She began with hesitation. "It goes against your Christian ways."

Margaret lowered her voice. "I believe in our Almighty and trust my soul to Him, but it doesn't mean I don't appreciate the faiths of others. We are connected in the afterlife. Now, don't tell our hosts I said such a thing. They may ask me to leave!" She smiled, teeth white, spared from the illness that had wreaked havoc upon her bones.

"Do you know much about the Ancients and our beliefs?"

"I'm afraid not."

"The foundation of our religion is to depend upon the Earth, to allow her to guide us in our actions. Certainly we've been influenced by the gods of men who have come to our isles for years," she said. "Many cultures have different gods for the elements. We've embraced the ones nature has bestowed. Eir guides my healing, and water is the power of Bylgia."

Margaret nodded and adjusted herself. "It's hard for any mortal to believe in such things they cannot see, even in our own Holy Trinity."

"My younger brother, Kendrick, he has the ability to feel the lifebloods of people around him. He sees into them and can sense good or bad, life or death, and even perceive their emotions. He says we emit colors of life."

"Very intriguing! Your gift is healing alone?"

She nodded. "Aye. My mother is also a Healer and has taught me the traditional herbals, but also the ways of Eir. We all harness the Earth's energy from Jörd." She swallowed before she added, "My sister Venora is a Seer."

"Oh, I've heard of them!" she said, her voice rising. "Even the Scots believe in such things. We may be Christians, but our ways are filled with superstitions. The priests have ways steeped in fantasy and their own perception as well."

"Indeed."

Margaret tsked. "Och, but don't tell them I said that." She sighed, pulled her cap off, and ran fingers through her brown hair, which looked far less frayed since the healing. "How do you do it?"

"My mother taught me the prayers, and I focus on the person's sickness, if it is known. I must focus on the specific area to be healed. I use water and this." She withdrew the stone from her pocket. "My mother has others like it. These stones came from the mouth of a powerful waterfall in the Cuillin mountains, or I've been told. Its radiating heat has always helped me with my healings."

"Hmm, may I?" Margaret reached for it.

Gwyn passed the warm, throbbing stone to her.

"It feels like a stone to me. Cold, smooth."

Gwyn smiled. "Och, it glows like fire for me."

"You should teach the priests about your gifts."

Gwyn sipped the quickly cooling cider beside her from her own goblet. "I worry they may not be as understanding as you, my lady."

"Men never are," Margaret said, smirking. "Now, my Simon, och, you've done something to him, dear Gwyn. I see it in his eyes, in his walk. He is besotted, and that is no charm, except perhaps the delicate persuasion of the female."

Delight filled her soul. His touch upon her skin was still fresh. "He pleases me, my lady."

Now Margaret laughed. "He's a stubborn ox! He pleases nobody or nothing but himself. He used to believe as you do, in healing and mercy. That time has long since passed." Her voice drifted. She turned serious. "There is good in him, Gwyn. There was, and there still is. Whatever madness he has planned, please—" She licked her lips and began coughing. She drew in a wheeze and placed a hand upon her chest.

It stirred a warning within Gwyn. "Margaret, what troubles you?"

"Nothing," she said, waving a hand.

They sat in silence while Margaret recovered from her coughing fit and sipped the cider.

Again, she said with her purposeful smile, "You'll stand by his side, Gwyn?"

"Of course, my lady. I am his wife."

"He seeks..." She pursed her lips. "Never mind. He's a moral man."

"I know."

"A mother always worries about her children. With my Desmond gone, Simon is all I have."

"I'll care for him."

"I know you will, dear. He may stumble, but he has a good heart."

Gwyn's own heart palpitated, reminding her how many breaths she'd already lost with her healing. If only love could heal the breaths lost.

Late afternoon came, and Simon's father did not. Surely he'd arrive upon the morn. His father wouldn't refuse the chance to confront Leidolf on their own terms. The presence of their captive penetrated Simon's soul and brought a heavy cloud upon the abbey, so a ride with Gwyn might do his spirit well. He loved to feel her in the saddle with him.

Heaviness would not leave his chest.

What had he become?

He had killed her kinfolk, Rothwell and Trygg. If Desmond hadn't intervened, he would have been the one to kill Gunnar. The truth darkened his spirit. He had been the one who started the fight on Uist. He wanted to hide from it. He would have killed Gwyn's brother. Without a blink of conscience. Instead, a man who hated to take up the sword, his brother Des, had been the one to kill Gunnar.

He was also was a thief, having stolen Gwyn.

And a liar. He'd promised to care for her brother Kendrick in return for her acquiescence. Now the lad was dead.

He didn't deserve her.

"Almost there," he said, shifting his focus to the ride.

Gwyn sat in front in their shared saddle. Her hair whipped his face, momentarily dislodging his blazing purgatory.

Farmland stretched over the ground in patterned flaxen patches similar to a quilt. Three hills dominated, standing mighty over the countryside. It was his favorite place, close enough to the serenity of the abbey, but far enough away from the clutches of his mother's illness.

An illness that was no more. Because of Gwyn. "Almost secretive in their allure," she said as they approached a cluster of oaks on a knoll.

"Interesting choice of words." As they reached the overlook, he dismounted and offered her a hand.

"Why?"

His hands lingered on her hips as she steadied herself upon the ground. He closed the space between them, resting his own hips against hers in a nearness he never would have ventured only weeks before with any lass. Gwyn was unlike any woman he'd met in tavern or merchant village. He tucked dancing waves of hair behind one of her ears, pausing to trace a finger down her neck. She was a glorious distraction from his misery.

"There used to be an old Roman fort here, at the foot of that tallest hill," he said, spinning them half a circle, one hand still on her hip. He pointed toward the highest peak. "Sometimes you can find the occasional gold coin here."

"The Romans?" She scrunched her brow. "Yes, I've read about them. Their conquests took them far."

He held in his response. He loved how his wife enjoyed reading and education. *His wife.* He shivered, reminded of their lovemaking.

He turned to Gwyn. Her eyes were lost in contemplation as she took in the sight before them. Gray clouds crawled across the sky, darkening the late afternoon sun, and the three peaks slowly became obscured.

She broke from his hold and sat on a large rock near the oaks. "Simon?"

There it was again. The way she said his name, like sweet butter on a fresh biscuit. The fine hairs on his neck prickled. He'd give a thousand breaths to have her say his name for the rest of his days. She didn't have a thousand breaths anymore though.

Because of him. Curse him. To the black clutches of hell may he be damned if he put another person in harm's way to appease his insatiable need for repentance. Not once had his mother expressed acrimony toward him for what had happened. He punished himself enough for it.

"Simon," her melodious voice said again, a pleasant jay in springtime.

"Hmm, aye?"

"You were mumbling under your breath. Is everything all right?"

He stared at her. "Aye."

He approached. She took his hand in hers. His was chilled from the day, and hers always seemed warm, from a mystical internal hearth.

"When do we return to Eilean Donan?" she asked.

"As soon as my father arrives, we can decide our best plan of action."

"Will you kill Leidolf?"

"I don't know." That was indeed the truth. Och, he could do this. Truth only. No more lies.

They sat in silence for a while, watching the clouds wave across the sky and the workers toil in the distance as wind rippled the fields. Gwyn had not asked about Kendrick recently. Christ, she trusted him. Had his selfishness also doomed Kendrick? Was Leidolf right? A shred of hope remained that Leidolf was a liar, that Kendrick was still alive.

"Simon."

If she said his name again he wasn't sure if it would pierce his heart with its tenderness or suspicion.

"Kiss me again," she said, chin up, eyes blazing.

Yes.

He could see why men spent hours in the arms of women. Gwyn numbed the pain. Even if only for a few moments, he could forget his daily hell.

He planted his lips upon hers, too eager to feel the release again. Och, did she heal with her body and tongue, too? He didn't care. He wanted every part of her. Pressing his hand into the small of her back, he pulled her closer. He cupped her chin with his other hand, and his mind nearly erupted when she moaned as he tasted her lips and mouth. Sweet heaven, that tongue.

Desire surged within him as their touching grew intimate. He would strip her naked if it weren't for the fact they were exposed on the knoll. No, he couldn't.

Instead, he ripped himself from her for but a moment. Her confused, tremulous smile asked him the question he wanted to answer with his body. "Come," he said. He stood and guided her, his arm around her waist, to a tree beside their grazing horse. With one hand, he dug into the satchel and withdrew a blanket.

He stepped from their embrace momentarily to spread it beneath the shade of a willow tree and behind the large rock. He'd always loved this tree, if it were possible for a man to love a tree. Never before had he brought a lass here, not even in his adolescent days before his life was shattered. Before he vowed to never love nor touch a woman.

Gwyn broke that into pieces.

He sat on the blanket and brought her into his lap. "Hmm," she said in a near purr.

"I need you again, Gwyn. Will you have me?"

"Here?"

Heat flooded his cheeks. He couldn't wait to make love to her in their own private chamber once they returned to Eilean Donan, and he didn't dare take her in that bed where Leidolf had pawed at her.

"Aye," he murmured with a lift of his palm to her cheek. He drew his hand slowly down her smooth skin, stopping at the nape of her neck. "Och, you are well."

She responded with another deep, soul-drenching kiss. He drew her head closer with both hands, winding his fingers through the waterfall that was her hair. Half of it had become unplaited, and he finished the job with a few swift movements.

She already had him. She'd had him from the first moment she healed him at the merchant's tavern in Loch nam Madadh. She couldn't know, but she'd captured his heart weeks ago. She'd stripped the shield away in a matter of seemingly tiny moments.

That they'd only begun to discover the bodily relationship between husband and wife didn't deter him from moving forward boldly. He'd always been a fast learner. He traced her collarbone with his lips. He moved to her ear and nibbled, teasing her with hot breath upon gooseflesh-covered skin. They moved as if longtime lovers, exploring each other's body through the fabric separating them. "Oh, Simon," she said, stroking his chin.

"Gwyn, you've about stolen all of me."

"I wish to steal more than your body."

"You have." He crushed her lips with his. Forget teasing. He needed her before he burst again.

Gasping, but returning the kiss, she reached one hand inside his tunic and found his chest. She rubbed her thumb over his nipple, bringing it to fullness, matching something much lower on him. He'd not allowed desire to rule his life for so long, but when she touched him, he lost all resolve. When he had joined his body with hers, plunging deep into her essence and bringing himself to a pinnacle of sensation, all the bandages from his old wound disappeared.

"Share your mercy with me, Gwyn," he whispered in her ear. She repositioned herself upon him so she straddled his legs, her skirts hitched up to her hips. They locked gazes. God, he couldn't let her see his frailty. He had to be strong. He had to—

"Simon..."

"Oh my God," he moaned as her fingers fell upon the top of his hose with no hesitation. He inhaled the earthy fragrance and sweet rosewater in her hair, muffling a curse as she slid a hand inside. He focused on her face. Her eyes were uncharted, heavenly stars.

Flashes of light burst behind his closed eyes as she caressed the length of him. He untied her gown layers with eager fingers, moving deftly through the lacings until her perfect breasts fell forth. He drew his mouth to one and sighed as she continued her fondling. She'd bring him to release in moments if she continued.

He changed tactic. As badly as he wished to see her fully naked again, it would have to wait until the sanctity of their own bedchamber. Arm around her waist, he shifted her and switched places with her, laying her back upon the blanket. He kissed her while his fingers roamed down to her stomach, then farther lower, beneath her skirt, to the smoothness of her thigh. He pushed the layers of skirts into a ruffled mess about her hips. He broke from their kiss and drew his mouth down to her thigh to taste her sweet nectar. She quivered beneath him and whispered words in Norse he didn't know. When she moaned, "Simon," it drove him further.

"When you say my name," he began between kisses on that soft flesh that defined her as a woman, "it drives me to sheer madness. You taste like, hmm..."

"Simon..."

She was everything he had imagined as he kissed the soul of her being, his tongue eager and exploring. He cupped her bottom, and her muscles pulsed around him. Her thighs clenched, her bottom rose, and her moan carried on the wind. Och, she was divine.

He nearly lost himself with her writhing but forced his mind and body to steady. He needed to be inside her. He needed to feel her.

He took her hand and guided her to sit upright with him. He leaned against the tree again. Her cheeks were flushed, her breathing rapid, and with a subtle rise and him lifting her hips, he guided her onto his lap...and onto him.

"By God," he said through gritted teeth as she swayed upon him, their bodies joined once again. He had never known it could be this way.

She released a whimper, saying his name again and again. "Simon, Simon, Simon...oh..."

He held her bottom, the heat of her flesh searing his fingers as he encouraged her faster, harder, until he could last no longer. He drew one hand to her neck and locked eyes with her as he gave in to the decadence.

She crumpled against him and rested her forehead upon his shoulder, their hearts thumping.

He closed his eyes and drank in her mercy as it poured through him, forever changed. He would do whatever was required of him so she could live the rest of her breaths with him at Eilean Donan. He would never let anyone steal the breaths from her again.

The day darkened with evening shadows when they finally made their way to the abbey. Gwyn's whole body still pulsed from Simon's lovemaking.

As they drew upon the edge of the meadow, where abbey grounds met forest, the horse grew agitated. Its ears twitched.

"Easy, easy. We're going back to the abbey. Hush, hush," Simon cooed.

Gwyn rubbed the horse's withers. Its skin trembled beneath her fingers. The horse snorted.

"What is it?" she asked Simon in a whisper. "Something's amiss."

They turned on the path.

"Hush, sweet thing. 'Tis fine. See? Your friends are there near the stable yonder." He pulled gently on the reins. The horse squealed. It startled the life from Gwyn.

"What the—" Simon said.

She fumbled in her seat and would have ended up dumped upon the ground if it weren't for her death grip on the pommel.

Gwyn almost vomited. In front of them, in a heap of white robes beside a tree, was a priest. Blood seeped into the ground.

The horse snorted, hard.

Simon dismounted, helped Gwyn, and then he drew the nervous horse away.

"Bloody hell. They waited for us to leave!" Without even checking on the motionless priest, he bolted for the abbey.

"Simon!" she hollered after him, but he was swift. "Wait!"

Leidolf.

Well, not him. He was locked away! Had it been one of his companions? Had they been watching all along? Waiting for Simon to leave? She fought her churning stomach. She knelt beside the priest. Compulsion drew her hand to the man's neck. No life beat. He was cold.

A lone priest with naught but a dagger guarded Leidolf, Simon had told her.

The abbey was no fortress mighty. It was penetrable and vulnerable. They had foolishly left it unguarded, the only able fighter gone on a ride with his wife. "Dear heavens," she muttered.

Visions of laughing Nordmen crashing through holy sanctuaries, upturning fonts and statues, digging through altars for gold and silver, and slitting crying priests' throats pervaded her mind as she stepped away from the dead priest. Had they been daft in their assurance Leidolf was well-guarded?

She made for the abbey.

Halfway across the meadow, pain seared her skull and brought her to her knees. She clutched her head and released a sharp cry. Her bones throbbed, and the pain coiled around her soul. What in the heavens was wrong with her? She blinked again, and yes, there it was. Nordmen all over the grassy lawn near the cloister, killing and laughing. Screams rang. She shuddered and covered her ears.

They are here.

She swallowed hard, released her hands, took two deep breaths, and the vision flickered away.

No. Nobody was there. Simon had already run ahead to the dungeon, leaving her dumbfounded in the middle of a grassy meadow.

She rose with weakened legs.

The wind whirled around her in an eddy, lifting her skirts. She patted them down.

She whispered as she struggled with the breath escaping her lungs, "Venora, is that you?"

The wind flexed its influence again, and she tightened fists at her sides to steady the trembles, firming her feet in place. A voice in the wind echoed.

Instantly regretting it, she closed her eyes. High-pitched, shrill, and urgent, Venora's voice swirled. She spoke in the Ancient ways. Gwyn didn't know her mother's tongue, aside from her Healer's chant. She was well-versed in other languages, but this, this she did not know! The words danced, teased, and enticed.

She grasped at the familiar but found naught but a string of garbled words.

"Venora, please! I don't understand!" she cried into the bellowing wind. *How* did Venora know such words? Their mother always said she'd teach them the complete Ancient language after she finished transcribing the books of Fire, Wind, Water, and Earth for their father.

The screaming wind changed to hooves pounding the ground. She collapsed again into the grass.

Arms grabbed her. She shrieked.

"Whoa! Gwyn! What the devil?"

She convulsed in Simon's arms as he held her. "Oh, Simon! It's horrible. I saw horrible things. Venora whispered deaths in my ear!" She sobbed into his chest. The ground rumbled. "Are they here? Are they still here?"

He stroked her head. "No, they are gone."

She struggled to make sense of it as she closed her eyes again, leaning against the comfort of him.

Nothing. It was gone. The vision and the hundreds of horses.

Ker-thump, ker-thump beat Simon's heart against her cheek and temple.

She had not seen a vision of the impending battle on the shores near Cumbrae, as Venora predicted. She had seen death and horrors here at the abbey.

Had it been a real vision? Or had Venora accessed the Silver Veil to communicate with her? Certainly the gifts of Jörd ran through their blood, connecting them in a bond. In her mind, she whispered, *tell me more.*

Nothing. She was gone.

"Simon!" a deep voice beckoned.

She belatedly opened her eyes as the ground stopped shuddering and the wind fell to a stagnant calm.

Alroy MacCoinneach hovered above them on his horse, a few men on horseback behind him.

"Father," Simon said, turning but not releasing her from his chest. Taut muscles in his arms flexed against her back, and his hand tightened on her waist. "Impeccable timing as always. It appears our captive escaped, leaving two dead priests in his wake."

Dear mercy, no.

CHAPTER TWELVE

James and Bernard had both been killed by a slice to the throat. Quick kills. They'd been as helpless as a hare trapped in a snare. By the footprints, it appeared there had been more than one of them.

As evening fell, Simon grimaced, standing in the chapter house over the two wrapped bodies while the priests gathered themselves in the cathedral for prayers. Quiet stillness blanketed him as images of former abbots on the plaster walls judged him from within stoically painted portraits. He prayed for the priests' souls. He prayed for forgiveness.

Was this his fault, too? He hadn't been the one to send their souls to the grave, but he *had* left the grounds unprotected. Too many deaths. "Christ, forgive me," he said in a strangled gulp. He could no longer outrun or outwit the guilt of always needing to kill.

He should have remained on the grounds. Should have checked the posts again. *Should have. Should have. Should have.* A priest with a small dagger was like leaving a child to guard a gold vault against marauders. He doubted

Bernard would have even wielded it if the situation called for it. And James? The priest had been on a stroll.

Nothing had changed. Mercy got you killed.

"I have news," his father said, appearing beside him after having taken care of his horses.

Simon found it hard to focus on the words his father spoke. He had brought death to the holiest of places. Today while partaking in the pleasures of the flesh with his wife, men of the holy cloth had been slaughtered like animals.

All he saw was blood.

Sticky blood puddled at the foot of an open cell door, the keys in the lock. A pool of blood seeped into the forest floor.

At least Leidolf hadn't found his dagger and sword, both stowed in the vault in the library. Abbot Oliver believed both attacks happened after the morning meal delivery. At least more men had not been senselessly killed. Two was too many.

His mind was a blur. Today had been filled with more intimacies with Gwyn than he could imagine. Yet, while he had been selfishly indulging, James and Bernard had been murdered.

"Simon," his father barked, bringing him to the present.

He jerked his head up and held his father's stony gaze.

"Good news."

"What news?" He gestured to the wrapped bodies. "These priests are dead. The Nordmen know we're here. Leidolf escaped!" He flung his hands out. "What could possibly be good?"

His father clapped a hand on Simon's back. "Come to the parlor. This calls for whisky."

Simon tossed a glance around. "I need to find Gwyn."

They walked through the hallway to the parlor. "She's with your mother," his father said. "She'll be well. I've put Henry on guard, and I brought two other men from Edinburgh to walk the perimeter. You remember William and Iain, Laird Campbell's sons?"

Simon nodded, numb.

"I'll be blunt."

"You always are," Simon snapped, falling into a seat beside the hearth in the parlor.

"I'll let your behavior pass, but remember your place," his father said, his tone sharpening.

"My behavior? Two men are dead!"

"Simon, we can't undo the past. I'm saddened to hear of their deaths. All we can do is pray for their souls and take action."

Simon gritted his teeth and shook his head. "You're unbelievable."

"I do what I must, and when you're laird—and you *will be* laird—you will make the same decisions for your people that I've had to."

They weren't lairds. They were stewards. He sighed. "What news comes from Edinburgh?"

"War *is* on the front, as we suspected."

"War is already here."

His father strode to the nearby table. He pulled out a cork from a flask and poured a goblet half full with Abbot

Oliver's special whisky. "I know when and where they will make landfall."

"You do? What if they change course? It's not next spring as we suspected?"

"The court has spies everywhere. Even among the Lochlanach themselves. It's time to root them from our country once and for all. They make shore near Cumbrae in a few days. Their ships were seen gathering by the isles. Their forces are converging into one greater fleet. King Haakon is sailing down. This is more than boastful ideas, Simon. It's why I took longer in Edinburgh than expected. I would bet Leidolf's presence is no coincidence either."

Simon rubbed his chin. "How do we proceed?"

"King Alexander is gathering forces and rallying lowland clans. Not all the Highlanders will make it. I'm to meet a brigade two days hence to lead the charge."

"Lead the charge? That's a great honor."

Instead of boasting or celebrating, a sober look crossed the shadows of his father's face. "Aye, it is. Time for a reckoning has come, Simon. Now is our chance to prove ourselves to our king and secure Eilean Donan's lairdship. We fulfill this duty for your mother as well. And to protect your wife and her family."

He swallowed, reminded of Leidolf's threat about Kendrick. "I go with you?"

"Of course."

"Have you seen Mother?"

The creases in his face deepened. The sorrow drew his brows downward. "She's in a stupor, is she not? I'll go speak with her shortly."

"No, Father. She is not."

His father raised his furry auburn eyebrows mid-sip. "What do you mean?"

"She's been healed."

Now it was his father's turn to be astonished. "Whatever do you mean? She is incurable."

"Not for a Healer." There. He finally said it with the full power it deserved. Gwyn was a god-gifted Healer.

"Mervyn already tried his tinctures. Same with the priests. She is in God's hands now, son. The sooner you accept that...," he said, heaving a sigh. "We can honor her virtue. Seek these men who did this to her." Fumes of whisky tumbled from his quickly stated words.

"I *have* accepted it! It's you who searches the countryside for her perpetrators!" he said, shaking his head. Had he not been doing the same thing all these years? Killing any Nordman crossing his path? Hoping that they had been *the one.*

His father sipped slowly, unfazed by Simon's outburst. "The Lochlanach who did this to her *will* be found."

"Seeking him is futile." *I gave up years ago,* he wanted to say. He was no better than his father. While his father sought the specific offender, Simon had killed Nordmen indiscriminately these past nine years. God, was he a hypocrite? Only moments before he had begged for the Lord's forgiveness, but now, he delighted in the thought of having killed many of them. How could he both love it and hate it?

His father muffled a guttural "Phmm" but said nothing.

He put it together in a heartbeat. "*That* is why you lead this charge? Not just for our lairdship. You hope to find this wolf among a sea of wolves!" Simon rose, passion brimming within him. "They are all wolves! They are all beasts! You seek something that cannot be found." He stormed from the room to the library. He flung open the vault, which of course was not locked, and withdrew Leidolf's weapons. With a heavy step, he returned to the parlor and dropped them upon the table in front of his father. "They are all wolves!"

"You remember *him*, don't you?" his father countered, not rising.

Simon inhaled sharply. "I would never forget his face."

"Those with him?"

Words he'd regret if he spewed them became lodged within his throat. He coughed. "Yes," he growled.

The wolf's eyes in the dagger nearest him twinkled with jest. They were amber in a sea of black. Leidolf was another wolf of many. Finding the man who had ruined his mother's life was a vain cause. He'd accepted that dismal conclusion years ago and chose to just kill instead. Kill, kill, kill. Bit by bit, cut them down.

He asked, "What about Blasius and the isle people? The clans?"

His father sighed. "Alan and Dubhgall MacRuaidhri are divided on this cause. The Ranalds are also an unknown. They may side with the Nordmen. You know how the Isles' clans can be." He shrugged and sipped again. "Both clans may also take sword with King Haakon's fleet. As for Mad Blasius, I don't know. What does it matter?"

Simon stared at him, mouth dropping open. "Because I'm married to his daughter, perhaps?" His head was infinitely heavy. Stars danced behind his eyes. "Wasn't the purpose of our marriage to get in favor with him and subsequently with the MacRuaidhris? Form a strong alliance for trade and security?"

"Yes, it was. That option is no longer possible. This news changes everything. I'm sorry the lass's brother got caught in the fray. Perhaps there is a chance to help him. Besides, you're sweet on her. Now you have a wife to love, Simon."

Simon swallowed guilt.

His father rose. "I must go see your mother. She is healed, you say? This was your wife's doing?"

"Yes, it was her doing. She is a Healer with powerful abilities far beyond yours or mine. She's healed me twice." He finally believed—she was indeed a Healer. *Dear God, she's lost much of her breath already.*

His father's eyes gleamed. "Then I must thank her. Can't you see, Simon? This is for us. This is falling into place. Your mother will be avenged, and we will secure our land for generations to come."

His stomach twisted with knots. He loved his father, and he knew his father did what was best for all. His mother's affinity for compassion and mercy had also softened his father's rigid beliefs.

His father was still a steward trying to gain a home.

Still, a husband trying to avenge his wife.

Yes, he saw. He saw very clearly.

Gwyn sat at Margaret's side. In silence.

Margaret had begun quilting a blanket. It lay across her lap on the bed as now nimble fingers worked a needle and thread. She hummed under her breath.

"For your children," she said to Gwyn.

Well, that stirred Gwyn from her stupor. She coughed despite having not taken a sip of anything.

Margaret smiled. "Och, I'm sorry. Getting ahead of myself. I've always wanted grandchildren, and Desmond and Meredith didn't have any. God took my son too soon..."

Gwyn didn't know what to say. Her mind had become overcrowded. Blood. Dead priests. Leidolf—gone. Pausing first, she said, "Children bring beauty to a marriage." It was a half-truth, considering what her father had done.

Despite the world she would bring them into, of course she wanted children, too. Strongly linked to her siblings, she wanted to share a life with a house full of her own bairns and with a man she loved. That had never seemed a possibility. Until now.

Och, but now. Now. Now what?

She briefly closed her eyes and inhaled deeply. "I can see it."

Margaret patted her hand and sighed. "I wish to see it."

She opened her eyes. "Why wouldn't you? You'll be returning to Eilean Donan soon after us?"

A frown parted Margaret's lips, and she whimpered, her hands stilling upon the needle and blanket. She exhaled.

"How are your spirits, my lady?" Gwyn evaluated: her eyes were clear, the pustules on her face had closed and had begun to scab over although they'd likely leave scars, and her chest moved in rested rhythm.

"It's my heart. It's never been strong." She waved a hand as Gwyn reached for her. "No. No, you may not. You've done enough. You've brought peace to my Simon."

Gwyn hovered her hand in the air, the other one lodged in her pocket on the stone in reflex. "I can. Let me get a basin of water." She moved to stand.

Margaret clutched her forearm. "No. Simon told me what happens to you when you heal. My heart is beyond healing. Yours is not."

Heat rushed up her throat and tightened it. "He shouldn't have said anything."

"Gwyn, dear. I am well. You've healed me, and I will enjoy these moments with my son and husband for however long I may have. I will not allow you to lose one more breath on me. You've healed my Simon's heart."

"I-I-I must."

"Your mercy has done much already. Don't fash over me, Gwyn. You may need your healing again."

That red-haired one, the son of MacCoinneach, he shall perish there. You can do naught about it. Venora's premonition prickled her skin, icicles spreading from her core down her arms to fingertips.

"Oh, Margaret," she said, feeling helpless.

Margaret returned to her sewing, glowing with contentment, her skin clearer and radiant, deep brown eyes fuller, and hair washed, fragrant, and brushed. "All shall be well. My Maker knows I'm coming."

The door opened, and Alroy MacCoinneach made an appearance. She'd wondered when he would come.

Simon entered behind him, silent and sulky.

Startled, she turned a stiff smile to both men. She rose. Simon shared a look with her. She took his meaning, curtsied, and left Alroy and Margaret alone. Perhaps one of their last moments together. Did Alroy know, too?

Why hadn't she dug deeper with her assessment of Margaret? Just as with Gunnar and Kendrick, she had failed. It crushed her spirit.

Simon returned with Gwyn to the refectory for a late evening meal alone. The priests were in the nave, and it would be hours before they broke to eat. His stomach bubbled with a mixture of hunger and acridness.

"Do you not wish to attend the funeral, um, what do you call it? The Mass?" Gwyn asked as they reached the large open room, with tables neatly set for supper, a meal cut short by the announcement of the priests' deaths. Empty trenchers were set for stew, along with platters of dried fruits and sliced hard cheeses, and pitchers of ale.

Simon's stomach threatened to erupt. He ran both hands through his hair, applying more pressure than was necessary to his scalp. Rigidity in his shoulders gave way, and he slumped into a chair. "No."

"Are you not allowed?"

"I'm allowed, but..." The lump in his throat would not dissipate. He didn't finish the sentence.

She laid a hand on his and sat beside him. "It's not your fault," she said.

Yet again. She needed to cease saying that.

He thumped a fist against the table, rattling the trenchers. He stood, hunger abated. "I can't. I can't."

She rose, too, and reached for him.

He waved her hand away. He doubted she'd want to touch him again after he told her his father's news and the truth about Kendrick. He had to tell her what Leidolf said. Even if it had been a lie, Leidolf was gone. What prevented him from unleashing his anger on Gwyn's brother now? "No, sit, eat. I'll bring you stew. I need to walk."

"Then I will walk with you. Food can wait." She looped her arm in his. Instead of comfort, he found guilt.

Gwyn ignored his hints. He grimaced, finding his eyes moistened. With a discreet finger, he dabbed at the corners of his eyes. "Aye, as you wish."

He led her to the library instead of outside, for the fingers of night were upon them. Would this day not end? Admittedly, he had wanted to revisit the dungeon. As if seeing the puddle of blood, Bernard's lifeless body, and the cell door wide open once hadn't been enough. No, he wanted to see it again. To investigate the struggle. To return to the scene. How many times had he done that after his mother's attack? Without thinking, he went to rub his knee, but it didn't ache. Habits had a way of never dying.

"Didn't you want to walk? Get air?" Gwyn asked.

"It's too late. Let's sit by the hearth. I need to speak with you. Are you parched?"

She sat on a cushioned seat. "No, thank you."

He remained standing. "My father brought information."

Her dark eyebrows shot up. "Aye?"

Now was the time to lay it out. "The Nordmen...," he said with a deep pause, intentionally not referring to them as Lochlanach. He curled his hands into a ball, diverted his gaze momentarily to the flickering flames in the hearth, and continued, "...traveling under King Haakon's orders, sail south to Cumbrae. Though they've always been present in the outer seas, they now congregate for war. Our king has tried to delay their landing, push it to winter to ground their ships or send them back home, but it seems more are coming. They will make landfall in a few days with a larger fleet of ships. Cumbrae is an isle west of here, along the coast. They wish to press inland, take back territories lost, and if successful make route for Glasgow and Edinburgh. I believe Leidolf's kin are among them."

"Are you certain?"

He looked over his shoulder at her. "Aye. My father's sources do not lie."

Her gaze burned into him. "There is more?"

Now he sat beside her on the bench. Took her hands in his. "I must go."

She inhaled but didn't retreat. "I assumed as much."

"Some isle clans, the MacRuaidhris and Ranalds, will be fighting, possibly on Haakon's side."

"My father?"

His fingers twitched in hers. "We don't know. What do you think he will do?"

"I don't know either. He's erratic in his decisions. Driven by a glory not his to take." Tears glimmered in her eyes.

"I need you to stay here with my mother."

She stood up, hands splayed. "No!"

"Gwyn, you can't possibly come with us."

"Why not?"

"Gwyn."

"Simon, I must. I'm a Healer. You can't go to battle without me!"

"There are others who can tend wounds."

She pursed her lips, and he sensed she wasn't telling him the full truth.

"Simon, you will die."

"That is always a possibility."

Shock widened her gaze. "How can you say that? After all we've shared? Do you wish—do you wish to die—" she stammered, but stopped.

Yes.

No.

He didn't know if life was worth living anymore. He rubbed a hand over his face. *Gwyn* had made life worth living. He was being a fool again.

"Gwyn, the foundation of marriage is honesty and trust. So, I must be honest with you," he said, gulping in air to give him the courage. "It's Kendrick. I sent Niall to Uist as I told you. Leidolf said…"

Damn him. Damn himself.

"What about Kendrick? Did word reach him? Is he safe at Eilean Donan? Please tell me he's safe. Did your father bring news?"

Simon shook his head. "I don't know. No word has come to me." *Spit it out, you dolt.* "Leidolf told me your father was going to kill Kendrick if he didn't return with you in hand. He told me this when he came to Eilean Donan. They know about Kendrick's condition." He hung his head in his hands. A hotness raced through his chest. "I'm sorry. In the dungeon, when I questioned him, he said Kendrick may already be dead. Gwyn, I didn't think—" He stopped himself from lying. He knew. He knew the Nordmen too well. "He may already be dead, Gwyn. I'm sorry."

"No! That can't be! Kendrick received word. He must have left. You can't be certain. You promised, Simon. You promised," she repeated as her confidence lost power.

He was wordless.

"You…knew…two weeks ago and said nothing?" she whispered in gulps.

"I've not heard any message from Niall. Messages can take a week to make it to Eilean Donan. We've been away."

She stepped away from him. "Oh, Simon, I begged you to let me go to him! I could've gotten him away and still honored our agreement. Now I'm your *wife* and for what? What was the point of the arrangement if we didn't secure peace? One of my brothers is dead. Now you're telling me Kendrick may be dead. Your brother is dead. You killed Rothwell and Trygg. These two priests are dead," she said, her face twisting with horror. "My people will be dead if we don't stop this war. You and your stubborn pride. I thought there was something different in you, but you're just like them, Simon MacCoinneach! All you do is kill. Death follows you."

"Gwyn—" He reached for her.

"No! Don't. This was always your father's intent. You knelt to his words and promises. You hunger for blood like the rest of them. There was never going to be peace. Did you lie about everything? Did you even send Niall with the letter?" she said through gritted teeth, her wrath a slice to his heart.

"Yes, yes I did!"

She paced.

Simon bit his lip until it hurt. "This was all my fault."

She held her arms tightly against her middle. "I can't possibly stay here. Stay here while you get yourself killed? No, I dare not. I *will* not."

"You cannot come, Gwyn." His pulse pounded in his head. "I will see things made right."

"I must go. Venora has seen it."

Dread expanded in his stomach. "Seen what?"

Pleading, silent, furious eyes. "The war...and your death."

The hearth crackled. Blood rushed from his limbs to his chest. His hands and feet numbed. "You knew about the Nordmen coming? All this time? I mean, you *had confirmation*? You didn't tell me. We asked you." Now it was his turn to be enraged. "We could've done much more. We would've had more time."

She turned away from him, shoulders hunched. "You lied about Kendrick."

"I sent help." He reached but found his fingers curling into a fist instead of squeezing her shoulder. He threw a punch at the nearest thing—the hearthside table. Pain shot through his knuckles. Another punch and the goblets and pitcher crashed to the floor and the thin wood table top split. He could have done more. So much more. "Kendrick is one man!"

"One man?" she fumed. "He is my brother! He's a good man! He is not a murderer like you, the Nordmen, or nearly every other man I've met! You knew...you knew what Leidolf would do if I didn't return and you brought me here anyway. All to cleanse your soul of guilt—at the loss of others!"

Her true words were a venom-tipped dagger, but it didn't strike him down—yet. "This war may take hundreds or thousands of lives! For a Healer intent on mercy and preventing death, I'd think you'd understand! How could you've not told me?"

She spun around, her hair loose, her face maddened. "Because I didn't care if the Nordmen and Scots die! Let them kill each other."

"Including me?"

"You were one of them...before...before...this," she said in gulps, her cheeks reddened enough to match the color of his auburn hair.

He stumbled and drew closer to the door. "Has your opinion of me not changed?"

"I believed in you. Now I don't know."

The cutting edge of her words went deeper, spilling blood into his entire chest cavity, breaking ribs.

Her face grew ashen. "Oh, Simon."

There was his name again but spoken in the way that attacked him.

He was steps from the door. Just another. So close. He had to ask. "Do you wish for the priests to annul our union?"

Now she stepped toward him, her hand outstretched and shaking. "No."

The door burst open behind them. His father entered. "What the devil is going on here, Simon?"

"Nothing," he said, sourness settling on his tongue.

"I can hear you down the hall. Your mother needs her rest."

"Aye." Simon nodded. His father turned, leaving Gwyn and Simon alone again.

A fog of emotion hung heavy in the room. "Gwyn," he said.

"Simon," she responded, her pained look saying it all. She approached him but stopped. He smelled the fresh rosewater of her hair. She blinked wet eyes, then departed the room.

The blade in his heart could not have gone any deeper.

Gwyn was already waiting in the stable when Simon, Alroy, and their men arrived to depart after a brief morning meal.

"No," Simon said.

"I *am* coming."

Alroy approached and gave her a cursory look. "What is this?"

"I'm coming," Gwyn said, firming her feet to the ground, expecting Alroy's rebuttal. "I'm a Healer. My place is on the battlefield."

Alroy didn't argue for once. "You did well by my wife, Gwyn. I thank you for it. Do as you wish, but you need to be aware of the dangers ahead."

She fisted her hands at her sides. "I am well aware."

"Do as you wish." He nodded and strode into the stable, giving choppy orders to the men. They didn't need them. All worked in procedural routine, preparing saddles, loading satchels, and mounting. Henry, one of the MacCoinneachs' best men, was to stay watch at the abbey.

"Gwyn, this is madness," Simon said, shoving past her to his own horse.

"I must come," she said again. Liar that he was, she couldn't let Simon go to his death either. Perhaps Kendrick was still alive. She *had* to see for herself.

"If you must." He moved through the motions of readying his horse, his posture as stiff as his voice. She stood behind him, chilled by his iciness.

How had their promising love quickly become such a tangle of thorns? Had she been a naïve fool, hopelessly strung along in a futile battle of man against man, and man against himself? "Simon, I—"

A gaze of hurt spun upon her. His voice was low, nearly a whisper. "I don't wish to speak of it." He ripped his look from hers, deftly cinched the saddle, and tied his satchel. With a small nod toward a saddle on the ground beside him, he said, "You can use that one, take this mare beside mine. She is gentle. We leave at any moment. Do you have all you need?"

She nodded. The heavy saddle wobbled in her slick hands. Her fingers slipped, and the saddle fell. She swore under her breath.

Simon came beside her wordlessly and helped her saddle the mare. Their fingers touched. She quenched the swelling ache in her chest. He moved with precision, his hands meticulous and calloused, always working.

"Gwyn." He stopped and rested his hands upon hers, the pair of them interlaced.

"Yes?"

"I don't want you to get hurt."

"I can't let you go alone, Simon. Not if I have the power to stop your death."

Perspiration beaded near his hairline. He took a throaty swallow. "I've always been ready for death."

"Living isn't that unbearable, is it?"

He squeezed her hand as he drew their intertwined fingers down to the space between them. "Not anymore. Not since I met you. Your own life, Gwyn. Your breaths. You can't give them for me."

She nibbled on her lip, mute, suffocating on her own doubts and fears.

The horse stomped an impatient foot beside them. "Come, I'll help you mount."

It was as close as two stubborn souls could get to a truce.

They were off. The vast lowlands, a fleet of ships, and a day of death awaited them.

CHAPTER THIRTEEN

S imon sloshed through the muddy ground as he and Gwyn set up their tent, two days later alongside a glen. The gathering of clans grew to an impressive size in the clearing not far from the western sea where they would meet the Nordmen if their plans unfolded in their favor. Men, and a few women, methodically set up tents, settled mounts, and prepared the evening suppers. Gwyn had shared few words with him since the abbey. She had shared no kisses. He deserved none.

Men moved about, conversing. Many clans had come. The Montgomeries, Cunninghams, Campbells, Sinclairs, and even Donalds from near Edinburgh gathered in the glen. They nestled into open dales and clearings. The convergence was massive, easily many hundred. When the king's men arrived, they would have nearly a thousand, Simon reckoned.

King Alexander had been on high alert the past few months as the numbers of Nordmen and ships grew along the Western Isles and shores.

It was finally happening. His pulse soared.

Fires blazed. Men conversed in excited voices. The chills and rush of prebattle prickled Simon's skin. He clenched and unclenched his fists to expend the riled energy within him. This was their land, and it was time to cull the beasts.

He glanced at Gwyn as she shifted to preparing a small supper on a fire beside their tent. He'd brought along food and drink, as well as her meager belongings: a second gown and undergarments, a brush from his mother's things, and her dagger, which he assumed was tucked in one of her pockets. She didn't have any of her special herbal things. No bandages. No ointments or tinctures.

She was displaced, aimless, and hurt. But not helpless.

Still, what could she do on the battlefield? He could no longer let her heal men with her gift. No. He refused. So long as she was his wife, he would press the issue. For her to lose her breaths of life to save another person? No. Call him an arse, but he forbid it. This was not her war. He would not let her save him.

She moved fluidly next to the fire as their dinner bubbled in an iron kettle. She yanked out her dagger and began shredding linens they'd acquired from the Cunninghams' keep for her to use. His mind raced. Perhaps she could gather medicinal plants from the surrounding area? Maybe he could escort her through the wood to forage in the early morning before their last leg to the coast.

Her gaze lifted. They shared a look, her eyes reflecting hurt. By God, there was hope. Even if a sliver. Perhaps

Venora was wrong. Maybe he wouldn't die, and he and Gwyn could raise fat bairns. Maybe. Blessings, maybe.

He turned and strode to the ring of men in conversation around his father. A scout who had come from the front proclaimed in an animated voice, "Well, my lairds, I counted at least thirty ships. Big warships, the kind holding a hundred men each. More than have been there all summer. The rest of his fleet has arrived. Ah ha! Though many small ones were run aground by the storm!" His face glimmered with excitement.

Murmurs.

"Here! Here!"

"God shines upon us!"

"Let's strike them now!"

The scout continued, "They're beached, broken, in disrepair. The townsfolk have fled. The larger ships afar have yet to make landfall. I saw King Haakon's golden lion on their sails. Most were positioned around the Isle of Cumbrae, and in the strait, closest to the village of Largs. I suspect they will make for the shore on the morn once the weather has cleared."

Laird Sinclair spoke with fervor to Simon's father. "Good. We'll send in archers to take out the Nordmen who are salvaging upon the shore. Give them a taste of what's to come!"

"Aye! Aye!" other lairds and commanders agreed.

"Shan't we wait for the king and surprise them? Use our proven tactics?" another laird asked.

"No! Let's send in our archers!"

"Aye!"

"Yes!" others voiced.

"Be ready. They'll have axes, swords, spears. Do not hesitate," his father added. "We must send our best archers."

More cheers.

Whoops of excitement.

"I've men, no' wi' bows like ye, but they hiv slingshots! They're braw at shootin' stones! Might help if we are to rattle 'em beasts on the shore?" one elder said. Simon wasn't sure which clan he hailed from.

"Aye!"

"Aye!"

His father took a moment to absorb the ideas. "Tomorrow we'll meet them, head on. We need to get there first, after the archers have culled the ones on shore. Be ready for the remaining ships to land. We'll leave before dawn. Let the men rest this evening. More of King Alexander's forces, many upon horseback, are gathering along the glen and will be arriving throughout the night. We shall ride and take back what has always been ours," he said, voice deadly calm. Lairds Sinclair and Campbell cheered and clanked flasks in agreement.

There was a flurry of movements as the lairds dispersed and rallied archers and men who could shoot stones. Within the hour, several hundred men strong had departed the clearing toward Largs.

So it had begun.

Heedful, Gwyn listened to the conversation as men gathered around the central fire while their elders encouraged and boasted in anticipation. Simon had long since left the rowdy men to sit with her.

Silence became a shiver-inducing mist over their small corner of the campground. Men around them readied for bed, roasted a freshly caught deer, laughed about the triumphs of past and future, while she and Simon sat, forcing bites of their last supper together. The meat had no taste. The stew, enticing moments before, was nothing more than liquid on a parched throat. It was nourishment for a soul depleted beyond repair and for a body already pushed to its limits with healing. Would she have strength tomorrow to heal once again?

She dropped her bowl and barely touched meal on a folded plaid in front of her. "Simon, I must find my family."

He stirred a spoon around in his bowl, not eating either.

She made to stand, and he stopped her with a squeeze on her knee. "You're not safe there, not with the Nordmen about. Not with your father within reach. Please, Gwyn. Stay here with me. I'll protect you. Please wait until tomorrow. If you insist, we can leave earlier than the rest of the men."

His hand lingered on her knee. The foggy peat of the fire made her cough. The smoke stung her eyes. "They sent archers, Simon. What if my family is with them on shore? What if they are hurt?"

A muscle flickered in his cheek. He drew his hand from her knee and took her nearest hand in his. A clammy palm squeezed hers. "There is naught we can do tonight, Gwyn. Come. We need sleep. Tomorrow is a day anew. We'll rouse before the rest of the men, aye? We can search for them. I daresay your family may not be with them, Gwyn, and I ask that you reconsider."

"How do you know?"

"I don't."

She buried her fears. "My father never journeys without my mother. What about Venora?" She didn't mention Kendrick.

"Our archers aim for the men only. No *non-fighting* woman will be harmed." Non-fighting, of course. Both knew that many Norse women took up shield and sword alongside their husbands.

"What about Kendrick?"

Then again, he might already be dead. She wept inside.

"Would your father be mad enough to bring the women and lad with him? *Into* battle?" Simon asked, clearly exasperated with the topic.

She shook wild hands. "Yes!"

He muffled a curse and something about *her* being here, too, under his breath.

After a quick clean-up of their meal and douse of their fire, she followed him into the pitched tent. With trembling knees, she stripped to her shift for easier sleep. Simon's body and a wool blanket would keep her plenty warm. He allowed her to lie first upon the bedroll, and he followed suit after removing his boots and hose. Lastly, he extinguished the small lantern at their feet and lay behind her, cradling her in his arms. He caressed her cheek.

This was it.

The night before it would end.

She closed her eyes as his slow, deep breathing synced with hers.

At some point in the bleak midnight hours, she awoke from a dreamless sleep to feel a hard longing behind her and Simon's heavy arm wrapped tightly around her waist. She stirred.

"Gwyn, I'm sorry," he whispered in her ear, his voice flowing into her soul.

Her words caught. She managed, "As am I."

"I should've done more to help Kendrick. There is still hope for him, Gwyn. I have hope that he has escaped your father's wrath."

She nodded. "Simon MacCoinneach has hope?"

"Sometimes."

"You did what you could. I should've told you about Venora's vision." She wanted to say more. To tell him about Leidolf's family. Or did he already know they had been the ones to violate Lady Margaret?

He stroked her cheek, brushing her disheveled hair, his finger lingering on her neck. "You did all you could. I was foolish to think I could...I could..." His hand traveled down her shoulder and paused, his own tremors vibrating into her bones.

His yearning pressed against her bottom, and without thinking, she curved her back to wiggle closer to him, closer to the security of him. "Simon."

"Every time you say my name, it crushes me."

His kisses fell upon her shoulder, and she shivered. "Why?"

"Well, och, I do enjoy your sweet birdsong, but it's not just that. I was named after Saint Simon, the Zealot. Do you know what saints are?" His lips moved downward, toward her spine, and she arched, his kisses arousing her through the thin shift.

"Yes, I've read about them before."

"Well, we know I'm no saint, but you're the one who has brought me mercy, Gwyn." He pushed the loose neckline of her shift down.

She sighed as he continued the trail, sweet pecks along her shoulders and back and nape. His hand slid slowly to her breast. She inhaled at the touch. "What else does your name mean, besides emulating a saintly man of mercy?"

Hot breath said, "God is heard."

"Ah." She wiggled deeper into his embrace, wishing his hands all over.

"I'm afraid I've not lived up to my name. I've failed."

She sank into the abyss of desire. She needed to feel him again. Perhaps for the last time. "No. Your journey has yet to begin."

She dropped a hand to the hemline of her shift and rumpled it upward, bringing her bare bottom against his exposed groin, for his shirt had already slipped up his waist as well. She then moved her hand behind her, where it fell upon something equally hard, equally longing. He inhaled with a groan.

"Simon, I am still yours," she moaned.

"I am yours," he said, his hand dropping to the heart of her.

His touch was as hot as the heat in her palms when she healed. It was smooth, urgent, loving.

Reveling in his strokes, she parted her legs for the hardest part of him. He gently glided into her, and they heaved with breathlessness. Tingles found their way to the most intimate parts of her body. They rocked and danced, slowly. She was entranced with the feel of their joined bodies as he made love to her.

His hand beneath her side held her breast, while the one on her hip drew her closer with each motion. He groaned behind her with the effort. The firmness of the earth beneath them, the moist inhalations in the dark tent encircling, and the slick smoothness of their moving bodies sent her over the edge.

"Simon, show me mercy," she said through gasps.

He moved quicker, harder. "Always."

"Always," he said again with one final thrust until they both moaned and he shuddered behind her.

A long moment passed where they lay still in the darkness, his pulse pounding against her back, and her heart nearly breaking loose from her ribs. He slid from her, and they lay entwined, neither wanting to dress or move. Finally, Simon smoothed her shift down and pulled the blanket back on them.

His breath tickled her ear. "My heart is yours until we both pass on to the next world. I love you, Gwyn."

"I love you, Simon."

He murmured quietly under his breath words she couldn't distinguish for they were a mix of Gaelic and Scots vernacular. He repeated, "I love you."

"You have all of me, Simon. I will return with you to your home, our home...and be yours until my last breath. If I shall pass before you, I'll be waiting on the other side of the Silver Veil. Until you come home to me." She hated saying it. She hated verbalizing the truth. If she saved his life tomorrow, it would cut her breaths by a hundred or more. She would be the first one to fall, not Simon.

More muffled murmurs.

Tomorrow would be the end of her father's realm. Tomorrow she would take whatever breath was needed to save Simon.

Leidolf drew himself upright onto a grassy mound, entranced by the fire on the beach. He scanned the shoreline, squinting as darkness diluted daylight. After riding out the storm in the comfort of whores at a tavern in Largs, he'd acquired a sail across the small bay to the Isle of Cumbrae. The fleet had been felled by a strong storm, some ships beached or sails torn. He didn't give them a second look. They'd recover. They always did. Odin was just testing them.

He had spent most of the afternoon canvassing the campsites in anything but an urgent manner while men worked and prepared after having lost their kin on the shore across from them near Largs. A thousand men or more roamed the rocky shoreline and hills. Not one sailed across the bay to help the men being taken out by the storming Scots on the mainland.

Leidolf didn't care either. Less to cull later if any should rise against his authority on Uist.

His head still thundered from Gwyn's strike at the abbey days ago. She would suffer for this. He teetered between wanting to kill her and keep her. He'd enjoy breaking her into submission. Her ability was an asset he could not deny, so he leaned toward keeping her.

Delaying the inevitable, he wandered around and shared stories with kinfolk while he momentarily parted ways with Donner and Steinthor. He partook in drinks and even allowed himself the pleasure of a scrawny thrall who tasted of sour mead. His father and the higher-ranked jarls would have finer thralls and be in the inner circle of Nordmen on the isle.

He hopped off his viewpoint, wobbled from too much drink, and made his way through the roaring crowd. He'd yet to locate Blasius or the isles' clans, but they'd be here. Their boats were not as fast and perhaps their journeys had been fraught in the inner sea.

The fires rose high, curling into the dark night. Flames of orange and red licked as massive timbers lit and hissed. Men tossed logs onto the glowing blazes. Smoke hazed the sky and seduced their souls. The cheers and jeers were of glory and blood as they passed around the bog myrtle ale and devoured the meats from the spit. As men got lost in the effects of the drink, the crowds grew rowdier. Each jarl had his own group on the beach of the isle, and Leidolf snaked his way closer to his father's campsite in the interior.

Thralls belonging to the highest ranked jarls, and even King Haakon himself, squealed and giggled as men drew them near and retreated into tents for carnal delights. None were ever taken by force, at least not by Leidolf. He paid well and always promised them a gratifying experience. Thin or thick-hipped, well bosomed or still blossoming, he didn't care. To plunge into one of them distracted him from the ache in his soul. He almost wanted another.

His fingers danced on the pouch at his side. The wolf's blood. He'd need it tomorrow.

His mood sank when he found his father's camp, for there was no mistaking Magnus of Reindalr's voice, nor Magnor and Hallbjorn's unassailable presence. Not always the loudest voices in the group, they stood at least a head's height taller than Leidolf. Magnor was laughing with a group beside him. The *úlfheðnar*. His father had brought his warriors, of course, decked in wolf furs and sharp spears. On the morrow they'd paint their faces, arms, and lye-bleached beards with berry-infused and animal-blood dyes. The bitter scent of hemp floated over to him as his brothers and others passed a pipe around.

Nobody noticed his arrival.

He cleared his throat.

His father shot him a half glance. He returned to his meal. "What news does my third-born bring?"

By Helheim, the goddess of the burning pit of hell, where oath breakers and cowards resided, he had nothing. All this time trying to forge an alliance with Blasius and, well, kill him after, retrieve his bride, and acquire any knowledge for his father...and he was left with nothing. All because of the whore and her red-haired lover. A Nordman never arrived empty-handed.

"I come ready to fight."

His father smirked and continued gnawing upon a fleshy bone with his teeth, the meat and gristle catching in his graying black beard. "We have men." He wiped the beefy back of his hand over his mouth, tossed the bone into the fire, and grabbed a jug from one of the men closest to him.

Leidolf played his only coin of knowledge. He prayed Steinthor and Donner's excursion to Edinburgh had proven the information to be true. He lifted his chin and stood erect. "The Scots' king knows we're coming. He's gathering men and will arrive by morn. The *king* will be at this battle." Or he hoped. Donner had been certain he'd heard it clearly, but he wasn't the most reliable. Steinthor had corroborated the information.

"You tell me nothing I don't already know," his father said, blue glare piercing.

His hope dwindled. Leidolf didn't dare spur him. His cheeks burned. He slipped a hand over his belt, caressing the holes. One, two, three. He lacked his sword and dagger. The red fox still had them at the abbey. Thank the gods they hadn't taken his pouch of wolf's blood.

"Oh, don't fret, my young, foolish wolf. I've my resources, too. There is no point in chasing that feral whore over hell's soil. We have something better."

Leidolf swallowed as his father barked, "Blasius!"

Mad Blasius emerged from a tent near the gathering, his older daughter Venora at his side. The woman was disturbingly ominous in her stature. Leidolf had kept his distance from her while in Blasius's village. There were no signs of Caoimhe or Kendrick. Had Blasius held fast to his threat to kill the young man when Leidolf hadn't returned with Gwyn? His coveted Healer wife couldn't be far. Leidolf's gaze darted around, but he didn't see them.

"Our victory has been seen," his father said with a snide grin and flick of a hand toward Venora.

Leidolf tightened his fists at his sides. He wished he had his dagger. He needed to feel the amber stones beneath his fingers. Blasius the bold—the fool, the truly delusional was more like it. What daft man would share such a treasure as the Seer daughter? Had his father seduced Blasius as well with promises of power? He bit his tongue, for he had the same quest. Once again his father had been quicker. "Oh?" Leidolf asked, feigning ignorance.

"Yes. The Seer has seen our victory tomorrow morning."

Venora held Leidolf's look, her eyes penetrating. "Has she?"

Blasius stepped forward in a huff, his own cheeks glowing from drink. "She has! You dare doubt her?"

"Never," said Leidolf, feeling his lips curl into a grin. "Where are the rest of your brethren?"

"I've brought my best fighters. Tomorrow, the strong bond of Nordmen and islefolk will unite and bring down the inferior Scottish force."

Leidolf directed his look to his father. "What of my fealty, Father? When we win?"

His father scoffed, "What fealty is that? You've not secured your bride, nor have you even managed to bring Blasius and his men to our battle. I had to do that myself. You bring me no new information on the eve of the day we shall conquer the Scots at last. What fealty? You're a third-born. You're a never-should-have-been-born! Go, be off. Prepare yourself for battle if you must."

Killing Blasius. Taking the village. Marrying Gwyn. Yes, he knew well the tasks he'd vowed to complete. Oath-breakers held a special place in hell. He ground his teeth. "I've broken no oath. All is going according to its path. Many shall see the tip of my sword tomorrow, including the MacCoinneach clan."

He refused to plead. Magnor and Hallbjorn stared at him, both wordless, both smirking. They could have been twins with their tall, muscular physiques, lye-bleached and jewel-adorned beards, clipped dark hair, and white-blue eyes. Scars from their triumphs spidered their brawny arms and crossed the bridges of their noses. Each was tattooed with war insignia on their chiseled cheeks. He shivered, instantly reminded of the hate they had unleashed upon him while he was young, the count-less times they terrorized him prior to his sail to Uist from the Nord Land. The years of hell. Perhaps they'd see the tip of his sword tomorrow, too, or if the gods chose it to be, would fall. They had their father's build and looks. Leidolf had been *blessed* to share the blond with his mother...a constant reminder to his father of the woman he'd lost after she birthed Leidolf.

They turned to their companions and fell into their own prebattle conversations of mirth and lust without verbal acknowledgment of their youngest brother's arrival.

Leidolf's mind buzzed as he departed to find a tent for the night and a new sword and axe. Tomorrow was the day. The whole of Blasius of Varteig's family would meet their end along with that red-haired fox. It was time for Leidolf of Reindalr to rule Uist with Gwyn the Healer by his side.

He fell into a broken sleep and before dawn's first light as the rest rose and readied to depart for the mainland, he slid his hand into his pouch, uncorked his vial, and swallowed half of the contents of his coveted wolf's blood.

Gwyn couldn't sleep.

In the wee hours, many men returned to the camp. There was no drowning their exuberance. The Nordmen on the shore had been driven away or killed by the archers and slingers. Some had managed to get their ships into working shape and returned to Cumbrae with the rest of the fleet.

She prayed her family had not been among those killed. She closed her eyes, whispered Venora's name, and waited. Nothing but a light breeze. *Venora, is that you?*

Nothing. She had no mystical connection to her sister. This was a fool's game.

The first skirmish had been won. More, oh, many more men were waiting. Were coming.

With the predawn birdsong, Simon rolled over and gave her a squeeze. She quickly dressed, her fingers fumbling with laces, her stomach a whirlpool. He mumbled his disapproval of leaving before the men, but he readied himself regardless. The shoreline had been cleared. It would be relatively safe. For now.

Other men stirred, but the entire camp was not set to leave for another hour or two. Gwyn stretched and gathered her things as Simon shuffled to a tent nearby.

"Brochan, hey, Brochan," he said, the lantern outstretched.

"Aye?" A ruddy-faced man with a mop of messy brown hair popped out of the tent.

"Tell my father we've gone ahead. No need to be alarmed. We'll meet at the set point. *Ehm*, we're scouting, gathering some needed things," he lied.

His friend nodded, and she and Simon departed, leaving the horses behind for other men.

Gwyn found it odd Simon hadn't awoken his father to tell him of their early departure. Then again, she doubted Alroy would want Simon to go ahead, even if he was a skilled fighter. They walked silently along a meager road through the forest. After a while, it opened to rugged sea hills. The crunch of their steps sliced the silence hovering between them.

They drew closer to the village, skirting the vast knolls. The sky turned gray with early light, and Simon extinguished the lantern in his hand. He stumbled, but Gwyn caught him by the arm.

"Och, sorry. My knee gave way. I don't know why. The weather is awfully foul."

"Oh, Simon. I'm sorry. Your knee…"

He waved a hand. "It's a spirit wound, Gwyn. Mervyn told me many times. The injury has long since healed since the attack. It only flares sometimes."

His bluntness never surprised her. "But—"

He drew his hand from rubbing his knee to a gentle stroke upon her cheek. "Dinna fash. I know you knew and that you didn't heal it."

"How?"

He shrugged. "Don't know. Just did."

She lowered her gaze.

"Gwyn."

She looked up. Sincere eyes stared back. "Not a worry, Gwyn," he said. "You were trying to help me."

Her teeth chattered. All she did was try to help. All she did was fail. "I can't heal phantom wounds."

"You've healed me in other ways, Gwyn."

They walked, burdened by what would come. They walked one step closer to death.

Finally, they reached the small, abandoned fishing village. Gwyn realized Simon had taken her on a roundabout way, avoiding the skirmish area on the beach. Not a soul was about as slivers of sunlight made way for day. She peered in the distance to the shore, where a few beached ships remained, but the rest had retreated. Then she saw the bodies.

Dead Nordmen.

She gasped and covered her mouth. Simon followed her gaze. "They're not there, Gwyn. I told you. No women would be harmed. I know your father is a madman, but he wouldn't bring them on the beach!"

"Yes, he would."

He sighed. "They're probably yonder on Cumbrae or on a larger ship, like I *said they may be*, mind you. They can still be back on Uist. There is naught we can do, Gwyn. I'll need to find a hiding place for you."

She stiffened. "Is that why we left early? So you could hide me? Simon, I must search the beach."

He exhaled. "I came as a favor to you. I *knew* they wouldn't be here. You insisted to see with your own eyes. So I brought you. Look about," he said with an irritated flourish, his voice steeling, their tender moment earlier quickly fading. "They're not here! Bleeding Christ, *you* should not be here. You should've stayed at the camp. You would've been safer there." He cursed again under his breath, shaking his head, thoroughly rattled now. "You should've stayed at the abbey!"

"You know I must be here."

He grumbled. "I know."

She hurried to a closer vantage point, Simon quick, but not opposing, by her side.

She rooted her feet. Squinted. A thorough scan of the beach confirmed only a few men's bodies. Nothing more. Most had indeed sailed back to Cumbrae.

Still.

Dead men. There would be so many more soon.

She turned and scanned the sea as the haze lifted. Pointed bows cut through the clouds. Thirty or more immense warships with sails catching the morning wind drifted across the sea toward them. They were a blur of brown hulls and massive red and flax-colored sails. Many flags were solid with animal emblems, others red and white striped. Her breath caught.

Truth struck her.

Was her family on one of those ships? Which? Her father's ship was nothing like these great warships. Was he sailing with the other Nordmen?

"They're coming," Simon said. He took her hand and scouted the edge of the forest where trees met dunes and seagrass. Clusters of cottages and fishermen's crofts composed the small town. "A croft or inn won't do. They'll ransack the town. By God's bones, where am I to hide you? You shouldn't have come!" he repeated, panic filling his normally steadfast voice. Gwyn's pulse quickened.

They spent far too long searching for somewhere safe enough, hidden enough. The ships grew closer. Robust hills painted the landscape. Grassy meadows. The forest lay farther away, only sprinkles of trees nearer to the beach and town. She could maybe make for the forest.

Farther. She wouldn't be close enough to save Simon, though.

She hugged her fingers around the dagger in her pocket. "Simon, I can fight."

A sad snort. "You wouldn't raise a blade to a soul, Gwyn. It's not who you are."

Gwyn's resolve faded. "I was a fool."

"No, you were hopeful," he said with despondency.

Where were they? Which ship? She paused and looked again instinctively for the snarling red wolf.

Closer, closer they came.

"What is it? What do you see?" Simon paused in his search. He came beside her and followed her gaze.

"Leidolf's kin," she rasped, the admission a relief, a pain to say. Tears found their way to her eyes. "There." She pointed to his longship.

Though she lacked a Feeler's ability, she *felt* Simon's tension. His ire. "The red wolf's banner? That is *his* kin?" he said, nearly growling like a wolf himself.

She sniffled, nodded. She gripped her middle, anticipating the consequence of her lie.

His voice cracked and his chin quivered. "You knew? Oh my God, Gwyn, you knew?"

"I'm sorry, Simon."

He balled his fist and pressed it against his forehead. "You knew. You knew. I told you about what happened and you..."

"It wasn't Leidolf!" she defended. "He was too young nine years ago, like Kendrick's age, and third-born. He never went on their pillages. He would have been home in the Nord Land—and as I said, I've never met his family!"

Simon pinched the bridge of his nose, and instead of evading, he closed their space. "No, 'twas not that bastard. They were older. Their leader had *úlfheðnar*, those wolf-hide-wearing beasts. I don't forget faces. No, it was not Leidolf. The beasts who attacked her all had dark hair, looked nothing like Leidolf. Black hair, blue eyes. Not a strand of blond."

She inhaled sharply. "His father? Magnus?"

Simon ground the words between teeth. "I. Don't. Know. Gwyn, honesty! That's all I asked for! How could you not tell me? After everything we discussed? After I told you *everything*? I thought we made amends."

She shifted on her feet, held her ground. He didn't touch her, but she could almost breathe in the betrayed pain. "I wasn't sure until you mentioned the red wolf banner. Their emblem was on correspondence from the Nord Land. Leidolf never goes with his family on plunders. My father told me. Only Leidolf's father and two brothers went on yearly pursuits abroad. That's all I know."

Plunders and pursuits? More like murdering, violating ventures. Gwyn's stomach churned.

"Does any other family share such a banner?"

She shook her head. "No. Each is unique. Their family is well-known."

"So it was one of them...his father or brothers. It was one of the leading men in their party. The others...*watched*."

Simon continued his searching.

"Simon, there is nothing here for me."

Sounds came from the nearby forest path. Horses and Scotsmen emerged and rode through the wide meadows and hills, drawing upon the beach in full force.

Alroy was one of the first to approach. "Simon."

"I've enlightening news, Father."

Alroy's eyebrows lifted. "Oh?"

"The red wolf banner is there." He pointed to the ship. "That is whom we seek."

"Oh?"

"Aye." Simon's chest rose and fell with a deep breath. "I never told you about the banner. That horrid red wolf is the banner those brutes traveled under when Mother and I were attacked." He added, "They are Leidolf's family."

Alroy was silent, a distant, focused smile directed toward the ships. He lifted his shoulders with a satisfied exhalation. "Good. You'll know the man if we see him?"

Simon scowled. "Aye. His father or older brothers, likely."

"Take positions!" Alroy hollered with an elaborate hand gesture to nearby commanders or lairds on horses. Those men rode off and relayed the orders to the hundreds of other riders and men afoot. The clansmen all moved like bees in a hive, forming predetermined rows along the meadow and beach. Far across the field, more men under new flags arrived. They, too, took position. Was this their king's men?

Henry had not left to join the formation.

Henry.

Her knees went weak. Simon saw, too. Henry had been left at the abbey to guard Margaret and the priests. *Oh, no. No, no, no!* she pleaded to Jörd.

Alroy caught their gazes. "I'm sorry, Simon. Henry arrived shortly after you left."

Simon steadied himself against a tree.

"Your mother has passed on, Simon. Her heart was too weak," Alroy said bluntly.

"No!" Gwyn cried.

Simon roared. "What? No! That's not possible! She was healed! How can this be?" He turned fierce eyes to Gwyn.

"I healed her!" Her head spun.

"The lass speaks the truth. Simon. Simon!" Alroy said. Finally, Simon turned to his father. "She's had a condition her entire life. We never told you. The disease, though Gwyn helped her, had progressed too much when it came to her heart. There was no saving her. There was nothing we could do. Healing gave her a few more days, that's all."

Simon targeted his glare at Gwyn. "You lied."

She stumbled, catching on a tree root. "No. No!" Her lungs constricted. She had just *been* with Margaret a few days ago. She seemed well...but had hinted at something deeper with her heart. How could she have died suddenly? She'd heard of old or frail hearts failing. Had Margaret been born with the condition, with her husband as her only confidant in this secret? Aye, she knew it well. For her own heart was linked to the breaths she lost. One day it would beat for the last time, all due to her healings.

"Did you know?" Simon questioned.

"Yes, well," she mumbled. She held up a hand to a pacing Simon. He wasn't one to hit a woman, but she cowered nonetheless. "But not until after I healed her, Simon. She wouldn't let me help with it! I didn't know it was that poorly."

"You knew, too? And never told me?" he said to his father. Alroy nodded.

Simon wheezed. "You led me to believe—"

Tears clouded Alroy's eyes. He firmed his voice. "I led you to believe nothing. Your mother wished for you and your brother to have a meaningful life. She saw the guilt plaguing you after the attack. She didn't want you to know about it. She was born with it. The Frenchman's disease worsened it. This is not Gwyn's fault. Now, come join us so we may taste revenge."

Henry came forward. "Master Simon? There is a place yonder," he said with a flick of his chin over his shoulder, "where you can hide Lady Gwyn. An old stone building with a well on the edge of the woods, near the path. It's set away from the village."

Given there were no caves and the homes in the village were too close to the shore, it was all they had. The skirmish would be on the beach and meadow, and if the Scots fared well, as they should, no loner should come this way. Or so she hoped.

Simon grabbed her hand in anything but a kind way. "Make haste."

A few moments later, they found the stone croft. It was set back from the shoreline, tucked behind the dunes and close to the forest's edge. It was abandoned.

"Your dagger, Gwyn. You'll need it," Simon said with a cursory look within.

Her hand instinctively fell into her pocket. She swallowed, her pulse racing. "Simon, please. Please forgive me. I didn't—" She cut herself off. Forgive her for what? Knowing about Leidolf's family? Knowing Lady Margaret was living on borrowed time? "There is nothing else. You know all. I'm sorry!"

He didn't allow her apology. "Do not hesitate if anyone approaches. You and I both know what they will do," he said with a throaty growl.

"Simon..."

He pressed his lips together, an angry scowl spread across his forehead. "No."

"I must be near you if I am to—"

He raised a hand. "No! Your sister has seen it, hasn't she? We can't change our fates. Just let me go. Let me die. It is my time, Gwyn. Let me fall. Do not save me."

He didn't even kiss her goodbye. He turned and left with Henry by his side as the Norse ships made shore. Though set back, she could see it all.

They were here.

CHAPTER FOURTEEN

Awe and shock kept Gwyn from leaving the doorway. She'd never seen such a fleet before.

Closer came death by sea.

Just like a month ago, when Venora warned her death would come by water. This time it was not the Scots. It was her father's people.

They would be the ones to fall, not the Scots. The fates favored them.

The dragon-headed ships made shore, as men barked orders and rowers grunted. Waves crashed against their wooden hulls. Men paced the decks.

So many of them.

More archers released arrows through the morning fog from the first line on the beach.

The warships responded quickly with their own archers. The next row of archers lit their arrows with fire, released, and aimed for sails. A few caught. More arrows. Back and forth.

One by one, the shallow-drafted longships beached directly onto the pebbly coast.

As the mist lifted, men grabbed hundreds of round shields from the rails. They deflected arrows as they spilled upon the shore, unleashing war cries. She'd always heard of the dirty, abrupt, and disorderly Norse ways, much unlike the methodical English and Scottish tactics. She shuddered, reminded of the murdered priests, James and Bernard. Her father's people held no regard for foreigners' holy ground or holy people.

Both sides rushed each other in a blur of weapons and bodies. Ships were aflame. Screams, so many screams.

She was too close to the battle. Too close. She saw it all.

Nordmen flung spears into the swarm of Scots. Many wore bear and wolf furs, leather vests and breeches, with bone-carved pointed daggers attached at their waists. Black and deep blood-red paint—or was it real blood?—decorated their faces and bare arms. Men howled, screeched, and clawed at each other like animals.

Those must have been Magnus of Reindalr's infamous *úlfheðnar*. There was no mistaking them.

Her pulse pounded in her head as axes and swords exchanged blows. Men wrestled each other to the ground. They slaughtered in fits of rage and glory.

She tightened her grip on the dagger. A drizzle began to fall. She'd need water. Yes, water. She had a small, empty flask in her other pocket. She poked in the croft, but there was no bucket or rope to get water from the well. A bubbling burn flowed nearby. She left the safety of her spot.

She quickly filled the flask and stood up. Her gaze fell upon the ships again. The Reindalr wolf was one of the nearer ships. She ventured a few steps closer, knowing it was unwise. She couldn't stand here and watch them die! Not her family.

A shockwave of grief flooded her veins. She thrust her hands into her full pockets. The Healer's stone burned. She twitched and paced. Men piled into mounds of limbs and bodies on the beach. Enraged Nordmen sliced through Scots, who fell like splinters.

Closer. She stepped closer, away from her shelter. Closer to death.

She searched the horde of fighting men. Norse women fought aside Nordmen as well, evidenced by their shriller cries. One shocked Scot was startled at the sight of a woman wielding an axe. It was his undoing. She cut through him with a grunt and carried on.

Too close. She hurried back to her hiding place.

From it, she lost sight of Simon's legion, and panic knocked her to her knees.

Venora's vision.

Through the haze, she thought she saw her mother and sister disembarking a ship. It was ablaze. "No!" she screamed. *Get back on the ship*, she wanted to cry. But they couldn't. Their long dark gowns were easily distinguished from the rest as they dashed through the men on the beach toward the village. She screamed again.

Then she saw him. He'd heard her. A Norse warrior, dressed in animal skins and painted with blood. Yes, that was blood, not dyes. He ran toward her, axe ready. Angry rapture filled his eyes. His face glowed with madness.

She had no time. She yanked out her dagger, and as he flung himself toward her, she ducked to the side. His axe hit the door and got stuck. It was her moment. She swiped blindly at his throat.

Instant death poured from his neck vein, all over her, all over the ground in front of the doorway. He fell forward, his one hand on his neck, his other grabbing the front of her gown with a tight fist. She screeched, ripped his hand from her gown, and stepped back.

Two others heard the commotion and ran toward her from the beach.

She couldn't fight two. She turned and fled to the forest behind her and toward the northern part of the village, away from the battle. She was faster, nimbler. The Nordmen gave up their pursuit and returned to the beach.

Legs shaking, soul breaking, she slowed to a walk. Farther away from the battle. Farther from her family. Farther from Simon. Was he already dead? Would the gods not even give her a chance to try? She paused, riddled with indecision.

The rain fell harder. With it, her tears.

A wind blew, whistling among the trees, rustling new leaves.

Gwyn.

She froze. It was Venora's voice.

Garbled words in the Ancient tongue again, or so she thought.

She strained to decipher snippets. Getting lost among the trees and bushes, she followed the sound. Venora's Seer's wind was her beacon.

Gwyn.

She hurried.

"Gwyn!"

Her mother's voice beckoned, and she almost lost her footing on slippery rocks. Righting herself, she changed direction. The call was far, barely audible among the chaos on the beach, but her heart told her it had been her mother's. She stopped for a long moment, having lost her bearing. Perhaps she had turned the wrong way.

She closed her eyes.

Venora's whispers returned. A direct and guiding wind. *This way.*

A few minutes later, Gwyn stumbled out of the trees upon a cottage, on the northern fringe of the village. There, her mother, sister, and Kendrick waited.

Kendrick!

She ran to them and embraced her mother.

"He brought you here? Why didn't you stay on the ship?" She shuddered in her mother's arms and fought the tears.

Her mother shrugged from the embrace but ran a smooth hand over Gwyn's forehead and then down her cheek to wipe the tears away. "Aye, he would never journey without his prized things," she said, her thin, pink lips downturned into a frown. Worry creased her high forehead. "Our ship caught fire. We had to flee."

Gwyn grabbed Kendrick's hand and held him close. "You were dead." Her mind raced as she remembered everything Simon had told her. "D-Did you get word? From Simon's messenger?"

Kendrick nodded. "Aye, we did. Gwyn—"

Her stomach dropped.

Cloudy blue eyes stared at her, connecting to her in his own unique way. He was feeling her lifeblood. He seemed older, no more a young lad. His hair was longer, messy. Dirt smudged his brow. Angst had creased lines into his forehead and around his grimacing mouth. His face was covered with new, healing bruises. "He's still alive, Gwyn. Simon. He's out there. I feel him."

Her heart lifted with relief. For now.

"What is it?" she asked, eagerly seeking truth in Venora's eyes, for her sister stood silently beside them, her own gaze locked on the distant bloodshed in unadulterated horror. In fact, she had never seen her sister so distraught. To live with the visions and then see them fulfilled...she couldn't imagine the pain.

"Come, Gwyn. Come. Take refuge here. We're not safe. We must get farther away. It's hurting Kendrick. All the death. He feels it!" her mother said.

Gwyn stood her ground. She couldn't hide. Simon was out there. "We've never been safe." She exhaled. "Where is Father?"

"Here," he said, appearing behind her.

She startled, belatedly dropping the blood-covered dagger that had been death-gripped in her hand. She made no move to pick it up. Protectively, stupidly, she stepped in front of Kendrick.

Her father wasn't fighting. Why would he have taken a sword to fight alongside his brethren?

"You've strayed, Gwyn," he said, stepping closer, face painted with spiral shapes to match the other Norse warriors. Oil streaked his hair into a greasy, spiked coif.

She clenched her hands to prevent the shakes from consuming her. "I am here, Father."

"You have allied with the *Scotsman*."

She gritted her teeth. "Have I? Then why am I here and not safe away in his castle? Why would I risk my life by coming here if I truly sided with him? He is filth," she lied.

Madness danced in his eyes, enraged by drink. The axe in his hand shook. His bare muscled arms tensed. "We received your warning from the messenger. You are no longer my daughter."

Palpitations seized her heart. Her breath shifted from resilient to panicked. "I came here to warn you." Meek lies. *Jörd, give me power.*

He stepped closer. She countered with her own motion, pushing Kendrick farther behind her. Futile, for if her father had wanted him dead, he would've already killed him. No, this time he came for her.

"You lied to me," he said. "You betrayed your people."

She opened her mouth to refute, but he continued.

"Kendrick. Oh, I know. Not only do I know about his blindness, I know of his power. What an asset for our new Norse-Ancient bloodline! I have one too many Healers though."

She caught Venora's look as her sister stepped aside subtly. Was she leaving? Was she *abandoning her own family*? Venora's face was placid, but she moved her head side to side ever so slightly. Just like in the market, Gwyn's own sister was leaving her again!

"Don't look to her. I'm afraid though, she will suffer the same fate as you for her help in this. Her curse has already been set loose."

Curse? What curse?

Kendrick whimpered. The shockwave from their father's rage and the massive carnage happening around them debilitated him.

"Step away from him," her father ordered.

"What more can you do to us? Our people will lose, Father."

Coarsely he said, "Our bloodline will prevail but without you." He raised his axe.

She closed her eyes, waiting for the blow. At least she could shield Kendrick with her body.

"We will see glory—" he cried in a gurgling moan on his own words.

She opened her eyes.

Her dagger was lodged through his neck. He dropped his axe and stumbled, fright upon his face. Blood poured from the death strike.

Venora stepped out from behind him. She lifted her chin with sickly pride.

Their father fell to the ground, dead, Gwyn's dagger stuck in his throat.

Kendrick's body gave way. He held his head and moaned. Their mother dropped to her knees beside him and laid a hand upon his forehead. Venora remained silent, numbed. She hugged herself.

"Kendrick, my sweet son, I must heal you, or you will die."

He bit his lip and nodded.

"What?" Gwyn sat on his other side, still reeling from Venora stabbing their father.

Her mother closed her eyes but took Gwyn's hand. "I must, Gwyn." She laid her hands upon Kendrick and began chanting as the patter of rain broke through the forest canopy. She reached one hand up, cupping rain in her palm, then ran her hand over Kendrick's eyes.

"No, no, no! You will die!" Gwyn cried.

"Gwyn, there is too much death here. He will die if it continues. You know he feels it *all*. I must. It is my time."

Kendrick writhed as her mother sang the song of gods.

Heat poured off his body, the rain sizzling and evaporating as it touched his skin. She ceased trying to reason with her mother, but her heart screamed in agony, aching with each beat.

It was over as quickly as it had begun, for Caoimhe the Graceful One, daughter of the Ancients, spell caster and Healer, sister of the goddesses, was divine in her abilities. Her mother's breath caught.

Venora knelt beside her and grabbed one hand, while Gwyn reached across and took the other. The women of the Ancients held each other one last time.

"Be strong. I love you all. There is always hope and mercy," their mother said. She then gasped and with one final breath, her hands went flaccid, and she fell upon her son's chest.

Gwyn cried, her soul ripped in two, and Venora was silent as they pulled their mother off Kendrick's body and laid her on the ground, pushing away soggy leaves and wet, dark hair.

Gwyn looked at her dead mother, numbed by the chill of the rain.

Kendrick then spoke. "I feel nothing."

She turned her attention to him and eased him to sitting. "You feel nothing?" she repeated.

He quaked. "It's gone," he said, voice grief-stricken. "I feel nothing, no lifebloods, no colors—not even yours."

His gift was gone.

He lifted a hand, his blue eyes no longer cloudy. They were sharp and directed toward hers. "You're beautiful."

"You can see me?"

He nodded and crumpled against her in an embrace. "But Mother..."

They sat for a long moment, lost in the sacrifice their mother had made. Finally, Gwyn stood. She hardened her resolve, ignoring her wobbly knees. "Stay here, be safe. I must go."

Venora didn't fight her but only said, "If ye heal him, yer own breaths will be taken. Ye won't die today, sister, but yer life will be cut short."

"My choice is made." She'd rather love and heal Simon than live a life of suppression and isolation without him.

If anyone had known it, her mother had. Caoimhe the Graceful One lay dead, the ultimate sacrifice, beside their stone-cold dead father.

Death surrounded Simon. Deafening rage engulfed the beach and meadow. He fought with dagger in one hand and broadsword in the other. Sticky blood soiled his skin and dripped down his chin.

More, more, more.

The animal in him unleashed. He focused on his need to be free of this burden.

His mother Margaret and her virtue. His brother Desmond.

The priests.

His soul.

His home and everything they'd worked for would be conquered if the Lochlanach from the icy north triumphed. They had usurped, raped, and destroyed. No more. The years of the Nordmen were finished.

He deflected, guarded, and pivoted in a dance of swords. In a dance of death. He advanced on two men.

Gwyn.

He still had Gwyn. He didn't look back. Taking his eyes off the men around him would seal a tragic fate.

A Nordman in a wolf skin approached, shrieking, his pupils pinpoints, teeth bared. Were his teeth chiseled to sharp points? Hell, they were! He had seen these men which no fire or iron could kill firsthand, nine years ago. They had been among the lot who attacked his mother. To hell with them. He rushed him. They locked arms and wrestled, each losing their grip on weapons. They rolled on the ground, punching, scratching, clawing. Simon fought with every morsel of remaining strength. Somehow, he found his dagger and went for the man's throat. A crunch, a gurgle, and the man was dead.

So much for their immortality.

Simon's heartbeat drummed in his ears, and his skull felt cracked from the fall. Yet he rose, ready for the next. And the next.

Soon, he found himself beside his father, fighting back to back, defending themselves against the throng of men surrounding them. Other clansmen swooped in and joined their defense. He sequestered his mind and allowed muscle to drive him. He whirled as he heard a cackle from behind.

The screech of a lunatic.

Within the chaos, he locked eyes with Leidolf, whose crazed face held the dilated pupils, edged smirk, and the look like the other *úlfheðnar*. He bore his teeth and lunged at Simon, growling like the wolf he claimed homage to. They exchanged sword blows in a strange prance of animals.

"Your death is now, red fox!" Leidolf said.

"Never! This is not your home, wolf!" Simon dodged.

"You stole my prize. She is mine, and you will die for it."

The thought of Gwyn distracted him for a moment, and Leidolf unsworded him.

Simon growled and barreled into him, dagger in his hand. Leidolf dropped his sword as they fell to the ground. Leidolf managed to smack Simon's daggered hand against a rock. Bones in Simon's hand cracked. The dagger fell. Simon punched Leidolf in the face with his already bloody hand. Leidolf scratched, grabbed a dagger from his own belt side, and swiped.

Simon rolled, avoided. "Go back to the dark hell you came from!" He punched. Caught Leidolf in the face again. Again and again. Fury drove him.

They rolled like animals on the beach. Pebbles scattered, and the waves crashed closer as they drew near the water.

"Death is too good for you!" Simon's father said to somebody else.

A twisted laugh erupted amid the shouts, clanging metal, and the aching in Simon's head and heart. Those laughs. Leidolf's and this man's matched. Even with all the wolf-embellished weapons Leidolf had in his possession, Simon hadn't made the connection. He had thought all Nordmen were wolves. No. Not all. Just Leidolf's kin. How had he not seen it?

A wave splashed against him. He scrambled to his feet, waterlogged clothes dripping and stuck to his skin. Leidolf stumbled, taking a moment to rise. Neither had the energy to continue—yet.

Simon scanned for his sword. As much as he'd like to strangle Leidolf, his hands were raw, his fingers could hardly move, and one hand was broken. Where was his damn sword?

Leidolf moaned, laughed, and reached toward a pouch at his side. He withdrew a clear vial from it; a thick, red liquid sloshed within the vial. He opened his mouth wide, uncorked it, and emptied its contents on his tongue. He smiled. "The blood of Fenrir flows in me! You will die, MacCoinneach!"

Simon heaved a recovery breath and glanced at his father's adversary while Leidolf chuckled and bent over, holding his middle.

The man locked in swordplay with Simon's father shared few physical traits with Leidolf, but Simon would never forget a face or a laugh. Leidolf's father. The man who had violated Simon's mother. Dark, now graying slicked back hair. Not blond and fair like Leidolf.

Clearly, Simon's father knew. He fought with passion and intent. He fought like a man who had lost everything.

Magnus of Reindalr moved with agility. They sparred with swords and curses. He was impressively taller than his youngest son, a wall of force to be reckoned with. He lacked the dyed markings and tattoos of his *úlfheðnar*, but he had a jeweled beard and numerous bracelets down his muscular forearms.

It *was him*. The man who had ruined his family's life.

It was as if Magnus had guzzled the juice of his gods. He laughed at each of Alroy's advances. Though Simon's father was also skilled, he was no match for the massive Nordman.

Magnus's deep-voiced boasting carried far. "We are the chosen! The land and its people are *ours* to do with as we please! Relent, MacCoinneach. You're no match! Odin would never put such inferior men on a land he did not wish for us to conquer! The gods' blood flows in our veins and spills upon this soil."

Their clanging swords pierced the air.

His father didn't speak even as Magnus continued to taunt him. "You fight like a *woman*, Alroy! Do you squeal like one, too?"

Thrusts. Guards. Jabs, grunts. Near bloody misses. Simon's father grew fatigued. No. No. His father was not to die in this battle! Simon searched again, fruitlessly, for his sword. Leidolf was still hunched over, but an animal-like moaning took over him as he shook his head, as if summoning spirits. What the bloody hell had been in that vial?

"Do you claw and slap, too? Just like your wife did? Where is that weak son of yours..." Magnus's words faded, lost on the wind and noise around them, but a fiendish glimmer lit the Nordman's eyes. Simon's father responded with greater effort to the spewed obscenities.

"...just like his father. You'll both die today!" Magnus continued. He spat blood. His father deepened his advance. He pivoted and passed back and front. Harder. Messier.

Somebody grabbed Simon from behind, jarring him to the moment. He struggled, but this beast was strong.

"Do we need to do your kills for you, too, Leidolf?" Another strapping man with a blood-smeared beard and grotesque facial tattoos said beside Leidolf. In a flash, they were surrounded by Nordmen on every turn. The man holding him released a heavy grunt and laughed at Simon's efforts to break loose.

"No, he is mine! Unhand him, Magnor. Father will see. Father will see!" Leidolf raged. He stood, brandishing an axe now.

Simon's head spun. What was he ranting on about? His axe. Dammit, it had been strapped to the fiend's back. Where was *his* own sword?

Leidolf paced, flaunting his chest in front of him, but hesitated. Had his fury worn off? Was he calculating his move? Had he become the coward?

Christ, just do it. Just do it.

Magnus spoke next between parries with Simon's father. "Leidolf, you're a despicable third-born with no honor, no power. You should be dead already. Why won't you die! The gods will not allow you into Asgard. Why do you persist? You're no better than a Scot! Strike that bastard down. Prove yourself!"

In a blur of hooves, several men on horses rode in, cutting through the Nordmen around them. Gaelic battle cries sounded. Shock lit Magnus's face.

The clansmen from Uist, led by Alan and Dubhgall MacRuaidhri, flanked Simon and his father, obliterating the Nordmen. Simon's muscles weakened, and his mouth went dry with relief. The man behind him tightened his grip on Simon's arms.

"We had an arrangement!" Magnus said. He stumbled over a fallen man.

"Our loyalty remains with the Scots and our king," Alan MacRuaidhri said.

Magnor, the Nordman holding Simon, groaned and spat. "Scot traitors!" The man beside Leidolf raised a sword to any Scot who approached.

The Scots cut through him like he was paper.

"Hallbjorn!" Magnor cried from behind Simon. He dropped his hold on Simon.

Simon was not fast enough. Bloody hell.

As if in slow motion, Magnor thrust his dagger up through Simon's back.

He lost his breath as the dagger punctured something. Lung? Kidney? Pain radiated through his upper back as the man slid the dagger out.

Simon gurgled on blood. He gulped for air. Not like this. Not like this. Where was his Gwyn? He needed to see her once more. He hadn't even killed Leidolf yet! Curse them all.

"No!" cried Leidolf.

Magnor roared. The brothers took weapons against each other. In a blink of an eye, Leidolf's demonic rage was greater than his brother's size. The large Nordman fell in a mighty thump.

In a possessed fit, and to Simon's still coherent surprise, Leidolf then took his axe and gutted his father Magnus in retaliation right then and there.

Shocked eyes and gasps took it in. Simon's father cursed and ran to his own son as his long-awaited duel, years of vengeful planning, ended at the hands of an ill-regarded third-born son.

Good. *Die, beast, die.* Simon's head roared as Magnus of Reindalr was chopped into a bloody pulp by Leidolf.

Simon's knees collapsed, and he slumped to the wet pebbly beach. A wave crashed upon him as he struggled for air. Aye, his lung. It whistled and rattled and gurgled with liquid.

He was next.

Simon's vision blurred. His chest and back burned. Everything grew muffled.

This was it. *Sweet Lord, take me now.*

Leidolf paced like an enraged animal. No others had drawn swords. Simon's father got to his feet, his own sword ready. Simon raised a hand in one final act of mercy. "No. Father. Help me. Let him go. Let him go."

Deafness numbed Simon. He tasted iron on his tongue. His lungs deflated. Cold arrested him. "Gwyn. I need Gwyn," he rasped. His gaze darted around. Not without her. He needed her. One last kiss. He needed her touch. His heart needed her mercy.

Tears. Inexplicable pain.

Leidolf rushed toward the meadow filled with men. A wave of fighting bodies swallowed him as he sought his last foray of glory and honor.

Simon closed his eyes. May God forgive him.

Oh, Gwyn. May she forgive him.

"I'm here, Alroy!" her voice rang.

He could almost feel her hands upon him, an angel's touch. Long, deft fingers danced across his chest, and he gulped air as fire poured into his core. The coldness in his fingers and toes was replaced with a blazing, almost intolerable heat. He cried as shards of glass punctured his lungs with his inhalation.

"Breathe in my life. Breath of my breath," her sweet voice said. Words he didn't understand sang in his ears. A rush of wind entered his lungs with her melodious words. He smelled fragrant heather, tasted salty rain, and felt only the comfort of her touch. It was like he was floating above the pebbled beach, wrapped in a blanket of relief.

Rain pelted him, waves soaked him, and his clothes matted against his quivering body.

Lips touched his. Hot, soul-filling breath.

This was it. The angel was his Gwyn. *Thank you, Lord. Thank you for gifting me with her.*

He let her heavenly body take him to his final resting place.

Simon ached everywhere. Perhaps he was in hell.

He was jostled about. Tried to sit.

"You need to rest," a sharp woman's voice said. She poked at his shoulder to push him down.

No angel song. Damn. Satan was a woman. Interesting.

"Och, leave me be, you ol' devil," he mumbled, moving about. He smelled hay. Something scratchy on his face. He went to swipe it, but his hand was bandaged.

"I'm no devil, Simon MacCoinneach."

He blinked and her blurry form came into focus.

Dark hair, pale skin. "Gwyn?"

"She's resting and because of ye, nearly dead."

His chest soared with pain as he exhaled, "Venora."

"Aye, ye bugger."

He swam in a murky consciousness. More jostling. *Gwyn.* She came to him in his sleep. Encapsulated him. He felt her touch, kissed her lips, wrapped himself in her embrace.

Time passed. He awoke again, bouncing. He cracked his jaw, repositioned himself to sit up, and took in his surroundings. Day was upon them, and he rode in the bed of a cart. Venora and another young man sat there, silent. His father and Henry drove the cart, their backs to them, equally silent. A wrapped body lay beside him. He nearly vomited.

No, Gwyn also lay beside him.

Immediately he touched her. "Gwyn? Gwyn!"

Venora smacked his uninjured hand. "She's asleep. She will rouse soon. Ye took many of her breaths."

He checked her pulse. Steady, slow.

"She's alive?" he asked, a frog caught in his dry throat. Venora handed him a flask. He drank and almost threw it up. His stomach twisted and hurt.

"For now," Venora whispered.

That brought him to full attention. He sipped the whisky again, slower, allowing the heady fumes and heavier taste to ease his throat, placate his mind. "For now?"

"I've seen her death."

The whisky burned. "Because of me?"

"Ye're not a fool, Simon. Of course because of ye."

He wished Magnor's dagger had killed him. Then Gwyn wouldn't have needed to heal him. He just sealed her early death. He looked at his open shirt and wrapped chest. It felt like he had eaten spoiled fish; his stomach roiled and rolled, but there was no blood on the bandage, and he would bet all the coin in the country—or all his cows; oh, how he thought of Desmond—the wound was healed.

"Her death. Does she know when and—and, blazes, how?"

"Nay. She won't let me share her path with her."

He didn't want to know *how*, but he had to know when. "How long does she have?"

"You will have some years together before she gifts you a son and daughter, born within minutes of each other. Three winters after your third child is born, Gwyn will cross over to the Silver Veil."

He attempted the calculation, but it hurt his head and depleted his spirit. How long was some? Five? Ten? Twelve? Was that all he'd have with her? Three bairns. A short life with Gwyn.

Venora must have sensed his unease. "Ye'll return to her when it's yer time, too. But ye've work to do. The war is no' over. There's another evil on the horizon that must be stopped. Ye'll have children to see grow."

"Another evil?"

She wrinkled her nose. "The king to the south."

He swallowed the noxious truth. Gwyn still slept.

His wife. So little time with her.

"One of yer children, she will have a gift, too. The oldest born child."

He lifted his head, regretting the quick movement.

His head throbbed. "She will?"

Venora's face glowed with esteem. "Aye, she will. She will become powerful. Be wise with her, Simon. She will be a Feeler like Kendrick," she said with a flick to the young man riding silently beside them. "Our brother wishes to return home with ye; he can explain this fire gift to ye more so ye're better prepared to embrace it."

Their bodies bumped in the wagon as the horses pulled the cart over unforgiving roads.

"There is more ye should know, Simon."

Did he want to? "I don't think I can bear it."

"Ye must."

He pinched his forehead. "Go on."

"Our mad father put a curse on our children."

He rubbed his face with his unbroken hand, aching for Gwyn to wake. He couldn't take Venora's truths. "You have children?"

"Not yet."

He sighed, it hurting his middle. He swallowed. "Tell me."

"Our father was not pleased with my hand in this," she said with a wave to him and Gwyn and Kendrick. The lad sat beside them, listening but mute. "He forced my mother to prepare a curse on us. Ye can't kill the living with a curse, but ye can torture the unborn."

"What?" His skin tingled and his thoughts were fuzzy.

"Yer children and grandchildren will hiv fulfilling lives and will find love, rest assured, Simon, but they must first overcome the curse. Och, there will be much sorrow associated with it. I'm sorry, I can't undo it. My mother's power was beyond me and Gwyn, and she took that power with her to the grave."

Kendrick stared in the distance, taking it in like a lad who had never seen it before.

Venora, ever astute, said, "Our mother healed him of his blindness and ability. She is dead because of it."

Lord, she was a blunt woman. Bless the man who married her.

Then again, he had thought the same thing at one time about the woman recovering beside him. Who had healed his body and soul, sacrificing her own.

Gwyn opened her eyes to the warmth of the new day's sun upon her face. She could hardly move her arms, let alone any part of her body. She yawned, a rattle escaping her.

"Rest, Gwyn. You've done much. So many breaths," Kendrick's voice said.

"Is it over? I'm still here?" she croaked, her throat raw.

"Aye."

"Simon?"

"Here."

Her pulse soared. "Simon!"

His voice came, groggy and diluted with weariness. "Here, my sweet Healer. Here." His hand found hers.

Tears flooded her eyes. "You're alive!" She fell against his shoulder.

He winced. "Aye, you're a Healer, but please, I feel like I've been gutted."

Kendrick smirked. "Och, you have."

"Did we win?" she asked.

"Yes. Well, the Scots did. You doubted?" Kendrick said, a youthful glow in his clearer eyes. She almost shuddered with their intensity.

"Venora?"

"Here, but I go home, Gwyn. I need to be with our people," Venora said. "I'll return with the MacRuaidhris to Uist."

"Mother?" Gwyn said, shifting upright, her head spinning. Blackness and orange starbursts danced before her and she closed her eyes.

"She is here with us. We will give her a proper burial."

Her chest constricted. Her soul was exhausted. *Och, her mother.* "And you, Kendrick?" she asked, clutching her aching head.

"My home is with you. I'll return to Eilean Donan with you and your husband," Kendrick said.

All of it rushed back to her. Her father. Her mother. The blood and injury. Simon. Her breaths. "Oh, Simon, I—we—"

He silenced her with a kiss, the delight of his now clean, prickly chin tickling all her senses. The last she had seen him he'd been covered in blood and filth and was near death, almost swallowed by the crashing surf. How much time had passed since then? He was clean and...whole. Life's energy rushed through her down to her toes. She exhaled. She had lost much breath in his healing. She could feel it in her bones. Venora's words echoed within her mind again. She began to sob. "Simon, I may not have many years with you. I may have ruined it. Your healing…"

He kissed her again, his lips trembling. "I told you not to heal me."

She sniffled. "You did."

"You're a stubborn woman," he said with a grin.

"I am."

"Gywn, you saved me." He took her hand and placed it on his chest, upon his strong-beating heart. "You saved all of me."

She inhaled the sweetness of fulfillment.

Solemnly he said, "I can never repay what you've given me. Not if I had all the time in the world, but as God as my witness, Gwyn, I will love you for all my days. I will give everything for you. Anything. You shall never want. We'll make every moment, every breath our own."

She nodded, holding his penetrating gaze with her own. "Aye."

She turned to her brother. "You don't want to return home?"

"My home is with you," Kendrick said.

Simon reached across and clasped Kendrick's hand, squeezed, then turned to Gwyn. "He is my brother, too." Simon stroked her face. "We are bonded by something far stronger than blood."

She smiled. "You've lived up to your namesake, my Simon, the merciful."

He sighed, a smile ruffling his face. He closed their space and kissed her again.

She tasted his lips, comforting, eternal.

"I hope I can earn it, Gwyn. I will show you."

"Then let us go home."

She didn't ask about Leidolf. She didn't care, but she did wonder about Lady Margaret's offenders. "Leidolf's father..." She couldn't say his name.

Simon understood. "They've all gone to meet their gods."

A long moment passed.

"Promise me one thing, my bonnie wife," Simon said.

"Anything."

"No more healing."

She opened her mouth to protest.

He held up a hand. "Herbs, aye. You have a fine gift that will be appreciated among our people. Your special ability. Please? I need every moment I can with you." Guilt plagued his eyes.

She nodded. Her time as Healer was over. "Aye, my last breaths are for you, Simon MacCoinneach."

He stroked her cheek. "And mine are yours. Now and forever."

EPILOGUE

Eilean Donan, Scotland, 1302

Domhnall yawned as he pulled himself upright. He sat perfectly still, the way Grandda Simon used to show him in Hall. "A keen laird sits, watches the people around him, friend and enemy. One doesn't need to be tall to be of stature. Sit upright, pay attention. An observant laird leads by learning. A laird is virtuous and merciful," Grandda would say.

The painting hanging on the wall at the top of the staircase called to him. Ma would not be pleased he'd slept here all night. He curled within his well-loved woolen blanket. He stood and ran a finger lazily over the black paint that fell down the sides of his grandmother's face. The waves of long hair reminded him of a waterfall. Her eyes shone, almost twinkling like the loch. She looked just like Ma.

The touch triggered another vision and a pinching on the bridge of his nose. He stumbled. A cool wind wrapped around him. It rushed and whirled, like the windiest day on the moor. Stronger than when the wind rippled the loch. He wasn't scared when the visions came anymore.

He'd grown used to them. He blinked and focused hard as the image revealed itself.

It was Grandda!

Grandda Simon smiled back, silver clouds surrounding him as he approached the long boat with the dragon's head. Ferocious teeth the size of Domhnall's hands were carved into the head and red gemstones in its eyes. It was both scary and compelling. He wanted to touch it. But he couldn't touch things in his visions. He knew it wasn't a dream because he was awake. Water slapped against the boat. His grandfather leaned over the railing and whispered.

Domhnall listened. He chewed on his thumb, the way Ma told him not to, lest she put that foul oil on it.

Yes, Grandda, I will tell them.

Then Grandda nodded in return. He appeared younger than Domhnall remembered, his hair less gray, thicker like a fox's brush, brownish-red and wild, and his beard was less speckled with white. Grandda looped his hand with...och, it was Grandma! Her seaweed blue eyes danced with laughter. Oh, Grandma, she looked like Ma, like her painting.

The clouds swallowed them, and the boat disappeared.

"Domhnall! What are you doing, sweetheart?" Ma said, approaching from Grandda's bedchamber. Her long skirt swooshed along the fresh spring rushes on the stone floor.

He stared at the painting again. His grandfather and the ship were long gone. All that remained was the painting of grandmother with bonnie pink lips, rosy cheeks, and long, dark hair like Ma's.

His mother crouched beside him. "Looking at Grandmother's portrait again, are you?"

He nodded. "When will Da return?"

His mother rubbed his shoulder. "Soon, sweetheart. Soon. Come, you need to eat. How long have you been sitting here?"

"Since last night. Your crying woke me."

She was quiet for a moment. He might only be five years old, but he knew when Ma was sad.

"Last night, Domhnall...your grandda, he's...well, he's..."

"With Grandma now. I know."

"He is. Yes."

Commotion in the kitchens stirred him. "Da!"

Ma smiled. "Yes, he must be home."

She couldn't restrain him as he hurried down the stairs to find his father. Halfway through the hall, his father sloshed in with wet boots. He wrapped his arms around his father's legs, inhaling the scent of horse and mud.

Da laughed. "Easy, lad. I missed you, too." Then he said quietly, as if Domhnall couldn't hear, but he always heard everything, "Deirdre, love, the messenger brought news and I returned as quickly as I could. Is he still—"

Ma whispered, "No. He passed last night. I no longer feel his lifeblood. He is gone."

Domhnall shifted on his feet. "I saw them."

"Saw who?" his parents asked in unison.

"Grandda and Grandma."

His mother added, "Oh, sweetheart, you mean Grandmother's painting?" She patted his head and leaned in to embrace his father. "You've never met your grandmother, Domhnall, sweetheart, although she would have loved you and your keen dreams."

Ma didn't know yet that they were visions. Not dreams. He saw things before they happened. He saw the dead. "No. I saw them together. They were moving through the silver clouds. They sailed away on a strange curved boat. Not like the boats we have here, but a different one. This was longer with many oars and round shields. It had a dragon's head with red eyes!"

Ma was quiet, her face alight.

"Grandda said to tell you he'd saved his last breath for her."

"For her?" Ma asked.

He nodded. "Uh-huh. He said *it* was love and mercy."

"That *what* was love and mercy, sweetheart?" his mother said, so softly a breeze would have swallowed it.

"Love and mercy brought him through the Silver Veil to Grandma. They are together again."

JOURNEY THROUGH THE HIGHLANDS...

People, clans, and places...oh my!

Want to learn more about The Hundred Trilogy? Visit my website (www.jeanmgrant.com) for some book extras. Learn about the MacCoinneach & Montgomerie family lineage, the clans, culture & lore, places, and so much more with a glossary, Scotland map, and family/lineage chart. Be warned! There may be spoilers. Read with caution...and sweet abandon.

Interested in continuing the journey through medieval Scotland? Read on.

The Hundred Trilogy

Norse invasions, Scottish wars for independence, and the plights of the mystical isles' people come together in The Hundred Trilogy. In each standalone book, delve deeper into the mystical powers of the MacCoinneach clan...a powerful family descended from the Ancients of the Isles. Each person is gifted with an ancient power—healing with water, intuition with fire, and prophecy with wind. But with each gift comes a curse. Can they overcome their afflictions to bridge peace...to find love?

A Hundred Breaths

1263

Gwyn of Uist is a merciful Healer but loses breaths of her life with every healing charm. She barters an alliance with a Scot bent on revenge against her Norse kin, in the hopes to save her brother from their abusive father. But can she and Simon MacCoinneach outwit her betrothed and bring an end to the Norse-Scottish bloodshed when it will take all her breaths to save Simon on the battle-field?

A Hundred Kisses

1296

Deirdre MacCoinneach feels the lifebloods of everyone around her...but vows to discover if her gift killed her husbands—twice. Under the façade of a trader, Alasdair Montgomerie travels to Uist with pivotal information for a claimant seeking the Scottish throne. A cruel baron hunts him, leaving little room for alliances with the lass he meets along the way. Amidst ghosts of the past, Alasdair and Deirdre find themselves falling together in a web of secrets and the curse of a hundred kisses...

A Hundred Lies

1322

Rosalie Threston's fortune-telling lies have caught up with her and she's on the run from a ruthless English noblewoman. Rosalie finds refuge in the halls of Eilean Donan castle deep in the Highlands, and in the arms of the laird's mysterious son, Domhnall Montgomerie.

Terrible visions plague Domhnall and he avoids all physical contact to temper them. When an accidental touch reveals only delight, he wonders if Rosalie is the key to silencing the Sight. Mystical awakening unravels with each kiss. But can Domhnall embrace his gift in time to save her life, even if it means exposing her lies?

Seeker

A novella, part of the Mortar & Pestle series

1322

Aileana Montgomerie lacks the mystical ability of the Scottish Ancients like her kin. She seeks a purpose but what good is her bow and arrow if she is denied the right to fight for her clan? Brodie MacDougall is ordained to be the next war chieftain of his clan. Chronic pain and nervous vapors force him to spend his days alone, not lift a sword and charge into battle. Can his strategic skills alone keep him one step ahead of his conspiring brother? After magic cast by mystical Mortar & Pestle, the seat on his brother's council is no longer dependent upon his health...but on Aileana's strength. With rumblings of unrest among their clans, will their love foster an alliance or be a step toward war?

ALSO BY JEAN M. GRANT

A Hundred Kisses

A Hundred Lies

Seeker

Soul of the Storm

Will Rise from Ashes

About the Author

Jean has a penchant for the misunderstood, be it sharks, microbes, or wounded characters. A scientist by training, she now spends her days as an author and champion for her children. She draws from her interest in history, science, the outdoors, and her family for inspiration. She serves on the local library board of trustees and is an advocate for community, inclusion, and diversity.

A nature enthusiast who adores the national parks, Jean also writes for family-oriented travel magazines and websites. When not writing, she enjoys gardening, tackling the biggest mountains in New England, and going on adventures with her husband and children, while taking snapshots of the world around her and daydreaming about the next story. If she were stuck on a deserted island, her three essentials (besides family, food, water, shelter) would be: coffee, lip balm, and endless pink sticky notes.

Find out more about her books by visiting her website: www.jeanmgrant.com

SCOTLAND
1263-1322